NIV Adventure BIBLE
Book of Devotions

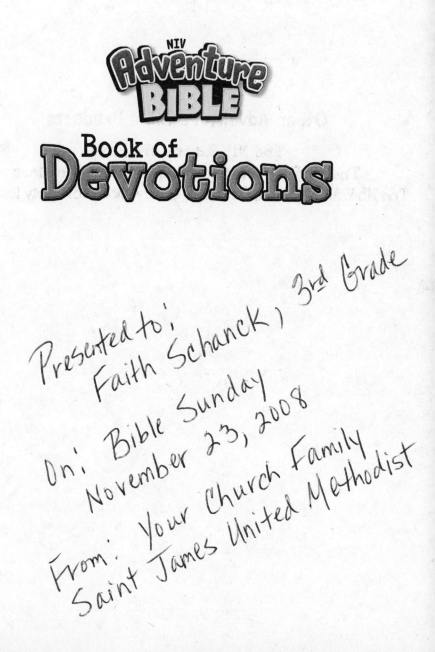

Presented to:
Faith Schanck, 3rd Grade

On: Bible Sunday
November 23, 2008

From: Your Church Family
Saint James United Methodist

Other Adventure Bible Products

The NIV Adventure Bible
The NIrV Adventure Bible for Early Readers
The NIrV Adventure Bible: Book of Devotions for Early Readers

NIV Adventure BIBLE

Book of Devotions

written by
Robin Schmitt

ZONDERkidz

ZONDERVAN.com/
AUTHORTRACKER
follow your favorite authors

This book is dedicated to
my wife, Helen,
our children, Alex, Jesse, and Audry,
and all of God's children.
Laus Deo!
—R.S.

 ZONDER**kidz**™

The NIV Adventure Bible: Book of Devotions
Copyright © 2008 by Zondervan

Requests for information should be addressed to:
Zonderkidz, Grand Rapids, Michigan 49530

Library of Congress Cataloging-in-Publication Data

Schmitt, Robin.
     The NIV adventure Bible : book of devotions / by Robin Schmitt.
       p. cm.
     Includes bibliographical references and index.
     ISBN 978-0-310-71447-7 (softcover : alk. paper)
     1. Christian children--Prayers and devotions. 2. Devotional calendars--Juvenile literature. 3. Bible stories,
English. I. Title.
     BV4870.S415 2008
     242'.62--dc22
                          2008026355

Art direction: Merit Alderink
Interior composition: Carlos Eluterio Estrada
Interior design: Matthew Van Zomeren

Printed in the United States of America

08 09 10 11 12 • 5 4 3 2

Contents

January

March

April

May

July

August

September

October

December

Swimming with the Polar Bears

The foolishness of God is wiser than man's wisdom.

1 Corinthians 1:25

It was New Year's Day, snow was falling, and Aaron and his sister were standing on the beach in their swimsuits. Many other people were doing the same. It was time for the Polar Bear Swim!

"I c–can't believe I'm d–doing this," said Aaron, his teeth chattering.

Shivering, Christina said, "D–don't wimp out n–now."

As a crowd of onlookers cheered, everyone ran splashing into the ocean. Aaron and Christina dove under the icy waves. They came up gasping and whooping, then raced back to shore to wrap themselves in towels.

A kid watching them shook his head. "You guys are crazy."

Laughing, Aaron replied, "W–we know!"

Naaman thought it was foolish to dunk himself in the Jordan River. But when he obeyed God and did it, he was healed of leprosy. (See 2 Kings 5:1–14.) Will you trust and obey God when he asks you to do something "foolish"? What if he wants you to tell the cashier she gave you too much change? Or to forgive someone who isn't sorry? Acts like these may not seem wise, but God knows they make you a better person.

People in Bible Times

One of Naaman's slaves, a young girl from Israel, believed that the prophet Elisha could heal Naaman. She may have thought it was foolish to try to give her master advice. But she trusted in God and did it.

Knocked off Your Feet

Be on your guard; stand firm in the faith.

1 Corinthians 16:13

"Link up, everybody," Lilly said. "We'll go faster!" Sitting at the top of the hill, she and four of her classmates grabbed each other's snow tubes. Another classmate, Denny, gave them a push, then jumped on his tube and held on to them. They started down the icy slope, laughing and yelling as they picked up speed. Lilly's school was having its winter party at a ski resort with six tubing lanes. She and her friends were careening down the steepest, bumpiest one.

"Woooeee!" shouted Katrina as they scored some air time. The group plummeted to the bottom of the hill and slid to a stop.

"Whoa, that was fast," said Denny. Grabbing his tube, he headed for the rope tow.

"Watch out!" Lilly cried. A rider in the next lane slammed into Denny's legs, flipping him over. "You gotta stay alert," Lilly said, helping him up.

Rubbing his head, Denny said, "Yeah. Guess I learned *that* lesson."

What knocks your faith out from under you when your guard is down? It could be something someone says on the radio. Or a comment someone writes in a magazine. Or maybe a remark from a friend who doesn't believe in God. Keep your guard up by remembering what the Bible says. Keep believing the truth, so doubt can't take you down.

Words to Treasure

It is by faith you stand firm.
2 Corinthians 1:24

Powerful Pull

[Jesus said,] "I, when I am lifted up from the earth, will draw all men to myself."

John 12:32

Sitting at the desk in his bedroom, Dylan wound copper wire around a large nail. "What are you doing, Son?" his father asked, walking into the room.

Dylan looked up. "Making an electromagnet. I saw the instructions for it in a book." As his dad watched, Dylan taped one end of the wire to the positive side of a D-cell battery. Then he taped the other end to the negative side. "Okay, I'm ready to test it," he said.

Scattering small nails on his desk, Dylan held the point of the large nail over them. They leaped up and stuck to it.

Some Christians are afraid to tell people about the gospel. They think others won't like hearing about how Jesus was nailed to a cross on the ground and then was lifted up to die. But when people understand that he died to save them, they see the cross differently. The love Jesus showed the world by dying on the cross draws people to him like a magnet. Don't be afraid to share the gospel with others! You'll help them realize how much Jesus loves them.

Life in Bible Times

To the people of Jesus' time, a cross was a symbol of death. But Jesus cared about sinners enough to die on a cross to save them. So the cross has become a symbol of love. (See John 3:16; 15:13.)

Angry Eruptions

> [Love] is not self-seeking, it is not easily angered, it keeps no record of wrongs.
>
> 1 Corinthians 13:5

As Rob walked along the road, he saw plumes of steam in the distance. They were rising from the Hawaiian coast. Suddenly Rob stopped. The road ended right in front of them! "This is where lava flowed over the street in 1990," Rob's dad said. "From this point we'll be walking on hardened lava." Rob and his family were hiking near Mount Kilauea, the world's most active volcano.

They started making their way over the smooth, black rock. "I can see hot lava!" said Rob's sister, Jamie, as they approached the shoreline. Rob could see it too. The molten rock was flowing into the sea, creating massive steam clouds. "What makes the lava come out?" Jamie asked.

Her mom replied, "Well, magma pushes up underground, building lots of pressure. Then the volcano erupts."

Grinning, Rob said, "Kinda like Jamie when she gets mad!"

Selfishness and bitterness will bubble inside you like red-hot magma, causing anger to erupt. Don't let either one into your heart. Think of others, and listen to people when you have disagreements with them. And forgive those who hurt you. Ask God to fill your heart with love, so *that* will flow out of you instead.

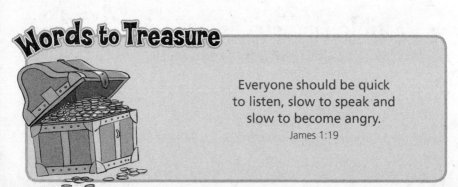

Words to Treasure

Everyone should be quick to listen, slow to speak and slow to become angry.
James 1:19

Taking a Tumble

Pride goes before destruction, a haughty spirit
before a fall.

Proverbs 16:18

A mber watched her brother ride his snowboard down the half-pipe. Holding
her own board, she was taking a break from the bunny hill. She was just a
beginner, but Bradley considered himself a master. He zipped up and down the
sides of the half-pipe, catching air at the top. She could tell he was showing off.

Then he raced toward a jump at the bottom of the hill, yelling, "Watch this!"
She rolled her eyes as he hit the jump. But it seemed that Bradley was more
focused on impressing her than on hitting the jump properly. He wiped out, tumbling head over heels several times.

While he brushed himself off, she applauded, laughing. "I liked that move!"

There's a difference between self-respect and pride. Pride will make you
tumble. It caused Satan, who was once a beautiful angel, to take a terrible fall. He
wanted to be God, so God threw him down from heaven. (See Isaiah 14:12–15
and Luke 10:18.) Don't let pride be your downfall. Choose self-respect, which
goes hand in hand with humility.

Did You Know?

Self-respect is loving yourself in a good, healthy
way. It's giving God the credit for your abilities.
Pride is thinking you're better than you really
are. It's taking all the credit for God's work in
you. (See Romans 12:3.)

Monster Mash

> [Jesus told his disciples,] "You know that the rulers of the Gentiles lord it over them, and their high officials exercise authority over them. Not so with you. Instead, whoever wants to become great among you must be your servant."
>
> Matthew 20:25–26

The indoor arena was filled with dirt for the monster truck rally. One of the big trucks spun in circles, kicking up clouds of dust. Skidding to a stop, it stood facing a line of automobiles parked side by side. As the driver revved its engine, Daisy and her brother Billy hollered, "Crush 'em! Smash 'em up!"

Spinning its huge tires, the truck lunged forward. The front wheels flew up in the air as it hit the side of the first car. Then the truck came crashing down on top of the automobiles. Bouncing and swaying, it crawled across the cars, grinding them up. "Monster trucks rule!" shouted Billy, pumping his fist.

Just because you're bigger than some other kids, don't roll all over them like a monster truck. In other words, don't bully people to get your way. Be gentle and considerate with younger siblings and other children who are smaller than you. Use your greater size and strength to serve others, not smash them. Follow Jesus' example. Being God, Jesus was bigger and more powerful than anyone. But instead of crushing people, he helped them.

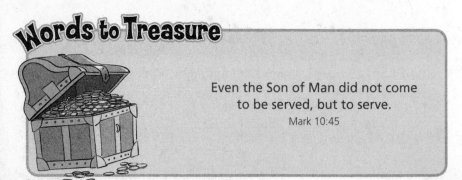

Words to Treasure

Even the Son of Man did not come to be served, but to serve.

Mark 10:45

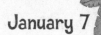

The Domino Effect

Without wood a fire goes out; without gossip
a quarrel dies down.

Proverbs 26:20

Chaz and his sister were building a huge domino display in their basement. At least they started with dominoes. Then they used their little brother's building blocks. Now they were using anything they could find.

"Wait'll Mom and Dad see this," Chaz said as he set up some books.

Lila nodded. "Yeah. They're gonna flip out!"

Chaz reached for another book.

"I'll bet they—oh no!" His elbow had knocked over the last book, and the others had started tumbling. Before he could grab them, they'd all fallen over, knocking down the DVD boxes. Next the CD cases began toppling. Quickly Lila put her finger on one that was still standing. Holding it upright, she stopped the damage from spreading any farther.

Gossip can travel quickly around your school, church, or neighborhood. When it does, it causes lots of damage. People argue, feelings get hurt, and relationships get broken. Don't be like other kids who fall for the temptation to pass along rumors. When gossip hits you, ask the Holy Spirit to help you stand tall and keep it to yourself. That'll stop the harmful domino effect that gossip creates!

Live It!

Make a domino display. Before you push over the first one, put your finger on the tenth. See how easy it is to stop the domino effect? Now have fun and knock down your entire display!

Frozen Waves

A fool gives full vent to his anger, but a wise man keeps himself under control.

Proverbs 29:11

Denise and her mom got out of the car near the beach. But first they put on hats and mittens. "Wait'll you see this, Denise," her mom said. "I love coming to Lake Michigan in the wintertime. It looks so different than in the summer!" They followed a path through snow-covered trees.

When they reached the beach, Denise saw an icy landscape. "Look, Mom. The waves are frozen!" All along the shore were large gray and white formations that looked like waves that had suddenly turned solid. They strolled along the shoreline, admiring the formations. "Did these waves just freeze all at once?" Denise asked.

"No," her mom said. "They built up over time. The shallow water freezes first. Then as waves splash on the ice, the formations get bigger and bigger. Some get huge."

"I know," Denise said, pointing. "That one looks like an iceberg!"

If you let anger build up inside you, it'll just grow bigger and bigger. Find ways to melt away your anger when it starts freezing over. Praying will help. So will talking with the person you're angry at. Ask your parents for ideas about good ways to express your anger. These are the best ways to get rid of the ice without losing your cool.

Words to Treasure

In your anger do not sin.
Psalm 4:4

The Real Thing

Put on the full armor of God, so that when the day of evil comes, you may be able to stand your ground.

Ephesians 6:13

Josh loved pretending he was someone else—a cowboy, a fireman, an astronaut. This made him a good actor, and he'd been in many school plays and church skits. Tonight was special, though. The community theater was doing *Camelot*, a musical about King Arthur. And he was going to be in it!

Wearing his costume, Josh hurried to the prop table. For weeks he'd been practicing with a toy bow, but this was the dress rehearsal. The prop man handed him a long wooden bow, saying, "Remember, this is real."

Josh examined the weapon. It felt heavy. Slinging the quiver of arrows over his shoulder, he stood before a mirror. Now he really felt like the character he was playing, Tom, a boy who wanted to be a knight.

It's fine to play with plastic weapons when you're learning about the armor of God. But remember: the weapons God gives you are real. Salvation really is a helmet. Faith really is a shield. And God's word really is a powerful sword you can use against the Devil, just as Jesus did. (See Matthew 4:1–11.)

Did You Know?

God gives real, strong armor to believers. The apostle Paul compared it to a soldier's armor. For instance, righteousness is a mighty breastplate that protects your heart. (See Ephesians 6:10–17.)

Time for a Change

"I will give you a new heart and put a new spirit in you," [says the Lord].

Ezekiel 36:26

This car weighs three thousand pounds," said Lisa's dad. "Are you ready to pick it up?"

Nodding, Lisa replied, "I'm ready."

Her father stepped aside. "Okay. Pull the lever!" Lisa pulled it down. She watched as the hydraulic lift raised the vehicle.

"That's good!" her father said, and she released the lever. She hurried over to him, curious to see what the bottom of a car looked like. It was Take Your Child to Work Day, and Lisa was spending the day with her dad, an automobile mechanic. He put a pan on the floor beneath the car. Then he set up a stepladder, handed Lisa a wrench, and helped her remove a nut under the car's engine. "Watch out, because oil will come out," he warned. Sure enough, when the nut popped off, black oil poured out. "Now, as soon as all that dirty old oil drains out, we'll replace the nut. Then I'll let you pump in some fresh new oil. That'll make this car a whole lot happier!"

When you've sinned, you don't have to clean yourself up inside before you draw near to God. Just come as you are. He'll take away the mess you've been hiding and pour brand-new life into you.

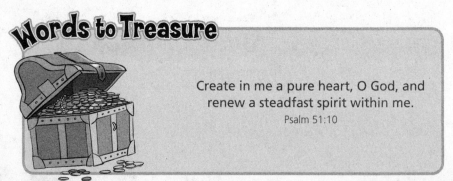

Words to Treasure

Create in me a pure heart, O God, and renew a steadfast spirit within me.
Psalm 51:10

Shaping Your Character

O Lord, you are our Father. We are the clay,
you are the potter.

Isaiah 64:8

At his mom's pottery studio, Alec was helping teach kids how to use a potter's wheel. "This isn't coming out right!" said a girl named Rhonda. She was trying to mold the clay as it spun on the wheel in front of her.

"What's wrong?" Alec asked.

She pointed at her bowl. "Look at how crooked the top is. You can't eat cereal out of a bowl like that!"

Alec examined her work. "I see what you mean. Don't get frustrated. As long as you keep the clay wet, you can keep working on it until it looks good to you." He showed her how to use her fingers, then watched her reshape the bowl. "That's better," he said. "I bet it'll hold your Froot Loops now!"

As God forms you into the person he wants you to be, don't worry. There's no permanent flaw in you that will ruin your usefulness to him. Just stay soft and pliable in God's hands. He'll keep reshaping your character until it's pleasing to him. God can and will make you into someone he can use.

Life in Bible Times

When a potter in ancient days made a bowl, he had a certain shape in mind. He kept forming the clay until it was just right. As long as the clay didn't harden, he could fix any problems in it. (See Jeremiah 18:1–12.)

One of the Good Guys

> Blessed are those who hunger and thirst for righteousness, for they will be filled.
>
> Matthew 5:6

Josh watched the action onstage at the community theater, his heart pounding. It was opening night for *Camelot*, and he was about to make his entrance. He was playing Tom, a boy who wanted to be one of King Arthur's knights. Josh could relate. It wasn't hard for him to pretend to be Tom, because Josh had always been inspired by heroes in stories. That's why he loved acting. He could make believe he was a hero.

Watching the man playing King Arthur, Josh waited for his cue. He loved this part of the play. In it, the king granted Tom his wish. The king had the boy kneel, tapped him with his sword, and made him a knight. Josh knew his own dreams would come true, because he'd decided to do whatever it took to be one of the good guys.

Do you root for the good guys in stories and in real life? Do you long to be one? This is part of what Jesus meant when he talked about being hungry for righteousness. If you're hungry like that, make up your mind to do whatever you need to do to be a good person. Ask God to show you how. He'll teach you what to do and help you become a true hero.

Words to Treasure

[The Lord] loves those who pursue righteousness.
Proverbs 15:9

The Best Name of All

[Jesus told his disciples,] "When you pray, say:
" 'Father ...' "

Luke 11:2

Kora was excited, because it was Bring a Parent to School Day. In her classroom, kids were introducing their moms or dads and talking about their jobs. Finally it was her turn. Smiling, she led her dad up front. "This is my father, and he's a judge," she said. "He works in a courtroom. When people have an argument, he decides who's right and who's wrong."

Raising his hand, Victor asked her dad, "Is it fun to bang your gavel?"

Grinning, he nodded. "Yes, it is!"

Tessa waved her hand. "Do people always call you Your Honor?"

Kora's father replied, "When I'm at work, everyone calls me that. When I'm playing golf with my friends, they call me by my real name, Harold." He put his arm around Kora. "But no matter where I am, this girl calls me by my favorite name—Daddy!"

Since ancient times, God has been known by various names, such as "Elohim," "Adonai," and "El-Shaddai." Today many Christians call him "God" or "Lord." The most important name to remember is "Father," because that one reminds you that you're his child.

Did You Know?

God's divine name is "Yahweh." That's a Hebrew word meaning, "I am." His other names are really more like titles. They describe who he is, what he is like, or what he does.

A Colorful Beam

Your word is a lamp to my feet and a light for
my path.

Psalm 119:105

Chris turned off the lights in his dad's home lab. He was helping his father, a science teacher, try an experiment. "Here," his dad said. "Use this flashlight and magnifying glass to shine a light beam through that prism."

Chris aimed the flashlight at a triangle-shaped piece of glass on the workbench. He focused the beam with the magnifying glass. A bright, rainbow-like spectrum appeared.

"People once believed those colors came from the prism," his dad said. "But Isaac Newton thought that the colors were in the light, and that the prism just split them apart. He proved it by putting the colors back together." Chris's dad set a second prism on the workbench. Using another magnifying glass, he directed the colored beams through it. Out came a beam of white light.

God's Word, the Bible, has been split up into many verses. That helps people study it. Different verses teach about different parts of life—such as friendship, prayer, or kindness. Keep studying and learning the verses of your Bible. Together they form a powerful light to guide you.

Live It!

Make a Scripture spectrum. Draw a rainbow. In each part of the rainbow, write a topic you want guidance on. Then write the reference of a Bible verse about that topic. This Scripture spectrum will remind you of what God's Word says about important areas of your life!

Dancing to a Heavenly Beat

Since we live by the Spirit, let us keep in step with the Spirit.

Galatians 5:25

Lights flashed and music pounded. Dawn and Sierra were dancing side by side on a machine at the video arcade. They were trying to keep up with the arrows scrolling on the screen in front of them. Laughing, the friends jumped up and down on the dance pad.

"Did it!" Dawn said, landing on two arrows to finish a combo move. Her side of the screen flashed, "Great." Sierra was struggling. She couldn't seem to do what the screen was telling her to do. Finally the song ended. Breathing hard, the girls checked their scores. "You did all right," Dawn said.

Sierra shook her head. "Not really. I just can't get the hang of it."

Dawn tried to offer some advice. "Well, you can't just watch the screen. You have to listen to the music too. That's how you get in synch with the beat!"

To live God's way, you need to do more than read his Word. You also have to listen to his voice. The Holy Spirit warns you when you're about to make the wrong moves (sinning). He reminds you what the right moves are (obeying God's laws). When you make the right moves, you're keeping in step with the Spirit. You're dancing to the music of heaven!

Words to Treasure

Live by the Spirit, and you will not gratify the desires of the sinful nature.

Galatians 5:16

Broadcasting the News

[Jesus said,] "Go into all the world and preach the good news to all creation."

Mark 16:15

Josh stood on the community theater stage, taking a bow. The opening-night performance of *Camelot* had gone well. Backstage, his mom said, "You were wonderful!"

A TV reporter approached Josh. "May I interview you?" she asked.

"Sure," Josh replied.

The cameraman switched on a bright light. Holding a microphone, the reporter said, "Josh, you play Tom, a boy who wants to be one of King Arthur's knights. How did you prepare for that role?"

Josh answered, "First, I learned my lines. Also, the director helped me understand what happens in my scene. He said that when King Arthur orders Tom to tell everyone about Camelot, it's like Jesus commanding his disciples to tell people about God's kingdom. That helped me play my part."

In the book *The Once and Future King*, King Arthur's idea to create a great kingdom is described as a burning candle. That candle lit up Tom's heart. The king told him to take it and light up the hearts of others. The gospel message works the same way. After it lights up your heart, God wants you to share it with other people. Then it sets their hearts on fire.

People in Bible Times

After the shepherds saw baby Jesus, they told people the Savior had come. The gospel had lit up the shepherds' hearts. They shared that light with others. (See Luke 2:8–20.)

Calm in a Crisis

Even though I walk through the valley of the shadow of death, I will fear no evil, for you are with me, [O Lord]; your rod and your staff, they comfort me.

Psalm 23:4

The bedroom filled with smoke, and Alyssa couldn't see. Getting on the floor, she started crawling straight ahead. When she felt a wall, she followed it to the door. Alyssa reached for the knob, then stopped and felt the door. It was hot. She couldn't get out that way. Now she was getting scared. "Mom!" she cried, crawling around blindly.

At that moment she heard her mother's voice. "I'm here, Alyssa. Don't panic. Think about what to do next." Alyssa thought hard. Then she went back to the wall. Following it in the other direction, she found a window. She opened it and scrambled out—onto the balcony of the Fire Safety House. It was a special motor home the fire department was using (with fake smoke) to teach kids how to escape from a burning home. Alyssa's mother followed her out. "Good job, honey. You did it!"

Psalm 23 describes God as a shepherd who guides and protects his sheep. When you're in danger, God guides and protects you. Call out to him whenever you're in trouble. He'll calm your fear and help you think clearly so you can do what you need to do.

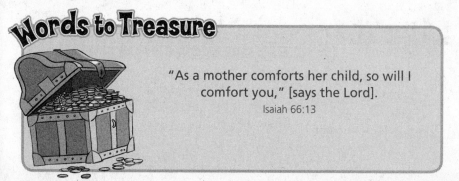

Words to Treasure

"As a mother comforts her child, so will I comfort you," [says the Lord].
Isaiah 66:13

Wholesome Nutrition

> Man does not live on bread alone, but on every word that comes from the mouth of God.
>
> Matthew 4:4

During the class trip to a pizzeria, Raymond was tossing dough to make a crust. "That's good!" said the restaurant owner. Taking the dough, he placed it on the counter. "Now we add the sauce." He ladled spicy tomato sauce over the dough. "Next, some mozzarella." Grabbing a grater, he piled on shredded cheese. "Finally, the toppings." He chopped up green peppers, onions, olives, and mushrooms. Then he sliced thin circles of pepperoni and arranged everything on the pizza. "Now it's ready to bake!" Slipping a wooden paddle under the pizza, he slid it into a hot brick oven.

Raymond's teacher said, "Okay, class. Who can name the food groups on our pizza?"

A girl raised her hand. "Bread, dairy, vegetables, and meat."

The teacher said, "Good, Joanna."

Smelling the pizza baking, Raymond grinned. "Mmm. That's what I call good nutrition!"

Healthy food is important for your body. In the same way, God's words are vital for your soul. Feed your body good food daily. And be sure to read your Bible and listen to God's voice, so your spirit will be well fed too.

Live It!

Go to www.mypyramid.gov and print a poster of the MyPyramid symbol. Write the words of Matthew 4:4 on it. Tape it on your refrigerator to remind your family to eat right *and* take in God's words!

Magic vs. Miracles

Do not practice divination or sorcery.
Leviticus 19:26

A Christian magician was performing for the children at Allison's church. He pointed at her. "Would you help me, young lady?" Allison went up on stage, and he handed her a birdcage. "This is empty, right?" he asked. She felt around inside and nodded. He covered it with a black cloth, clapped his hands, and asked her to remove the cloth. Allison whisked it away, and there was a dove, flapping its wings!

The magician spoke to his audience. "Kids, the kind of magic I do is illusion. That means I trick your eyes so you think you see something impossible happen. It's fun, and it's different from divination or sorcery. That's where people wanting help or guidance try to tap into some source of supernatural power besides God's. Doing that is dangerous, because it gets you involved with evil spirits." Pulling the bird out of the cage, he held it up. "I used a dove for this trick because it's a symbol of the Holy Spirit. When you need help, don't go to spirit boards, horoscopes, séances, or witchcraft. Go to God!"

Evil spirits want to hurt you and mislead you, not help you. God loves you and wants you to come to him for direction and help. His wisdom and power are unlimited. They're greater than any you could tap into anywhere else.

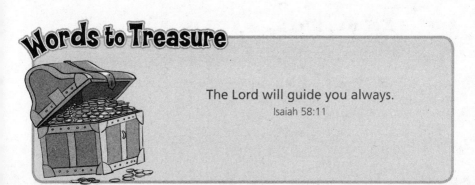

Words to Treasure

The Lord will guide you always.
Isaiah 58:11

From Generation to Generation

The righteous man leads a blameless life;
blessed are his children after him.

Proverbs 20:7

Hayden slid into a booth at Farrell's Ice Cream Parlour. "Your grandfather took me to one of these restaurants when I was young," his dad said. The room was bright and colorful. Servers wore old-fashioned striped shirts and flat round hats. A player piano banged out music.

Looking around, Hayden smiled. "This is great, Dad."

Suddenly a bell clanged. "Ladies and gentlemen," a server announced, "a birthday party just ordered a Zoo sundae—the largest sundae in the world!" As a siren blared, two servers ran around, carrying a tray with a huge silver bowl full of ice cream and toppings.

Hayden laughed. "I love this place!"

Grinning, his dad said, "I'm glad. Maybe someday you'll bring your kids here."

If you have godly parents, be thankful. God is blessing you because of them. Listen to them and follow their example, because they're trying to share with you something very special. Nothing would make them happier than to pass their faith along to you, and see you pass it on to your children.

Life in Bible Times

The Israelites did many things to pass down their faith. They wrote God's laws in places where their children would see them. They had celebrations so their children would remember great things God did. They set up memorials to remind their children about God's faithfulness.

Learning by the Book

All Scripture is God-breathed and is useful for teaching, rebuking, correcting and training in righteousness.

2 Timothy 3:16

In Crystal's basement, Crystal and her friend Dana were juggling beanbags. Watching them, Crystal's brother said, "You guys are good!"

"Thanks," Crystal replied as they stopped to rest for a moment. "Dana found this great book that's teaching us. It was written by a master juggler."

Starting to juggle again, Dana said, "Let's practice passing." They tried throwing beanbags to one another. But each time, they both dropped other ones while trying to catch the pass.

Crystal checked the book. "It says we have to juggle at the same speed and watch each other." She set the pace. "One, two, three, four … one, two, three, four …. Now, when I say, 'Pass,' throw me a beanbag. Ready? Pass!" Watching Crystal, Dana threw one. At the same time, Crystal threw one to her. This time they caught them cleanly. "Great!" Crystal said. "Keep going! Pass, two, three, four … pass, two, three, four …"

Many experts have written books that show you how to do all kinds of things. But God is the ultimate expert, and the Bible is the ultimate how-to book. Through the Bible, God can teach you everything you need to know about living. Keep your Bible close at hand, and refer to it daily.

Words to Treasure

The unfolding of your words gives light, [O Lord]; it gives understanding to the simple.
Psalm 119:130

Seekers = Finders

"You will seek me and find me when you seek me with all your heart," [declares the Lord].

Jeremiah 29:13

Duncan got up early Saturday morning. His dad had promised him and his sister that they'd do some fun things together while Mom was away. On Duncan's door was a yellow sticky note that said, "Bet you can't find me!" It was signed, "Dad."

Duncan woke up Alicia and showed her the note. Grinning, she said, "He's probably in the bathtub!" Racing through the house, they checked all the usual hiding places. They found notes that said, "You're cold" or "Getting warmer." The one in the hall closet said, "You're on fire!" Rushing into the garage, they looked in the SUV. Then Duncan noticed the tool cabinet in the corner. They yanked open the doors.

"You found me!" their dad said, grabbing and tickling them. "Come on, I'll make you some chocolate-chip pancakes."

God wants to know that you really want to spend the day with him. Show him you do, by seeking him. The inside of your Bible is a good place to start, and prayer is a great way to keep looking. If you seek God wholeheartedly, you'll find him. He's not far away, and he wants to be found.

People in Bible Times

The magi looked for Jesus earnestly. They followed a bright new star all the way to Bethlehem, looking for the new King. When they found Jesus, they rejoiced. (See Matthew 2:1–12.)

The "Candy Machine"

Do you not know that your body is a temple of the Holy Spirit?

1 Corinthians 6:19

Entering the diner, Emma looked around. Her family had been driving for hours through the middle of nowhere, heading out West to go snowmobiling in the mountains. "Look, Reid," she said, pointing at an old vending machine. They went to check it out.

"It's full of cigarettes!" Reid exclaimed. He started pulling the knobs.

"What's that?" their dad asked.

Emma turned. "It's a cigarette machine! We didn't know you could buy cigarettes this way."

Their dad smiled. "First you'd have to prove to the cashier that you're old enough. But even if you could get cigarettes easily, you shouldn't smoke. God doesn't want you putting harmful things in your bodies."

Later, as Emma sat sipping a malt, she said, "I wish that machine sold candy. I'd love a Snickers bar."

Her dad laughed. "Sorry, sweetheart. God doesn't want you eating too many goodies either!"

Did you know that the temple in Jerusalem during Jesus' time had golden spikes on its roof? They kept birds from making a mess all over the place where God's Spirit dwelled. Today the Holy Spirit lives in your body. Don't mess up God's new temple with tobacco smoke, drugs, alcohol, or even too many snack foods. God cares deeply about what you put into your body—and what you do with your body as well.

Words to Treasure

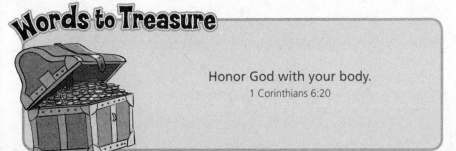

Honor God with your body.
1 Corinthians 6:20

A Panoramic View

> The devil took [Jesus] to a very high mountain and showed him all the kingdoms of the world and their splendor. "All this I will give you," he said, "if you will bow down and worship me."
>
> Matthew 4:8–9

Tyler and his dad stepped into the glass elevator. "Seventy-third floor, please," his father said. They were in the Peachtree Plaza hotel in Atlanta, Georgia. Tyler's dad had brought him along on a business trip. As the elevator rose, Tyler gazed outside. "I have a surprise for you," his dad said when the elevator stopped. "We're eating in a revolving restaurant!" They got out, and Tyler's jaw dropped. The restaurant was round, and the tables were slowly moving past huge glass walls.

"Dad, this rocks!" For an hour, they enjoyed lunch while admiring a view of the entire city.

When the Devil showed Jesus all the world's kingdoms, he was tempting Jesus with something he didn't even own. Jesus knew that Satan is a liar. (See John 8:44.) He also knew that the *real* owner of the world is God. And Jesus knew that only God is worthy to be worshiped. When the Devil tempts you, remember the truth you've learned from the Bible. Don't fall for his lies!

Did You Know?

Satan twists the truth. When he tempted Jesus, Satan quoted part of the Scriptures so his challenge seemed sensible. Jesus wasn't fooled, because he knew *everything* God's Word said. (See Matthew 4:1–11.)

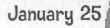

Searching Deep

Search me, O God, and know my heart; test me and know my anxious thoughts. See if there is any offensive way in me, and lead me in the way everlasting.

Psalm 139:23–24

Bryson and his father trudged across the frozen lake. "This looks like a good spot," his dad said. He set down their fishing equipment, then used an auger to start drilling a hole.

"Can I try?" Bryson asked.

His dad looked up. "Sure! You can finish the job." Straining to turn the auger, Bryson finally broke through the ice. "Good work!" his dad said.

Bryson noticed a device in his dad's hand. "What's that?"

Grinning, his father replied, "Our secret weapon. It uses sound waves to find fish." Into the hole he dropped a small, oval-shaped object on a wire. Then he turned on the fish finder. "There's the lake bottom," he said, pointing at the screen. "And those blips are fish. This *is* a good spot!"

God can look deep into your heart and see things you can't. For example, let's say you have an argument with someone. You might think you've done nothing wrong. But if you ask God to search your heart, he'll show you whatever sin is there. Then you can ask him—and the person you fought with—for forgiveness. Dealing with the sin in *your* heart is the best way to settle your differences with someone else.

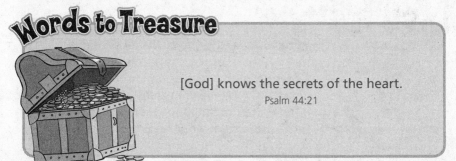

Words to Treasure

[God] knows the secrets of the heart.
Psalm 44:21

A Fountain of Goodness

> [Jesus said,] "Whoever believes in me, as the Scripture has said, streams of living water will flow from within him."
>
> John 7:38

Missy stood beside the kitchen table, eyes closed. "Don't peek," her mother said. Then Missy heard a humming sound, and all of her friends oohed and aahed.

"What is it?" she asked.

"It's a birthday surprise," said her mom. "Okay, you can look." Missy opened her eyes. On the table was a chocolate fountain.

"Oh, wow!" she exclaimed. The fountain was three feet tall. Melted chocolate was flowing over four tiers and falling into a silver basin.

"It looks like a chocolate waterfall," said Angelina.

Missy said, "Dip in, everyone!" Around the fountain were strawberries, marshmallows, graham crackers, ice cream balls, and little squares of cake. Using toothpicks, everybody dipped the treats into the fountain and ate them.

"This is sweet!" said Mara. Missy giggled. Her friend's mouth was covered with chocolate.

When you believe in Jesus, you become like a fountain. Then God blesses others through you. He fills you with "living water"—in other words, his Spirit. God's beautiful presence in you overflows, and then everyone around you is touched by it too.

Live It!

With your parents' help, throw a fondue party. Borrow or rent a chocolate fountain. Or simply melt chocolate and serve it in a nice bowl. While your guests enjoy the goodies, tell them about the wonder of God's presence in your life.

Pen Pals

Abraham ... was called God's friend.

James 2:23

Luke burst into the kitchen, opening an envelope. "We got a letter from Miguel!"

His mother smiled. "That's wonderful. What does it say?" Luke's family had decided to sponsor a needy child from another country. They'd agreed to send money each month to an organization called Compassion International. That way, the organization could feed Miguel, help him stay healthy, help educate him, and tell him about Jesus. And the best part was, Luke and Miguel were going to be pen pals!

"There's Miguel's handwriting," Luke said, "but it's in Spanish."

His mom asked, "Isn't it translated into English?"

Luke flipped the letter over. "Oh yeah. Here it is." He read it. "Wow. Miguel goes to school like me, and he loves baseball too." Luke lived in Minnesota. Miguel lived in Nicaragua, which was in Central America. Using the Internet, Luke and his parents had learned a lot about Nicaragua. Luke wanted to go there someday and meet Miguel in person. Meanwhile, it was cool having a friend in another country. Grabbing a pen, Luke said, "I'm gonna write back and tell Miguel all about me!"

Prayer allows you to be "pen pals" with God. Although you can't see God now, you can build a friendship with him through prayer. And someday, with faith in Jesus, you'll meet God face-to-face.

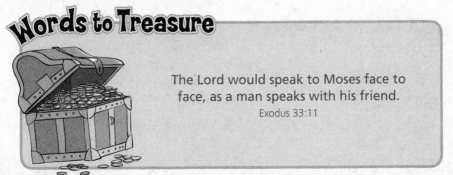

Words to Treasure

The Lord would speak to Moses face to face, as a man speaks with his friend.

Exodus 33:11

Seeing a Miracle

[O Lord,] you created my inmost being; you knit me together in my mother's womb.

Psalm 139:13

Where's the baby?" Devin asked, staring at the monitor. He and his sister Amanda were at the hospital, watching their mother get a sonogram.

The sonographer smiled as she moved an instrument over their mom's belly. "Don't worry, the baby's in there. It's harder to see things in sonograms. They're not like photos. Photographs use light to make an image, but sonograms use sound."

Suddenly Devon pointed. "Is that the baby's head?"

"Yes," the sonographer replied, "and there's a hand."

Amanda bounced on her feet. "The baby's moving around!"

Their mom laughed. "Just like you do when I take your picture."

Looking at Amanda, the sonographer said, "Sounds like this little girl is a lot like you."

Amanda gasped. "Did you say *girl*?"

The woman nodded. "That's right—it's a baby girl." Amanda gave a cry of glee. As she hugged their mom, Devin marveled at his new sister.

Every person is a miracle created by God. That includes you. Long before anyone saw you, God was forming your body. And he was doing it in ways only he understands. Whenever you look in a mirror, remember that you are a very special being. After all, you were made by an amazing Creator!

Words to Treasure

I praise you because I am fearfully and wonderfully made; your works are wonderful, I know that full well.
Psalm 139:14

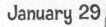

Karaoke Choir

Sing to the Lord, praise his name; proclaim his salvation day after day. Declare his glory among the nations, his marvelous deeds among all peoples.

Psalm 96:2–3

At Angie's birthday party, Laurel sat in a pizza place with twelve other guests. "Let's all go up and do a karaoke song!" Angie said.

Laurel asked, "What'll we sing?"

Angie smiled. "How about 'Our God Is an Awesome God'?"

Glancing around, Laurel cringed. "Do they even have any Christian songs here?"

Laughing, Angie said, "I don't know. Let's find out." She went to the DJ and spoke with him. He nodded, and she waved for the others to join her onstage. As the music started, they stood around the microphone. Watching the words on the monitor, they joyfully sang God's praises. The audience didn't exactly go wild, but they didn't throw tomatoes either. And Laurel noticed a few people singing along.

Don't be afraid to praise God wherever you are. It doesn't matter whether you're singing or speaking. God is worthy to be worshiped anywhere. He's especially honored when you praise him in public. That way, everyone can hear. And you never know whose heart you may touch, or who may join you.

People in Bible Times

Paul and Silas sang praises to God in prison! There was an earthquake, and all the prisoners could've escaped. But they didn't. As a result, the jailer put his trust in Jesus. (See Acts 16:25–34.)

Watch Your Step!

Make level paths for your feet and take only
ways that are firm.

Proverbs 4:26

Standing on a ladder, A.J. poked his head into the attic. His father needed his help while he did some work in there. "Come on up," his dad said, aiming the flashlight in front of A.J. "Just be careful. Stay on these wooden planks."

A.J. scrambled up. "It's creepy in here," he said, following his father along the walkway.

"Yeah," his dad replied. "Kind of dark and stuffy." He shone the flashlight around. "Those crisscrossed boards are called trusses. They hold up the roof above us and the ceiling below."

A.J. asked, "What's that pink stuff all over the floor?"

Pointing the flashlight down, his dad said, "That's insulation. It keeps heat inside the house in the wintertime. Don't step on it. The only thing underneath the insulation is the plasterboard ceiling. That won't hold your weight. If you try to walk there, you'll end up flat on your back in the middle of the living room floor!"

God's laws are like sturdy, level planks you can step on with confidence. If you walk on them as you make your way through life, they'll keep you from falling. Learn God's laws well, so with all the steps you take, you'll know right where to set your feet.

Words to Treasure

Blessed are they whose ways
are blameless, who walk
according to the law of the Lord.
Psalm 119:1

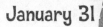

Eye on the Ball

A discerning man keeps wisdom in view.
Proverbs 17:24

In the center of the racquetball court, Angelica's mother turned to her. "Ready?"

Standing in the back of the court, Angelica said, "Go ahead!" They'd been playing racquetball at the health club a lot during the winter. Angelica was getting good at it, and their games were getting competitive. Her mom served the blue rubber ball. *Thwoing!* It made the strange, echoey noise that Angelica thought was so funny. The ball hit the front wall, then bounced toward the back corner. Angelica lunged, making a backhand shot. It hit the front wall and rebounded to her mom's right. Her mother hit the ball again. Then she stood in the center of the court, facing forward. Angelica chased the ball and made a solid forehand shot. It hit her mom right in the back of the head! "Sorry, Mom," Angelica said, trying not to laugh. "Are you okay?"

Rubbing her head, her mom said, "Guess I should've kept my eye on the ball!"

In sports, it's important to keep your eye on the ball. In life, you have to keep your focus on wisdom. That'll keep you from stepping off God's path and doing something foolish. How do you keep wisdom in view? By reading the Bible daily. By remembering what it says. And by staying tuned in to the Holy Spirit.

Words to Treasure

Preserve sound judgment and discernment,
do not let them out of your sight.
Proverbs 3:21

Raising Your Hand

> I heard the voice of the Lord saying, "Whom shall I send? And who will go for us?" And I said, "Here am I. Send me!"
>
> Isaiah 6:8

"Hey, Mom," Chad said after church. "Mr. Lewis visited our Sunday school class. He needs some kids to help him with a project, so I volunteered."

"To do what?" Chad's mom asked.

Chad shrugged. "I don't know. He didn't have time to explain." Chad's mom called to get more details. It turned out Mr. Lewis, an artist, needed some models for a painting. When Chad learned that, he was glad he'd raised his hand.

Later, when they arrived at the studio, Mr. Lewis said, "Come in. I'm painting the scene where Jesus blesses the children. I want it to be filled with kids running around, having fun." Chad put on the costume Mr. Lewis gave him. He had a great time wrestling another boy on the set while Mr. Lewis took pictures of the group.

Whenever God is looking for somebody, be eager to say, "I'll do it!" You may wind up delivering food to the needy. Or going on a mission trip with your family. Or doing something you never thought of before. God will lead you on exciting adventures if you're willing to serve him.

People in Bible Times

None of the Israelite soldiers were brave enough to face Goliath. David knew God was looking for someone to fight the giant. So he volunteered. And God gave David a great victory! (See 1 Samuel 17:1–58.)

A Peek at Paradise

[The angel] showed me the Holy City, Jerusalem, coming down out of heaven from God. It shone with the glory of God, and its brilliance was like that of a very precious jewel.

Revelation 21:10–11

Look, Mom," Rachel said, staring out the living room window. "It's beautiful!" Her mother came over to see. "That was quite an ice storm last night," she said.

Rachel hurried to the closet. "I want to see this up close!" Putting on her winter clothes, she went outside. The cold stung her face, but she was too dazzled to care. The sky was perfectly clear, and morning sunlight sparkled through the trees' icy branches. Everything—the mailbox, the fence, a car across the street—was coated in shimmering ice. The whole world glittered as if it were made of diamonds. Rachel felt like a princess in a crystal kingdom.

Sometimes this world offers a hint of what heaven is like. The Bible reveals even more. It says heaven is lit up with God's glory. And all that marvelous light blazing from God is reflected off golden streets, golden buildings, gates made of pearls, a crystal-clear river, and walls decorated with jewels. God gives you "glimpses of heaven" so you'll realize what a wonderful place it is. That way, you'll want to live with him there forever.

Words to Treasure

The city [of heaven] does not need the sun or the moon to shine on it, for the glory of God gives it light.
Revelation 21:23

Doing the Drills

> No discipline seems pleasant at the time, but painful. Later on, however, it produces a harvest of righteousness and peace for those who have been trained by it.
>
> Hebrews 12:11

Sitting in the music store, Timothy couldn't wait to start taking guitar lessons. But he learned that playing a guitar wasn't easy. "Hold down the strings firmly behind the frets," his guitar teacher said. "That way, the strings won't buzz." He demonstrated, playing a nice, clear chord on a guitar. Timothy tried it on his instrument. The notes sounded buzzy. His teacher adjusted his fingers, telling him to press harder. This time the chord sounded better.

Timothy smiled. "I did it!" Rubbing his hand, he added, "But it hurts."

His teacher nodded. "Practice the exercises I gave you. Your fingers will get stronger and more flexible, and your fingertips will toughen up. Then you can make sweet music."

God disciplines people in two ways. One way is by giving them consequences for doing the wrong thing. The other way is by helping them practice doing the right thing. It can be very hard to do what's right, like being patient when your younger brother doesn't understand the rules of a game. But the more you practice doing the right thing, the better you get at it.

Did You Know?

God's discipline trains you to be righteous. This spiritual training has great worth for your life on earth and for your future life in heaven. (See Hebrews 12:11; 1 Timothy 4:7–8.)

Turnaround

[The Prodigal Son said to himself,] "I will set out and go back to my father and say to him: Father, I have sinned."

Luke 15:18

Bianca and her family were visiting relatives in Melbourne, Australia. It was Bianca's first trip "down under"—that is, below the equator. Last night her cousin Kerry had shown her a constellation called the Southern Cross. He'd said it was only visible from the lower half of the world! Today he was teaching her how to throw a boomerang. "Hold it straight up, with the blade pointing away from you," he said, standing beside her in his backyard.

"Like this?" she asked.

He nodded. "That's right! Now throw it overhand. It'll flatten out and curve around back to you." Bianca threw the boomerang. Spinning through the air, it traced a big circle in the sky and landed at her feet.

When you sin, never say to yourself, "Well, I blew it. God doesn't love me anymore. I might as well keep on sinning." Instead act like a boomerang! Spin around and head back to your heavenly Father. Confess your sin to God and ask him to forgive you. He will. He loves you so much that he sacrificed his Son, Jesus, on the cross so you *could* return to him. All you have to do is turn around and go back, just like the Prodigal Son.

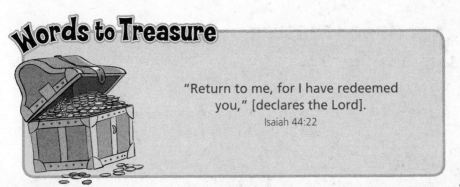

Words to Treasure

"Return to me, for I have redeemed you," [declares the Lord].
Isaiah 44:22

Gone for Good

> You will tread our sins underfoot and hurl all our iniquities into the depths of the sea.
>
> Micah 7:19

A buzzer sounded at the indoor ice rink. Struggling to stay on his skates, Ian said, "Aw, I was just getting good at this!"

His dad laughed. "It's time for the Zamboni to come out." Everyone left the rink, and a large, rectangular vehicle rolled onto it. A man rode it around, smoothing out the ice.

When the man drove off the rink, Ian and his dad asked him if they could look at his machine. "Sure!" the man said, climbing down. He pointed out the blade that scraped off the rough ice, and the tank where it was collected. "Come on," he said, climbing back up. "I'll show you what we do with the old ice." They followed him into a back room. There he pulled a lever. The front of the Zamboni machine tilted, dumping the ice on the floor. It looked like snow. "We call this room the snow pit," he said. "Here the bad ice melts and goes down the drain."

When God forgives you and takes away your sins, he doesn't keep them someplace. He never pulls them out again to remind you of them. He gets rid of them completely, so neither of you ever has to think about them again.

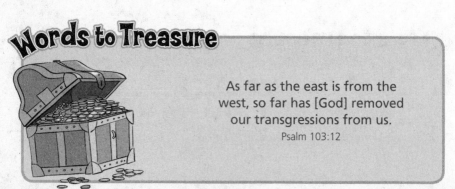

Words to Treasure

As far as the east is from the west, so far has [God] removed our transgressions from us.
Psalm 103:12

Pulling Together

We rebuilt the wall till all of it reached half its height, for the people worked with all their heart.

Nehemiah 4:6

When C.J. and her brother Todd got home from school, their parents were busy cooking. "What are you making?" C.J. asked.

Her dad put down a spoon. "Well, I have a special activity planned. Your mom and I are ready to open our own flower shop. Now, the whole family will need to pitch in to make this new business a success. So we're having a taffy-pull party, to remind us all to keep pulling together." He showed them how to stretch the warm taffy again and again to make it light and chewy. "Grab a handful, everyone!" Soon they were all laughing and pulling, helping each other stretch the gooey candy.

In Nehemiah's day, the wall around Jerusalem was broken. The Israelites needed to rebuild it. So families pulled together to get the job done. That's what God wants to happen today in your family—and his. Do your part to make your family a success. Work at it with all your heart. And pull together with the members of God's family to help build his kingdom on earth.

People in Bible Times

Families in Jerusalem worked as teams to fix the city wall. Each family repaired the part of the wall near their home. By pulling together, the people rebuilt the wall in fifty-two days. (See Nehemiah 2:11–6:16.)

Keeping Harmony

Love … is not rude.

1 Corinthians 13:4–5

As colored lights flashed, Conrad played his big drum solo in front of thousands of screaming fans. The other band members had left the stage, because it was clear that the audience wanted to hear only him. He beat the drums furiously, his hands moving at lightning speed. People were stomping and clapping and chanting his name: *Conrad! Conrad!*

"CONRAD!" his mother yelled.

The stage, lights, and crowd disappeared. Conrad found himself back in his basement, practicing on his new set of drums. He stopped playing, then grabbed the cymbal to silence it. "What, Mom?"

Coming downstairs, she gave him a stern look. "Your sister is upset. She said she asked you to stop so she could listen to the TV. Didn't you hear her?"

Sighing, Conrad said, "Yeah, but I just got these drums, and I wanted to play them."

His mom held out her hand. "You'd better turn in your drumsticks until you can learn to be more considerate. It's rude to only think about yourself. I don't mind a little banging around here, as long as there's harmony in our home!"

Part of loving people is caring about their well-being as much as your own. This helps keep your relationships with others pleasant and peaceful. So don't be rude. Show people you love them, by being considerate of their wants and needs.

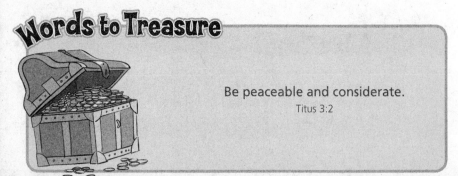

Words to Treasure

Be peaceable and considerate.
Titus 3:2

The Gateway

> Small is the gate and narrow the road that leads to life, and only a few find it.
>
> Matthew 7:14

Gage and his family entered the odd little vehicle, filling its five seats. The tram car at the Gateway Arch in St. Louis, Missouri, was the strangest "elevator" Gage had ever seen. For one thing, it was shaped like a sideways tube. The car began rising inside the arch.

"Wait a minute!" Gage said. "Aren't we gonna tip over?"

His dad replied, "No. These cars stay level, like Ferris wheel seats."

When the tram car stopped, they all got out to see the view. Looking down, Gage gulped. There was nothing under them now but the ground 630 feet below. But it was cool being on top of the glistening steel arch. The monument stood beside the Mississippi River, in the middle of the United States. It was a reminder that St. Louis was once the gateway to the West for American explorers and pioneers.

Your family's set of rules is like a gateway and road your parents chose. Sometimes that road may seem too narrow. Especially when other parents' rules aren't as strict! But remember, Jesus said that the narrow road is the best one to take. That's the road of following him and living God's way.

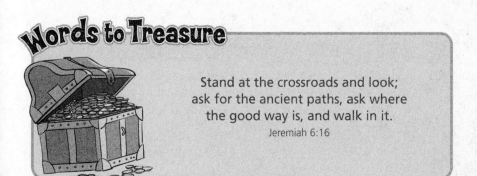

Words to Treasure

Stand at the crossroads and look; ask for the ancient paths, ask where the good way is, and walk in it.
Jeremiah 6:16

Be Ready

> Always be prepared to give an answer to everyone who asks you to give the reason for the hope that you have.
>
> 1 Peter 3:15

Carissa sat in the fire truck, hands on the wheel. Grabbing the radio microphone, she said, "We're ready to roll!"

Her uncle George, a fireman, laughed. "You look like a real firefighter."

"Which switch turns on the lights?" Carissa asked.

He pointed. "That one. Go ahead and push it." Carissa did, and red lights began flashing.

Her uncle showed her around the station. Upstairs he pointed out the kitchen, living area, and sleeping quarters. "Firefighters spend some time here," he said. "But they also spend lots of time caring for their equipment and practicing their skills. That way, they're ready when the alarm rings." He showed her a brass pole. "If necessary, they slide down this to get to the truck quickly."

Carissa said, "I wanna try it!"

What if someone asked you how you could be so sure you were going to heaven? Would you be prepared to tell the reason? Spend some time practicing how to explain the gospel. Memorize verses like John 3:16. Then you'll be ready to share the good news with someone who needs to hear it.

Did You Know?

Jesus died so people who believe in him won't have to die for their sins. He's like a brave firefighter who gave his life to rescue others. That's the good news of the gospel! (See John 3:16.)

Honestly, You Guys!

They acted with complete honesty.

2 Kings 12:15

Drew stared at the figure of a boy sitting on a fence outside a log cabin. "Looks real, doesn't he?" said someone behind Drew. It was another boy his age.

"Yeah," Drew said. "Think he actually looked like this as a kid?" They were at the Abraham Lincoln Presidential Library and Museum in Springfield, Illinois. There they were exploring an exhibit about Lincoln's childhood home.

The boy shrugged. "What I wonder is, was he really so honest? I heard he walked five miles barefoot through the snow just to return a penny."

Laughing, Drew said, "I don't know if that story's true or not. But I did a project on Lincoln once, and I learned he was pretty honest. He didn't make much money as a lawyer. If he hadn't been so honest, he could've been a lot richer."

The boy nodded, then said, "Hey, have you seen the 'Ghosts of the Library' show? It's cool. A guy on stage talks to a hologram of Lincoln!"

God wants you to be totally honest. And he'll reward you for your integrity. So go out of your way to return a wallet you find on the ground. If necessary, walk a few blocks through the snow to repay money you owe. Just be sure to wear your boots!

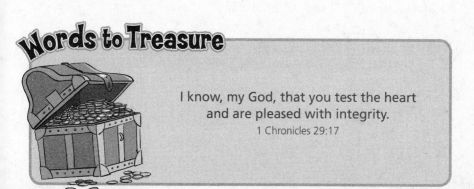

Words to Treasure

I know, my God, that you test the heart and are pleased with integrity.

1 Chronicles 29:17

Using What You've Got

> [The kingdom of heaven] will be like a man going on a journey, who called his servants and entrusted his property to them. To one he gave five talents of money, to another two talents, and to another one talent.
>
> Matthew 25:14–15

Counting out bills, Sally gave everyone lots of money. It was Monopoly night, and she was the banker. Her mom, dad, brother, and little sister arranged their cash on the kitchen table. "Let's let Maddie go first," Sally's mom said, "since it's her first time playing this game."

Maddie rolled the dice. "I got eight!" She moved her little dog token eight spaces, landing on Vermont Avenue.

"Wanna buy it?" Sally asked. Maddie said no. They all took turns rolling the dice and moving their tokens. Everyone bought properties—except Maddie. She just moved around the board, collecting two hundred dollars every time she passed Go.

Finally Sally said, "Maddie, you can't just stuff all your money under the board. You have to buy properties and build houses and hotels if you want to win!"

God gave you talents and abilities. Don't hide them, the way one of the servants in Jesus' parable hid his "talent" (money). Use them to bless others and glorify God. Then someday God will tell you what the master in the story told his two loyal servants. He'll say, "Well done!"

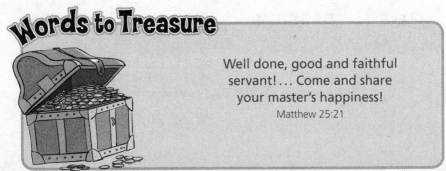

Words to Treasure

Well done, good and faithful servant!... Come and share your master's happiness!
Matthew 25:21

Programming Your Processor

Whatever is true, whatever is noble, whatever is right, whatever is pure, whatever is lovely, whatever is admirable — if anything is excellent or praiseworthy — think about such things.

Philippians 4:8

Levi shrugged off his backpack. "Dad, I'm home!" Going downstairs, he found his father sitting on the floor of his office. His computer was in front of him, its cover off.

"What are you doing?" Levi asked.

His dad replied, "Installing a new CD-ROM drive." He showed Levi the inside of the computer. "That's the processor, which is the computer's 'brain.' This is the hard disk drive, where the computer stores information. And these cards are for sound and graphics."

Looking at all the circuits and wiring, Levi said, "So that's what makes computers so smart."

"It's nothing compared to the brain God gave you," his dad said, smiling. He tapped Levi's head. "Speaking of which, you'd better get after your homework!"

A computer will only think about what it's programmed to think about and the data entered into it. Your mind can do much more than a computer can, but in some ways it's similar. God wants you to program your mind to think about good things. And he wants you to fill it with good things to think about.

Live It!

The next time you watch TV, count how many times you see or hear ungodly things. Make a commitment to choose TV shows that fill your mind with godly things.

Advancing to the Next Level

Let us leave the elementary teachings about Christ and go on to maturity.

Hebrews 6:1

Amelia tightened her purple belt. Then she bowed to her *sensei*, the woman who was teaching her karate. "Show us your stuff, Amelia," she said.

Amelia nodded. Assuming her ready stance, she faced another instructor. He was holding up a wooden board. Amelia focused on it intently. She'd already performed the karate moves she'd learned. And she'd demonstrated her kicks and punches. *This is it!* she thought. *If I break this board, I earn a blue belt.*

Swiveling on her left foot, she gave a mighty kick with her right one, yelling at the same time. Her heel split the board with a loud crack. Amelia bowed to her *sensei*. Then she smiled as everyone applauded.

A karate student doesn't want to wear a white belt forever. That color is the mark of a beginner. Karate students want to move up to higher colors. As a young Christian, you also want to progress. You want to grow more mature in your faith. So you need to develop patience, diligence, self-control, and other godly qualities. (See Galatians 5:22–23 and Colossians 3:12–14.) That's how you move up to higher levels of spiritual maturity.

Did You Know?

Christians can measure their spiritual growth each time God tests them. For example, God may make them wait for something. Then they learn if they're becoming more patient.

Drifting Over

Religion that God our Father accepts as pure and faultless is this: to look after orphans and widows in their distress.

James 1:27

Jeremy and Jeffrey entered the garage, where their father was gassing up the snowblower. "Dad, Mrs. Williams' car is buried!" Jeremy said.

"Yeah," Jeffrey added. "All that snow last night drifted right over it."

Their dad tightened the gas cap. "Well, why don't you boys drift over there and dig it out? She's been alone since her husband died. Your help would really be a blessing to her." He yanked the cord, and the snowblower roared to life.

The boys grabbed shovels and went to Mrs. Williams' house. Wind had driven snow across her driveway, covering her car up to the roof.

"You dig out the back. I'll do the front," said Jeremy. The boys dug for an hour. It was hard work, but it was fun watching the vehicle slowly appear. And it felt good to do something nice for their neighbor.

Being a Christian means more than just believing in God and Jesus. It also means caring about the people God cares about and doing what you can for them when they need help. God wants your faith in him to give you compassion for others. (See James 2:14–26.) Let your faith be a wind that blows you toward good deeds.

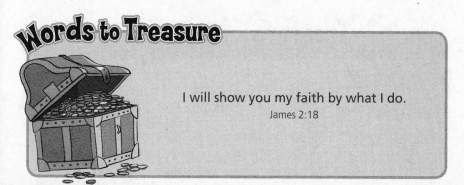

Words to Treasure

I will show you my faith by what I do.
James 2:18

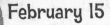

When Trouble Pops Up

We take captive every thought to make it obedient to Christ.

2 Corinthians 10:5

Standing on one side of an arcade game, Dawn put a token in the slot. Then she picked up the mallet. On the other side, Sierra did likewise. Together the friends waited. "Here they come!" Dawn said as little brown moles began popping up in front of them.

She and Sierra started whacking their heads. "Get 'em!" Sierra yelled. Laughing, the girls hammered away at the rodents. They hardly gave the critters a chance to see daylight. Moments later the creatures gave up, and Dawn and Sierra put down their mallets.

As tickets came streaming out of the machine, Dawn said, *"That's* how you handle those pests!"

When wicked thoughts pop into your head, you have to deal with them quickly. For example: A classmate gets a camera phone for her birthday. You think, *I never get anything that good.* That's a jealous thought. Grab it! Stop and remind yourself that Jesus doesn't want you to envy others. Make that jealous thought obey him. Change it to something like, *I'm glad she got such a cool present.* This isn't easy, so ask the Holy Spirit for help. With the two of you "whacking" evil thoughts, they can't cause you any trouble.

Words to Treasure

The mind controlled by the Spirit is life and peace.
Romans 8:6

Something Worth Everything

The kingdom of heaven is like a merchant looking for fine pearls. When he found one of great value, he went away and sold everything he had and bought it.

Matthew 13:45–46

Wayne walked into the coin shop with his dad, carrying his coin collection. It was worth a lot. "Can I help you?" asked the owner.

Wayne said, "Yes. I want to trade all this for your gold eagle."

While the man examined the collection, he let Wayne look at the coin. It was a ten-dollar piece made of solid gold. The coin was slightly bigger than a quarter but much heavier. On its front was Lady Liberty; on its back an eagle. It was old but in good shape. "Just imagine, Dad," Wayne said. "This was used during the Gold Rush and the Civil War. Coins like these were found in a ship that sank in 1865!"

Wayne's dad whistled. "Think it's worth your whole collection?"

Wayne held the coin up to the sunlight. "Definitely!"

Is God asking you to give up something? You may wonder if his kingdom is worth it. It is! God's kingdom is more valuable than everything you own. Being part of it is worth any sacrifice you have to make.

People in Bible Times

Jesus told a ruler he needed to give up his wealth to be part of God's kingdom. The man went away sad. He didn't realize God's kingdom was worth everything he owned. (See Luke 18:18–30.)

A Different Viewpoint

> "As the heavens are higher than the earth, so are my ways higher than your ways and my thoughts than your thoughts,"[declares the Lord].
>
> Isaiah 55:8

Y ou'll love this, Madison," her grandfather said. "They have one of the world's largest model railroads!" They were entering Northlandz, in Flemington, New Jersey. Soon Madison saw why her grandpa was so excited. The model railroad filled the three-story building. Madison stared up at mountains thirty feet high. They were connected by bridges up to forty feet long. Model trains were coming out of tunnels, passing towns, factories, and fields. Then they'd cross bridges and disappear into more tunnels.

"This is amazing, Grandpa!" Madison said. The walkway kept going up and up. Finally Madison was above the tallest peaks. She peered down into the valley at the river far below. There she saw other visitors at ground level. She knew her viewpoint was now much different from theirs.

God sees things differently than people do. He thinks differently too. Some things that are important to people aren't important to him, and vice versa. For example, looks matter a lot to people, but not to God. He cares more about a person's heart. (See 1 Samuel 16:7.) The Bible and the Holy Spirit help you see things from God's viewpoint. They help you think like he does.

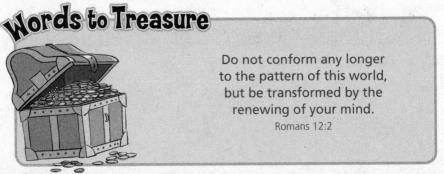

Words to Treasure

Do not conform any longer to the pattern of this world, but be transformed by the renewing of your mind.

Romans 12:2

Seeing Others as People

Show proper respect to everyone.

1 Peter 2:17

Dwayne's fencing opponent thrust his sword at Dwayne's chest. Dwayne parried, knocking the thin blade aside with his own weapon. Then he jabbed his opponent in the shoulder, scoring a hit. The crowd applauded. *Now I'm only down by one*, Dwayne thought. Circling his opponent, Dwayne studied him. Like himself, the other contestant was wearing white protective clothing. A steel-mesh mask hid his face. *He looks like a robot*, Dwayne thought. Faking a thrust, Dwayne tricked his opponent into swinging his sword to block it. That left him open to attack, and Dwayne scored another hit. The crowd applauded again. Both boys lifted their masks and respectfully saluted each other with their swords. This was customary when the score was tied and one more hit would determine the winner. Dwayne got a good look at his opponent's face. The two boys grinned, then lowered their masks and went at it again.

Whenever you interact with another human being, show him or her respect. It starts with remembering that he or she is a person too. This is someone created in God's image, just like you. Are you working with somebody on a class project? Are you competing against someone in a sport? Give him or her the respect every person deserves.

Words to Treasure

God created man in his own image,
in the image of God he created him;
male and female he created them.

Genesis 1:27

Ask and Learn

> "When your children ask you, 'What do these stones mean?' tell them that the flow of the Jordan [River] was cut off."
>
> Joshua 4:6–7

As she helped her mom dust the bookshelf, Corinne picked up an odd-shaped object with strange markings. "What *is* this?" she asked.

Her mother turned. "Oh, that's my souvenir from Africa. It's a water bottle made from a gourd."

Corinne blinked. "You were in Africa?"

Laughing, her mom said, "Don't look so shocked! Yes, I was. I spent a summer in Kenya while I was in college. I stayed with a missionary and his family. We visited people in remote places, telling them about Jesus. This souvenir is my little memorial, reminding me of how God watched over me then."

Staring at the water bottle, Corinne said, "Wow, Mom. I never knew you did anything so exciting!"

The pile of stones beside the Jordan River was a memorial. God wanted children to ask about it. Then they'd learn about how he helped their parents cross the river to enter the Promised Land. Start asking about memorials *you* see. This includes symbols and ceremonies at home and at church. You'll hear great stories about God, his people, and your own parents' journey of faith.

Live It!

Read about Samuel's memorial in 1 Samuel 7:7–12. Then write a message on a stone, reminding you of a time when God helped you. Keep the stone where you'll see it daily.

Our Great Big God

> [King Solomon wrote,] "The temple I am going to build will be great, because our God is greater than all other gods. But who is able to build a temple for him, since the heavens, even the highest heavens, cannot contain him?"
>
> 2 Chronicles 2:5–6

Brennan couldn't believe the size of the screen in the IMAX theater. It was five stories high! "Let's sit in the middle," he said. His sister looked nervous.

"Don't worry, Elissa," their mom said. "You'll enjoy this."

Brennan led them to the center seats. As they sat, the lights dimmed. "Just in time," Brennan whispered. They slipped on their 3-D glasses. The movie started, taking them for a ride on the Space Shuttle as it blasted off.

"This is great!" Elissa said. Brennan felt as though he were really in outer space. He was amazed at how big it looked. Then he remembered he was just watching a movie, and he realized how big space must actually be.

The word *great* can mean "very good." It also can mean "very big." With God, it means both! But in many ways, people try to put God in a little box. They only think about him on Sundays, for instance. Or they only believe he is powerful enough to do small things. Always remember that God is much greater than you can ever imagine.

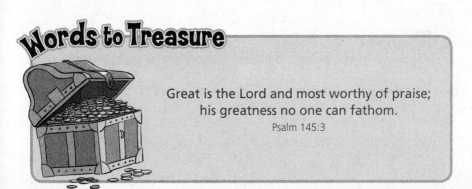

Words to Treasure

Great is the Lord and most worthy of praise;
his greatness no one can fathom.
Psalm 145:3

Nobody's Perfect

All have sinned and fall short of the glory of God, and are justified freely by his grace through the redemption that came by Christ Jesus.

Romans 3:23–24

In the fancy restaurant, Elyse and her parents applauded. A boy had just finished playing a prelude on the grand piano. Elyse's piano teacher stood. "Next, Elyse Patterson will play Beethoven's *Moonlight Sonata*." Wearing a pretty blue gown, Elyse walked to the piano. She placed her hands on the keys, then took a deep breath. She wanted so much to perform perfectly! As Elyse began playing, the lovely melody filled the air. Suddenly she fumbled some notes, lost her place, and had to stop. She sat there, horrified. Then she felt a hand on her shoulder.

"I'm sorry," Elyse said, trying not to cry.

"It's okay," her piano teacher whispered. "Just start over and try again."

Nobody's perfect, but don't let that stop you from trying to live God's way. You're his child. He loves you. And he won't abandon you when you make a mistake. Remember, Jesus took care of all your failures on the cross! When you've done something wrong, admit it to God. He'll forgive you and encourage you to keep trying to live a holy life. And as you do, you'll get closer and closer to being perfect, like him.

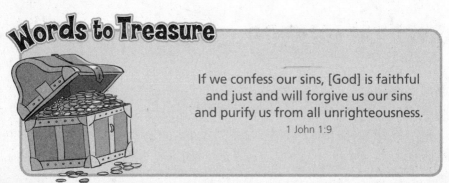

Words to Treasure

If we confess our sins, [God] is faithful and just and will forgive us our sins and purify us from all unrighteousness.

1 John 1:9

Bad to the Bones

A heart at peace gives life to the body, but envy rots the bones.

Proverbs 14:30

Dennis lay on his back, a large machine aimed at his body. Alone in the room, he kept perfectly still. He heard a brief buzz, then a door opening and footsteps. "Good going, Dennis," the radiologist said. She raised the machine.

Dennis sat up, swinging his legs off the table. "Can I see the X-ray?"

Helping him down, the woman said, "Sure. I'll call your mom in, and we'll all look at it together." Soon the three of them were gathered in front of a computer monitor. Dennis was amazed. He could see his arm bone! The black-and-white image showed the bone clearly.

"Is it broken?" his mom asked.

The radiologist shook her head. "No, it seems to be fine."

Did you know that obeying the commandment "You shall not covet" protects your health? (See Exodus 20:17.) Coveting means envying others because you want something they have. This hurts your relationship with God. It causes you heartache. And it can even affect your physical condition. The cure is to be satisfied with what you have and thankful for it. So take good care of yourself. Don't covet. Be content! (See Philippians 4:11–12.)

People in Bible Times

When Joseph's brothers saw his special robe, they were filled with hatred and jealousy. That's not a recipe for happiness and good health! They should have chosen to be content. (See Genesis 37:1–11.)

Leaning over the Line

> Just as [God] who called you is holy, so be holy in all you do.
>
> 1 Peter 1:15

Sidney knocked on the door of her father's home office. "Come in," her dad said. Opening the door, she saw him standing next to his desk. He was throwing darts.

"I thought you were working," she said.

He walked over to the dartboard. "I'm just taking a break. Wanna join me?" Pulling out the darts, he handed them to her.

"Sure!" she said. He'd never let her try his darts before. They were the real kind, with sharp steel tips.

"Stand sideways, with your foot behind the line," he said as she got ready to throw. "That puts your body closer to the dartboard. Then lean forward."

Sidney tried throwing a dart that way, but she lost her balance, and the dart stuck in the wall. "Oops. Sorry, Dad!"

When you're throwing darts, you want to stand as close as you can to the line. Then you want to lean as far as you can over it. This is *not* what you want to do when you're trying to be holy like God. The best way to do that is to stay far away from the line that separates good from evil. Stand as close as you can to God, and lean on him.

Words to Treasure

In the paths of the wicked lie thorns and snares, but he who guards his soul stays far from them.
Proverbs 22:5

Growing Up

The child [Jesus] grew and became strong; he was filled with wisdom, and the grace of God was upon him.

Luke 2:40

Josh was thrilled. He'd been chosen to play the main character in the community theater's next show, *Peter Pan*. At today's rehearsal, the child actors were learning to fly! A technician checked Josh's harness and cable. "Ready to take off?" he asked.

Josh grinned. "Oh yeah!" The technician gave a signal, and Josh rose into the air. He flapped his elbows and crowed, making everyone laugh. The technicians flew Josh around the stage as he waved his sword. Then they swung him high out over the seats where the audience would be. Finally they brought him down. "That was incredible!" he said.

While other kids flew, the girl playing Wendy talked with him. "It must be fun playing someone who never grows up," she said.

Josh nodded. "It is. But I'm not really like Peter Pan. I *want* to grow up!"

Nobody expects you to be all grown up now. But you should be growing up. Jesus matured, and God wants you to be like him. Are you becoming more patient? Are you becoming more compassionate? Are you becoming wiser? Some people stay immature all their lives. Be like Jesus instead.

Live It!

On a physical growth chart, write Scripture references to help you measure your spiritual growth. For example: Philippians 2:4 (selflessness); Ephesians 5:15 (wisdom); 1 Peter 3:8 (compassion).

Sweet Rewards

> The Lord will reward everyone for whatever good he does.
>
> Ephesians 6: 8

At her uncle's farm in Vermont, Helen was helping her cousin collect sap. It was late winter, and the ground was snowy. Helen and Kathryn emptied buckets into a tank, then hung them back up under spouts in the trees. "We're finished," Kathryn said. "Let's head to the sugar shack."

Helen grinned. "Okay. I'm whipped!" They walked to a building with steam billowing out of it. Inside, Helen's uncle was making maple syrup.

"So, you're back," he said. "Fetch a bucket of clean snow, and I'll reward you for your labor." They did as he asked. He poured boiled sap on the snow, making little puddles that hardened.

"What's that?" Helen asked.

Reaching into the bucket, Kathryn said, "Maple candy! We call it 'sugar on snow.'" She handed Helen a piece.

It was sweet and chewy. "Mmm," Helen said. "This makes all the work worthwhile."

Her uncle laughed. "Wait'll you taste my syrup on your pancakes!"

When you live your life for God, doing the good things he wants you to do, he rewards you. His rewards come here on earth and later in heaven. And they're wonderful! One of the best rewards God gives you is the knowledge that you've served him faithfully. That's a sweet sense of satisfaction.

Words to Treasure

> Always give yourselves fully to the work of the Lord, because you know that your labor in the Lord is not in vain.
>
> 1 Corinthians 15:58

Shooting Yourself in the Foot

The body is a unit, though it is made up of many parts; and though all its parts are many, they form one body. So it is with Christ. For we were all baptized by one Spirit into one body.

1 Corinthians 12:12–13

It was dark and foggy in the laser tag arena. Landon was wearing a plastic vest with glowing green panels on the front, back, and shoulders. Peeking through a bunker window, he aimed his phaser and waited.

Suddenly a figure stepped into view. Landon pulled the trigger, shooting in rapid-fire mode. A stream of laser beams struck the person's chest. Then Landon realized that the other player's vest was green.

"Hey, I'm on your side!" the boy shouted. "Our team loses points when we hit each other!"

Hurting someone in your family or church isn't good. In fact, it's a lot like zapping your teammate in a game of laser tag. The Bible compares a group of believers to a body with different parts. So maybe it's more like shooting yourself in the foot! However you look at it, everyone suffers. When you do something that hurts a member of your family or church, show the person that you care. Say you're sorry, and ask for forgiveness. He or she will feel better, and so will you.

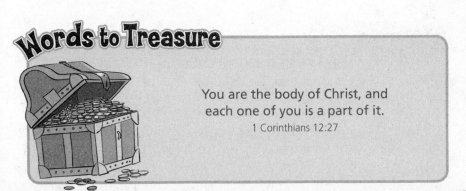

Words to Treasure

You are the body of Christ, and each one of you is a part of it.
1 Corinthians 12:27

Above and Beyond

> We fix our eyes not on what is seen, but on
> what is unseen. For what is seen is temporary,
> but what is unseen is eternal.
>
> 2 Corinthians 4:18

Biting her lip, Jennifer gripped the control stick. She was losing her battle to keep the F-18 fighter jet steady as it streaked over the ocean.

"Watch out!" warned her copilot, Danielle. "You're rolling us over!"

Both girls screamed as the aircraft flipped upside down. Jennifer felt the blood rush to her head. Then they were upright again, but now the jet was in a dive, with the water approaching fast. Struggling to pull up, Jennifer cried, "We're not going to make it!" There was a lurch, and the windows went black. For a moment everything was still, and then the hatch of the flight simulator popped open. The girls stepped out into the Air Zoo museum in Kalamazoo, Michigan, laughing and discussing what to do next.

The world you live in isn't pretend at all. It's very real. Yet the Bible says there's a greater reality beyond what you can see, hear, touch, taste, and smell. And just as the navy uses flight simulators to train pilots to fly real jets, God is using this world to prepare you for the next.

People in Bible Times

The apostle Paul trained hard, like an Olympic athlete. But he wasn't after a gold medal. Paul knew that the prize for training yourself to be godly lasts forever. (See 1 Corinthians 9:24–27.)

The Wind at Your Back

May our Lord Jesus Christ himself and God our Father ... encourage your hearts and strengthen you.

2 Thessalonians 2:16–17

Reece and Rianna sat in the front of the airboat as it sped through the Florida Everglades. Their parents were seated behind them. On a raised platform in the rear sat the driver. And behind him, a huge propeller created the powerful wind that was moving them across the wetlands. Slowing down, the driver pointed out some exotic birds. Then he said, "Take a peek down to your right."

Reece turned. "Mom, Dad, look! Alligators!" The large reptiles floated nearby, staring at them.

As the boat slid through some tall grass, Rianna said, "Dad, what keeps us from getting stuck in this stuff?"

Her father replied, "Well, the boat is flat on the bottom. The rudders use air to turn it, so there's nothing sticking into the water. And with that big propeller behind us, we can go through anything!"

No matter what you're going through, God is always behind you, propelling you along. He encourages and strengthens you by reminding you of his promises. He guides you and gives you what you need. As you travel through life, let God be the wind at your back.

Life in Bible Times

In the desert, God encouraged and strengthened the Israelites in many ways. He guided them. He gave them food and water. He even kept their sandals from wearing out! (See Nehemiah 9:19–21.)

Lion and Lamb

> One of the elders said to me, "... See, the Lion of the tribe of Judah, the Root of David, has triumphed...." Then I saw a Lamb.
>
> Revelation 5:5–6

Gavin shielded his eyes against the blizzard. Suddenly Bryce slumped in the snow. "Just leave me."

Gavin shouted, "No!" Pulling his brother up, Gavin dragged him forward.

Then he saw their house through the snow. And he heard their mom call, "Lunchtime!" Gavin dropped Bryce, and they raced to the door, laughing. Their mom said, "I'm glad you're enjoying your 'arctic expedition.' It may be your last one this winter. The month of March comes in like a lion and goes out like a lamb."

Bryce kicked off his boots. "What does that mean?"

Smiling, his mom replied, "It means that when March arrives, it's wintry and powerful, like a lion. But by the time it leaves, it's springlike and mild, like a lamb."

Jesus is a lion, strong and mighty. He's also a lamb, gentle and meek. You can see both his strength and his meekness in John 18:1–13. With three words, Jesus knocked a bunch of soldiers to the ground. Yet he let them arrest him so he could die to save the world. When you worship Jesus, remember that he is the Lion of Judah and the Lamb of God.

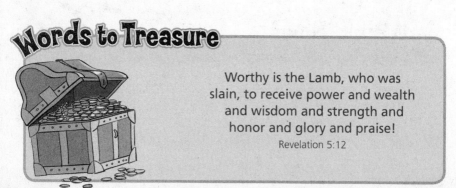

Words to Treasure

Worthy is the Lamb, who was slain, to receive power and wealth and wisdom and strength and honor and glory and praise!
Revelation 5:12

A Driving Force

Christ's love compels us.

2 Corinthians 5:14

Lying on a bodyboard, Megan paddled out into the Caribbean surf. She and her parents were vacationing in the Bahamas. Her mom and dad had rented the bodyboard for her at the hotel, and she was trying to ride it as they relaxed on the beach.

Bobbing in the water, Megan saw a good-sized wave cresting just ahead of her. She turned and paddled quickly toward land, glancing over her shoulder. The wave picked her up and propelled her forcefully all the way to shore.

"Looking good, Megan!" her father said. "You're really getting the hang of it."

Megan picked up the bodyboard and smiled. "Thanks, Dad. It's fun when I catch a wave just right. I can feel the power as it pushes me along!" Turning, she ran back into the ocean to find another big wave.

Jesus' love is like a strong wave that drives Christians forward. It compels them to share the gospel with others. Do you feel the power of it hit you when you meet people who don't know him? Learn more about Jesus' love by reading the New Testament. Let his love compel you to tell others about how he died so they can live.

People in Bible Times

God was going to punish his people. But he still loved them, so he compelled Jeremiah to warn them to repent. God's message burned so hotly in Jeremiah's heart, he couldn't hold it in. (See Jeremiah 20:8–9.)

Dealing with Darkness

> Do not be overcome by evil, but overcome evil with good.
>
> Romans 12:21

The blizzard that had canceled school continued to rage Friday night. Gavin and his family were watching a DVD. Suddenly everything went black.

"What happened?" Bryce asked. Gavin could hear his brother but not see him.

"The storm must've knocked down a power line," their dad said.

Gavin got up off the couch. "I'll get the flashlight!" Sticking his hands out, he started making his way toward the kitchen.

"Do you know where it is?" his mom asked.

Fumbling in the dark, Gavin said, "Yeah. Underneath the sink." He bumped into the dinner table. Then he turned and took a few steps, feeling around for the countertop. When he touched it, he followed it around to the sink. Opening the cabinet, he found the flashlight. He pulled it out and switched it on. Instantly the light pierced the darkness, and he could see.

Good always defeats evil, the way light overcomes darkness. Sadly, the world can seem pretty dark at times. Especially when the news is reporting something evil that happened. Evil events can make you feel afraid or depressed. But remember, Jesus is the Light of the World. He defeats all darkness! Let his light shine through you. Do good things to help overcome evil in your part of the world.

Words to Treasure

[Jesus said,] "In this world you will have trouble. But take heart! I have overcome the world."
John 16:33

Hearing Things

Eli realized that the Lord was calling the boy.
1 Samuel 3:8

In the Bahamas, Megan and her parents were walking along a beach. "What's that?" Megan said, spotting something on the sand. Running ahead, she picked it up. "Look, I found a conch shell!" The big brown shell had a spiky top. Inside, it was smooth and pink. As her parents caught up, Megan held it to her ear. "I can hear the ocean!"

She handed the shell to her mom, who listened. "I can too."

Megan's dad smiled. "I hate to burst your bubble, guys, but that's not the ocean you hear. It's all the sounds around us, resonating inside the shell." Just then they heard a large wave crash on the shore, and he said, "Now, *that's* the ocean!"

If you think God is speaking to you, ask older, godly people to help you make sure. They'll help you compare what you think God is saying with what the Bible says. That's important! God will never tell you something different from what he's said in the Bible. For example, he won't tell you to cheat or steal. A wise person can also help you understand God's message, when God really is talking to you.

in Bible Times

When God spoke to Samuel, the boy thought Eli was calling him! Eli was the old priest Samuel lived with in the tabernacle. He helped Samuel understand that God was talking to him. (See 1 Samuel 3:1–18.)

One of a Kind

> [God said,] "Before I formed you in the womb I knew you, before you were born I set you apart."
>
> Jeremiah 1:5

The winter storm had knocked out the power in Gavin and Bryce's neighborhood. The brothers huddled in blankets near the fireplace, sipping hot cocoa their mom had made over the fire. "I've got the perfect book for a snowy evening," their dad said. "Have you guys ever heard of the Snowflake Man?" Holding a lantern, he pulled a book out of the bookshelf. Then he opened it on the coffee table. "His name was Wilson Bentley, and he lived from 1865 to 1931. At his family's farm in Vermont, he figured out how to photograph snowflakes through a microscope. This book, *Snow Crystals*, is filled with his pictures." Everyone gazed at the beautiful photos.

"This is amazing!" Gavin said. "All the snowflakes have six branches, but they're all different."

His dad nodded. "Mr. Bentley's photographs started the whole idea that no two snowflakes are exactly alike."

God makes snowflakes so much alike and yet so different. He does the same with people. If you ever start thinking you're nothing special, remember snowflakes! Then praise God that he made you such a unique individual.

Live It!

Check out the book *Snow Crystals* by W. A. Bentley. Or find images of snowflakes on the Internet. Try drawing some snowflakes. Hang them up to remind you that you're unique and God loves you a lot.

Harmony among God's Creatures

God created the great creatures of the sea and every living and moving thing with which the water teems.... And God saw that it was good.

Genesis 1:21

Hurry up, Dad!" Megan said, putting on her mask and fins. They were with a group on a boat in the Caribbean Sea. Megan had spotted dolphins riding the bow waves as the boat entered their territory. They looked eager for her to join them in the water.

"I'm ready!" said Megan's dad. He stuck his snorkel in his mouth and grinned. She giggled. As they got into the water, Megan was thrilled. It was so clear, she could see the sandy bottom thirty feet below. All around her were dolphins! She heard them clicking and whistling underwater. They swam about gracefully, coming close enough for her to touch them. Megan swam beside them, pretending she was a dolphin too. Being in the water with them was so peaceful—and exciting!

In the beginning, all the creatures God made were good and got along. There was harmony between animals and people. Adam and Eve's sin changed things. But some animals, like dolphins, still get along well with people. Someday God will make a new world. Then all of his creatures will live together peacefully again.

Words to Treasure

The wolf will live with the lamb, the leopard will lie down with the goat, the calf and the lion and the yearling together; and a little child will lead them.

Isaiah 11:6

Invincible!

> The name of the Lord is a strong tower; the righteous run to it and are safe.
>
> Proverbs 18:10

Gavin and Bryce struggled to move a huge ball of snow for the wall of their fort. "Push!" Gavin shouted. They slammed into the snowball, and it finally rolled next to the others. "That'll work," Gavin said.

His younger brother nodded. "Good thing. I don't think we could move it any more."

"Let's go," Gavin said. "We've got to get ready before the other kids attack." Quickly they built their fortress. Soon the walls were taller than they were.

"This is perfect," Bryce said. "They'll never get us in h—" A snowball hit the top of the fort, shattering overhead.

"Here they come!" Gavin yelled. Grabbing the snowballs they'd stockpiled, they began hurling them. Suddenly there was a thud, and one side of the fort caved in. Two neighbor boys invaded the stronghold. Soon they were all wrestling on the ground, laughing and rubbing each other's faces in the snow.

Nothing can protect you the way God can. When you're in trouble, run to him for shelter. Calling God's name in prayer is like entering an invincible fortress. God is able to protect you in many ways. He can change your circumstances. He can send someone to help you. Or he can give you wisdom and strength to get through a crisis.

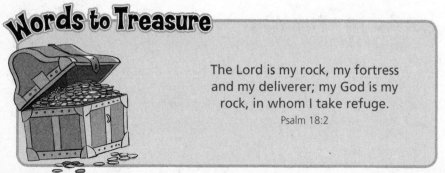

Words to Treasure

The Lord is my rock, my fortress and my deliverer; my God is my rock, in whom I take refuge.
Psalm 18:2

Going All Out

> Be very careful to keep the commandment ... to love the Lord your God, to walk in all his ways, to obey his commands, to hold fast to him and to serve him with all your heart and all your soul.
>
> Joshua 22:5

I got it!" Kennedy yelled. Holding her fists together, she hit the volleyball. This set up a shot for Daphne, who blasted the ball across the net. A girl on the other team tried to return the ball, but it hit the net and dropped to the floor. "Nice spike, Daphne!" Kennedy said.

Their phys ed teacher announced, "The score is ten to nine."

Kennedy faced the net as a girl behind her served the ball. The players on the other team hit it once, then smashed it back. Diving, Kennedy landed on the floor. Her hands slid under the ball, popping it up. Daphne slammed it into the corner on their opponents' side.

Helping Kennedy up, Daphne said, "Wow, when you play volleyball, you really give it your all!"

Are you going all out when it comes to loving God, obeying him, and serving him? Offer God your wholehearted effort and devotion. Throw yourself into living for him, giving it everything you've got.

People in Bible Times

Caleb followed God with all his heart. Although he saw giants in the Promised Land, Caleb was ready to charge in and fight them, as God had commanded. God rewarded him for his faithfulness. (See Joshua 14:6 – 9.)

Every Kid for Himself?

Each of you should look not only to your own interests, but also to the interests of others.

Philippians 2:4

"I'm king of the mountain!" Gavin said, standing on a gigantic pile of snow at the end of his street.

His younger brother, Bryce, and two neighbor kids, Randy and Darryl, took up the challenge. "Not for long!" shouted Bryce as they clambered up the hill to take Gavin down. Bryce, the smallest boy there, was also the quickest. He almost reached his brother first. But Darryl grabbed Bryce's foot, making him fall. Bryce slid halfway down while Randy tried to claw his way over Darryl. Gavin laughed as the others fought among themselves. His laughter died when Darryl shook Randy off, made it to the top, and lunged. Gavin and Darryl grappled at the summit, struggling to keep their balance. Suddenly Randy plowed into them, and all three tumbled to the bottom. When Gavin shook the snow out of his eyes, Bryce was standing at the top. "Ha! Who's the king now?" he taunted. Shouting, Gavin and the others scrambled up to get him.

Playing king of the mountain is fun when it's just a game. But God doesn't want you to live that way. As you're "climbing up the mountain" in life, God wants you to be considerate of others. Give them a hand up whenever you can, so everyone reaches the top.

Words to Treasure

Love your neighbor as yourself.

Leviticus 19:18

An Awesome Sight

> Mount Sinai was covered with smoke, because the Lord descended on it in fire. The smoke billowed up from it like smoke from a furnace, [and] the whole mountain trembled violently.
>
> Exodus 19:18

Standing on the balcony of her grandparents' condo in Florida, Chrissie stared at the island ten miles away. A huge cloud of smoke appeared on it. Chrissie saw the fire from the rocket engines as the space shuttle blasted off. "There it is!" she shouted, pointing. She could hear the roar and feel the vibrations. The spacecraft rose faster and faster into the sky. Then, with a loud boom, it broke the sound barrier. Seconds later it was out of sight. "That was incredible!" she said.

Her mom grinned. "How'd you like to be one of those astronauts?"

Shaking her head, Chrissie replied, "I don't know. It'd be awfully scary to be in the middle of all that!"

God is an awesome, powerful being. When he showed up on Mount Sinai, there was lightning, thunder, fire, smoke, and a violent earthquake. It was more astonishing than a shuttle launch! The Israelites were very afraid. It's good to have a healthy fear of God. That's called reverence, and Proverbs 9:10 says it's the beginning of wisdom.

Did You Know?

God revealed his power and majesty at Mount Sinai so his people would have a healthy fear of him. That fear, or reverence, would help keep them from sinning. (See Exodus 20:18–21.)

Glad to Go?

> I rejoiced with those who said to me, "Let us
> go to the house of the Lord."
>
> Psalm 122:1

On Sunday morning, Gavin and Bryce were putting on their snowsuits. "Where are you going?" their dad asked.

Gavin looked up. "Snowboarding!"

Their dad frowned. "What about church?"

Bryce said, "Aw, can't we skip it?"

Chuckling, their dad said, "No, but here's what you can do. I'm giving you permission to think about snowboarding at church today." The boys glanced at each other. He explained, "Let's say your Sunday school teacher talks about God's wisdom. You can think about how wise God must be to create snow and gravity and leg muscles. If he compares God to a father, you can consider what a loving father God must be to want his children to have fun. Get it?"

Grinning, the boys nodded. "Good," he said. "Then, when it's time to worship, sing praise and thanks from the bottom of your heart."

Are you looking forward to going to church this week? If not, take a moment to really think about the things you'd rather do. Remind yourself that everything you enjoy in life was given to you by God. Then go worship him with a grateful, joyful attitude.

Life in Bible Times

Some of God's people lived far from Jerusalem. Three times a year, they'd travel there to worship. They sang songs like Psalm 122 to show their joy while approaching God's temple.

Following Instructions

Be careful to do what the Lord your God has commanded you.

Deuteronomy 5:32

C ourtney stared at all the parts on the garage floor. "I'm supposed to build a race car out of *this*?" She'd just unpacked the kit she had to assemble so she could compete in the Soap Box Derby.

Smiling, her dad said, "Come on, I'll lend you a hand." After studying the instructions, they got started. Courtney's dad handed her some bolts, and she fastened them onto the floorboard with a wrench. She and her dad worked for hours. Courtney didn't always understand why she was doing things. But she followed the instructions carefully. As the car took shape, things made more sense. Finally she attached the wheels. Then her father helped her add the red fiberglass shell, which formed the car's body.

Climbing into the racer, Courtney tested the steering wheel and brake pedal. "Everything works!" she said.

It's important to follow God's instructions. And it's important to follow them *carefully*. As you read the Bible and listen to God, pay close attention to what he's telling you to do. Your life will turn out well if you follow his instructions to a T.

Life in Bible Times

Noah had never built a boat before. Moses had never built a tabernacle. Solomon had never built a temple. But they all followed God's instructions carefully, and things turned out great.

Weak Spots

The Spirit helps us in our weakness.

Romans 8:26

Chris held a glass rod over a beaker of water as his dad heated the tip with a propane torch. Chris was helping his dad, a science teacher, try a new experiment in his home lab. "What are we making?" Chris asked.

"Prince Rupert's Drops," his dad replied. "They're little glass beads that are very strong. But they have a surprising weakness." Some molten glass fell into the cold water and quickly hardened. It had formed a long tail, like a tadpole. "The nephew of the king of England invented these in the 1640s," said Chris's dad. "The king used them to play pranks on people." When the glass drop cooled completely, he hit it with a hammer. It didn't break. "See how strong it is, Chris? But watch this." He snapped off the tail, and the drop exploded into tiny pieces.

Even strong Christians can have a weak spot. They hold up under most temptations, but there's one that causes them big trouble. What's your weak spot? Maybe you get impatient a lot, or disobey your parents, or tell lies. Whatever your weakness is, if you ask God, he'll help you overcome it.

People in Bible Times

Samson was a strong man, but he had a weak spot that caused him great trouble. He kept falling in love with ungodly women. Sadly, Samson never asked God to help him overcome this weakness. (See Judges 13–16.)

A Treasure-Hunting Tool

Send forth your light and your truth, [O God,] let them guide me; let them bring me to your holy mountain, to the place where you dwell.

Psalm 43:3

Teresa rode in her father's Jeep through a remote forest. She was staring at a handheld device. "We're getting close, Dad." They were on a high-tech treasure hunt called geocaching. On the Internet, they'd learned where a "cache" was hidden. They'd entered its coordinates into a GPS receiver. And the device was guiding them to the treasure.

"We'd better walk now," said Teresa's dad, pulling off the dirt road. After hiking for several minutes, they reached a clearing in the woods.

"It must be around here somewhere," Teresa said. Spotting an old, hollow tree stump, she ran to it. Inside was a plastic container. "We found it!" she shouted. The container was filled with trinkets, a logbook, and a pen. After signing the logbook, Teresa pulled out a keychain.

Her dad said, "Don't forget to replace it with something else. That way, the cache will stay full."

Teresa grinned. "I know." She took a toy compass out of her pocket and dropped it in the container.

The Bible is like a GPS device that will lead you straight to God. That's the greatest treasure you could ever hope to find. Keep studying your Bible every day. It'll take you right to your heavenly Father!

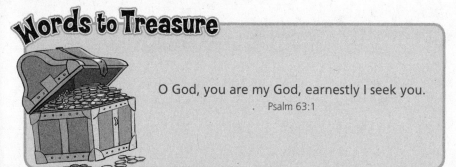

Words to Treasure

O God, you are my God, earnestly I seek you.

Psalm 63:1

Pitching Pennies

Put your hope in the Lord both now and forevermore.

Psalm 131:3

Chip and his parents stood outside a restaurant. As they waited for a table, Chip's stomach growled. "Here, you can hold this," his father said, handing him an electronic gadget.

"What is it?" Chip asked.

His dad replied, "It's a pager the hostess gave me. When our table's ready, it'll vibrate." Chip examined the gizmo, then stuck it in his pocket. Leaning over a rail, he gazed into the small pond near the door of the restaurant. He could see coins glittering at the bottom.

"Dad, can I have a penny? I wanna make a wish."

His father gave him one, saying, "You'd better read this coin first."

Chip held it up. "It says, 'In God we trust.'"

His dad nodded. "Right. So when you toss it in, maybe instead of making a wish, you should say a little prayer!"

Grinning, Chip said, "Okay." He paused a moment, then flipped the coin into the water. Suddenly he felt a little jolt on his leg. "Whoa! I think our table's ready!"

Which do you do more often, wish or pray? And when good things happen to you, do you think, I'm so lucky or I'm so blessed? Put your hope in God instead of trusting in luck. And when God blesses you, be sure to give him the credit—and the thanks!

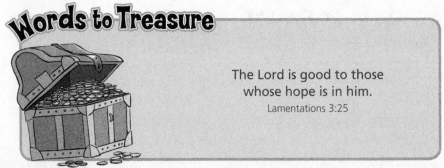

Words to Treasure

The Lord is good to those whose hope is in him.
Lamentations 3:25

One Jump at a Time

Fix these words of mine in your hearts and minds.

Deuteronomy 11:18

Wearing her helmet and pads, Catherine was ready to try her new pogo stick. "Watch this!" she told her parents. Hopping on, she started bouncing on the driveway. After two jumps she lost her balance and hopped off.

"That'll take some practice," said her mom, smiling.

As her parents headed inside, her dad said, "Keep trying. You'll get the hang of it."

Catherine kept practicing, and later she rushed into the house. "Mom! Dad! I bounced sixty-four times!"

Her mom looked doubtful. "Really?"

Catherine said, "Come on, I'll show you."

Outside, her dad counted out loud as she bounced. She made it to seventy-two. "That's amazing, honey," her mom said.

Catherine grinned. "Pretty soon I'll do a hundred!"

You may think you could never memorize long passages of the Bible. But it's a lot like learning to use a pogo stick. Try taking them one word at a time. You'll be amazed at how fast you can learn long Bible passages by heart. And having key passages of Scripture fixed in your heart and mind is important. It helps you avoid temptation and live God's way.

Live It!

Bounce on a pogo stick or skip with a jump rope. As you do, try to recite Philippians 4:4–9. Each time you bounce or skip, say one word of the passage. If you stop or forget a word, start over!

Knowing Who You Are

> You are light in the Lord. Live as children of
> light (for the fruit of the light consists in all
> goodness, righteousness and truth).
>
> Ephesians 5:8–9

Mickey and his father stood outside the Philadelphia Museum of Art. They were admiring the statue of Rocky Balboa. "This is it, Dad!" Mickey said. "This is where they filmed that scene in *Rocky*. Remember, when he runs to the top of the steps?"

Mickey's dad nodded. "I know. I love that moment. He's still training for the big fight, but he already knows he's a champion."

Heading for the famous stairs, Mickey said, "C'mon, let's do it!" He raced up the stone steps, his dad hurrying to keep up. At the top, Mickey jumped up and down, thrusting his fists in the air.

Laughing, his dad said, "Way to go, champ!"

An athlete who wants to be a champion starts with believing that he *is* a champion. Then he trains and competes like a champion. Becoming a godly person works the same way. It starts with knowing that you're the child of a holy, perfect God. Your heavenly Father is all light and goodness. There's no darkness and evil in him. Knowing that you're his child gives you the confidence and power to live a godly life.

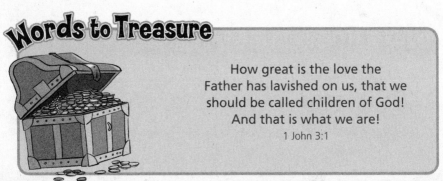

Words to Treasure

> How great is the love the
> Father has lavished on us, that we
> should be called children of God!
> And that is what we are!
>
> 1 John 3:1

Saved!

The Lord preserves the faithful.

Psalm 31:23

Rene sat with her mom in a horse-drawn carriage as the driver gave them a tour through the quaint little town. It was a sunny day, and Rene was enjoying the fresh air and scenery. As they traveled along the main street, she looked at all the shops and people. At the edge of town the road crossed a river, and Rene saw that they were approaching a covered wooden bridge. "This bridge was built in 1871," the driver explained. "It's been carrying traffic over the river for over a hundred years." He guided the horse inside, where its hooves clip-clopped loudly on the planks. "A few years ago the bridge was in bad shape, and it was almost demolished. But a group of people who loved it worked hard to preserve it. They convinced the town to have the bridge restored, and now it's a treasured landmark."

When they emerged into the sunlight again, Rene turned for one more look at the faithful old structure. "Isn't it beautiful?" said her mom, who was admiring it too.

Rene nodded. "Yeah. I'm sure glad they saved it!"

The word *salvation* means to save something or someone from being destroyed. That's exactly what God does for his people. When you believe in Jesus and faithfully follow him, God saves you from death. He preserves your life forever!

Words to Treasure

My shield is God Most High, who saves the upright in heart.
Psalm 7:10

There When You Need It

Be prepared in season and out of season.
2 Timothy 4:2

As Gordon's dad drove him home from his Boy Scout meeting, the ride started getting bumpy. "What's that?" Gordon asked.

Frowning, his dad pulled over. They discovered that one of the tires was flat. Gordon's father opened the trunk and asked, "Can you earn a merit badge for learning how to change a tire?"

Gordon grinned. "I don't think so."

"Well, it's a good skill to have anyway," his dad said. "You may need it when you're old enough to drive." He lifted the floor of the trunk. Gordon saw a spare tire in the area below.

"Wow, I never knew that was there!"

Laughing, his dad said, "It fits the Boy Scout motto: Always be prepared." He set up the jack and let Gordon pump the handle to raise the back of the car. They changed the tire, and soon they were on their way again.

The Boy Scout motto, which reflects 2 Timothy 4:2, is a good rule to live by. And the best way to prepare yourself for life is to store God's words in your heart. Memorize as many Bible verses as you can. They'll come in handy down the road!

People in Bible Times

Timothy learned God's Word when he was a child. When he grew up, he was prepared to do the work God wanted him to do. That made him an excellent partner for the apostle Paul. (See 2 Timothy 3:14–17.)

Achieving Glory

Not that I have already obtained all this, or have already been made perfect, but I press on to take hold of that for which Christ Jesus took hold of me.

Philippians 3:12

D errick and his dad were in an open field, preparing to launch a model rocket. They were using the largest solid-fuel engine they could. "Wouldn't it be cool if it went into orbit?" Derrick said.

"That *would* be cool," his dad agreed. Derrick attached a wire to the igniter in the engine, then placed the rocket on the launch pad. He ran to his dad, who handed him the launch controller. After Derrick inserted the safety key, his dad began the countdown. "Ten … nine … eight …" At zero, Derrick pushed the button. With a *whoosh*, the rocket shot into the air. Soon it was so high, they couldn't see it anymore. Then Derrick spotted its parachute as it floated back to earth.

God wants you to be perfect and holy, like him. (See Matthew 5:48 and 1 Peter 1:16.) That's a very high goal. Even if your own goodness were big enough to shoot you into space, you couldn't reach that goal by yourself. But with faith in Jesus you *will* reach your goal. So keep trying! Jesus' goodness is the rocket engine that'll make you perfect and holy.

Words to Treasure

I press on toward the goal to win the prize for which God has called me heavenward in Christ Jesus.
Philippians 3:14

Getting Through

At that moment the curtain of the temple was torn in two from top to bottom.

Matthew 27:51

On the tenth hole at the miniature golf course, Kayla set her yellow golf ball down. Holding her putter, she watched the blades of the windmill go around. She had to time her shot just right. That way, her ball would go under the windmill to the hole on the other side. Kayla was ahead of her mom and her grandma by two strokes, and she wanted to win. She hit her ball. It headed straight, looking good—until a spinning blade knocked it away.

"Too bad, honey," her mom said, putting down her pink ball. She took a shot, with the same result.

Kayla's grandmother stepped up. "I'll show you how it's done." She hit her green ball, and a windmill blade stopped it cold. "Well," she said, "looks like nobody's getting through today!"

There once was a barrier that kept people away from God. It was a heavy curtain hanging in the temple, in front of the Most Holy Place. But when Jesus died on the cross, the curtain was torn in half. This was a sign that anyone who believed in Jesus could now get through to God. As a Christian, you have full access to God, anytime.

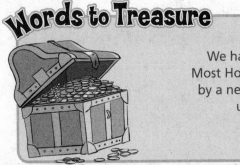

Words to Treasure

We have confidence to enter the Most Holy Place by the blood of Jesus, by a new and living way opened for us through the curtain.

Hebrews 10:19–20

Staying High and Dry

Have nothing to do with the fruitless deeds of darkness.

Ephesians 5:11

As Hunter and his parents walked toward the massive waterfall, he could hear its roar. "There it is," his dad said. "Niagara Falls! It was worth taking a little detour to see this." They'd made a side trip to the falls on their way to visit Hunter's grandparents in New York state.

Hunter watched the water rush over the brink and plunge toward the river 170 feet below. "I'd hate to go over the edge," he said.

His dad looked down. "Me too."

"How far upriver do you have to stay to keep from getting swept over the falls?" Hunter asked.

His dad laughed. "Son, the best way to keep from going over a waterfall is to stay out of the river!"

Telling small lies. Cheating just a bit. Taking little things that don't belong to you. It's not a good idea to wade into wrong behavior like this. And not just because you might slip over the waterfall into some really *big* sin. Any contact with sin is bad, and God wants you to stay away from it completely. Keep your toes dry!

Live It!

Play "Over the Waterfall." Draw a line on the ground. Have your friends close their eyes and see how close they can walk to the "waterfall" without going over. Then tell them the farthest one from the edge wins! Explain why, showing them Ephesians 5:11 in your Bible.

Rough Bounces

> [The Lord] shielded him and cared for him; he guarded him as the apple of his eye.
>
> Deuteronomy 32:10

Look how high I can go!" Keith said, jumping on the trampoline in Leon's backyard. He bounced higher and higher, waving his arms to keep his balance.

Leon and Camille, a girl who lived nearby, stood watching him. Halfheartedly Leon said, "You rock, dude."

Hands on her hips, Camille said, "Can *we* have a turn now? You've been jumping a long time."

Keith wasn't ready to quit, though. "I wanna try one more move. Watch this!" With that, he did a knee drop, bounced up, landed on his back, and came up again, trying to land on his feet. Instead he pitched forward, arms flailing. Camille gasped as he flew off the trampoline—right into the safety net around it. "Glad that was there," Keith said sheepishly, climbing down. "Okay, I've had enough. Next!"

Bouncing on a trampoline is fun. But things aren't as pleasant when life starts bouncing you around and it feels like you're headed for a nasty fall. Maybe your family is going through a rough spot now, or things aren't going well at school. At these times, it's good to remember that God has you covered. He surrounds you like a safety net. You're precious in his sight, and no matter which way life throws you, he'll be there to catch you.

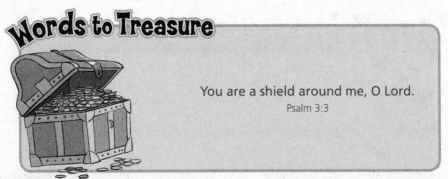

Words to Treasure

You are a shield around me, O Lord.
Psalm 3:3

Good Things from Above

[Jesus said,] "Which of you fathers, if your son asks for a fish, will give him a snake instead?... If you then, though you are evil, know how to give good gifts to your children, how much more will your Father in heaven give the Holy Spirit to those who ask him!"

Luke 11:11–13

A im right!" someone yelled. Eliza swung the stick again, this time striking her target. The crowd cheered.

"Time's up!" said Joy's mom. "It's the birthday girl's turn now."

Removing the blindfold, Eliza looked at the piñata hanging from a tree. The colorful bull was battered but still intact. Eliza handed the stick to her friend, saying, "It's ready to break."

Joy grinned. "I'll finish it off!" She put on the blindfold, and her mom spun her around. Then Joy started swinging. On her fifth try she hit the bull, and it exploded. All kinds of goodies rained down as the kids scrambled for them.

Parents don't fill piñatas with bad things—they fill them with good things like candy and toys. God is the same way. If his children want something good to eat, like a fish, he doesn't give them something that would hurt them, like a snake. He's a loving Father who showers his children with wonderful gifts. Thank God today for all of his blessings—and especially for his Spirit inside you!

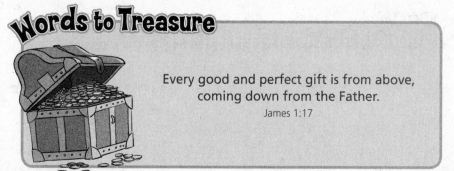

Words to Treasure

Every good and perfect gift is from above, coming down from the Father.

James 1:17

Taking Time

> "Love the Lord your God with all your heart and with all your soul and with all your mind." This is the first and greatest commandment. And the second is like it: "Love your neighbor as yourself."
>
> Matthew 22:37–39

Standing beside a dirt track, Craig and his father watched the BMX race. As the bikers hit the hills, they flew into the air, then disappeared behind the mounds in front of them.

Suddenly one of the riders lost control and wiped out. He rolled to a stop and lay there. The other bikers swerved around him. In a moment the pack was gone, leaving the injured rider in the dust.

"Look at that, Dad," Craig said. "Nobody stopped to see if he was okay!"

His father nodded slowly. "Well, they're all focused on winning the race."

What are *you* focused on as you race around every day? The most important thing in life is to love God; the second most important thing is to love others. Are you taking time for people? Are you willing to stop and help someone in need? That's hard to do in these busy times. But if you focus on what's really important, you'll always take time for people!

People in Bible Times

In one of Jesus' parables, a Samaritan took time to help a wounded man. Taking the man to an inn, he paid the innkeeper to care for him. Only then did the Samaritan continue on his trip. (See Luke 10:25–37.)

Tripping Up Others

Make up your mind not to put any stumbling block or obstacle in your brother's way.
Romans 14:13

Benjamin placed the big red picnic cooler near the swing set in his backyard. He spread a blanket over some folding chairs. Then he took logs off the firewood pile and lined them up on the ground.

"What are you doing?" asked Stevie, a little boy from the neighborhood.

Benjamin said, "Making an obstacle course. Wanna try it?"

Grinning, Stevie replied, "Yeah!"

Benjamin pointed out the route. "You have to climb the ladder, go down the slide, jump over the cooler, crawl under the blanket, and walk across the logs. I'll time you." At Benjamin's signal, Stevie started the course. But he didn't get far. Tripping over the cooler, he fell flat.

The Bible gives lots of guidance about living God's way. But it doesn't spell out everything people should and shouldn't do. For example, it doesn't say which TV shows are okay to watch and which aren't. People must decide those things for themselves with the Holy Spirit's help. Don't put obstacles in front of people by tempting them to do things they think are wrong. It might trip them up! For instance, when your friends visit, don't watch TV shows they believe they shouldn't watch. Instead of putting a stumbling block in front of people, set a good example before them. (See 1 Timothy 4:12.)

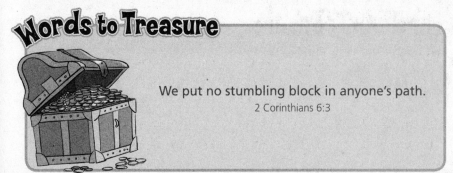

Words to Treasure

We put no stumbling block in anyone's path.
2 Corinthians 6:3

Leaders without Vision

> If a blind man leads a blind man, both will fall into a pit.
>
> Matthew 15:14

One evening as dusk fell, Maggie and Chuck were playing blind man's bluff with their cousins. Eyes closed, Maggie walked around the yard with her hands out, trying to tag the others.

"Here I am!" said someone behind her, giggling.

"No, over here!" said someone else. Recognizing Olivia's voice, Maggie headed in her direction. Then she lunged forward, waving her arms.

"Gotcha!" she said, opening her eyes. It was Olivia, all right.

"I have an idea," said Ralph. "Let's play a new version of follow the leader! I'll be the leader." Everyone lined up behind him. "Okay, close your eyes, grab the person in front of you, and follow me!" The kids laughed as he led them around. They played this game for a long time. Finally Ralph said, "We'd better quit. It's getting so dark, even I can't see!"

Some children are natural leaders, and others tend to follow them. But just because a kid has a knack for leadership doesn't mean you should fall in line behind him. Anyone who doesn't know Jesus is spiritually blind and will lead you into trouble. If none of the leaders your age are Christians, don't follow any of them. You know Jesus. You're not blind. You be a leader!

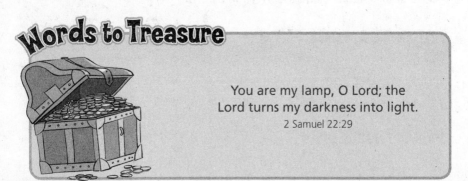

Words to Treasure

You are my lamp, O Lord; the Lord turns my darkness into light.
2 Samuel 22:29

Following the Blueprint

By wisdom a house is built, and through understanding it is established; through knowledge its rooms are filled with rare and beautiful treasures.

Proverbs 24:3–4

mitchell ran upstairs to the second level of the house, then stood there blinking. The sunlight blinding him wasn't coming through a window. The house didn't have a roof yet! Mitchell was helping his dad build their family a new home.

"Did you find those nails?" his dad asked.

"Yeah," Mitchell said, showing him the box.

"Good," his father said. "You nail down this piece of floorboard while I check something." Grabbing a hammer, Mitchell got to work. Meanwhile his dad unrolled a big sheet of paper.

"What's that?" Mitchell asked.

His dad replied, "This is the blueprint for the house. I just wanted to make sure we're doing things right!"

You're building a life for yourself right now. That life will be the "house" you'll live in. Build wisely with the choices you make and the actions you take! That way, your life will be well constructed and filled with good things. God gives you wisdom through the Bible, through his Spirit, and through the advice of godly people. Follow that wisdom—it's your blueprint!

Life in Bible Times

People in ancient times used wisdom to build good houses. For example, windows were big enough to let out smoke from the fire. But they were small enough not to let in a thief.

Redecorating

> Above all, love each other deeply, because love covers over a multitude of sins.
> 1 Peter 4:8

What are all those people doing?" Erika asked. She and her dad were out for a walk. They were approaching an old building covered with graffiti.

"I don't know," he replied. "Let's go see." They went up to the crowd near the building. Several people were painting over the graffiti.

A woman walked over. "Hello, I'm Celeste."

Erika's dad shook her hand. "Hi, Celeste. I'm Robert, and this is Erika. What's going on?"

Celeste smiled. "I wanted to make our neighborhood more beautiful, so I got permission to paint a mural on this building. When I began painting, people offered to help." She showed them her design for the mural. It was a field of wildflowers near a river and mountains.

"That's pretty," Erika said. "Can I help too?"

Nodding, Celeste replied, "Sure! You can work on the bottom." She handed Erika a smock and a brush, then showed her where to paint. Erika worked beside her neighbors all afternoon, covering ugly words and drawings with bright, colorful flowers.

You can make life more beautiful by covering people's wrongs with love. Sometimes people make the world ugly by saying or doing hateful things. You'll only make it uglier by responding the same way. But you'll brighten things up if you show love and forgiveness instead.

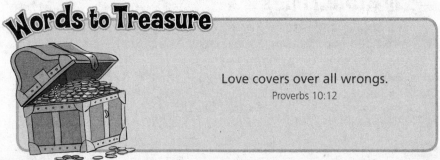

Words to Treasure

Love covers over all wrongs.
Proverbs 10:12

The Secret Recipe

It is by grace you have been saved, through faith.

Ephesians 2:8

I'm hungry," Jerry said. His family was driving through Kentucky.

Jerry's dad glanced at him in the rearview mirror. "I know. My stomach's growling too."

"Hey!" said Jerry's mom, pointing at a billboard. "Up ahead is the place where Colonel Sanders invented Kentucky Fried Chicken. Now it's a KFC restaurant and a museum. Let's eat there." Jerry's dad drove into the town of Corbin. He parked near a building with a sign that said Sanders Cafe. Inside they saw the kitchen where Colonel Sanders developed his special method of cooking chicken. There was also a display of items from his first restaurant.

Jerry said, "Look. It's a barrel of the eleven herbs and spices the Colonel used in his secret recipe!"

His father laughed. "I notice there aren't any ingredients listed on the label."

God's recipe for being saved is no secret. There are only two ingredients: grace and faith. People are saved by God's grace and through faith in Jesus. Sometimes Christians forget this simple recipe. Always remember it! It's the only way to be part of God's kingdom on earth and in heaven.

Did You Know?

Some people try to save themselves by obeying God's laws perfectly. That recipe doesn't work! When people accept God's grace by putting their faith in Jesus, God saves them. Then the Holy Spirit empowers them to obey God's laws.

March 31

A True Wonder

> Your word, O Lord, is eternal; it stands firm in the heavens.
>
> Psalm 119:89

Zoey squirmed in her chair. The sky was dark here at the Giza Plateau, just outside Cairo, Egypt. She couldn't see the gigantic monuments in front of her. Suddenly music filled the air, and the scene came alive with colored lights. "There it is, Mom. The Great Pyramid!"

Her mother was applauding with everyone else. "Isn't it beautiful, Zoey?" The pyramid stood over 450 feet tall, with two smaller ones beside it. The Great Sphinx guarded its entrance. While the music played, the lights painted the monuments different colors.

"Mom, do you realize that the Great Pyramid is the last of the original Seven Wonders of the World? My class studied them. There were two giant statues, a huge lighthouse, and other incredible things, but they're gone now. So the whole world voted to pick seven new wonders."

Zoey's mom smiled. "They should've made the Bible number one. God's Word is the most amazing thing on earth, and it'll be around after everything else has disappeared!"

What makes your Bible so wonderful isn't its paper or ink. That'll be gone someday. Your Bible is special because it contains the words God has spoken. They tell us who God is, what he thinks, how he feels, and much, much more. They are precious, important words, and their truth will last for all eternity.

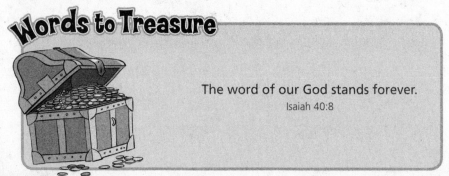

Words to Treasure

The word of our God stands forever.
Isaiah 40:8

The Jokester

A man reaps what he sows.

Galatians 6:7

In the kitchen alone, Darin slipped a rubber band over the handle of the sprayer on the sink. Then he began setting the table. As the family ate dinner, he couldn't wait for everyone to finish. "Whose turn is it to do the dishes?" his mom asked, getting up to clear the table.

"Elizabeth's," Darin said, grinning.

His sister said, "No way! It's Dad's turn tonight." Darin's grin faded.

"Guess I'd better get at it," his dad said, heading for the sink.

"Uh, Dad—," Darin said. But just then his father turned on the faucet and got blasted with water.

"Hey!" he cried. Everyone looked at Darin.

"Gotcha," Darin said sheepishly, and they all laughed.

Wiping himself off, his dad said, "You'd better watch out. Next time it's your turn!"

A harmless practical joke now and then can keep your home life lively. It's something else, though, to say and do things to make members of your family truly upset. That's like "sowing" (planting) weed seeds in your own garden! What you'll "reap" (harvest) is your family's anger. Sow seeds of love, peace, and joy instead. That will please God and keep things fun.

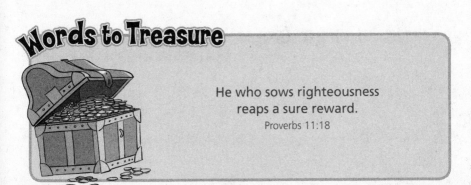

Words to Treasure

He who sows righteousness
reaps a sure reward.
Proverbs 11:18

Justice and Grace

> In [Jesus] we have redemption through his blood, the forgiveness of sins, in accordance with the riches of God's grace.
>
> Ephesians 1:7

The judge looked down at the man. "I find you guilty of speeding in a school zone. The fine is one hundred dollars." Kailey watched with her classmates, fascinated. The judge banged his gavel. "This court is in recess." Everyone stood as the judge rose and approached Kailey's group. "Welcome, class. I hope you're enjoying your visit to my courtroom. Any questions?"

Kailey raised her hand. "Your Honor, why did that man have to pay a fine? He said he always obeys the speed limits. That day while he was going past the school, he just forgot it was time for kids to get out."

The judge replied, "In our society there are laws that must be obeyed. When people break those laws, they have to pay the penalty. It's the only way to maintain justice, to keep things fair."

Justice is important to God. But he also loves you. Although you've broken his laws, he doesn't want you to die. (Death is the penalty for sin.) So he sent Jesus to die on the cross to pay your penalty for you. This way, justice is maintained. And now God can bless you instead of punishing you. That's called grace!

Words to Treasure

[God] loved us and sent his Son as an atoning sacrifice for our sins.
1 John 4:10

Holding Up under Pressure

The one who is in you is greater than the one
who is in the world.

1 John 4:4

As snow swirled, Leo and his dad pulled their golf clubs out of the SUV. "This isn't the kind of weather I was hoping for during spring break," Leo said.

His dad grinned. "I know. But we're making the best of it!" Closing the hatchback, he said, "Let's go hit a bucket of balls."

Leo followed his dad inside the big, white dome of the indoor golf center. It was made of a soft, tentlike material.

Gazing overhead, Leo asked, "How does this thing stay up?"

His dad replied, "It's inflated with air. See those blowers? The dome stays up because the air pressure inside is greater than the air pressure outside."

Satan puts pressure on you to sin or to be afraid. But you have the Holy Spirit inside you! That gives you the strength to hold up under this pressure. God's Spirit enables you to stand up under other pressures too, for example, the pressure of worrying you'll do poorly on tests or in sports. God's Spirit in you is mightier than any pressure you feel from the outside.

People in Bible Times

The Jewish leaders ordered Peter and
John to stop preaching about Jesus. But
Peter and John were filled with God's
Spirit. That gave them the courage to
declare that they wouldn't stop.

The Empty Tomb

> [The angel at the tomb said,] "You are looking for Jesus the Nazarene, who was crucified. He has risen! He is not here."
>
> Mark 16:6

Under the dome of the ancient church, Kip pointed at a large, square structure. "Is Jesus' tomb in there?" He was inside the Church of the Holy Sepulchre, in Jerusalem.

"Yes," replied his father, an archaeologist working in the Holy Land. "This church was first built three hundred years after Jesus died. Christians living in Jerusalem back then believed he was buried here. So this structure was erected over the tomb they found."

Kip's sister Mira asked, "But what about the Garden Tomb?" They'd just come from that place. It was a vault cut into a stone hillside.

"Some people think Jesus was buried there," said Kip's father.

Smiling, Kip's mom said, "Whichever tomb is the right one, I'm glad it's empty!"

Nobody knows for sure where Jesus was buried. But it helps to remember that his death, burial, and resurrection were real events that happened in real places. Jesus really did die. He really was buried. And he really did rise from the dead! That truth gives all Christians the hope of eternal life.

People in Bible Times

When an angel rolled the stone away from Jesus' tomb, the guards were so scared that they passed out. Later they said the disciples stole Jesus' body while they were sleeping! (See Matthew 27:62–28:15.)

The Place to Be

> [God] has qualified you to share in the inheritance of the saints in the kingdom of light.
>
> Colossians 1:12

During spring break, the weather wasn't springlike. Leo shivered in the blowing snow as he walked across a parking lot at night. "It's freezing out here!" he said. He and his family were headed for an indoor water park.

Leo's dad pointed ahead. "This place will cheer you up."

Through large windows, Leo saw a different scene. It was bright and colorful. Everyone was wearing swimsuits and having a great time. He saw a waterslide, a vortex pool, a floating obstacle course, and a zip line. "That's more like it!" he said, walking faster. Soon they'd changed into their suits and joined the fun. Glancing outside at the dark, snowy night, Leo grinned. "Being in here sure beats being out there!"

Satan will try to convince you that his kingdom is better than God's. He'll make sinning seem more fun than living God's way. He'll even make spending eternity with him sound more exciting than spending it with God. But the truth is, Satan's kingdom is a place of darkness and misery. (See Colossians 1:13.) God's kingdom is *much* better. It's the kingdom of light—and warmth and fun and laughter and love and joy and peace and life!

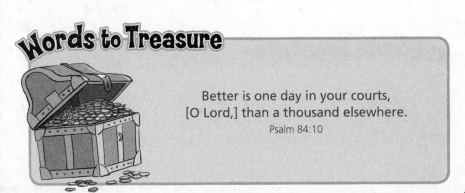

Words to Treasure

> Better is one day in your courts, [O Lord,] than a thousand elsewhere.
>
> Psalm 84:10

April 6

Signs of Life

> There before me [in heaven] was a great multitude that no one could count, from every nation, tribe, people and language.
>
> Revelation 7:9

Isn't this beautiful?" Alayna said. She and Libby were walking through the apple orchard behind Alayna's house. It was spring, and the trees were in bloom.

Libby breathed deeply. "Yeah, and the air smells so good!"

Alayna twirled a couple of times, just for fun. "I love coming out here every spring. The blossoms are my favorite sign of Easter." She ran her hand through them.

Libby said, "Mine is chocolate eggs." They both laughed. Then Libby asked, "Why are these your favorite?"

Picking a blossom, Alayna said, "Because they make the trees look alive again." She looked around. "And because there's so many of them. It reminds me of all the people who'll be in heaven because of Easter. The Bible says there'll be too many to count!"

What's your favorite sign of Easter? Does it help you remember the real meaning of the holiday? Easter is a celebration that Jesus rose from the dead. Because he did, there'll be many joyful people in heaven. And you'll be one of them! If your favorite sign of Easter doesn't remind you of that, why not choose a new favorite? The real meaning of Easter is too good to forget.

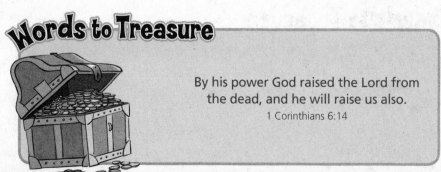

Words to Treasure

By his power God raised the Lord from the dead, and he will raise us also.

1 Corinthians 6:14

An Uplifting Experience

Peter got down out of the boat, walked on the water and came toward Jesus. But when he saw the wind, he was afraid and, beginning to sink, cried out, "Lord, save me!" Immediately Jesus reached out his hand and caught him.

Matthew 14:29–31

Brandon and Hailey stood on the boat in the waters near Sarasota, Florida. Fluttering behind them was a colorful parasail.

"Bon voyage," said their mother as a man let out the rope.

Their father added, "Next stop: eight hundred feet over the Gulf of Mexico."

Brandon felt his toes leave the deck. The parasail lifted him and his sister higher and higher. "This is cool!" Hailey said. They cruised along the coast, enjoying the view.

Suddenly Brandon glanced at Hailey. "The boat's stopping. We're going down!" The waves rushed at them. As their feet hit the water, the kids moved their legs as if they were running across the ocean. Then the boat's engine revved, and they shot up into the air again, laughing.

Peter's faith in Jesus was going full blast when he stepped out of the boat and walked on the water. But when Peter got scared, his faith slowed down, and he began to sink. Whenever things look bad, keep your faith in Jesus moving full speed ahead. And if you feel afraid and start doubting, call to him the way Peter did. Jesus will pull you up every time!

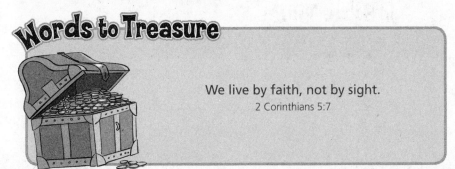

Words to Treasure

We live by faith, not by sight.
2 Corinthians 5:7

Hitting the Mark

The battle is the Lord's.

1 Samuel 17:47

Pulling back the stone in his new slingshot, Ted took careful aim. That was no ordinary tin can on the stump in his backyard. It was a loud-mouthed, giant tin can, the champion of the tin-can army. A giant tin can challenging anyone to come fight him. Ted squinted through one eye. *No problem, big guy. Take this!* He released the stone. It whistled past the giant's head.

"Keep your arm steady," said Ted's dad.

Picking up another stone, Ted put it in the pouch. "Okay." He aimed again. The slingshot twanged, and the stone ricocheted off the stump. Ted shook his head. "I don't know how David took down Goliath with just one stone. I can't hit a can with a whole pile of 'em!"

When David faced Goliath, he wasn't alone. David knew God would help him defeat the enemy. He told the giant, "This day the Lord will hand you over to me, and I'll strike you down." (See 1 Samuel 17.) David attacked Goliath with all his skill. But he knew the battle really belonged to God. Are you living like David, doing your best and trusting God to give you victory?

Life in Bible Times

Ancient slings were different from slingshots. Their pouch was connected to two long cords. One cord was released as the stone was swung in circles. Slingers could hurl stones at high speeds over long distances, with great accuracy.

Waiting for Sprouts

[The apostle Paul wrote,] "I planted the seed, Apollos watered it, but God made it grow."

1 Corinthians 3:6

Cheryl wanted to plant a garden in the backyard. So her dad was using a rototiller to prepare the ground. As Cheryl and her mom watched, the machine's spinning blades loosened up the dirt. Finally Cheryl's father shut off the engine. "Well, *my* job's done," he said, wiping his forehead. "Now you two can get started."

Cheryl's mom patted his shoulder. "Nice work! Okay, Cheryl, you're in charge. Where do we begin?"

Looking at her plans, Cheryl pointed. "The beans go along that side." She walked around the garden. "Here's where the carrots go, and the squash go there ..." Soon she and her mom were on their knees, digging dirt and planting seeds. Cheryl marked the places where the different vegetables were. Then she watered the garden. "That's it," she said, rolling up the hose. "Now we just have to wait!"

Once you plant a vegetable seed and water it, your work is finished. But it's different with the seed of the gospel. First you plant this seed in someone's heart by telling him or her about Jesus. Then you water the seed by loving the person the way Jesus does. After that, there's still one more thing to do. You pray that God will make the seed sprout into faith.

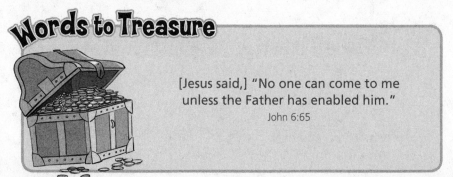

Words to Treasure

[Jesus said,] "No one can come to me unless the Father has enabled him."

John 6:65

Morning Glory

> From the rising of the sun to the place where
> it sets, the name of the Lord is to be praised.
>
> Psalm 113:3

Gazing at the huge Civil War memorial carved on the side of Stone Mountain, Justin yawned. Not because he wasn't excited. It was early in the morning, before sunrise. He and his family were in a cable car, swaying over the treetops near Atlanta, Georgia. They were traveling to the top of the mountain for a special Easter celebration.

"Look at the stars," said Justin's sister Lydia. "It still looks like the middle of the night."

Justin nodded, shivering. "It's still cold out too."

Soon they were sitting on a blanket on the mountain's summit. A pastor spoke about the wonder of Jesus' resurrection on the first Easter morning. As he did, the starry sky gave way to a glorious sunrise. The sun appeared, shining brilliantly, and Justin's heart overflowed with love and praise for God.

Sunrise and sunset are wonderful times for praising God. Yet they're not the only times made for worshiping him. Psalm 113:3 says you can praise God in the morning, in the evening, and anytime in between. So praise him all day long!

People in Bible Times

God chose some Levites to be priests. The rest were to be the priests' helpers. One of the duties of these Levites was to stand and praise God every morning and evening. (See 1 Chronicles 23:28–31.)

From Pollywogs to Bullfrogs

Anyone who lives on milk, being still an infant, is not acquainted with the teaching about righteousness. But solid food is for the mature, who by constant use have trained themselves to distinguish good from evil.

Hebrews 5:13–14

Torrey and Drew were down at the pond, catching pollywogs. Scooping scummy water into a glass jar, Torrey held it up. "Look how many I got!"

His sister admired his catch. "Wow, you got a bunch. Look at mine!" Torrey examined hers. Then they started walking up to their house.

"It'll be fun watching them turn into frogs," said Drew.

Torrey nodded. Suddenly a thought struck him. "What'll we feed them?" They stopped and looked at each other.

Drew shrugged. "Well, I guess they'll just eat the green stuff in the water. I don't think they're ready for flies yet!"

Like pollywogs, babies can't handle solid food. Some Christians can't handle it either. They still haven't learned the simple, "baby's milk" truths about living God's way. Their behavior proves they're not ready for the "meatier" truths. You're young, but you can handle a hamburger, right? Do all the basic things you know God wants you to do. Show him you're ready for more!

Live It!

Play Ten-Commandments leapfrog. Have each person say the first commandment and hop over everyone else. Then have each person say the second, and so on. By the way you live, show God that you know these laws.

No Strings Attached

The Lord God formed the man from the dust of the ground and breathed into his nostrils the breath of life, and the man became a living being.

Genesis 2:7

In the school gym, a puppeteer was putting on a show. He had hand puppets, marionettes, and a dummy named Charlie who sat on his knee. Kara watched, mesmerized, as he made them come alive. "Want to hear a knock-knock joke, Charlie?" the man asked.

Charlie replied, "Sure!"

The man said, "Okay, you start."

Charlie cleared his throat. "Knock, knock."

The puppeteer said, "Who's there?"

Charlie opened his mouth, but nothing came out. Then he said, "Hey!"

Everyone laughed. Putting Charlie away, the man said, "Now I need volunteers." Kara's arm shot up, and he chose her and two others. He gave them marionettes, then had them perform a zany skit on the puppet stage. Kara had fun making her puppet walk, hop, and dance. And the audience laughed as the three kids tried to act out the story the man told.

When God made people, he wanted real, live children, not puppets. He loves people, and he wants them to love him and obey him so he can bless them. But he wants them to do it because they choose to, not because he's making them do it. Have you chosen to love God and obey him and be his child?

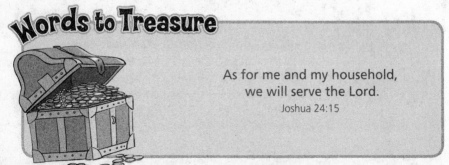

Words to Treasure

As for me and my household, we will serve the Lord.

Joshua 24:15

Going Exploring

In keeping with [God's] promise we are looking forward to a new heaven and a new earth,
the home of righteousness.

2 Peter 3:13

"We could build a fort out here," Jacklyn said. She and her brother were exploring the woods behind their new house.

"Or maybe—" Carson stopped. "Do you hear that?"

Looking around, Jacklyn said, "What?" She started walking in a new direction.
"What is it?" Jacklyn asked, trying to catch up.

"It sounds like water," Carson said. "There must be a river."

Jacklyn was eager to see what they'd discover. Now she could hear the noise
too. As they climbed a hill, it grew louder.

Reaching the top, Carson said, "Check this out!" Jacklyn joined him. They
were standing on a steep bank. Below them, a wide stream wound through the
woods.

Jacklyn pointed at a flat, grassy area on the other side. "There's an excellent
place for our fort!"

Imagine how thrilling it'll be to explore heaven. You'll discover all the exciting things God has in store for you there. Some of it will be familiar. Some of it
will be like nothing you've ever imagined! All of it will be new and perfect and
wonderful.

Did You Know?

Here are some things you'll be able to explore in
heaven: A great mountain. A crystal-clear river.
A city made of gold. You'll see a sky lit up with
God's glory. Best of all, you'll see God himself!
(See Revelation 21:1–22:5.)

Building Homes

> He who is kind to the poor lends to the Lord,
> and he will reward him.
>
> Proverbs 19:17

Jesse climbed out of her mom's minivan near a small crowd in a grassy lot. She saw her teacher, Mrs. Evans, with a young girl. "Hi, Jesse," Mrs. Evans said. "This is Nicole. Her family is moving into the house that'll be built here. Nicole, Jesse helped raise money for your new home." Nicole said hello.

"Hi," Jesse said, holding out a gift bag. "This is for you. It's one of the birdhouses we made to sell. I'm not old enough to work on your house. But I had fun building these! I thought you'd like to put one outside your window."

Nicole hugged her and said, "Thank you!" Jesse smiled.

"Look, the groundbreaking ceremony is beginning," said Mrs. Evans.

They watched as a person spoke. He was with Habitat for Humanity, the organization helping Nicole's family build their house. Nicole's father thanked everyone. Then he dug up a shovelful of dirt, officially starting the construction project.

You're not too young to make a big difference in someone else's life. There are many ways for kids your age to get involved in efforts to help others. God is pleased when you lend a hand to people in need.

Live It!

Make a difference. Get involved with efforts to help the needy. Maybe you could participate in a car wash or bake sale to raise money. Remember to pray for the poor!

Throwing Away the Key

Commit yourselves to the Lord.

1 Samuel 7:3

Zach stood on the Great Wall of China, his eyes following the wall as it snaked up the mountain. He and his parents were sightseeing in the city of Beijing. Tomorrow they were going to pick up Sophie, the little Chinese girl his family was adopting.

"This is the biggest manmade structure in the world," said their guide, a young Chinese woman. "It's four thousand miles long."

Zach looked at the highest watchtower on that section of the wall. "Let's go up there!"

Smiling, the guide said, "First, watch this." She pointed at a man and woman at the wall's edge. "They just got married," she explained. "What they're doing now is meant to show that their love will last forever." As Zach watched, the couple snapped a padlock on a thick metal chain attached to the stone and then tossed the key over the wall.

The most important commitment you'll ever make is the one you make to God. Lock yourself to him now and throw away the key! Promise God not to let anything ever pull the two of you apart. Then ask him to help you keep that promise.

People in Bible Times

Jacob committed himself to God at Bethel. After God appeared to him there, Jacob set up a stone to remember the place. He vowed, "The Lord will be my God." (See Genesis 28:20–22.)

Time for It to Go

There is a time for everything, and a season for every activity under heaven: ... a time to tear down and a time to build.

Ecclesiastes 3:1, 3

Using a crowbar, Abigail's father pried another board off the old deck behind their house. "Here you go, Abby," he said, tossing the board beside her. She was using a hammer claw to pull nails out of the boards. "Hey," her dad said, "remember when we watched that wrecking crew demolish the house down the street?"

Abigail looked up. "Yeah. Their excavator looked like a T. rex taking bites out of the roof!" She pulled out another nail. "Why did they tear down the house, anyway?"

Struggling to pry off another board, her father replied, "They're building a better one."

Abigail dropped the hammer, shaking her hand. "Well, I'm glad we're only replacing our deck."

Her dad laughed. "I wouldn't mind having a dinosaur to help with this job, though!"

Often in the Old Testament, God's people tore down bad things so they could build good things. They destroyed altars to false gods so they could worship the true God. Is there anything *you* need to tear down (for example, selfishness or pride) so you can build a better relationship with God?

People in Bible Times

King Hezekiah wanted to build up the Israelites' relationship with God. So he tore down sacred stones and Asherah poles, which were used to worship false gods.

The Meeting Place

My soul thirsts for God, for the living God.
When can I go and meet with God?

Psalm 42:2

Jack pounded a nail into the roof of the tree house he and his friends were building in his backyard. "More shingles!" he shouted.

Trevor loaded the shingles into a box with a rope attached. "All right, Willie, pull 'er up." Standing in the tree house, Willie hauled on the other end of the rope, which went over a pulley tied to an upper branch.

When the box was high enough, Jack grabbed it. "Okay!" He set the box on the roof, pulled out a shingle, and started nailing it down.

"Well, we're almost done," Willie said, climbing onto the roof.

"Yeah," Jack replied. "You guys coming here after school tomorrow to hang out?"

Willie handed him another shingle. "Are you kidding? We're gonna be here every day—reading comic books, listening to music, playing games ..."

From below, Trevor hollered, "And eating munchies!"

Do you have a special time and place to meet with God regularly? Your relationship with the Lord will grow if you hang out with him for a while every day. Spend time with God daily. Read the Bible, talk to him, and listen to what he says to you.

People in Bible Times

Daniel was busy. Still, he met with God regularly. Daniel's special meeting place was in his room. Next to the windows facing Jerusalem, Daniel prayed every day. (See Daniel 6:10.)

Checking Things Out

> [The Lord told Abraham,] "Go, walk through the length and breadth of the land, for I am giving it to you."
>
> Genesis 13:17

As the minivan pulled up to the large, two-story house, Regan and Troy were bouncing in their seats. Their mom laughed. "You guys are really eager to see our new home."

Regan said, "We can't wait to check it out!" She and Troy jumped out and ran across the big front yard. A moving van was parked in the driveway. Regan waved at her dad, who was helping the movers. Inside the house, the kids scurried up the steps to inspect their bedrooms. Regan's had a cool window seat. Troy's had a built-in bookshelf. Downstairs, they examined the living room, kitchen, and dining area. And in the walk-out basement, they checked out the large recreation room.

"It's gonna be great living here," Troy said.

Regan peered out the sliding glass door. "Let's go see the backyard," she said. "It looks huge!"

When God showed Abraham the Promised Land, he wanted him to explore it. There were boundary lines, but within them was a wide-open place full of opportunity. Your life has boundaries too—God's laws. But within those laws is a wide-open space where you'll find freedom and adventure. Explore the life God has given you, and make the most of it.

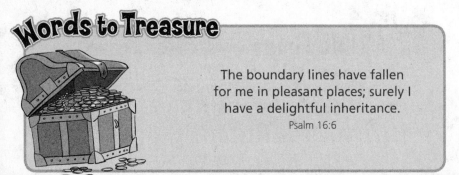

Words to Treasure

The boundary lines have fallen for me in pleasant places; surely I have a delightful inheritance.

Psalm 16:6

Building Bridges

Do not be proud, but be willing to associate with people of low position.

Romans 12:16

In the woods behind their house, Jacklyn and Carson pulled a small tree trunk across the stream. They hauled one end of the tree trunk onto the flat, grassy bank where they planned to build their fort. The other end rested on the steep, rocky bank on the opposite side of the stream.

Together they rolled the log against others that were already there. Then, using rope, they lashed all the tree trunks together.

"Wanna try it out?" asked Carson.

Stepping onto the logs, Jacklyn walked across their new bridge. "It's bouncy," she said, "but it works!"

Forming a friendship with someone is like building a bridge. It's easy if the other person is a lot like you. But it can be harder if he or she is different. What if the other person isn't as good-looking or rich or talented or smart? God doesn't want you to go through life only hanging around with people who are just like you. And he doesn't want you looking down at others. Jesus built bridges of friendship with people who had less status than he did. Are you willing to do the same?

People in Bible Times

In Jesus' day, tax collectors were near the bottom of the social ladder. That's because they often cheated their own people. Yet Jesus became friends with them. (See Matthew 9:9–13.)

Inside and Out

> Man looks at the outward appearance, but the Lord looks at the heart.
>
> 1 Samuel 16:7

Zach and his parents were about to climb the Great Wall of China. As they headed for the large stone steps, a man approached. Speaking Chinese, he held up his camera and pointed at Zach. "I think he wants your picture," said Zach's mom.

Their guide, a young Chinese woman, explained. "People here are interested in anyone different from them. Haven't you noticed everyone watching Zach?" Zach and his parents looked around. People were staring at him, pointing and talking.

"What's so weird about me?" Zach asked.

The guide smiled. "It's your hair. There aren't many red-headed people in China." She looked at the small crowd gathering around them. "Okay if they take your picture?" Zach nodded and posed with his parents, smiling. He enjoyed all the attention, but it was strange having everyone think he was different. He didn't *feel* different.

When you meet someone who looks different from you, ask God to help you see that person the way he does. God doesn't focus on things like skin color or clothes or handicaps or scars. He focuses on the person underneath—who's really a lot like you.

Did You Know?

God told Samuel he'd chosen one of Jesse's sons to be king of Israel. Samuel thought it was Eliab, who looked kingly. But God had chosen David, because of David's character. (See 1 Samuel 16:1–13.)

The Platform

Who is like the Lord our God, the One who sits enthroned on high, who stoops down to look on the heavens and the earth?

Psalm 113:5–6

"Aren't the giraffes beautiful?" Suzanna said. She and her mom were at the African savanna exhibit at the zoo. It was a wide, grassy area with scattered trees. Giraffes, zebras, and antelope roamed freely.

"They sure are graceful," Suzanna's mother agreed.

Suzanna sighed. "I wish we could see them up close."

Her mom said, "Well then, you'll like what's up ahead." They followed the trail through the savanna, spotting animals and birds along the way.

Then Suzanna saw a large wooden structure. "What's that?"

"It's a feeding station!" her mom replied. "They've built a platform so we can get up to the giraffes' level." A ramp led them to the top of the platform, where there were coin-operated machines full of giraffe food. With a handful of treats, Suzanna approached a giraffe that was looking over the railing. She laughed as the friendly animal gobbled up the food with its long tongue.

God sits high up on his heavenly throne, holy and majestic. Because of sin, people can't get up there close to him. (See Romans 3:23.) But like a platform, Jesus lifts people up to God's level. When you pray, thank Jesus for making you holy, so you can be with God!

Words to Treasure

Humble yourselves before the Lord,
and he will lift you up.
James 4:10

Don't Be Duped

> From infancy you have known the holy Scriptures, which are able to make you wise for salvation through faith in Christ Jesus.
>
> 2 Timothy 3:15

Willie watched Jack nail another shingle to the roof of the tree house. Jack finished pounding, then looked up. "You could help, you know."

Grinning, Willie said, "That's an idea." He hollered down, "Hey, Trev! Find me a left-handed hammer so I can help Jack."

Trevor stood up. "Okay!"

As Trevor ran into Jack's house, Willie snickered. "Let's see how long this takes." He handed Jack another shingle. Shaking his head, Jack laid it down and started hammering.

Willie watched him finish ten more shingles before Trevor returned. He was carrying an ordinary hammer. "Very funny, guys. I looked all over. Finally I asked Jack's dad if he even had a left-handed hammer. He said there's no such thing!"

Nobody likes to be duped. Especially in important matters. Get to know the Bible well, so you'll become wise. Then you won't be misled about the things that really count in life. You won't fall for Satan's tricks. You won't believe lies about what's right and what's wrong. And you won't be fooled when someone tells you the Bible says something it doesn't really say.

People in Bible Times

The Bereans were excited when the apostle Paul told them about Jesus. But before they believed Paul, they made sure the Scriptures backed up what he said. (See Acts 17:11.)

Nothing to Fear

[Jesus told his disciples,] "I have given you authority to trample on snakes and scorpions and to overcome all the power of the enemy; nothing will harm you."

Luke 10:19

Inside the insect house at the zoo, Suzanna saw some kids gathered around a zookeeper. "What's going on?" she asked.

Her mother shrugged. "Let's go see."

As they approached the group, Suzanna froze. A huge, hairy spider was crawling on the man's hand! It was black, with red patches on its legs. "Spiders are actually arachnids, not insects," the zookeeper was saying. "This is a Mexican redknee tarantula. Many people keep these as pets."

Suzanna leaned forward. "Aren't they deadly?"

The zookeeper replied, "No. Their bite would hurt, but it wouldn't kill you. Want to hold him?"

Suzanna hesitated, then nodded. The zookeeper gently placed the spider in her hand. As it moved around, she giggled. "It tickles!"

Satan is sort of like a tarantula. He has a scary reputation, but he's not as powerful as people think. Satan never was as powerful as God, because God created him. And whatever power he had was destroyed when Jesus died on the cross. (See Colossians 2:15.) Satan has been defeated and disarmed. He can't harm you. All he can do is lie to you, tempt you, and try to scare you. And God will shield you even from that!

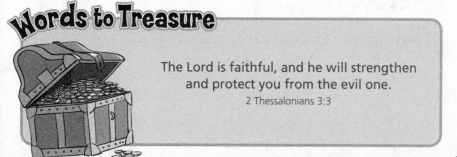

Words to Treasure

The Lord is faithful, and he will strengthen and protect you from the evil one.

2 Thessalonians 3:3

Facing Guilt Head-On

> There is now no condemnation for those who are in Christ Jesus.
>
> Romans 8:1

The mounted knight wearing blue charged toward Garret, his lance lowered. Garret imagined he was the other knight, in red, riding hard to meet him. The knights were jousting at the Renaissance fair, a festival being held near the city where Garret lived. It was a colorful event, with flags and banners everywhere. Minstrels and jugglers wandered about, and the smell of roasting meat filled the air. Dressed in medieval costumes, Garret and his family stood beside the arena. They were cheering on the contestants. "Knock him off!" Garret yelled.

His sister, Kelly, shouted, "Go! Go!" Dust flew as the horses galloped toward each other. The blue knight looked unstoppable, but the red knight rode on. They collided, and the blue knight's weapon shattered. His opponent's lance caught him squarely in the chest, and he was thrown to the ground. The crowd cheered as the red knight turned his horse and raised his fist, his silver armor gleaming.

The Devil often charges at you, accusing you of wrongs you've done. You can face him head-on, wearing the breastplate of righteousness. (See Ephesians 6:14.) Just confess your sins. God won't condemn you. Instead he'll forgive you. He'll cover you with Jesus' perfect goodness. It protects you like armor, so the Devil can't knock you down with guilt.

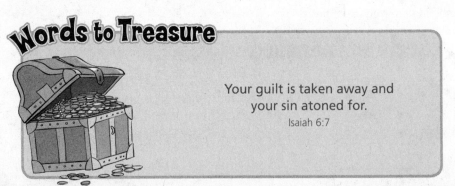

Words to Treasure

> Your guilt is taken away and your sin atoned for.
>
> Isaiah 6:7

Certified Hero

Jesus said, "It is finished." With that, he bowed
his head and gave up his spirit.

John 19:30

Zach reached the sixth watchtower on the section of the Great Wall of China he
was climbing. He leaned against the stone building, breathing hard and waiting for his parents.

He wanted to go to the highest watchtower on this mountain. Their guide had
said, "To Chinese people, anyone who climbs up there is a hero." She'd told Zach
that if he made it, he could get an official hero certificate.

"Whew!" his dad said, catching up. "I'm glad our steps at home aren't this
big."

By now Zach felt rested. He stood up straight, saying, "We can't stop now.
We've got to go all the way to the top."

His father laughed. "All right, hero boy. Just give me and your mom a minute
to catch our breath!"

When Jesus climbed the hill called Calvary, he became the greatest hero of
all time. There he accomplished the mission God gave him. He died on the cross
for the sins of the world and saved everyone who believes in him. Want to read
Jesus' hero certificate? Take a look at the Scripture passage below.

Words to Treasure

[Jesus] humbled himself and became
obedient to death—even death on a
cross! Therefore God exalted him to the
highest place and gave him the name that
is above every name, that at the name
of Jesus every knee should bow.

Philippians 2:8–10

Listen Carefully

Listen to advice and accept instruction, and in the end you will be wise.

Proverbs 19:20

Allie's parents were going out for the evening. "Bye, honey," her mother said. "Enjoy your movie night at home!"

"Bye, Mom," Allie replied. After they left, she went into the kitchen with Karen, the sitter. Unwrapping a bag of popcorn, Allie unfolded it and put it in the microwave.

"Is it right side up?" Karen asked.

"Yup!" Allie said, closing the door.

"Good," Karen said. "Set the timer for four minutes." Allie pushed the buttons. The oven hummed, the bag rotated, and the corn began to pop. Karen said, "Now listen carefully. When the popping slows down, shut off the microwave."

Allie nodded. "Okay. But why do we have to listen?"

"So we don't scorch the popcorn," Karen replied. "The first time I made microwave popcorn, I didn't listen. I smelled something burning, and when I opened the door, smoke came out. Then the smoke alarm went off. I had to open all the windows to air out the kitchen—in the wintertime!"

It's important to listen. People learn to talk when they're toddlers. But sometimes they never really learn to listen. Get good at listening to others. Especially when you're arguing! (See James 1:19.) Most importantly, learn to listen to people who are godly and wise. If you listen to people such as parents, teachers, and pastors, you'll become wise like them.

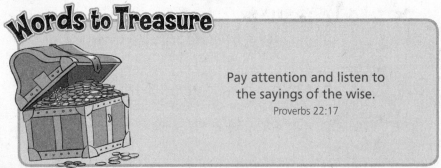

Words to Treasure

Pay attention and listen to the sayings of the wise.

Proverbs 22:17

In a Bind

Let us throw off everything that hinders and the sin that so easily entangles.

Hebrews 12:1

After watching the joust at the Renaissance fair, Garret and Kelly were arguing about what to do next. "You never want to do what I want to do," Garret said. "You're such a loser."

His mom began lecturing him about calling his sister names. But his dad interrupted. "I know how to handle this." He marched Garret over to a man dressed like a medieval judge. "This scoundrel insulted a young maiden," Garret's dad complained.

The judge frowned. "To the pillory!" He led them all to a platform. There a scruffy-looking man was standing with his head and hands sticking out of holes between two heavy boards. The judge put Garret on a wooden crate and stuck him in the pillory too.

Turning his head, the man said, "I stole a watermelon. What did you do?"

Laughing, Garret told him his crime. The pillory seemed fun at first, but soon it grew uncomfortable. Eventually Garret promised not to call Kelly bad names anymore, and the judge released him.

Sin will always get you in a bind—even if you're not punished. Think about what happens when you hurt others with unkind words, for instance. Your relationships get all tangled up with anger and bitterness. That's no fun! Get rid of sin, so you'll be free to live God's way.

Words to Treasure

Those who are righteous will go free.
Proverbs 11:21

The Password

> [Jesus said,] "By this all men will know that you are my disciples, if you love one another."
>
> John 13:35

Sitting up in the tree house in his backyard, Jack heard a knock. "What's the password?" he asked.

Willie's voice answered. "Terabithia."

Jack got up and lifted the door latch. "Hey, Willie," he said.

His friend entered, carrying a large bag of potato chips. "Hey. What's going on?"

Sitting down again, Jack said, "Nothing yet. You see Trevor?"

Willie plopped into a chair. "No, but he knows I've got these, so he'll be here." As he ripped open the bag, another knock sounded.

Jack called out, "What's the password?"

They heard silence, then Trevor's voice. "I forgot. Wait a minute ... Oh yeah. Terabinthia."

Willie groaned, saying, "It's not Tera*binth*ia! You gotta say it right."

The door started rattling. "Come on, guys! Why do we need a password, anyway? You know it's me!"

Jesus gave his disciples a kind of password. It's a sign that proves they're his followers. But it isn't something they say; it's something they do. Everyone can tell who Jesus' true disciples are by the way they love each other. Do *you* know the password? If you do, show it!

Did You Know?

The Gileadites used a password to tell friend from foe after a battle. The password was "Shibboleth." If a man said the word right, the Gileadites knew he was one of them. (See Judges 12:4–6.)

Being a Pawn

Don't let anyone look down on you because you are young, but set an example for the believers in speech, in life, in love, in faith and in purity.

1 Timothy 4:12

Kelly stood on a giant chessboard at the Renaissance fair. She'd been chosen to be a pawn in a human chess match! As part of a show, two noblemen were playing the game. "Bishop takes rook!" said the nobleman controlling the black "pieces." The black bishop moved three squares diagonally to replace the white rook.

Kelly feared her side was losing. But the other nobleman said, "Pawn to knight's eight." He meant her! She moved ahead one square. Then she understood. When a lowly pawn reaches the end of the board, it can become a powerful queen. A crown was placed on her head, and now she had the black king trapped.

"Checkmate!" an official declared.

Never imagine you don't matter because you're little. A pawn can win a chess game! Likewise, God can use a young kid like you to make a big difference in the world. God is making great changes in your heart. The way you talk and act as a result sets a powerful example for others. You can inspire people (even adults) to live a more godly life.

People in Bible Times

Young Timothy made a big difference in the world. Traveling with the apostle Paul, Timothy helped spread the gospel. And his behavior set a good example for others. (See Philippians 2:22.)

Joining God's Family

> In love [God] predestined us to be adopted as his sons through Jesus Christ.
>
> Ephesians 1:4–5

At the orphanage in Nanchang, a small city in China, Zach waited with his parents. His family was adopting a Chinese girl named Sophie. For Zach, coming to get her had been full of adventures. He'd flown for sixteen hours to visit a country where hardly anyone spoke English. He'd seen many amazing things. But meeting his new sister was the biggest adventure of all.

"Here she is!" said a woman, handing Sophie to Zach's mom. As his parents hugged Sophie and talked to her, Zach noticed she wasn't smiling. He thought of all they'd done to adopt her. They'd spent lots of money, made room for her in their home, and traveled far. What if she didn't want to join their family?

"Say hello to your new sister!" his mom said, putting Sophie down.

"Hi, Sophie," said Zach. She just stared at him. So he made a funny face—and she laughed.

God went through a lot to adopt you! He did everything that needed to be done so he could call you his own. All you had to do to become one of God's children was to respond to his love. You did that by putting your faith in Jesus. Tell your friends they can become God's children too!

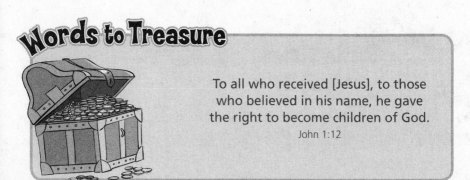

Words to Treasure

> To all who received [Jesus], to those who believed in his name, he gave the right to become children of God.
>
> John 1:12

A Message of Praise

Her children arise and call her blessed; her husband also, and he praises her.

Proverbs 31:28

Dressing for school, Miranda heard her mother call, "Breakfast is ready!" She glanced at her clock, then hurried to the table. Her brother Travis was just sitting down. He checked his watch.

Miranda said, "Mom, could you turn up the radio?" Her mother was listening to their favorite Christian station while she packed everyone's lunches.

"Sure," she said, adjusting the volume.

"Good morning, everybody," said Miranda's father, entering the kitchen. He looked at the clock, then winked at Miranda and Travis.

Just then the song ended, and the DJ said, "This morning the Meyer family wants to wish Carol a happy birthday."

Next they heard a recording of Miranda's voice: "Mom, thanks for everything you do. Like making us breakfast, lunch, and dinner every day. You're the best—and tonight we're taking you out to eat!"

The fifth commandment says to honor your mother. (See Exodus 20:12.) Find ways to show her how much you appreciate her. Think of special ways to thank her for everything she does. And remember to tell her what a great mom she is. According to Proverbs 31, your mother deserves some praise.

Live It!

Proverbs 31:10–31 is called "The Wife of Noble Character." It could also be called "The Wonderful Mother." Make a card for your mom, listing the ways she is like the great mother in this passage.

Grab Hold!

I pray that out of [God's] glorious riches he may strengthen you with power through his Spirit in your inner being.

Ephesians 3:16

With a clang of its bell, the cable car stopped in front of Rudy. He was in San Francisco, visiting his great-uncle Don. "Hop on!" Uncle Don said, stepping onto the running board and grabbing one of the poles. Rudy did the same.

"We get to ride on the *outside*?" Rudy asked.

His uncle nodded. "Cool, huh?"

The bell clanged again, and the car began moving up a steep hill. Rudy's great-uncle explained how the cable car worked. "There's a slot in the street between the tracks," he said. "In there a cable is constantly moving. When the operator wants to go, he pulls a lever. Then a device called a grip grabs the cable, pulling the car along. That's how the car can climb this hill!"

Like a cable car, you have a source of power available to you. But there's a difference. You have the power *inside* you. It's the mighty power of God's Spirit, who lives in the heart of every Christian. Learn to grab hold of that power, so you can accomplish the things God wants you to do.

Did You Know?

Christians grab hold of God's power inside them by believing it's there. They ask God to enable them to grasp it. Then they trust him to answer that prayer. (See Ephesians 1:18–19.)

Life Goes On

[Jesus said,] "I am the resurrection and the life. He who believes in me will live, even though he dies; and whoever lives and believes in me will never die."

John 11:25–26

Hold still!" Leah said. "One landed on you!" Kristen froze. Carefully she turned her head. On her shoulder was a beautiful butterfly. She and Leah watched it, fascinated. Then the insect took off. The girls followed its flight above their heads, where many butterflies were fluttering. Kristen's class was at the Frederik Meijer Gardens and Sculpture Park in Grand Rapids, Michigan. Thousands of butterflies had been brought to the conservatory, a big glass building full of tropical plants.

As the girls admired all the butterflies, their teacher walked up. "Have you seen the chrysalis display?" he asked. "A butterfly is coming out."

Kristen and Leah went to watch the insect struggle to get free. Eventually it broke loose, then opened its wings. "Isn't that amazing?" Leah said. "First it was a caterpillar, and now it's starting a whole new life as a butterfly!"

A caterpillar seems to die. That's because it goes into its chrysalis and is never seen again. But actually it doesn't die. Instead God changes it into a butterfly. For believers, what looks like death is the start of a great new life.

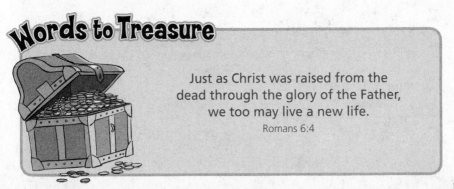

Words to Treasure

Just as Christ was raised from the dead through the glory of the Father, we too may live a new life.

Romans 6:4

Quick Trip to the Top

Do not put the Lord your God to the test.

Matthew 4:7

As the elevator doors closed, Jason's heart started pounding. "Get ready, guys," his dad said. "These elevators are really fast. In just a few seconds we'll be on top of Sears Tower, the tallest building in America."

Jason braced himself and looked at his sister. "Hang on, Sarah. Here we go!" Suddenly they were whooshing upward. Jason felt his ears pop, and he knew they were climbing higher than he'd ever been in his life. He watched the numbers change rapidly.

Sarah shouted, "We're already a hundred stories up!" The elevator slowed, then stopped. Jason's legs felt a little wobbly as he stepped out—but he forgot about that when he saw the view. They were 1,353 feet above the ground, and Jason could see the city of Chicago, Illinois, below him.

Jesus had a similar experience when the Devil whisked him to the highest part of the temple, the tallest building in Jerusalem. There the Devil told him, "If you really are God's Son, prove it and jump. God said he'll protect you." (See Matthew 4:1–11.) But Jesus didn't fall for that trick. He knew that although you can trust God to protect you, you should never test God by doing something foolish.

Life in Bible Times

The temple where Satan tempted Jesus wasn't the one King Solomon built. The Babylonians destroyed that temple. Later King Herod built a bigger, grander one.

Pulled Both Ways

[Abraham] did not waver through unbelief regarding the promise of God, but was strengthened in his faith.

Romans 4:20

"Pull!" Keenan yelled, holding the rope and digging his feet into the ground. He felt himself sliding forward. His teammates struggled to help him yank the rope back. It was field day at school, and some kids were playing tug-of-war.

"We're losing!" Cynthia shouted. The red ribbon tied onto the middle of the rope was getting close to the other team's line. Keenan pulled harder. His teammates did too, and he felt the momentum shift. Feet scrabbling, he took a few steps backward, and the ribbon moved toward his team's line.

"Keep going!" Raul hollered. Suddenly the rope lurched forward. Keenan and some of his teammates fell. They were pulled through the grass as the ribbon crossed the other line.

Getting up and brushing himself off, Keenan told Raul, "We need a really big kid on our side."

Are you in a tug-of-war between faith and doubt? Your faith in God's promises is pulling you in one direction. But your doubt is pulling you the other way. God can strengthen your faith. Let him be the "anchor" on your team. That's the big guy who holds the end of the rope, plants his feet on the ground, and doesn't budge! Ask God to increase your faith and help you defeat unbelief. (See Luke 17:5 and Mark 9:24.)

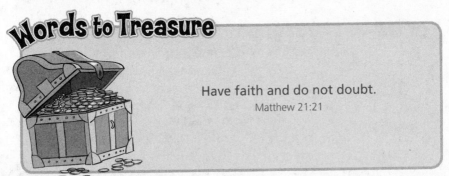

Words to Treasure

Have faith and do not doubt.
Matthew 21:21

A Colorful Scene

> There before me [in heaven] was a great multitude that no one could count, from every nation, tribe, people and language.
>
> Revelation 7:9

Tammy used a big piece of chalk to finish the picture she'd drawn on the pavement. It was an ocean scene, with palm trees, sand, and seashells. Putting down the chalk, Tammy sat back and admired her work. Then she looked at her little sister's picture. "Your horse looks beautiful, Kendra!"

Still coloring, her sister smiled. "Thanks. I'm almost done."

Tammy stood and looked around. Other kids were drawing pictures next to theirs. In fact, the plaza was full of all kinds of people—young and old, short and tall, black and white and Hispanic and Asian. Everyone was helping to draw a giant, colorful mural at the city's arts festival.

You're part of a great mural God has been creating since the beginning of time. It tells a beautiful story. God has an important purpose for you in this story. There's a part of the mural that he wants you to draw. God's story is about saving his children. It's also about making everything perfect again. The mural shows God's whole family gathered in heaven, praising him for what he's done. And you'll be in that colorful scene!

Words to Treasure

You are a chosen people, a royal priesthood, a holy nation, a people belonging to God, that you may declare the praises of him who called you out of darkness into his wonderful light.

1 Peter 2:9

A Snake in the Grass

I am afraid that just as Eve was deceived by the serpent's cunning, your minds may somehow be led astray from your sincere and pure devotion to Christ.

2 Corinthians 11:3

H ey, guys," Willie said, entering the tree house he and his friends had built.

Jack looked up from a game of Battleship. "Hey."

Staring at his game board, Trevor muttered, "Hi."

Willie unzipped his backpack. "Look what I found!" Jack and Trevor crowded around him as he pulled out a magazine.

Instantly Jack said, "Where'd you get that?" It was the kind of magazine his dad had warned him not to look at.

"I found it out behind our school," Willie said, opening it. "Some older kids must've been looking at it."

Jack grabbed the magazine and stuffed it back into Willie's backpack. "Get rid of it," he said. "Go throw it in the trash bin by the road."

Some pictures or videos show images that stir up a sinful desire to look at nakedness. These images are like a snake in the grass. Even though you aren't looking for them, you can stumble upon them easily. You could find a magazine somewhere. A friend could show you one. Or unwelcome images could pop up while you're surfing the Internet. These images attack quickly. When they grab you, they drag you away from God. If you come across one, get away fast!

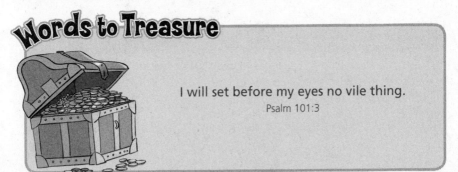

Words to Treasure

I will set before my eyes no vile thing.
Psalm 101:3

Big and Wide

I pray that you ... may have power, together with all the saints, to grasp how wide and long and high and deep is the love of Christ.

Ephesians 3:17–18

Jenna placed one foot on the glass floor of the Grand Canyon Skywalk. "Don't worry, it'll hold you," said her aunt Carla. She started jumping up and down on the U-shaped observation deck. "See? It's safe!"

Laughing nervously, Jenna said, "Now you're *really* scaring me."

Aunt Carla led her to the end of the platform. Jenna glanced down, shuddering. They were far above the Colorado River. "Look at that view!" Aunt Carla said, spreading her arms wide. "Just imagine. This canyon is more than a mile deep at its deepest point. It's over fifteen miles wide at its widest spot. And it's 227 miles long! Have you ever seen anything so beautiful?" Jenna looked around, thinking she'd never seen anything so *big*.

You can measure the Grand Canyon in miles. But to measure Jesus' love for you, you'd have to use light-years—at least! The truth is, the amount of love Jesus has for you is too big to measure. All you can really do is be amazed by it, let your heart be filled with it, and love him back in return.

Did You Know?

Jesus showed how big his love is by dying on the cross for people's sins. According to John 15:13, there's no bigger love than that!

Tackling a Task

Diligent hands will rule.

Proverbs 12:24

On the ground behind their house, Owen's dad marked a rectangle eight feet long and six feet wide. "There, Owen. This shows where the hole needs to go and how big it has to be. Think you can dig it for me, six feet deep?"

Grabbing the shovel, Owen said, "No sweat!" He looked at the rectangle again. "Well, maybe a little."

They were burying a plastic tank to catch and store rainwater. The idea was that rain falling on the roof would flow into the gutter, down the downspout, and into the tank. Then it could be pumped out whenever Owen's mom wanted to water her flower garden.

Owen worked hard, but it was fun. He'd never dug a hole this big! Soon he was in over his head, flinging dirt out of the hole.

"Wow, you're really going at it," his dad said. "That's one of the things I like about you, Son. You know how to get a job done!"

The Bible reveals the secret of being a good worker. You have to be diligent. That means working wholeheartedly, giving it your all. It means steadily working hard at a job, not letting up until it's finished. When someone gives you a task, show that you know how to tackle it!

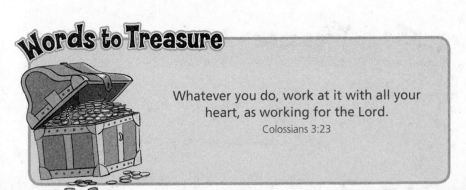

Words to Treasure

Whatever you do, work at it with all your heart, as working for the Lord.
Colossians 3:23

Pass It On!

[God] comforts us in all our troubles, so that we can comfort those in any trouble with the comfort we ourselves have received from God.

2 Corinthians 1:4

Where are they?" Kendra whimpered, gripping Tammy's hand as they searched through the crowd. Tammy looked down. Her little sister was about to cry. Tammy was pretty upset herself. At the arts festival in the city, they'd gotten separated from their mom and dad. The festival was huge. Thousands of people had come to view artwork, listen to music, and enjoy the food. How was she going to find her parents? Tammy prayed silently. She told God how worried she was. She asked him for help. Then Psalm 23 came to her mind, and the image of God as a shepherd reassured her.

"Don't worry, Kendra," she said. "God's with us, and he'll lead us back to Mom and Dad." Kendra smiled at her. A few minutes later Tammy spotted an information booth. "Look, Kendra! They can make an announcement, and Mom and Dad will be able to find us."

God comforts you when you're in distress, because he loves you. He also does it so he can comfort others through you. People you know may be facing the same troubles you are. Or they may be struggling with problems you've faced in the past. Share with them the comfort God has given you.

Words to Treasure

The Lord comforts his people.
Isaiah 49:13

Guardrails

[Lord,] I will never forget your precepts, for by them you have preserved my life.

Psalm 119:93

We need to cut these posts so they're three feet long," Troy's dad said. He tossed Troy a tape measure. Troy measured each post, marking them with a pencil. He and his father were building a guardrail for the basement stairs. That way, Troy's three-year-old sister, Pauline, wouldn't fall off them.

"All done," Troy said.

His father nodded. "Good. Now, the cuts have to be made at an angle, so we can attach the handrail. I've set the correct angle for you on the miter saw."

Troy laid a post in the miter box, lining up his mark with the saw blade. Then he held the post and sawed back and forth. When he finished cutting them all, Troy's dad said, "Great job! Now let's make a railing that'll keep Pauline safe."

Some kids think of God's laws as fences God built to pen them in and keep them from having fun. But really they're guardrails God put up to shelter you and keep you from harm. That's one reason why the author of Psalm 119 wrote 176 verses about how much he loved God's laws!

Life in Bible Times

Ancient Israelites built pens for their sheep. The walls were often made of stone. Within these pens the sheep were safe, because of the walls and because a shepherd guarded them.

No Bend or Break

> We are receiving a kingdom that cannot be shaken.
>
> Hebrews 12:28

From the Skydeck in Sears Tower, Jason and his sister stared down at the city of Chicago. They were 103 stories high. Their dad said, "They call Chicago the Windy City, but I'm glad it's calm out today. I've heard that if you're up here during a strong wind, you can feel the building sway."

Jason turned to him. "You mean this thing *moves*?" He'd felt nervous at first about being up so high. But the building seemed so solid that he'd started to relax. Now he was worried again. Sarah looked scared too.

"It's okay, guys," their dad said. "Skyscrapers like this one are designed to sway in the wind, like trees. If a tall building didn't sway, a powerful gust could knock it down." He patted the glass wall in front of them. "We're actually safer up here because the building *does* move."

Shuddering, Sarah said, "I wish it was so strong that it didn't even have to bend!"

God's kingdom—like God himself—can't be shaken by anything. It stands perfectly sturdy. It doesn't "sway in the wind" as times change or as evil forces attack it, and it'll never fall. God's kingdom will go on standing forever. And since you're part of it, you don't have to bend or break either.

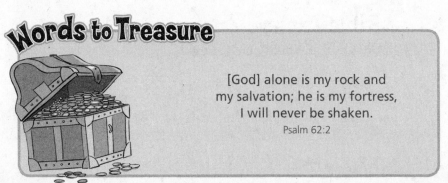

Words to Treasure

[God] alone is my rock and my salvation; he is my fortress, I will never be shaken.
Psalm 62:2

Mule Train

> "Even to your old age and gray hairs I am he,
> I am he who will sustain you. I have made you
> and I will carry you," [says the Lord].
>
> Isaiah 46:4

Jenna chewed her lip as her mule made his way down the narrow, rocky trail leading into the Grand Canyon. "Steady there, boy," she muttered. The mule train Jenna and her aunt Carla were riding with had reached a switchback. That was a part of the trail that zigzagged sharply. *What if there are loose stones?* Jenna thought. *Or a snake?* Glancing down, she caught her breath. The mule was walking so close to the ledge, her foot was dangling over it!

"Jenna, you're missing the view," Aunt Carla said.

Their guide turned in his saddle. "Don't worry. Dusty's the most experienced, sure-footed mule around. He's carried hundreds of people safely down into the canyon. Relax and enjoy the ride."

Jenna forced herself to look up. The magnificent sight made her breathless again — this time with awe.

For thousands of years, God has been carrying people on their journey through life. He has carried you since you were created, and he'll keep carrying you until he takes you home with him to heaven. Don't miss the wonders of this life by worrying all the time. Trust God to carry you all the way.

Words to Treasure

[The Lord] tends his flock like a shepherd: He gathers the lambs in his arms and carries them close to his heart.
Isaiah 40:11

Stay Out of Prison

If [Jesus] sets you free, you will be free indeed.
John 8:36

Climbing into the helicopter, Rudy sat next to his dad. Rudy's great-uncle Don was sitting across from him. The pilot closed the door, then got into the cockpit. "Everyone buckled in?" he asked. They all gave him a thumbs-up. Grinning, he turned and flipped a switch. "Here we go!" The engine began to whine.

"Have you ever flown in a helicopter, Dad?" Rudy asked.

His father nodded. "Once. You're in for a treat!" The noise grew, and Rudy felt the aircraft rise. It banked left, carrying them out over the bay.

Rudy looked down at the city of San Francisco. His great-uncle, who lived there, pointed out landmarks. "That tall, pointed building is the Transamerica Pyramid. And there's the Ferry Building, near the waterfront." As they headed toward the Golden Gate Bridge, Uncle Don said, "See that island? That's Alcatraz, the prison where famous gangsters were kept. You wouldn't have wanted to be locked up there. Several inmates tried to escape from it, but none ever could."

You were once in a prison called sin. It's a nasty place, like Alcatraz. But when you became a Christian, Jesus set you free. You're no longer Satan's prisoner. So don't break God's laws and get locked up again. Stay out of prison by living God's way, and enjoy the freedom Jesus has given you!

Words to Treasure

It is for freedom that Christ
has set us free.
Galatians 5:1

Keep It Simple

When you pray, do not keep on babbling like pagans, for they think they will be heard because of their many words.

Matthew 6:7

W hat's that contraption?" asked Chris's mom.

Chris's dad replied, "It's a Rube Goldberg machine, which is a device that uses a complicated process to do something simple. I'm going to demonstrate it at school." He was a science teacher, and Chris was helping him in his home lab.

"We're ready to test it," Chris said. He pushed a steel ball down a ramp. It rolled into a bucket hanging from a pulley. As the bucket lowered, it flipped a switch. A fan blew a sailboat toward a helium-filled balloon. A pin popped the balloon, which was holding up a lever. The lever dropped, lighting a match that ignited a can of cooking fuel. Ice on a metal tray began melting, and water trickled into a glass. "It worked!" Chris shouted.

Laughing, his mom said, "If you're thirsty, why don't you just go to the sink for some water?"

Don't make prayer complicated, like a Rube Goldberg machine! You don't have to use big words or say a lot to impress God or anyone else. Just pray sincerely, from your heart. Simply praise God, thank him for his blessings, confess your sins, and make your requests.

Did You Know?

The Lord's Prayer is a short, simple prayer Jesus taught his disciples. It has only fifty-two words. Jesus taught his disciples to speak to God plainly, as they would to a father. (See Matthew 6:9–13.)

Working as a Team

> May the God who gives endurance and en-
> couragement give you a spirit of unity among
> yourselves as you follow Christ Jesus.
>
> Romans 15:5

In a raft floating down the Colorado River, Nathan and his stepfather listened to Marty, the guide. Their group was out West on a father-son church retreat. "There's some serious whitewater ahead," said Marty. "It's a class three rapids with major obstacles. This is what we've been practicing for. Ready, team?"

Everyone raised their paddles and shouted, "Yeah!" Nathan and his stepdad grinned at each other. Then Nathan adjusted his glasses and gripped his paddle.

As they rounded a bend, the water got rougher. "There's our first obstacle!" shouted Marty, pointing at a huge, jagged rock. "Now, follow my commands. Left turn!" Nathan obeyed the guide's orders, doing his part to steer the raft. At times paddling forward, at times back paddling, he kept pace with everyone else. The guys all cheered as they passed the boulder, and Nathan was amazed at what they'd accomplished together.

Your sports team, your class at school, your family, and your church all need unity. When a group has unity, everyone is working together. They're all following the same leader. Are you cooperating with your teammates, your classmates, your siblings, and your church group? Are you obeying your coach, your teachers, your parents, and Jesus?

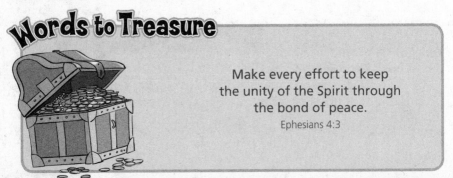

Words to Treasure

Make every effort to keep
the unity of the Spirit through
the bond of peace.
Ephesians 4:3

Merging Together

You, though a wild olive shoot, have been grafted in among the others.

Romans 11:17

Libby watched Alayna's father. He was standing on a ladder, sawing off a small branch from one of the trees in his apple orchard. "What're you doing?" she asked.

"I'm grafting a new branch onto this tree," he said.

"He's trying to develop a new kind of apple," explained Alayna, who was Libby's friend. "We're hoping he'll make one that's bigger, sweeter, and crunchier!" Alayna's dad wedged another branch into the spot where the old branch was. Then he wrapped the grafted area with tape.

"What happens now?" Libby asked.

He grinned. "After a while the new branch will become part of the tree. Then it'll grow apples, just like the other branches."

God's family started with Abraham and his descendants, the Jews. If you don't come from a Jewish background, then you are a *Gentile*. (That word simply means you're not a Jew.) But the good news is, you've been grafted into God's family tree! Because of your faith in Jesus, God has welcomed you into his family. Keep that in mind the next time someone joins your school, your church, your sports team—or even your home. God accepted you. Be willing to accept others.

People in Bible Times

The apostle Paul explained that Jews who didn't believe in Jesus were like branches cut off of God's family tree. Gentiles who had faith in Jesus were like branches grafted into it.

Home, Sweet Home

[God has] set eternity in the hearts of men.

Ecclesiastes 3:11

Jeanie watched as thousands of salmon climbed a fish ladder to get past Bonneville Dam. The dam was on the Columbia River, near Portland, Oregon. Having left the ocean, the fish were swimming upriver to their birthplace to lay eggs.

"I saw one jump!" Jeanie told her mom, pointing. The ladder was a stairway made of water. To go up a step, the fish swam through the water flowing over it or leaped to the next level.

"Let's go down to the other viewing area," Jeanie's mom said. There they looked through large windows right into the water.

Gazing at all the fish, Jeanie asked, "How do they find their way home?"

Her mom shrugged. "Nobody knows. Somehow God puts the desire in them to go there, and then he shows them the way."

God put a desire for eternity in your heart. You want to be home in heaven with him someday and live with him forever. The good news is, your faith in Jesus puts you in God's kingdom right here on earth. Your eternal life has already started! Heaven will be better, of course. But you can start enjoying your eternity with God now.

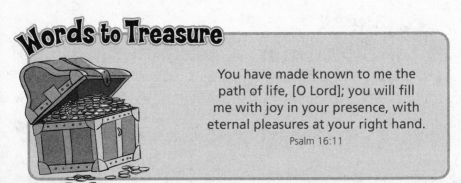

Words to Treasure

You have made known to me the path of life, [O Lord]; you will fill me with joy in your presence, with eternal pleasures at your right hand.

Psalm 16:11

Taking the Controls

Prepare your minds for action; be self-controlled.
1 Peter 1:13

Mike watched his dad work the remote control, trying to land the radio-controlled airplane. "Bring the nose up!" said his dad's coworker, Carl. He'd just sold the plane to them. The aircraft bounced on the grass, then flipped over.

"Guess I need practice," said Mike's dad.

Carl inspected the plane. "No damage. Wanna try a takeoff, Mike?"

"Yeah!" Mike replied. His dad handed him the remote.

Setting up the plane, Carl asked, "Do you know what you need to do?"

Mike nodded. "I push the left stick forward to make the plane go faster. I move it left and right to keep the plane on the runway. I pull back on the right stick to take off."

"Attaboy," Carl said, starting the engine.

Mike moved the left joystick forward, and the aircraft began rolling. He guided it down the runway. As it picked up speed, he pulled back the right stick, and the plane rose into the air.

Flying an RC plane and growing spiritually both require you to take the controls. You have to decide what you must do and then do it. To become an honest person, for instance, you need to make up your mind to always tell the truth. As you practice doing that, you grow in the area of honesty.

Words to Treasure

Each of you should learn to control his own body in a way that is holy and honorable.
1 Thessalonians 4:4

Listening with Your Spirit

Love the Lord your God, listen to his voice, and hold fast to him.

Deuteronomy 30:20

Sarah and her family were in Chicago, Illinois, walking along Navy Pier. It was a shopping mall and amusement park built on a wharf sticking out into Lake Michigan. The day was calm and sunny, and lots of people were out. "Look, a mime!" Sarah said. Next to the walkway stood a man with his face painted white. He wore a black-and-white tuxedo and held a closed umbrella. As they passed him, he smiled and tipped his hat. Then he began walking beside Sarah, acting as though he were chatting with her.

Her brother Jason laughed. "You made a friend, Sarah!" The mime frowned, looked up, and stuck out his hand. Then he opened his umbrella and held it over Sarah.

Giggling, she said, "Thanks." Suddenly the umbrella shot forward, as if caught by a strong wind. The mime struggled with it, but it dragged him along. Finally he just gave a little wave and let it carry him away.

God isn't mute, like a mime; he can speak to you. But God doesn't talk to you the way people do. Instead his Spirit speaks to your spirit. This can happen anytime, especially when you're reading the Bible or praying. Listen for God's voice, and ask him to help you recognize it.

Words to Treasure

If he calls you, say, "Speak, Lord, for your servant is listening."
1 Samuel 3:9

Sorting Things Out

> The kingdom of heaven is like a net that was let down into the lake and caught all kinds of fish.... [The fishermen] collected the good fish in baskets, but threw the bad away.
>
> Matthew 13:47–48

Using a net on a long pole, D.J. fished around in the pond. Then he pulled out the net and looked inside. There were six golf balls. "I got some more!" he said.

Across the pond, Trent was fishing around with his net. "Keep trying. Let's get as many as we can before dark." They were on the golf course Trent's father owned.

"Will your dad really pay us for these?" D.J. asked, dropping the balls into a bucket.

Trent pulled his net in. "Uh-huh. But only the good ones."

Peering into the bucket, D.J. said, "How do you tell the good ones from the bad ones?"

Trent laughed. "That's easy. The good ones aren't all scratched up."

Someday God's angels will separate the good people from the bad ones. But everyone has been damaged by sin. So how will the angels know the difference? That's easy. Jesus will have redeemed the people who put their faith in him. They'll be perfect, like brand-new golf balls. Be thankful, because that includes you!

Did You Know?

One meaning of the word *redeem* is to make something like new again. In the beginning, people were perfect. Then sin damaged them all. Jesus restores people to the way God first created them.

Good Traction

> The Sovereign Lord is my strength; he makes
> my feet like the feet of a deer, he enables me
> to go on the heights.
>
> Habakkuk 3:19

Nathan adjusted his glasses and strapped on his bicycle helmet. Today their church group was going mountain biking in the Rockies. "Here's your bike, Nathan," his stepfather said, bringing over a red bicycle from the rental office. "Hop on and see if it fits."

"Okay, Dad," Nathan said. Grabbing the handlebars, he climbed on the bike. "It feels good to me."

His stepfather grinned. "Okay, then. We're ready to ride!"

Nathan stared down at the wide, knobby tire in front of him. "Why are the tires so big?"

Climbing on a blue bicycle, his stepfather replied, "Mountain bikes are designed to go places regular bikes can't. They have large tires to give them good traction, so they can handle rough terrain. When we get going, you'll be glad those tires are so big and rugged. They'll help keep you on the trail!"

Mountain bikers rely on their tires for good traction. Christians rely on God. When you're walking on the path of righteousness, there's always the danger that you could slip. Temptation could make you slide off into sin. But if you rely on God, he'll give you the traction you need to stay on the path.

Words to Treasure

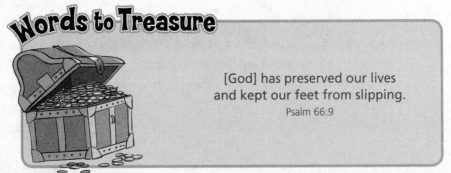

> [God] has preserved our lives
> and kept our feet from slipping.
>
> Psalm 66:9

God's Tools

In a large house there are articles not only of gold and silver, but also of wood and clay; some are for noble purposes and some for ignoble.

2 Timothy 2:20

Abigail was helping her father build a new deck behind their house. He was drilling holes in the floorboards. She was using a screwdriver to fasten screws in the holes. "I'm almost done with this power drill," her dad said. "Then I'll put in a screwdriver bit so you can use it."

Abigail gasped. "I don't believe it! You're going to let *me* use one of your power tools?"

Her dad laughed. "Yes, I think you're ready." Acting as if there were spies watching, he knelt beside her. "But remember, this is the mighty Tool of Power! It can accomplish great good, like building a deck for us all to enjoy. It's also capable of terrible evil. Why, it could easily take apart your little brother's swing set! Only you can decide how it will be used." Giggling, Abigail gave him a little punch and took the drill.

God gave you a wonderful body and an incredible mind. He also gave you the freedom to choose what to do with these powerful tools. Will you allow God to use them for noble purposes? Are you willing to keep them clean from bad thoughts and behaviors so he can?

Words to Treasure

Offer the parts of your body to [God] as instruments of righteousness.

Romans 6:13

Belly Flops

> Sovereign Lord, you have made the heavens and the earth by your great power and out-stretched arm. Nothing is too hard for you.
> Jeremiah 32:17

Rudy watched thousands of jelly beans pour into a large drum. He, his father, and his great-uncle Don were visiting the Jelly Belly candy factory. It was near San Francisco, where Rudy's great-uncle lived. "What does this do?" Rudy asked.

His father replied, "Listen to the tour guide, and you'll find out." Rudy had already seen how the soft middles of the jelly beans were made. And he'd learned how their hard shells were produced. Now the tour guide explained that the large drum was separating the perfectly shaped beans from the misshapen ones. Those would be sold as Belly Flops.

Rudy said, "Boy, I wish *we* could bag up everything that goes wrong and sell it."

His dad laughed. "Me too."

Smiling, Uncle Don said, "You gotta hand it to this company. They sure can turn lemons into lemonade!"

God is powerful and sovereign. That means he rules over everything! For this reason, he can take all the bad stuff that happens in the world and use it for good. When something goes wrong for you, trust God to make it work out right.

People in Bible Times

Joseph's brothers sold him as a slave. God used that bad event to put Joseph in power in Egypt. In that way, God saved many people from starving during a famine.

Dealing with Pests

[Jesus] called his twelve disciples to him and gave them authority to drive out evil spirits.

Matthew 10:1

Dad! There's a mole in my garden!" Cheryl said, running into the house.

Looking up from his newspaper, her dad asked, "How do you know?"

Cheryl waved her arms. "I saw it! I was pulling weeds, and it popped out of the ground." Shuddering, she added, "It had great big hands and no eyes! Ugh!"

Her dad stood up. "Let's have a look." Cheryl led him out to her vegetable garden in the backyard. She pointed at a mound of dirt near the carrots.

Her dad said, "It's a mole, all right. Well, I know how to handle this." He drove Cheryl to a lawn-and-garden store. There he bought a large metal spike.

"What's that?" Cheryl asked.

Her father handed it to her. "It's a sonic mole repeller. You stick it in the ground, and it sends sound vibrations through the soil. This will drive that pest away!"

When the Devil or his demons bother you, start praying. Jesus gave his disciples power and authority over evil beings. Every time you pray, you're like a sonic repeller that drives Satan and his demons away.

Life in Bible Times

A vineyard owner in ancient Israel had to deal with foxes. The foxes would come and eat grapes off the vines. They were like Satan and his demons, who come to steal and destroy. (See Song of Songs 2:15.)

Your Place in God's Kingdom

God raised us up with Christ and seated us
with him in the heavenly realms.

Ephesians 2:6

In the garage, Troy watched his father use a belt sander on their kitchen table. Troy's three-year-old sister, Pauline, had scribbled on the table with a marker. His dad shut off the sander. "Want to give it a try?" he asked.

Troy said, "Sure!"

His father showed him how to hold the power tool. "Keep moving it around, sanding evenly," he said. "We have to remove all the black marks and old varnish before applying new varnish."

As Troy put on a dust mask, his dad patted the wood. "This old table means a lot to me. I always sat on one end, across from my dad. Like you do now. That was my spot, and no matter where I went, I knew it was always there waiting for me."

You have a special place with God and Jesus in the kingdom of heaven. It's reserved for you. You're like one of King Arthur's knights. However far a quest took them, they knew there was a seat for them at the Round Table. *Your* seat proves you're a child of God. If you remember that, you'll always know who you are and where you belong. You're part of God's royal family!

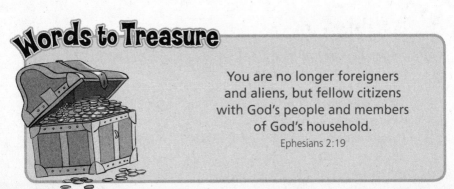

Words to Treasure

You are no longer foreigners
and aliens, but fellow citizens
with God's people and members
of God's household.
Ephesians 2:19

Official Spokesperson

We are ... Christ's ambassadors, as though God were making his appeal through us.

2 Corinthians 5:20

The Memorial Day parade rolled through the small town. Lights flashing, a fire truck sounded its siren. Behind it, Becca sat on the edge of the 4-H float, throwing candy to children. As they scrambled for the goodies, she laughed. "Don't fight. There's plenty for everyone!"

Becca's older sister, Kelsey, had been chosen as the 4-H queen this year. The king and queen and their court always rode on the 4-H float. Some of their younger siblings did too. Dressed in a pretty gown, Kelsey stood in the center of the float, smiling and waving.

After the parade, Becca proudly watched her talk to a local TV reporter. Kelsey spoke about the wonderful things the 4-H club had to offer. "Kids, come out and join us," she invited. "You'll love it!"

You may not be old enough to be a 4-H king or queen. But as a Christian, you've been chosen to represent Jesus on earth. You're an official spokesperson for God! It's a great honor. It's also a big responsibility. Study the message God wants to tell the world. Then deliver it boldly and earnestly to people who need to hear it.

Live It !

Many people are children when they choose whether or not to become Christians. Be a good ambassador for Jesus. You may inspire kids to follow him for the rest of their lives!

Useful Differences

> We have different gifts, according to the grace given us.
>
> Romans 12:6

Trent was teaching his friend D.J. how to play golf. Standing on the practice range, he pulled a large club out of his bag. "This is the driver," he told D.J. "It hits the ball the farthest." Teeing up a ball, Trent hit it past the 150-yard target. Then he pulled out a smaller club. "This is a seven iron. It hits the ball higher but not as far." Again he demonstrated. This time the ball flew higher, landing near the 100-yard marker. Trent pulled out two more clubs. "This one's a sand wedge. It's for hitting the ball out of sand traps. And this is the putter. It knocks the ball in the hole."

D.J. pointed at another item in Trent's bag. "What does that club do?"

Laughing, Trent said, "That's not a club. It's for getting your ball back after you hit it in the water!"

Different golf clubs do different things. Yet a golfer uses them all to play golf. Likewise, people with different spiritual gifts serve God differently, but God uses them all to build his kingdom. Don't compare yourself with others, in terms of what gifts you have or how you can serve God. Just be joyful in doing what God created you to do!

Words to Treasure

There are different kinds of gifts, but the same Spirit. There are different kinds of service, but the same Lord.

1 Corinthians 12:4–5

A Name That Fits

[Jesus said,] "To him who overcomes, I will give ... a white stone with a new name written on it."

Revelation 2:17

As Corey wiggled a toy mouse on a string, the kitten crept forward. Then it leaped, catching the mouse before Corey could pull it away.

Laughing, Myra said, "He's quick!" Their family was adopting a pet at the Humane Society. After looking at all the animals, they'd chosen a black kitten with white paws. "What should we name him?" Myra asked.

Corey turned to her. "Well, he likes to sneak up on things, and his feet look like tennis shoes. Let's call him Sneakers."

Myra didn't reply. She was looking over Corey's shoulder. Just then, Corey felt the kitten pounce on his back.

Giggling, Myra said, "Sneakers is the perfect name for him!"

God gave Abram the name Abraham, which means "father of many." Jesus gave Simon the name Peter, meaning "rock." Have you ever wondered what name God has for you? If you stay faithful to him, someday you'll find out. God has a perfect name for you because he knows you well and has a special purpose for you. Ask God to start showing you what his plan for you is, so you can begin living up to your name.

People in Bible Times

Gideon was just a normal guy. But an angel called him "mighty warrior." God planned to make Gideon into a great leader of Israel's army. (See Judges 6–7.)

Dogfights

> [Jesus asked his disciples], "What were you arguing about on the road?" But they kept quiet because on the way they had argued about who was the greatest.
>
> Mark 9:33–34

Mike and his dad were at the RC air show. There people were showing off their radio-controlled model airplanes. They were also competing in different events. In one contest, pilots flew their planes high into the sky. Then they turned off their engines to see who could keep their plane in the air the longest.

"What's going on now?" Mike asked. Airplanes were taking off with long streamers behind them.

"It's a dogfight," his dad replied. "They'll try to cut off each other's streamers with their propellers." Climbing into the sky, the planes started swooping and diving. The crowd roared whenever a streamer fluttered down. Everyone gasped when planes crashed into the ground or collided in midair.

"Dogfights are cool," Mike said. "But they're pretty hard on the dogs!"

RC plane owners compete to see who's the best pilot. Jesus' disciples argued about which of them was the most important. What do *you* fight about when you argue with your siblings and friends? Most arguments are caused by selfishness and pride. People fight because everyone's trying to be number one. Jesus said if you really want to be better than others, stop fighting with them and start serving them!

Words to Treasure

If anyone wants to be first, he must be the very last, and the servant of all.
Mark 9:35

Rolling with the Changes

Peter and his brother Andrew ... were casting a net into the lake, for they were fishermen. "Come, follow me," Jesus said, "and I will make you fishers of men."

Matthew 4:18–19

Sylvia laced up her inline skates. Then she glided to the trail, where her dad was waiting. "Which way should we go?" she asked.

He pointed left. "Let's go south. The trail crosses an old trestle bridge that way, then runs along the river." They started down the asphalt path. "This used to be a railroad track," her dad said as they skated past some joggers.

"Really?" Sylvia said.

He nodded. "Uh-huh. The railroad company abandoned it. So the state made it into a park that people can use for fun and exercise. It's called a rail trail."

"Wow," Sylvia said. She waved at some people on bicycles. Then she said, "I'll bet this train track never dreamed it'd become a park!"

You may keep changing your mind about what you want to be when you grow up. That's okay. But always keep following Jesus. He'll take your interests and skills and mold you into something he can use. If he can make fishermen into disciples, imagine what he can do with you!

Did You Know?

Many of the disciples were fishermen before they met Jesus. Levi was a tax collector. But like the fishermen, Levi left everything to follow Jesus. (See Luke 5:27–28.)

Please and Thanks

> "Have faith in God," Jesus [said.] ... "Whatever you ask for in prayer, believe that you have received it, and it will be yours."
>
> Mark 11:22, 24

Sam sat on his bed, watching his mom pack his clothes for summer camp. "Are you still nervous?" she asked.

Sam shrugged. "A little. I'm excited about shooting rifles and stuff. But I'm worried I'll get homesick."

His mom nodded. "I know. But we've been asking God to fill your heart with peace and joy while you're away. I believe he will! Let's pray about it again. But this time, we'll pray a little differently." Sam's mom took his hands. She prayed, "Father, we know you'll give Sam the peace and joy we've been asking for. Thank you for that. Help Sam to encourage others in his cabin who feel homesick. That way, they can enjoy camp too!"

Praying with faith is all about trusting God. It's about knowing that he's a loving Father who listens to his children and gives them what they need. He promised to! Jesus prayed with faith. He said, "Father, I thank you that you have heard me. I knew that you always hear me" (John 11:41–42). As God's child, you can say "please" and "thanks" when you ask him for something. Believe that God will give you what you need. It's the way Jesus taught people to pray.

Words to Treasure

If you believe, you will receive whatever you ask for in prayer.
Matthew 21:22

Daybreak

> This is the day the Lord has made; let us rejoice and be glad in it.
>
> Psalm 118:24

Mindy felt someone shake her shoulder. "Honey, it's time to get up." For a minute she didn't know where she was. Then she remembered. She was at her grandmother's house on the Jersey Shore. "The sun will be rising soon," her grandma said.

Mindy raised her head. "Okay, I'm awake." Her grandmother left to get dressed. Pulling on some clothes, Mindy went downstairs. There she found her grandma waiting at the door. They followed the sandy path through the beach grass to the shore.

Above the Atlantic Ocean, the horizon was glowing yellow and orange. Mindy and her grandmother strolled along the shoreline as the colors in the sky grew more intense. Finally the sun burst into view, making the water sparkle.

Mindy's grandma smiled. "Now, that's the way to start a day!"

God starts every morning with a sunrise to light up your day. Respond to him with thanks and praise. Tell him how happy you are to have another twenty-four hours to spend with him. Showing God your gladness and joy in the morning lights up *his* day.

Live It!

Set your alarm clock early so you can get up and watch the sunrise. It's fun to see the sky get brighter and change colors. As the sun peeks over the horizon, praise God and thank him for a new day.

"Camping Out"

> If you make the Most High your dwelling—even the Lord, who is my refuge—then no harm will befall you, no disaster will come near your tent.
>
> Psalm 91:9–10

Lights out, kids," Corey's father called from the doorway. Inside their pup tent, Corey and Myra tried to stop giggling.

"Okay, Dad!" Corey yelled. He shut off the flashlight, and the two of them lay there, whispering in the dark. A slight glow outside the tent cast shadows on its sides. Corey rolled over and was about to close his eyes when he heard a noise. "What's that?" he whispered, sitting up.

Myra half-rose, leaning on one arm. "Huh?"

Corey pointed at the side of the tent. "Look!" One of the shadows was moving.

Myra started yelling. "Dad! Dad!"

They heard the door open and their dad's voice. "What's going on?" As they crawled out of the tent, a bright light went on. Corey saw his father at the top of the stairs, looking down at their tent in the basement. He also saw a black-and-white cat dash up the steps.

"Never mind, Dad. It was just Sneakers."

In your heart, make God your dwelling place. Then no matter where you are, you'll always be under your heavenly Father's protection. It's like "camping out" inside your parents' house. You'll feel secure, knowing nothing can bother you.

Words to Treasure

> He who dwells in the shelter of the Most High will rest in the shadow of the Almighty.
>
> Psalm 91:1

Home Team

Be patient, bearing with one another in love.
Ephesians 4:2

Jordan's little sister hit the baseball and ran toward third base. "No, Brittany!" Jordan said, scooping up the ball. "You have to go to first!" He tagged her. "That's three outs. Now it's my turn to bat." None of Jordan's friends were around for a game of baseball. So Jordan was playing with his two younger sisters. He'd set up his old T-ball tee and some bases in the backyard. "Ready?" he asked, after helping the girls put on their gloves and showing them where to stand.

Both of them hollered, "Ready!"

Jordan hit a slow grounder to Alana. But as he ran for first, he saw her chase a butterfly instead of the ball. "Alana!" he shouted, trying not to get mad.

Watching from the deck, his father laughed. "This reminds me of when I was teaching you how to play baseball."

Jordan shook his head, saying, "How did you keep from tearing your hair out?"

It's important to be patient and forgiving when people make mistakes. Patience is one of the qualities of love. God loves you, so he's patient with you. (See 2 Peter 3:9.) Show your siblings and friends and classmates that you love them. Don't get angry when they do things wrong. It's okay to correct them, if you need to, but do it with kindness and respect.

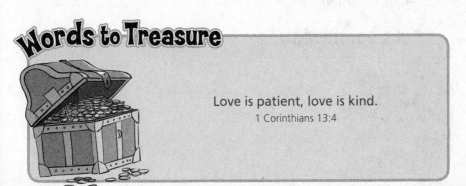

Words to Treasure

Love is patient, love is kind.
1 Corinthians 13:4

A Beautiful Change

[O Lord,] you turned my wailing into dancing; you
removed my sackcloth and clothed me with joy.

Psalm 30:11

mindy was walking along the beach near her grandmother's home on the Jersey Shore. She noticed a glint of color in the sand. Bending over, she picked up what looked like a light-blue stone. It had irregular edges and an almost see-through appearance. "Look at this, Grandma."

Her grandmother peered at it. "Oh, you found a piece of sea glass! I've been collecting those for years."

Mindy turned it over in her hand. "What's sea glass?"

Her grandma replied, "They're pieces of broken bottle that get tumbled over the sand by the waves. Eventually their edges are smoothed and they get that frosty look. I've found many different colors."

Mindy handed her the piece. "Here, you can add this to your collection."

Smiling, her grandmother said, "Thanks, dear. I'll show you my big jar full of sea glass when we get back. It's very pretty. I think it's amazing how the ocean can turn broken bottles into something so lovely!"

Like the ocean, God can create beauty out of brokenness. Even in the worst situations, he changes sadness and despair into hope and joy. When you're grieving and heartbroken, lean on God. Trust him to make this beautiful change in you. In time he'll turn your tearful face into one that's smiling and bright.

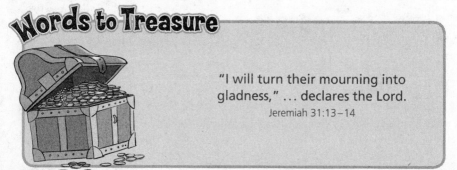

Words to Treasure

"I will turn their mourning into
gladness," ... declares the Lord.
Jeremiah 31:13–14

Awesome Angels

> Then I saw another mighty angel coming down from heaven. He was robed in a cloud, with a rainbow above his head; his face was like the sun, and his legs were like fiery pillars.
>
> Revelation 10:1

At the air show, Eric pointed at the sky. "Here come the Blue Angels!"

Four blue-and-yellow fighter jets approached the airfield. They were flying in a diamond formation. As the F/A-18 Hornets flew past, they rolled over, keeping the diamond shape intact. Then they roared off.

Moments later the squadron did a knife-edge pass. Two planes flew straight at each other, rolling to their sides briefly to avoid colliding.

"Watch this," Eric's dad said. "The next jet will be traveling at seven hundred miles per hour. That's almost the speed of sound!" Eric saw the aircraft coming fast, but there was no noise. The jet blazed past the crowd. It was nearly out of sight before Eric heard the scream of its engine.

The Blue Angels are exciting to watch. But seeing a *real* angel would be much more thrilling! Angels are supernatural beings created by God to serve his people. They help you in ways you aren't even aware of. Thank God for sending these powerful guardians to watch over you.

Did You Know?

God doesn't want people to worship angels. The apostle John started to worship one once. But the angel said, "Do not do it! ... Worship God!" (Revelation 19:10).

Shine Bright

[Jesus told his disciples,] "You are the light of the world."

Matthew 5:14

Mindy read the sign at Barnegat Lighthouse State Park, then looked up at the tall red and white tower. "Can we go to the top, Grandma?"

Her grandmother looked up too. "You go ahead, Mindy. My lighthouse-climbing days are over." With a wink, she walked over to a bench. Hurrying inside, Mindy started up the spiral staircase. She wanted to see if she could climb all 217 steps. Counting as she went, she made her way round and round. At a small window halfway up, Mindy stopped, breathing hard. She rested a moment and pressed on. When she reached step two hundred, she sprinted the remainder of the way. Standing on the walkway that circled the top of the lighthouse, Mindy waved to her grandmother. Then she looked all around at Long Beach Island, New Jersey, where the lighthouse stood. Gazing out over the Atlantic Ocean, she imagined nights long ago when the great beacon shone brightly, guiding sailors through the darkness.

Peer pressure can be bad or good. When kids at school or in your neighborhood push you to do things you shouldn't do, respond with some peer pressure of your own! Stand solid and tall, like a lighthouse, and let your commitment to God shine. You'll keep yourself out of trouble, and you may lead someone else in the right direction as well.

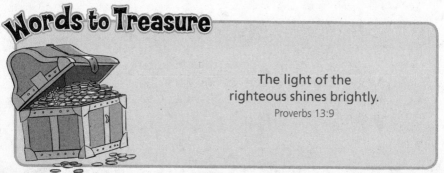

Words to Treasure

The light of the righteous shines brightly.
Proverbs 13:9

Spinning Like Crazy

"Be still, and know that I am God; I will be exalted among the nations, I will be exalted in the earth."

Psalm 46:10

A carnival worker strapped Braden into the giant gyroscope. It was made of three big rings that swiveled in different directions. A person inside it could spin in unlimited ways. "Are you scared?" asked Braden's sister Mackenzie.

Braden grinned and shook his head. "Nope."

Pulling the last strap tight, the worker said, "Ready, kid?"

Braden nodded. "Let 'er rip!" The man gave him a push, and Braden rolled over backward, turning to his left. "Whoa!" he shouted as he began spinning every which way. One minute everything looked upside down, the next he was seeing the sky.

"You okay?" his mom called. Braden could only catch glimpses of her.

"Yeah ... I think!" Finally the worker stopped him. Wobbling as he got off, Braden said, "Oh, man. I have to find my center of gravity again!"

Life's busyness and stress can make your head spin. All the images and noise from TV and video games can add to your dizziness. Soon you're wondering which way is up! Spend some quiet time focusing on God each day. Remind yourself that he's the maker of the universe and the center of it all. When you find your center of gravity in him, it'll calm your soul. Then you can face the world with your head on straight.

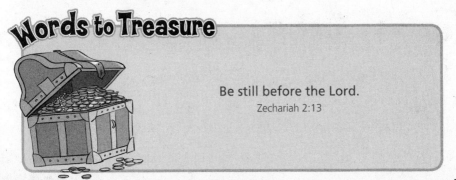

Words to Treasure

Be still before the Lord.
Zechariah 2:13

Rocks between Your Toes

A righteous man may have many troubles, but
the Lord delivers him from them all.

Psalm 34:19

Lynette's family was visiting Acadia National Park, on the rugged coast of Maine. She and her brother stood near Thunder Hole, a huge cleft in the rocks next to the ocean. "Here comes a big one!" Barry shouted as a large wave approached. Lynette squealed as the wave hit the cleft, crashing loudly and spraying water high into the air. The ocean breeze blew the mist all over them.

"Okay, guys, time to boogie!" called their dad.

Laughing, Lynette and Barry ran to join their parents. "Where are we going now?" Lynette asked.

Her mom replied, "Let's take a walk down the shoreline." As their parents strolled along the coast, the kids scrambled on the rocks closer to the water. It was fun, but it was also tough going.

Picking her way with care, Lynette said, "This isn't anything like the beaches we're used to!"

Sometimes life is a smooth, sandy beach. And sometimes troubles make it a rugged shoreline. When you find yourself walking on jagged rocks instead of soft, warm sand, call out to God in prayer. Trust him to rescue you from your problems. He'll either clear away your difficulties or help you climb over them. Either way, God will get you back to level ground.

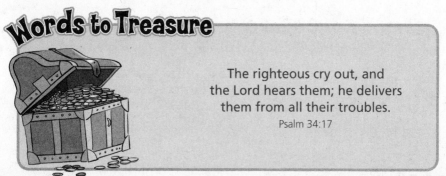

Words to Treasure

The righteous cry out, and
the Lord hears them; he delivers
them from all their troubles.

Psalm 34:17

Sandy Feat

Serve one another in love.

Galatians 5:13

Austin's dad was teaching him how to bodysurf. "As a wave hits you," he said, "dive toward shore and let it carry you."

Austin threw himself in front of a big wave, arms outstretched. With a rush of power, it propelled him toward the beach. He hit sand and stood up, laughing. "I felt like a torpedo!"

They bodysurfed together until Austin's mom called. "Time to get back to camp," she said. "Austin, please help Kyle and Tina clean up."

Austin went to his younger siblings, who were playing at the water's edge. "Come on, guys." Leading them to the campsite, he grabbed a bucket of water and began washing sand off their feet.

Although Jesus was God, he came to earth to serve others. (See Mark 10:45.) Jesus served people in many ways. He taught them, fed them, and healed them. Before he died, he washed his disciples' feet to show his followers they should be servants like him. (See John 13:1–17.) There are lots of ways you can serve others. For example, you can help your brother and sister put on their coats, do homework, or clean up their rooms. If their feet get dirty, you can even wash their toes!

Live It!

At the Last Supper, none of the disciples wanted to wash feet. So Jesus did it. Think of a job nobody wants to do at your house. Then do it, following Jesus' example to serve others.

Flying Straight

[The Lord] made me into a polished arrow and
concealed me in his quiver.

Isaiah 49:2

Standing thirty yards from the target, Sam fitted an arrow on the bowstring.
With his left arm, he held the bow. Three fingers of his right hand held the
bowstring, one above the arrow, the others below.

"Remember, Sam," said Mack, his camp counselor, "at this distance you have
to aim higher. Keep your left arm steady and release the arrow smoothly."

Sam nodded. "Got it." He raised the bow and drew back the arrow. Aiming at
the top of the bull's-eye, he let the arrow fly. With a *thwack*, it struck the edge of
the center circle.

"Excellent shot!" Mack said. "See if you can do it again." Sam drew another arrow out of the quiver on the ground. But he noticed it was crooked, so he tossed
it aside and grabbed a straight one instead. Putting the arrow on the bowstring,
he drew it back and released it. This time he hit even closer to the center.

God needs straight arrows! You can be a valuable arrow in God's quiver if you
let him straighten you, polish you, and guide you in everything you do. He does
this through his Word (the Bible) and his Spirit. Then God can use you, because
straight arrows fly straight and true.

Words to Treasure

Teach me your way, O Lord; lead me
in a straight path.
Psalm 27:11

Skimming the Surface

Love the Lord your God with all your heart and
with all your soul and with all your mind and
with all your strength.

Mark 12:30

Searching the lakeshore, Janie spotted a good stone. It was round, flat, and smooth. "Did you find one?" called her brother, Seth.

Janie ran back to the water's edge. "Yeah. This one's perfect!"

Seth held up his stone. "Great. Now, grab it like this. Then throw it side-handed, just above the water. Like this." He threw his stone so that it hit the lake at a shallow angle. It skipped across the water.

"That's so cool!" Janie said. "Let me try." She threw her stone the same way. It hit the water and skipped several times, skimming over the lake.

"You did it!" Seth said.

Skipping stones is fun. But don't let it be a picture of your relationship with God. He wants you to love him much more deeply than that. Instead of skimming through the Bible, dive into God's words. Rather than just singing along at church, worship God with all your heart. If you only think of God once in a while, keep reminding yourself that he's always with you. Don't be a skipping stone. Go deeper with God!

People in Bible Times

The Pharisees' relationship with God
was very shallow. God said about
them, "These people honor me with
their lips, but their hearts are far from
me" (Matthew 15:8).

Important Positions

> God has arranged the parts in the body, every one of them, just as he wanted them to be.
>
> 1 Corinthians 12:18

Jordan wound up and threw another fastball. *Thwack!* It hit the catcher's glove. "That's enough," said the coach, making notes. Jordan returned to the bench.

"Think he'll let you pitch?" Clay asked.

Jordan shrugged. "I don't know. I can throw hard, but not always accurately."

The coach approached the team. "Okay, here are your positions. Kirk, first base. Clay, second. Jordan, shortstop ..." After practice, the coach put an arm around Jordan's shoulder. "I know you're disappointed about not pitching. But you're great at fielding the ball, so I need you at shortstop. Remember, every position counts. If everyone on the team were pitchers, we wouldn't have any outfielders!"

Being on a sports team is like being a hand or an eye that's part of a body. So is being in the cast of a school play. Or being a member of a family or church. Every part of the human body is important. And God has put each one where he wants it. Likewise, each role you play in a group is important. And God has put you in that role for a reason. He knows what you can do, and he has a purpose for you to fulfill. Do your best wherever God puts you, because what you do really matters.

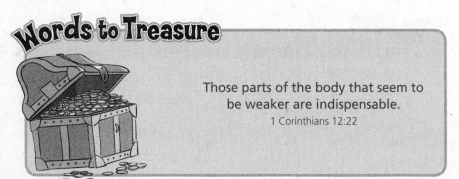

Words to Treasure

> Those parts of the body that seem to be weaker are indispensable.
>
> 1 Corinthians 12:22

A Whale Tale

> [God told Jonah,] "Go to the great city of Nineveh...." But Jonah ran away from the Lord and headed for Tarshish.
>
> Jonah 1:1–3

Lynette stood in the bow of the large boat speeding across the water. Her family was visiting Bar Harbor, Maine, where they'd boarded the boat to go looking for whales.

There was a shout, and Lynette felt the boat slow down. People pointed to the open water.

Lynette looked about eagerly. Then she saw it—a huge, dark form rising to the surface. "There it is!" she hollered. A blast of mist shot up. The whale glided past the boat, then dove. As Lynette watched, its tail rose above the water, then slipped back under the waves.

When Jonah set sail, he wasn't looking for giant sea creatures. But he found one! His story shows God's wisdom and power. God wasn't fooled when Jonah ran away; he knew where Jonah was all the time. And God controlled the storm at sea and the fish that swallowed the prophet. Jonah's story also shows how important it is to obey God. If you don't, it's not likely you'll get away with it. But if you do obey God, you can be sure that he's able to guide you and protect you and provide for your needs.

People in Bible Times

The Ninevites were enemies of Israel. That's why Jonah didn't want to go preach to them. He was afraid they'd repent and God would forgive them instead of destroying them.

A Clear Self-Image

> Do not think of yourself more highly than you
> ought, but rather think of yourself with sober
> judgment, in accordance with the measure of
> faith God has given you.
>
> Romans 12:3

Braden and his sister entered the funhouse at the carnival. At first they played inside a huge rotating barrel. Then Braden walked up to a curvy mirror. "Hey, check this out!"

Giggling, Mackenzie said, "You look so short and fat!" She stood in front of the next mirror. "This one stretches me all out." Raising her hands, she said, "Look, I'm Elastigirl!"

Braden laughed. They goofed around in front of the mirrors for a few more minutes. Finally he said, "We'd better move on. If I do this much longer, I'll forget what I really look like."

It's important to have a healthy self-image. You don't want to go through life thinking too highly of yourself—or too lowly. So you need a good mirror. The Bible is a perfect one. It'll show you exactly what you look like, so you can see yourself the way God sees you. The Bible will reveal all your sins. But it'll also show you how great you look after you confess those sins and God washes them away.

Life in Bible Times

Ancient mirrors were made of polished brass, not glass. So their reflections weren't very good. The Bible is a perfect mirror. It lets Christians see themselves clearly.

Bug Buffet

John's clothes were made of camel's hair, and he had a leather belt around his waist. His food was locusts and wild honey. People went out to him from Jerusalem and all Judea and the whole region of the Jordan. Confessing their sins, they were baptized by him in the Jordan River.

Matthew 3:4–6

Troy and his sister were bug hunting in their backyard. Spotting an insect, Troy pounced with his net. "What'd you catch?" Regan asked.

Troy put the bug in their glass jar. "It's a grasshopper." Showing her the jar, he said, "Can you believe John the Baptist ate bugs like this?"

Regan's eyes got big. "What?"

Laughing, Troy said, "It's true! He ate locusts and honey—and locusts are a kind of grasshopper."

Regan made a face as she looked at the insect through her magnifying glass. "Honey sounds good. But I couldn't eat one of these!"

The Bible doesn't say people have to eat bugs, the way John the Baptist did. But it does tell everyone to be baptized. Ask your parents and Sunday school teachers about baptism. Learn what it means and how your church does it. Find out whether you're old enough to be baptized in your church. If so, and you haven't been baptized yet, ask yourself, your parents, and God whether you're ready to take this important step.

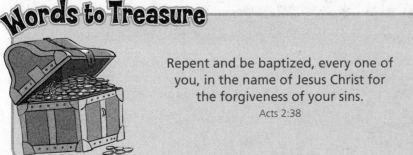

Words to Treasure

Repent and be baptized, every one of you, in the name of Jesus Christ for the forgiveness of your sins.

Acts 2:38

Spotting Each Other

Two are better than one, because they have a good return for their work: If one falls down, his friend can help him up.

Ecclesiastes 4:9–10

Floating in the lake, Brodie grasped the rope handle and struggled to keep his ski tips up. He was learning to water-ski. "Ready?" his friend Drake called from the back of the boat. Drake's dad was driving, and Drake was the spotter.

Before the ski lesson began, Drake's dad had explained to Brody, "The spotter watches the skier and lets the driver know if he falls."

Brodie signaled Drake that he was ready. "Okay!" Drake said, and his father gunned the engine. Brodie started moving. This time, instead of standing up too quickly and falling face-first into the water, he let the boat pull him up. Shaking the hair out of his eyes, Brodie grinned—and managed to stay up two minutes before taking a nosedive. Coming to the surface, he saw the boat circle around. "Ex-cel-lent," Drake said, helping him into the boat. "Now you can spot me!"

If you have a close Christian friend, you can spot each other. That means watching out for one another and helping each other when needed. If your friend nosedives into wrong behavior—using bad language, for example—you can help him or her get back up. And vice versa!

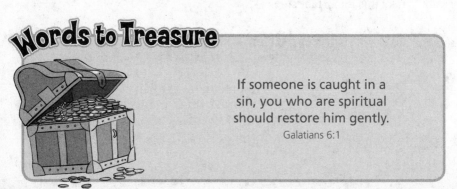

Words to Treasure

If someone is caught in a sin, you who are spiritual should restore him gently.

Galatians 6:1

Awake at the Wheel

He who watches over you will not slumber.

Psalm 121:3

Tanya gazed out the windshield of her dad's semi-trailer truck. They were traveling west through Kansas, and the land was flat and covered with wheat fields. Yawning, she asked, "Are we there yet?"

Her father grinned. "Very funny. C'mon, this is supposed to be fun." He'd invited her to ride with him on one of his cross-country runs.

Leaning her head back, Tanya closed her eyes. "It's been lots of fun, Dad," she murmured. "I'm just getting sleepy."

He chuckled. "Then it's a good thing you're not driving! Take a nap if you want."

Tanya snuggled into the seat. Soon the engine's hum lulled her to sleep. When she awoke, her dad was as alert as ever. "Hey, sleepyhead!" he said. "We've made some progress while you snoozed."

Tanya looked outside. The land was still flat. But in the distance she could see the Rocky Mountains.

It's only human to need sleep. But God doesn't have that need. While you're dreaming, God is wide awake, watching over you, taking care of you. His hands are always on the wheel, even while you rest.

People in Bible Times

Elijah challenged the prophets of Baal to a contest, to prove that Baal was a false god. The prophets shouted to Baal to light a fire, but nothing happened. Elijah made fun of them, saying, "Shout louder! Maybe he's sleeping." He knew that the *real* God never slept.

Warning Signs

> Do not forsake wisdom, and she will protect
> you; love her, and she will watch over you.
>
> Proverbs 4:6

"Watch out for ripples in the water," said Caleb's dad. "That means there's a rock or log just under the river's surface."

Caleb was barely listening as he and Jessica put on life jackets. He couldn't believe their parents were letting them ride in a separate canoe. *This'll be great*, he thought. *We even have our own cooler with drinks and snacks.*

At first everything went smoothly. Then Caleb splashed Jessica with his paddle.

"Hey!" she protested, splashing back. That started a water fight.

Too late Caleb saw the ripple. "Look out!" he shouted as the canoe hit a rock and capsized. When Caleb came up, he saw his sister, the cooler, the soda cans, the granola bars, and the upside-down canoe bobbing with him down the river.

If you're wise, you'll spot the warning signs that'll help you steer around problems. Your parents can teach you to see the signals that indicate danger ahead. Then you'll know when a friend is having a bad influence on you. You'll see that a situation is getting you into trouble. God gave you parents to train you to be wise, so take advantage of the wisdom they offer.

Words to Treasure

"Honor your father and
mother" —which is the
first commandment with a
promise —"that it may go well
with you and that you may
enjoy long life on the earth."

Ephesians 6:2–3

On the Ropes

Encourage one another and build each other up.
1 Thessalonians 5:11

Sam struggled to climb the big cargo net. It led up to the high platform at the beginning of the ropes course at summer camp. "Almost there!" said Mack, his counselor. Sam knew that the other boys from his cabin were watching him. They'd all become friends during the week, doing lots of fun stuff together.

"Go, dude!" Scott shouted.

Resting a moment, Sam shouted back, "This is harder than it looks!" With a burst of effort, he pulled himself onto the platform. The group cheered, and he did a victory dance.

"Okay, Sam," Mack said, laughing. "Let's see you tackle the high wire."

"Aye, aye, Captain," Sam said, turning around. Short ropes dangled above a cable that stretched to the next platform. Grabbing the first rope, he stepped onto the cable. It swayed and he lost his balance, pitching forward. He hung there awkwardly, holding the rope, his feet still on the cable.

"Don't give up, dawg!" Jimmy yelled. Regaining his balance, Sam slowly worked his way across. The group cheered again. This time Sam only grinned, too tired to dance.

When people around you are struggling, God can use you to encourage them. Your words of support will lift their spirit and give them confidence. Can you think of someone you know who needs encouragement?

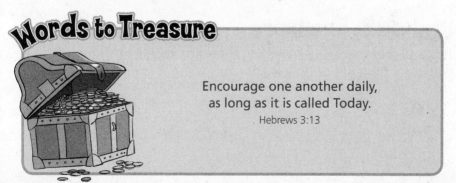

Words to Treasure

Encourage one another daily,
as long as it is called Today.
Hebrews 3:13

A Sure Thing

Having believed, you were marked in [Christ] with a seal, the promised Holy Spirit, who is a deposit guaranteeing our inheritance.

Ephesians 1:13–14

At a carnival booth, Braden tossed red plastic rings at bottles on a table. The rings kept bouncing off. "I think the idea is to get one of them to stay on a bottle," his mom said, grinning.

Braden went on tossing, trying to keep his focus. "I know that, Mom!" Finally he threw his last ring. It bounced off just like all the rest.

Chuckling, his dad said, "Well, that was a quick way to spend five bucks."

Braden's sister Mackenzie pointed at a booth across the midway. "Maybe you should try that one." Braden turned to look. It was a dart game with lots of balloons. On the front of the booth was a big sign that read, A Winner Every Time!

Counting the money he had left, Braden sighed. Then he shrugged. "Maybe that's not such a bad idea," he said, walking over to the other booth.

Being a Christian isn't like playing a carnival game you could win or lose. It's more like playing a game that guarantees you'll win the grand prize. Keep trusting in Jesus. You're certain to get the eternal reward God has promised to every faithful believer. God has guaranteed it!

Words to Treasure

[God] put his Spirit in our hearts as a deposit, guaranteeing what is to come.

2 Corinthians 1:22

Growing and Growing

Jesus grew in wisdom and stature, and in favor
with God and men.

Luke 2:52

The ride attendant stopped Macey when she was getting on the Superman:
Ultimate Flight ride at Six Flags amusement park. As he held up a measuring stick, Macey waited patiently.

"You can go," he said, and she and her brother climbed aboard.

"I'm glad you can ride this now," said Tyson.

Strapped in next to him, Macey grinned. "Me too."

Their seats swung back, putting them in "flying" position. Then they started climbing the hill. "Up, up, and away!" Tyson said. The next three minutes were a blur of high-speed dives, twists, spirals, and loops.

Getting out of her seat, Macey said, "That was incredible!"

Tyson grinned. "Wanna go on Batman: The Ride?"

"Yeah," she said. "Now that I'm fifty-four inches tall, I'm going on every ride in the park!"

Are you growing in height only? Or are you also growing in the other ways Jesus did? Like him, are you growing in wisdom, in your relationship with God, and in your relationships with others? You eat right, exercise, and get plenty of sleep so your body will grow up big and strong. Do everything you can to foster your spiritual growth as well.

People in Bible Times

Jesus grew in wisdom by learning
the Scriptures. Jesus grew in favor
with God by obeying him. He grew in
favor with others by showing them
compassion and serving them.

Triple Play

> Peter was hurt because Jesus asked him the third time, "Do you love me?" He said, "Lord, you know all things; you know that I love you." Jesus said, "Feed my sheep."
>
> John 21:17

It was the top of the fourth inning, with runners on first and second base, and no outs. Playing shortstop, Jordan yelled, "Strike him out, Rusty!"

He watched Rusty throw a pitch. The batter hit the ball, sending it flying toward Jordan. The runners took off, thinking it would sail over his head. But Jordan leaped high and caught the ball, stepped on second base, and then tagged the runner coming from first.

"Nice triple play!" the coach said, slapping Jordan's back as he jogged off the field. "Bang, bang, bang—three outs, just like that!"

Jesus made an awesome triple play after he rose from the dead. (See John 21:15–17.) Peter had gotten scared when Jesus was arrested. *Three times* Peter had lied, telling people he didn't know Jesus. Now Peter was feeling guilty. Jesus forgave all three of Peter's sins—bang, bang, bang, just like that. You may have let Jesus down many times. But he'll forgive you if you keep loving him and doing your best to follow him.

Did You Know?

How did Jesus tell Peter he was forgiven? Jesus didn't tell him, "I forgive you." He said, "Feed my sheep." This meant that he still wanted Peter to follow him and serve him. Peter knew he was forgiven!

Water! Water!

My soul thirsts for you, [O God,] my body longs for you, in a dry and weary land where there is no water.

Psalm 63:1

Damien took a long drink from his water bottle. "Wow, it's hot!"

Nodding wearily, his sister Robyn said, "Let's go to the water park." They were enjoying the rides at the amusement park, but the heat was getting to them.

"Okay," their dad said. "Follow me."

When they reached the adjoining water park, Damien said, "Look at all the people waiting to go on the water slides!"

His mom pointed at the water funhouse. "You should go there instead. It doesn't have a line." After putting on their swimsuits, Damien and Robyn took her advice. In the funhouse, they went through hallways full of spray, soaked each other with water cannons, and got drenched by the huge bucket on the roof. Soon they'd forgotten all about the blazing sun.

Water is very refreshing, whether you're drinking it or playing in it. And just as your body needs water to live, your soul needs God. Spend time with him each day. It'll perk up your spirit like a cold drink of water, reviving your soul like a cool splash on a hot summer day.

Did You Know?

Jesus offered a woman a better kind of water than she could get from a well. Called "living water," it was satisfying and life-giving. Jesus was talking about the Holy Spirit. (See John 4:1–15.)

Safe in God's Shadow

He who dwells in the shelter of the Most High
will rest in the shadow of the Almighty.

Psalm 91:1

The voice on the radio repeated, "The National Weather Service has issued a tornado watch ..." But Brianna, her little brother Patrick, and Molly, their sitter, were already watching. Brianna stared out the sliding glass door, listening to the thunder and wind. When lightning flashed in the darkness, she saw the large trees thrashing.

"It's just a thunderstorm," Molly said. "We'll be okay."

As Molly turned up the radio, Brianna thought, *She sounds nervous.* Suddenly the wind howled, lightning flashed again, and Brianna saw one of the trees fall over!

Molly saw it too. "Let's go, guys!" the sitter said. "To the basement, quick."

Patrick started crying as Molly hurried them downstairs. "Is it a tornado?" he asked.

Brianna was scared too. She took her brother's hand. "Don't worry, Patrick. We have a big, strong house. And we have God to protect us."

Experts say the safest place to be during a tornado is in the basement of a sturdy building. The Bible says the safest place to be—always—is in God's shadow. Whenever you're facing one of life's storms, run to God. He'll be your shelter every time.

Words to Treasure

O Lord, you preserve both man and beast. How priceless is your unfailing love! Both high and low among men find refuge in the shadow of your wings.

Psalm 36:6–7

Bugging God

Jesus told his disciples a parable to show them
that they should always pray and not give up.
Luke 18:1

C'mon, Dad," Tyson said. "Go with us on Kingda Ka."

His sister, Macey, nodded. "Yeah, Dad. It's the tallest and fastest roller coaster in the world!"

Looking up at the huge ride, their father cleared his throat. "You know, I loved going on these things when I was a kid, but they were a lot smaller back then."

Tyson and Macey pulled his arms. "Please ride with us, Dad," Macey said.

Resisting the tugs, their father replied, "I don't know, guys. This old body may not be able to take it."

They kept pleading and pulling. Finally he laughed. "Look, I'm thinking about it, okay? But if you keep bugging me, I'm not going."

Kids often pester their parents to do stuff. But it's not good to push too hard! Things are different with God. It's impossible to bug him too much about something. God's never going to answer your prayers with, "Go away and stop bothering me." So don't be afraid to keep coming to him again and again in prayer. Never give up until he gives you what you need.

Did You Know?

Jesus taught that it's good to be bold and persistent in prayer. In one of Jesus' parables, a man kept bugging his friend for bread. Because the man wouldn't give up, he got what he needed. (See Luke 11:5–10.)

Tossed About

> We will no longer be infants, tossed back and forth by the waves, and blown here and there by every wind of teaching.
>
> Ephesians 4:14

Tumbling through the water, Robyn held her breath. Then she swam back to the surface. People were shouting and splashing. But her brother was gone. "Damien!"

Treading the rough water, she looked around. Another large wave hit her, flipping her underwater. This time she swam to the surface more slowly. Her arms and legs were getting tired. "Damien!" She started to panic. He wasn't as good a swimmer as she was.

Suddenly a buzzer sounded and the waves stopped. As people headed to "shore," Robyn spotted her brother on the other side of the wave pool. "There you are!" she said, laughing, and swam to him.

You're a big kid now. But how *mature* are you? Can you handle it when someone starts telling you that God isn't real or that it's okay to bend the rules? Or do you suddenly feel as if you're being tossed about by giant waves? Being mature makes you like a mighty ship that stays on course no matter how big the waves are. The Bible helps you become mature by teaching you what's true, what it means to be good, and how to tell right from wrong. (See Hebrews 5:12–14.)

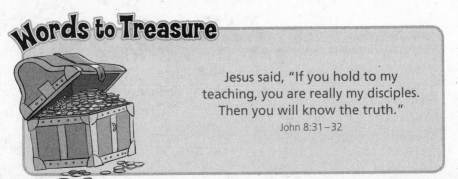

Words to Treasure

Jesus said, "If you hold to my teaching, you are really my disciples. Then you will know the truth."
John 8:31–32

A Hopeless Situation

We have this hope as an anchor for the soul, firm and secure.

Hebrews 6:19

The fishing boat skimmed over the water as Shawn revved its outboard motor. His mom and dad were traveling, and he was spending the week with his grandparents. They lived next to a lake. Today his grandfather was taking him fishing—and letting him drive the boat.

"There's a great spot near the other shore," his grandpa said. They crossed the lake, with Shawn's grandfather pointing the way. When he held up his hand, Shawn slowed the boat. "This is good," his grandpa said, and Shawn shut off the motor.

His grandfather reached for something in the front of the boat, then turned to Shawn. "Oh no! I forgot to bring the anchor." They tried fishing for a while, but the boat kept drifting away from the spot where the fish were. "We'll never catch anything this way!" Shawn's grandpa said. So they headed back to get the anchor to hold the boat in place.

What is "this hope" that Christians have? It's the confidence that God will keep his promises, because he always has. That kind of hope is greater than optimism or wishful thinking. It's an anchor that'll make you secure. It'll keep you from drifting into worry. And it'll encourage you in any situation.

Words to Treasure

Not one of all the good promises
the Lord your God gave you has failed.
Every promise has been fulfilled.

Joshua 23:14

A Grain (or Two) of Wisdom

How precious to me are your thoughts, O God!
How vast is the sum of them! Were I to count
them, they would outnumber the grains of sand.

Psalm 139:17–18

Using wet sand, Leslie made the last turret on the huge sand castle. "I'm done, Brian. How's the doorway coming?"

Her brother was lying down, his arm stuck all the way inside the entrance. "That's as far as I can dig from this side," he said, pulling out a handful of sand. "Now I'm gonna make a back door, so the hallway will go all the way through."

He moved to the other side of the castle and began digging again. Peering into the front door, Leslie saw his hand break through the sand. Brian got up, saying, "Okay, we can dig the moat now."

Leslie examined their work. "First, let's make the castle even bigger."

Looking around at the beach, Brian grinned. "Why not? We have enough building material!"

God gave Solomon a lot of wisdom. In fact, it was "as measureless as the sand on the seashore" (1 Kings 4:29). God has an unlimited supply of wisdom to give. So whenever you need some, ask him. He'll give you enough to deal with any situation you face.

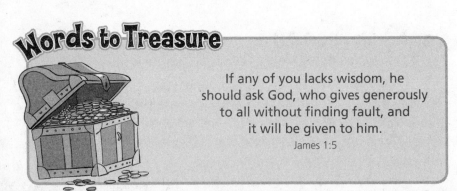

Words to Treasure

If any of you lacks wisdom, he
should ask God, who gives generously
to all without finding fault, and
it will be given to him.

James 1:5

Working It Out

Settle matters quickly with your adversary who
is taking you to court.

Matthew 5:25

Outside the kayak rental office, Ryan and his sister were arguing. "I want the red one!" Ryan said.

Melissa replied, "I grabbed it first."

"I called it first!" Ryan said, yanking the boat away.

Melissa started yelling, "Dad! Dad!"

Then Ryan remembered how much trouble fighting had gotten them into before. He tried to calm her down. "Wait. Let's settle this with a game of rock, paper, scissors."

Melissa thought about it. "Okay. That's fair." They pumped their fists as Melissa counted. "One, two, three!" Ryan kept his fist clenched, and Melissa laid her hand out flat. "Paper covers rock!" she said.

Ryan grinned. "Okay, you win."

Just then their dad came out of the office, carrying paddles. "What did you call me for?" he asked.

"Never mind," Ryan said. "We worked it out."

Learn to settle disputes peacefully. It's part of becoming more mature. And it's better than fighting about something until an adult has to get involved. Sharing and taking turns are great ways to work things out. If all else fails, remember: rock beats scissors, scissors beat paper, and paper beats rock. And all three beat getting into trouble!

Life in Bible Times

The Israelites often cast lots to settle matters. Casting lots was probably like drawing straws or flipping a coin. It was a fair, efficient way to work things out.

Leap of Faith

Without faith it is impossible to please God.
Hebrews 11:6

Sam stood on a platform high above the bank of a large river. He'd reached the end of the ropes course at summer camp. Mack, his counselor, was buckling him to the zip line that ran to the other riverbank. "All set," Mack said. "Can you handle this, big guy?"

"No sweat," Sam replied.

Mack slapped his shoulder, saying, "Have fun!"

Sam hesitated. It was a long way across—and a long way down. And this was no peaceful river. The white water rushed over jagged rocks.

"It'll carry you across," Mack said. "The ride's a rush, but you have to jump."

Sam grabbed the rope attached to his harness. *Here goes!* he thought and leaped. The zip line whirred as he shot across the water, and he whooped as he reached the far side of the river.

The main thing God wants from you is faith. He wants you to believe that he is real, he is good, and he keeps his promises. Every day of your life, keep leaping out in faith. Keep putting your trust in God, showing him by what you say and do that you believe in him.

People in Bible Times

When God told Abraham to leave his country, Abraham obeyed. How could Abraham make such a great leap of faith? He believed God had the power and faithfulness to keep his promises.

The One Thing That Matters Most

One thing I ask of the Lord, this is what I seek: that I may dwell in the house of the Lord all the days of my life.

Psalm 27:4

At circus camp, Kierra was practicing her juggling routine. "Good, Kierra!" her trainer said. "Now let's work on your riding skills."

Kierra replied, "Can't I keep practicing this? It's fun."

Chuckling, her trainer shook his head. "Remember, you'll be performing that on a unicycle. If you can't ride well, it won't be much of an act."

Kierra caught the balls. "Okay, okay." She put the balls away and grabbed a unicycle. Two of her trainer's assistants, riding their own unicycles, held her as she climbed on. Then they rode with her around the ring. When she was ready, they released her. She kept going, wobbling a little.

Her trainer applauded. "Great job, Kierra!"

The one most important thing to a unicycle rider is the wheel beneath her. Everything else in her act is based on that. Your relationship with God should be like that for you. Don't let anything else become more important. As you juggle school, sports, hobbies, and friendships, always remember the one thing that matters most. Make spending time with God your number one priority!

Life in Bible Times

Moses knew the Israelites would have many good things in the Promised Land. He told them not to forget God! He said, "It is [God] who gives you the ability to produce wealth." (See Deuteronomy 8:18.)

Lesson Number One

The fear of the Lord is the beginning of wisdom.
Psalm 111:10

Toby and his father lay on a blanket in the city park, waiting for the fireworks to begin. "You know, I visited a fireworks factory once," Toby's father said.

Toby sat up. "Really? What was it like?"

His dad propped himself up on one elbow. "It was interesting. I watched them make the round shells that shoot up and explode." He grabbed a handful of caramel corn, then continued. "They pack the shells full of gunpowder and 'stars.' Those are dime-sized pellets that burn brightly, like sparklers. When a shell explodes, the stars ignite and scatter. That's the part you see light up."

Sipping his soda, Toby said, "Wish I could've gone there."

His dad popped some caramel corn into his mouth. "The first thing I learned about making fireworks was that you've got to have a healthy fear of gunpowder. Those guys in the factory obeyed the safety rules, because they had a lot of respect for how powerful gunpowder is."

Toby nodded. Just then the sky lit up with glorious color. A second later came a thunderous boom. "All right!" Toby yelled. "It's starting!"

The first lesson truly wise people learn is to have a healthy fear and respect for God. That's because he's so awesomely powerful. When you fear God, as the Bible says to, you'll honor and obey him because he is the Lord.

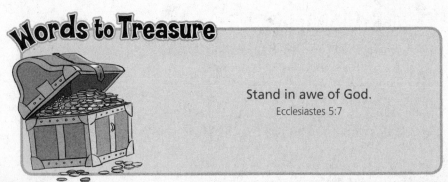

Words to Treasure

Stand in awe of God.
Ecclesiastes 5:7

184

Dangerous Duds

If you think you are standing firm, be careful that you don't fall!

1 Corinthians 10:12

Tommy's family was having a cookout with their neighbors on the Fourth of July. Everyone had enjoyed sitting around the fire pit, roasting hot dogs and making s'mores. "Okay, it's dark enough," Tommy said. "Time to light my fireworks!"

His little sister Bonnie clapped her hands. "Yea! Can I light some?"

Wiping chocolate off Bonnie's face, Tommy's mom said, "No, honey. This is Tommy's show." Tommy started setting off the fireworks he'd bought. They shot showers of sparks, whistling and crackling. He lit a big one, but it fizzled out. Thinking it was a dud, his dad tossed it in the fire pit. Tommy kneeled to light another one. Just then the fire pit started popping and whistling. Flames and sparks shot high into the air!

The apostle Paul warned believers to keep watching out for sin. That's because sin can cause trouble at any time. Now, some sins may seem like duds to you. In your life, they don't seem likely to start "going off" like fireworks. Maybe you've never committed certain sins, like cheating or stealing. Or maybe you used to, but God helped you stop. That's great! But stay alert so these sins don't flare up suddenly. Keep guarding against "dud" sins as well as the ones that *do* seem likely to explode.

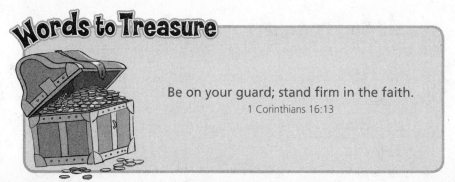

Words to Treasure

Be on your guard; stand firm in the faith.
1 Corinthians 16:13

A Piece of the Pie

A generous man will himself be blessed, for he shares his food with the poor.

Proverbs 22:9

April waited for the signal with eleven other kids. They all sat at a table with their hands behind their backs. In front of each of them was a cherry pie. "At the sound of the dinner bell, you may begin," said the judge of the pie-eating contest. "Good luck, everyone!"

He rang a steel triangle. Plunging her face into the pie, April gobbled as fast as she could.

The crowd cheered. Her brother Tim yelled, "Pig out, April!"

The middle of the sweet, tangy pie went down easily. Working on the edges, April glanced at her opponents. Their faces were covered in red goo and chunks of crust. With two-thirds of her pie gone, April started slowing down. Finally she sat back and groaned. Looking at the judge, she joked, "Can I share some of this with my brother?"

Picture all the food you eat in a year as one big cherry pie. Would you be willing to share a slice of it with others? God blesses people who are generous. Pray about ways your family can cut back on the amount of money you spend on food. That way, you can give the money you save to an organization that feeds the hungry.

Words to Treasure

[Jesus said,] "Whatever you did for one of the least of these brothers of mine, you did for me."
Matthew 25:40

The Catcher

> [O Lord,] your arm is endued with power; your hand is strong.
>
> Psalm 89:13

At circus camp, Kierra stood on a high platform. All week she'd been mastering basic moves on the flying trapeze. But now she was about to attempt a half turn. That meant she had to swing backward, let go of the trapeze bar, and turn in midair. And she had to trust Earl, the catcher, to be there and grab her outstretched arms.

"Ready when you are, Kierra," he called, swinging upside down. "You can do it!"

Holding the bar, she nodded. On his next swing toward her, she jumped. She sailed high into the sky, facing forward. Then she turned around and headed back toward the platform. Swinging out again, backward, she thought, *This is it.* She couldn't see Earl, but she released the bar and spun around, reaching for him. His hands grasped hers, and he held her as they flew through the air together.

When it's time to take a leap of faith, you can always trust God to catch you. He'll be right where you need him to be. He'll grab you with his quick, strong hands, and he'll carry you with his powerful arms.

People in Bible Times

Before Jesus was born, his mother Mary sang about great deeds God had done with his mighty arms. She told how God pulled kings off thrones, fed the hungry, and helped his people. (See Luke 1:46–55.)

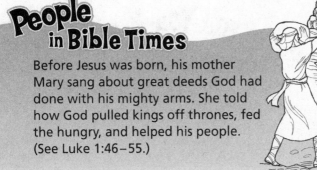

Hey, Batter, Batter!

Do not merely listen to the word, and so deceive yourselves. Do what it says.

James 1:22

Jordan swung at the baseball as it flew by. "Strike three!" the umpire called. Jordan walked back to the bench, shoulders drooped.

The coach said, "Nice try, Jordan. But you're not swinging level, like I told you."

Dropping the bat, Jordan replied, "Yes, I am!"

The coach shook his head. "No, you're not. You're still swinging upward." He clapped a hand on Jordan's shoulder. "If you swing level, you'll have a much better chance of hitting the ball."

Jordan sat and took off his batting helmet. He'd heard the same thing a million times during practice. He knew what he needed to do. *The next time I step up to the plate*, he decided, *I'm going to do it!*

The easy part about being a Christian is reading the Bible. Or listening to someone read it to you. It's a simple matter to learn what God's Word says. The hard part is *doing* what it says. Knowing a lot about the Bible doesn't make you a godly person. You have to put what you know into practice.

Did You Know?

Jesus met all kinds of people. He could always tell which ones were godly. He didn't recognize them by how well they knew God's Word. He recognized them by what they did with what they knew.

A Trustworthy Voice

Let him who walks in the dark, who has no light, trust in the name of the Lord and rely on his God.

Isaiah 50:10

"Turn left and take two steps," one voice said.

"No, Sam!" urged another. "Take three steps straight ahead." Blindfolded, Sam hesitated. He didn't recognize the first speaker—it must've been a camp counselor he hadn't met. But he knew the second one. It was Mack, the counselor from Sam's cabin. Sam started to step forward.

"Wait!" said the first voice. "Mack's trying to trick you! He wants to give everyone a big laugh!" Sam stopped. He knew that many kids were watching. His friends wanted him to make it. But others would love to see him fall into one of the slime pits in front of him.

"Sam, you can trust me," he heard Mack say. "Have I let you down before?" Sam thought about that. All week Mack had been encouraging and helpful. He was always looking out for Sam's best interests. Sam took three steps forward—and found himself on solid ground.

The Devil tries to convince people that God is against them, not for them. That's how he fooled Adam and Eve into disobeying God in the Garden of Eden. Always remember that God is on your side. Trust him and obey his commands, because he wants what's best for you.

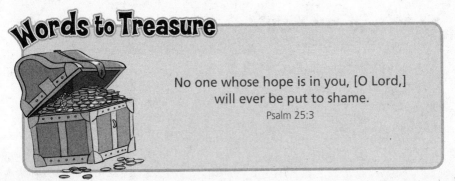

Words to Treasure

No one whose hope is in you, [O Lord,] will ever be put to shame.
Psalm 25:3

Testing, One, Two, Three

The Lord tests the heart.

Proverbs 17:3

At the pool in Morgan's neighborhood, the lifeguard blew his whistle. "Break time!" he said. As everyone got out, he turned to Morgan. "Ready for the swim test?" She nodded. Standing beside her was her next-door neighbor, Natalie. She'd told Morgan about this test. Kids had to take it if they wanted to swim in the deep end without a life jacket. The lifeguard needed to make sure they had the skills to do that safely.

"Okay, Morgan," the lifeguard said. "First, hold your breath underwater for thirty seconds. After that, tread water for five minutes. Then swim the length of the pool." Jumping in, Morgan stayed underwater, counting to thirty in her head. Then she treaded water while the lifeguard timed her. Finally she swam to the shallow end and back. "Good," he said, smiling. "You've passed with flying colors."

As Morgan climbed up the ladder, Natalie said, "Yea! Now we can swim anywhere in the pool together."

God tests everyone's heart. He's looking for qualities such as faith, love, honesty, and obedience. If you don't have these qualities, ask God to help you develop them. He'll teach you about them through the Bible and help you practice them every day.

Words to Treasure

Test me, O Lord, and try me, examine my heart and my mind; for your love is ever before me, and I walk continually in your truth.

Psalm 26:2–3

How Low Can You Go?

Above all else, guard your heart, for it is the wellspring of life.

Proverbs 4:23

Vince was at Allen's "beach bash" birthday party. And it was his turn to do the limbo dance! Caribbean music played. The other kids stood in line on the sand, joking and laughing. Leaning back, Vince scurried under the pole that Allen's parents were holding up.

"That was easy," he told Julie, joining her in line.

"It'll get harder!" she replied.

Sure enough, when they reached the pole again, it was lower. Julie gave it a try, barely scraping underneath. Vince did his best—but landed flat on his back.

These days, there is a lot of sexuality, violence, and bad language in TV shows, movies, and magazines. Knowing this, there are two ways you can respond to God's call to keep your heart pure. Like a limbo dancer, you can try to see how low you can go. That is, you can watch and listen to bad things you think you can handle. Then you can hope they don't get into your heart and cause you to sin. Or, like a pole-vaulter, you can try to see how high you can go. In other words, you can avoid as much bad stuff as possible. Then it has no chance to affect your heart. Which way do you think God wants you to choose?

Words to Treasure

Blessed are the pure in heart,
for they will see God.
Matthew 5:8

Tuning In

> [The shepherd] goes on ahead of them, and his sheep follow him because they know his voice.
>
> John 10:4

Dylan tightened a screw. Almost done! He was putting together a radio all by himself in his bedroom.

His dad had helped him build a simple crystal radio once, and that was exciting. So Dylan had saved up to buy a bigger, better radio kit. This one had a vacuum tube and a tuning knob. He wanted to surprise his dad with the radio when he got home from work. Then they could listen to the baseball game on it together.

Dylan tested the radio, turning the knob slowly. At first he heard static, then music. It worked! He kept turning the knob, listening.

Finally he heard the announcer's familiar voice: "A swing and a miss makes it two balls, one strike ..." Dylan also heard the front door open. Running from his room, he yelled, "Dad! Check this out!"

When you follow Jesus, you learn to recognize his voice. Reading your Bible and praying helps you tune in to it, like adjusting the knob on a radio. Keep tuning in to Jesus' voice every day. That way, you'll always hear it clearly.

People in Bible Times

In Jesus' day, a shepherd would call his sheep when it was time to lead them to pasture, water, or shelter for the night. Recognizing the shepherd's voice, his sheep would follow him. (See John 10:3–4.)

An Inner Glow

[Moses'] face was radiant because he had
spoken with the Lord.

Exodus 34:29

It was dusk. Anita and Juan were out in their backyard, trying to catch fireflies. But every time one lit up, it would stop glowing by the time they reached it. "Man, this is impossible!" Juan said.

Sitting on the patio, their parents chuckled. "Take a break, niños," their mom said. "Have some lemonade." The kids plopped down on the patio swing, and she poured them drinks.

The fireflies kept flickering in the twilight. "What makes them glow?" Anita asked.

Her dad replied, "A chemical reaction in their abdomens. It helps them find each other."

Just then Juan's stomach growled loudly. Grinning, he said, "Something's happening in my abdomen too. I'm getting hungry!"

Fireflies shine because of chemicals in their bodies. Moses shone because he spent time with God. Every time Moses met with God, his face would glow. In fact, it shone so brightly that he had to cover it with a veil. (See Exodus 34:29–35.) God wants you to shine in a similar way. He wants you to spend time with him in prayer so he can change you on the inside, making you more and more like him. Then people will sense something special about you. It'll be as if they can actually see God's glory in you!

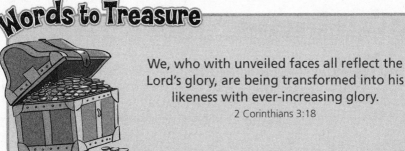

Words to Treasure

We, who with unveiled faces all reflect the
Lord's glory, are being transformed into his
likeness with ever-increasing glory.

2 Corinthians 3:18

Off the Hook

> Peter came to Jesus and asked, "Lord, how many times shall I forgive my brother when he sins against me? Up to seven times?" Jesus answered, "I tell you, not seven times, but seventy-seven times."
>
> Matthew 18:21–22

Look, Grandpa," Shawn said. "I caught him *again!*" Sitting in his grandfather's fishing boat, Shawn held up his line. A small bluegill squiggled at the end of it.

Shawn's grandpa laughed. "That's the third time! Well, he hasn't grown much in the last five minutes. You'd better throw him back again."

Taking the fish off the hook, Shawn said, "Maybe I should put him in the bucket. He keeps eating my worms!"

"That doesn't change the rules," said his grandfather with a shrug. "We're supposed to throw 'em back if they're not big enough."

Shawn sighed, then held the fish up. "All right, little guy, I'm letting you go. But stop taking my bait!"

Forgiving someone who keeps sinning seems unfair. It feels like you're just letting that person off the hook. But it'll keep *you* from getting hooked by bitterness and a desire for revenge. God doesn't want you to be full of bitterness and anger. (See Ephesians 4:31.) And he doesn't want you to become obsessed with trying to settle the score. (See Romans 12:19.) Just keep letting sinners off the hook, and trust God to set things straight.

Words to Treasure

Be kind and compassionate to one another, forgiving each other, just as in Christ God forgave you.
Ephesians 4:32

Balancing Act

Let your eyes look straight ahead, fix your gaze
directly before you.

Proverbs 4:25

The kids at circus camp were putting on a show. In a sparkly costume, Kierra carefully walked on the high wire. She was holding a pole to help her balance.

Her trainer stood on the platform ahead. Keeping her eyes on him, Kierra slowly moved across the arena. Finally she reached the platform. As the audience cheered, she smiled and waved.

"You made it, Kierra!" her trainer said. "You're a circus star!"

The Flying Wallendas are a famous family of tightrope walkers. On their website, Tino Wallenda wrote, "When I was seven years old, my grandfather, Karl Wallenda, put me on a wire two feet off the ground. He taught me all the elementary skills: how to hold my body so that I remained stiff and rigid; how to place my feet on the wire with my big toe on the wire and my heel to the inside; how to hold the pole with my elbows close to my body. But the most important thing that my grandfather taught me was that I needed to focus my attention on a point at the other end of the wire. I need a point to concentrate on to keep me balanced.... The Bible says that we need to focus our eyes on a fixed point. We need to fix our eyes on Jesus."

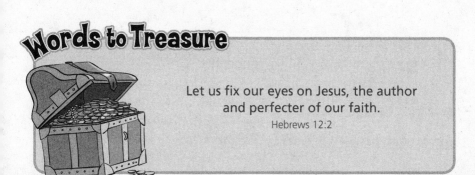

Words to Treasure

Let us fix our eyes on Jesus, the author
and perfecter of our faith.
Hebrews 12:2

Are These Your Clothes?

Clothe yourselves with compassion, kindness, humility, gentleness and patience. Bear with each other and forgive whatever grievances you may have against one another. Forgive as the Lord forgave you. And over all these virtues put on love.

Colossians 3:12–14

The kids at summer camp were doing flips off the diving board on the lake. Sam looked at the high dive. Nobody had attempted a flip off that. He told Jimmy, "I gotta try it." Climbing the ladder, Sam stepped onto the board. Before he could change his mind, he jumped. Turning and falling, he hit the water—feet first! When he came up, he heard cheers. In the changing room later, everyone congratulated him.

But Sam's grin faded when he realized his T-shirt was missing. His counselor threw him a wadded-up shirt. "Is this yours? It was on the floor." Sam checked the collar. There was his name, written in permanent ink.

The Bible says compassion, kindness, humility, gentleness, patience, mercy, and love are clothes for Christians to wear. Look closely at each of these godly qualities. Is your name written on them? If not, ask God to write it on for you, making these clothes yours. Then put them on every day.

Live It!

Decorate some T-shirts. On each one, write the name of a godly quality from Colossians 3:12–14. Whenever you wear one of the shirts, ask God to help you put on the quality it represents.

A Good Leader

We all, like sheep, have gone astray, each of us has turned to his own way.

Isaiah 53:6

Jayden strolled along the boardwalk, near the ocean shore. She loved coming here with her family. It was like being at a carnival. "Hey, look," said her brother, Conner. "Let's get an old-time picture taken! We could all dress up like cowboys."

Their mom smiled. "Why not?"

They went into the studio. Jayden and Conner had so much fun in their costumes, they wouldn't sit still for the photo.

"Listen up, you hooligans!" said their dad, drawing his six-shooter. He tapped his badge. "I'm the sheriff around here, and I'm a-tellin' ya to settle down!"

In the Wild West there was a lot of lawlessness. People went their own way, doing whatever they wanted to do. Back then a town needed a good sheriff to keep everybody in line. The Bible says everyone tends to ignore God's laws and go their own way. People are like straying sheep, and they need a good shepherd to lead them. Thankfully, God sent his Son, who said, "I am the good shepherd" (John 10:11). Don't go your own way through life. Go God's way, by following Jesus!

Words to Treasure

The Lord is my shepherd, I shall not be in want. He makes me lie down in green pastures, he leads me beside quiet waters, he restores my soul. He guides me in paths of righteousness for his name's sake.

Psalm 23:1–3

Linking Up with Greatness

Enoch walked with God.

Genesis 5:24

Jordan waited near the dugout, pounding his fist into his glove. The minor-league baseball game was about to start, and the players on Jordan's Little League team were escorting the hometown players onto the field. The name of the shortstop, Jordan's favorite player, was announced. Then Jordan heard his own name over the loudspeakers!

"Hey, Jordan," said Ron, the shortstop, as he came out of the dugout. He put out his hand. Grinning, Jordan slapped it. As they ran out together, the crowd roared. "How's your team doing?" Ron asked after they took their position.

"Okay," said Jordan. "We won two games." They talked baseball until it was time for the national anthem. Removing his cap, Jordan thought about how cool this was. Some people were elsewhere, paying no attention to the game. Some were listening on the radio, at home or in their cars. But he was right here at the ballpark, standing beside one of his heroes.

Genesis 5 says, "Enosh lived.... Kenan lived.... Mahalalel lived...." But then it says, "Enoch *walked with God*." Some people live their lives apart from God, not knowing him at all. Some have a long-distance relationship with him. Enoch had a very close relationship with God—and so can you.

People in Bible Times

Noah had a very close relationship with God. He did everything God told him to do. God was pleased with Noah, and he saved Noah and his family from the flood. (See Genesis 6–8.)

Follow the Leader

[Jesus said,] "Come, follow me."

Mark 1:17

At the NASCAR race, Corbin watched the cars roar past. They were traveling in a tight pack as they headed into the curve. "Why do they follow each other so close?" Corbin asked.

"That's called drafting," said his dad. "The lead cars have to cut through the air as they go around the track. By staying right behind the lead cars, the other cars have it easier. A lot of the air goes around them. Their drivers are trying to save fuel, so they won't have to make many pit stops."

As the cars thundered past again, Corbin said, "Wow, Dad. You should drive like that! We'd save money on gas."

His dad laughed. "If I did, I'd get a ticket. The police have another word for that kind of driving. They call it tailgating."

A NASCAR driver follows the car ahead of him closely to save fuel. In Jesus' time, a disciple followed his teacher closely to learn from him. The disciple would follow his teacher everywhere. He'd listen to his teacher's words, watch his actions, and try to be like him. Are you following Jesus that closely?

Life in Bible Times

An old Jewish proverb said, "Follow the rabbi, drink in his words, and be covered with the dust of his feet." Faithful disciples followed their rabbi, or teacher, very closely. They walked in the cloud of dust he kicked up!

Cool Water on a Hot Day

[The Lord] opened the rock, and water gushed out; like a river it flowed in the desert.

Psalm 105:41

Rod and his friends sat on the steps outside his family's brownstone apartment, trying to keep cool. The heat wave in the city made it hard to do much else. Rod had his shirt off. Pete was drinking lemonade. Nora was fanning herself with a magazine. A door slammed, and Rod looked up. "Look, here comes Michael. Hey, Mike!" All the kids scrambled down to the sidewalk.

Michael was a young fireman who lived across the street. He was carrying a large wrench, and Rod guessed what he was up to. "Hi, guys," Michael said. "You looked hot out here. So I thought I'd help you cool off." He crouched next to the fire hydrant on the curb. Turning the wrench, he said, "Stand back, everyone!" Water sprayed into the street, and the kids cheered. As Michael watched, grinning, they frolicked in the geyser.

God is a faithful, powerful provider. When the Israelites needed water in the desert, he made it gush out of a rock! Does your family have a need? Gather together and pray. Remind each other how God provided for his people in the past. Remember God's promises to take care of his people always. And have faith that he'll provide for your family now.

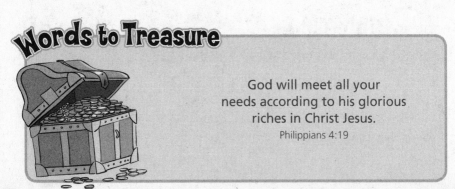

Words to Treasure

God will meet all your needs according to his glorious riches in Christ Jesus.

Philippians 4:19

Straight to the Finish

Do not swerve to the right or the left; keep your foot from evil.

Proverbs 4:27

Courtney's bright-red racer picked up speed as she zipped downhill. She was at the All-American Soap Box Derby in Akron, Ohio. In the middle lane, flanked by two drivers, she focused on steering straight. When she built the racer, she hadn't done anything illegal to it to make it go faster. And her car had passed inspection before the race. *I'm glad I didn't try to bend the rules*, she thought.

Now as she flew past stands full of cheering spectators, she was determined to keep doing things right. Courtney knew that steering straight would help her go faster. It would also keep her from veering out of her lane, which would disqualify her. Approaching the finish line, she glanced at the other cars. *I'm ahead. I might win!*

Seconds later she'd beaten them. But was her time good enough to make her the national champion?

Never try to bend God's rules. They don't bend. If you try to bend God's rules, you may *think* you're succeeding. But what really happens is that they stay perfectly straight, and you swerve away from them. Obey God's laws, and steer straight down the path of righteousness!

Did You Know?

One thing that helps Christians steer straight is *wisdom*. Wisdom teaches believers the difference between right and wrong. It keeps them from swerving off God's path. (See Proverbs 2:1–15.)

Hard to Starboard!

> Although [ships] are so large and are driven by strong winds, they are steered by a very small rudder wherever the pilot wants to go. Likewise the tongue is a small part of the body, but it makes great boasts.
>
> James 3:4–5

A stiff breeze propelled the Butterfly sailboat across the water. Holding the tiller, Max did his best to steer the craft. His friend Andrew was teaching him to sail. "The tiller is connected to the rudder, which is in the water," Andrew said. "And the rudder controls the sailboat." He turned to watch their progress. "You're doing great." Max started feeling more confident. Then Andrew said, "There's a kid in a Sunfish coming toward us. Better turn to starboard."

Max hesitated, then asked, "Which way is starboard again?"

"To the right," Andrew said. Max pushed the tiller right. Their boat veered left. "No, no!" Andrew shouted. "To go right, move the tiller left!" Max pulled the tiller left, and the Butterfly swerved right, just missing the smaller sailboat.

Like a boat's rudder, your tongue is important. The words you say set your life's direction. Your words can hurt others or help them, and that affects your relationships. Even the way you talk to yourself matters. You'll steer toward success if, instead of "I can't," you say, "With God, I can." (See Philippians 4:13.) Learn to control your tongue!

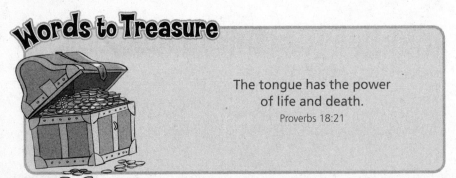

Words to Treasure

The tongue has the power of life and death.
Proverbs 18:21

Sneak Attack

[King David] and his men marched to Jerusalem to attack the Jebusites, who lived there. The Jebusites said to David, "You will not get in here." ... Nevertheless, David captured [Jerusalem].

2 Samuel 5:6–7

Sam, Scott, and Jimmy crouched on the platform for the zip line, high above the river. Mack, their counselor, was with them. Everyone at summer camp was playing capture the flag, with all the campers and counselors split into two teams. Sam had thought of a plan to help his team win. "Are you guys sure this will work?" Scott whispered.

Jimmy shushed him. "Quiet! We don't want anyone to hear us."

Mack finished helping Sam into the harness. "Okay, Sam. Go!" Leaping off the platform, Sam sped over the river. The zip line ended behind the other team's base. No one would expect an attack from that direction! Unbuckling himself, Sam sneaked through the woods, grabbed the other team's flag, and raced to his own base.

King David was faithful and obedient to God. So God helped him defeat his enemies. God gave David the wisdom to come up with a clever plan to capture Jerusalem. And it worked! Be faithful and obedient to God. He'll help you win your battles against evil.

Did You Know?

How did David capture Jerusalem? Jerusalem had high walls. But it got water from two springs outside those walls. David sent his soldiers through a tunnel connecting one of the springs to the city.

Going with the Flow

Do not worry about tomorrow, for tomorrow
will worry about itself.

Matthew 6:34

Wearing a swimsuit and sunglasses, Penny lay back, relaxed. She and her friends were tubing down a slow, wide river. Some adults were along to keep an eye on them. The girls had brought snacks and drinks, and everyone was having fun just floating along. Suddenly a blast of cool water hit Penny. "Wake up, lazybones!" Helena said with a giggle.

Startled, Penny sat up. "Hey, knock it off!" She kicked some water at Helena, and then they splashed each other for a few moments. The water felt good.

"Does anyone know what time it is?" Janine asked, floating behind them.

Splashing Helena one last time, Penny replied, "Why do you want to know?"

Janine looked up. "Well, the sun's getting lower. What if it gets dark before we reach the landing?"

Helena laughed. "Janine, you have to chill out. You worry too much."

Once you've chosen God's plan for your life, you don't have to worry about your future. Like a steady current, God will guide you and carry you along through life. He knows what lies ahead around each bend in the river. You still need to make decisions and work toward your future, of course. But you don't have to be anxious about it. Just trust God, relax, and enjoy the journey.

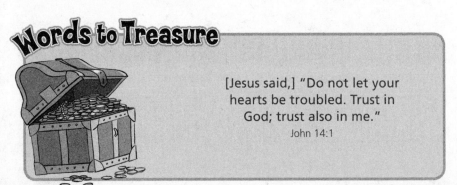

Words to Treasure

[Jesus said,] "Do not let your
hearts be troubled. Trust in
God; trust also in me."
John 14:1

Feeling Dizzy

They read from the Book of the Law of God, making it clear and giving the meaning so that the people could understand.

Nehemiah 8:8

Standing near first base, Jordan put his forehead on the end of a bat and started spinning. His Little League team was at the minor-league baseball field, watching the game. It was between innings, and Jordan was doing the dizzy bat race. At third base, one of his teammates was spinning too. After ten turns Jordan tried to run to second base. He stumbled sideways and fell. Trying again, he staggered in the other direction. Across the infield, his teammate was also struggling. As Jordan's dizziness faded, he steered himself onto the base path. Then he sprinted toward the goal, reaching it two steps ahead of his opponent.

Sometimes the Bible is hard to understand. It can make your head spin! But there are study guides to help make its meaning clear. Also, your parents and Sunday school teachers can help explain things to you. Most importantly, the Holy Spirit will help you comprehend God's Word. Don't give up trying to understand the Bible. You can't walk straight in life when you're dizzy and confused about what it says!

People in Bible Times

An Ethiopian was reading part of the Scriptures. It spoke of a man being sacrificed like a lamb. The Ethiopian couldn't figure out who it meant. Philip explained that the passage was about Jesus. (See Acts 8:26–38.)

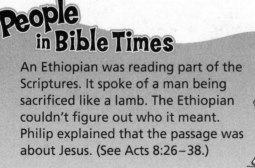

Are We There Yet?

> The people complained about their hardships in the hearing of the Lord, and when he heard them his anger was aroused.
>
> Numbers 11:1

Trying to sleep in the backseat, Kylie wasn't having much success. Her brother Paul kept jostling her as he tried to get comfortable. "When are we going to get there?" he complained.

Kylie sighed. "Yeah, Dad. How much longer? I hate these road trips." The family was heading for the Wisconsin Dells, the "Water Park Capital of the World." They'd chosen this spot for their summer vacation, though it meant a long drive.

"Quit complaining, you two," their dad said over his shoulder. "That's all you've been doing since we left. Think of the fun we'll have. Water slides, wave pools, mini golf, go-karts. Plus the waterskiing show. And touring the rock formations along the river in one of those Duck boats that can travel on land. It'll be great! But you need a better attitude."

Kylie laid her head back again. "Okay, you're right. But next stop, can I switch places with Mom?"

The Israelites' road trip through the desert shows what God thinks about grumbling. Imagine how God felt. He rescued the Israelites from Egypt, and all they did was complain! If you gripe a lot, try changing your attitude. Focus on all the great things God has done for you. God would be so pleased to hear you express some thankfulness for a change.

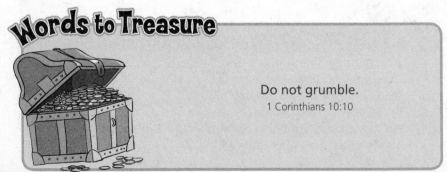

Words to Treasure

Do not grumble.
1 Corinthians 10:10

Hang On!

Hold fast to the Lord your God.

Joshua 23:8

From the back of the speedboat, Brodie climbed onto the big blue inner tube. His friend Drake was already floating on a yellow one. Brodie and his parents were enjoying a day at the lake with Drake's family, who owned a cottage there. Drake's dad was taking the boys tubing.

"There are lots of boats out making waves in the big part of the lake," he told them. "It's going to be bumpy at times, so hang on tight."

Brodie and Drake grinned at each other. "We will!"

The boat pulled away, taking up the slack in the ropes. Then it surged ahead, pulling the boys along. At first the ride was smooth, but then waves began bouncing them like crazy. Laughing, Brodie and Drake held on for all they were worth.

The Christian life isn't always a smooth ride. Sometimes the water gets pretty rough. That's when it's especially important to hold fast to God. Keep your faith in him. Trust his promises. Believe what the Bible says. And continue to live God's way, obeying his commands. Don't let things like problems, peer pressure, or other people's sins make you fall away from God!

People in Bible Times

Joshua clung to God from the time the Israelites left Egypt until they reached the Promised Land. Even when Joshua saw how big the people they had to fight there were, he never let go of God.

Peaceful Purposes

> They will beat their swords into plowshares
> and their spears into pruning hooks.
>
> Isaiah 2:4

Kylie sat with her family in the odd-shaped vehicle that was taking them through the Wisconsin Dells. The vehicle held about twenty people. It was boxy and heavy-looking, with low sides and a fabric top. As the wind tossed her hair, Kylie enjoyed the scenery along the wooded trail. Her brother, Paul, pointed ahead. "We're almost to the river. Get ready for the splashdown!"

Kylie braced herself. As the vehicle plunged into the water, a whoosh of spray exploded in front of them. "That was great!" she said, laughing. Their vehicle was one of the famous Wisconsin Ducks. Floating down the river, it continued the tour as if nothing had happened. Kylie admired the sandstone rock formations all around them.

"These vehicles were built for the military," her dad told her. "During World War II, they were used to transport troops and supplies over land and water."

Grinning, Kylie said, "The way we're using them now is lots more fun!"

In times of peace, the Israelites reshaped their weapons into farming tools. When wartime came, they changed their tools back into weapons. (See Joel 3:9–10.) The same piece of metal could be used for battle or for peaceful purposes. Think about your hands and your mouth. Are you using them to fight with others or to help and encourage people?

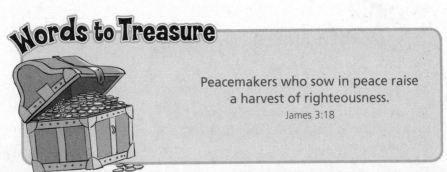

Words to Treasure

> Peacemakers who sow in peace raise
> a harvest of righteousness.
> James 3:18

Taste Test

Taste and see that the Lord is good.

Psalm 34:8

Shawn's grandmother started clearing the table. "How about homemade ice cream for dessert?" she suggested.

Shawn was staying with his grandparents while his parents traveled. "You guys can make ice cream?" he asked.

His grandfather replied, "Sure! It's work, but the result's worth it. If you've never tasted homemade ice cream before, let's make some." He got out a wooden bucket with a crank on top. "You have to turn this machine by hand," he said. Shawn's grandmother put milk, cream, sugar, and vanilla flavoring in the container inside the bucket. Then his grandfather poured ice and salt into the bucket, around the container. "As the salt melts the ice, it freezes the ingredients," he explained. "While it does, we have to mix the ice cream so it stays smooth." They took turns cranking the handle. Shawn went first. "Told you it's work!" his grandpa said.

When the ice cream hardened, Shawn's grandma scooped out a spoonful. Shawn tasted it. "Good, isn't it?" she said.

He nodded. "It sure is!"

Have you truly experienced God's goodness? "Taste" it by reaching out to him in prayer. You'll discover he really is as good as the Bible says he is. After you've experienced God's goodness, invite your friends to give it a try. Then they can "taste and see" for themselves.

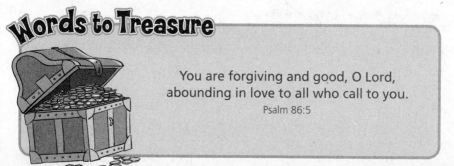

Words to Treasure

You are forgiving and good, O Lord,
abounding in love to all who call to you.
Psalm 86:5

Choose Your Weapon!

> David said to [Goliath], "You come against me with sword and spear and javelin, but I come against you in the name of the Lord Almighty."
>
> 1 Samuel 17:45

Jess peered around the corner. "Incoming!" he hollered. He and Jenny ducked as water balloons splatted against the side of the house. Then both kids charged, pumping their Super Soakers.

Laughing, their parents ran around the corner of the garage. "They're out of balloons!" Jenny said as she and her brother chased them. "C'mon, let's—"

Racing around the corner, the two of them stopped suddenly. "Uh-oh ...."

"Gotcha!" their mom shouted as she blasted them with the garden hose. Their dad threw a bucketful of water on them, drenching both kids from head to toe.

"All right, we give up!" Jess yelled, dropping his Super Soaker.

Jenny dropped her weapon too. "You guys win!"

"Well, that settles it," their dad said, handing Jess the bucket, some soap, and a sponge. "And remember, whoever loses the water fight has to wash the car."

Some weapons are greater than others. And the name of the Lord is the greatest weapon of all. As a Christian, you'll face spiritual battles. For example, you'll have to deal with temptation. Call on Jesus' name! It unleashes God's power in you so you can defeat evil. It's like fighting squirt guns with a fire hose.

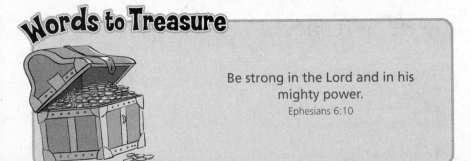

Words to Treasure

Be strong in the Lord and in his mighty power.
Ephesians 6:10

Plans and Results

The plans of the Lord stand firm forever, the purposes of his heart through all generations.

Psalm 33:11

Carrying fishing poles, Cole and Ethan walked onto the dock. Cole held a can with holes in the lid. The friends had spent all morning catching crickets to use as bait. They'd never tried using crickets before.

Cole opened the can and pulled one out. Ethan grabbed one too, then picked up his hook. "We're gonna catch a bunch of fish," he said, poking the bug. "I bet—ow!" He shook his hand, and the cricket sailed into the lake. "It bit me!"

Baiting his own hook, Cole laughed. "No way. Crickets don't—ouch!" His insect went flying, and he dropped the can.

Crickets started hopping all over the dock, and in moments they were all in the water. The boys stood there, stunned. Finally Cole said, "Great. We planned to go fishing, and instead we just fed the fish!"

People's plans sometimes don't work out, but God's plans always do. His purposes never fail. That's good news for you if you're trusting in God's plans for the world, and in his purposes for your life. You're sure to see excellent results.

Did You Know?

Before he made the world, God decided he'd send Jesus to save sinners. God plans for every believer to be made blameless, holy, and perfect. He plans for the whole world to be put under Jesus' leadership.

Petrified Lightning

> When [God] thunders, the waters in the heavens roar; he makes clouds rise from the ends of the earth. He sends lightning with the rain and brings out the wind from his storehouses.
>
> Jeremiah 10:13

The big red vehicle carried Alexis, her parents, and fifteen other people up and down the sandy hills. It was a topless truck with five rows of seats, run by Mac Wood's Scenic Dune Rides. At the top of the dunes, Alexis had a great view of Lake Michigan. "It looks as big as the ocean!" she told her mom. As the vehicle sped downhill, everyone raised their hands and shouted. Alexis laughed.

Later, after the exciting ride ended, she and her parents browsed in the gift shop. "Look at these," Alexis said, reading about some strange-looking objects on display. They were pieces of fragile tubes, rough and sandy on the outside, smooth on the inside. "They're fulgurites," she told her parents. "This says they're formed when lightning hits the sand. The lightning is so hot that as it branches out through the sand, it turns the sand into glass. When the glass cools, it's like petrified lightning buried in the dune!"

Fulgurites are evidence of the power of lightning. And lightning is evidence of the power of God. The next time you see a thunderstorm, let it remind you of how awesome God is. Then take a few moments to praise him.

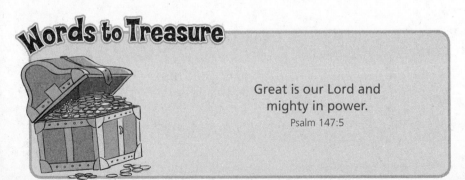

Words to Treasure

> Great is our Lord and mighty in power.
> Psalm 147:5

Stoking the Fire

Fan into flame the gift of God, which is in you.
2 Timothy 1:6

Sam and his friends at summer camp were spending a night in the woods. Their tents were pitched in a clearing about a two-mile hike from their cabin. Mack, their counselor, was helping them build a campfire. "Okay, Jimmy. That hole's good," Mack said. "Sam, you arrange the sticks, and Scott can light the fire."

Sam laid two medium-sized sticks across the hole. Then he stacked smaller sticks across them. On top he added some pine needles. That created a tinder pile above the ground, so air could move through it. Around this he made a tee-pee of larger sticks. Striking a match, Scott lit the tinder pile from underneath. The pine needles started smoldering. "Somebody fan it a little," Mack said. Sam grabbed a paper plate and fanned the embers, and soon they had a blazing fire.

Ask the Holy Spirit to show you what your spiritual gifts are. Then fan them into flame by practicing them. First Peter 4:10 says, "Each one should use whatever gift he has received to serve others." Do you have the gift of encouragement? Then start encouraging people who need it. Do you have the gift of teaching? Begin teaching others what you know about the Bible. God's gifts aren't meant to smolder. They're meant to burn brightly, so they can help your classmates, neighbors, and friends.

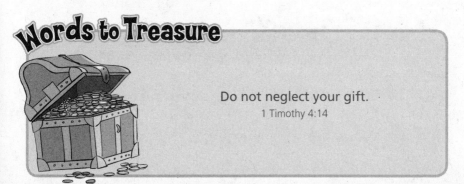

Words to Treasure

Do not neglect your gift.
1 Timothy 4:14

Raise the Sails!

> The God of Israel gives power and strength to his people.
>
> Psalm 68:35

ikayla sat on the deck as her dad's boss steered his large boat out of the marina. He'd invited her family to go sailing for the day. When they reached the open water, he said, "Let's get the sails up. There's a good breeze blowing, and we won't get far puttering along with our little motor."

Mikayla's father stood. "What are your orders, Skipper?"

His boss replied, "Keep the boat headed into the wind while Mikayla and I hoist the sails."

"Aye, aye, sir," Mikayla's dad said, taking the helm.

Her dad's boss unlashed the big sail in the middle of the boat and handed Mikayla a rope. "Here, start pulling on this." She obeyed, watching the sail climb the mast. Then together they raised the smaller sail in front.

Following orders, Mikayla's dad turned the boat a bit to the left, then switched off the motor. The sails filled with wind, the boat leaned over, and soon they were racing through the waves. "Now we're moving!" Mikayla shouted.

Like a wind that never stops blowing, the Holy Spirit is always there to help you live God's way. He'll give you the strength to resist temptation. And he'll empower you to accomplish the things God wants you to do. But you have to "raise your sails" by praying and asking for his help!

Words to Treasure

The Sovereign Lord is my strength.
Habakkuk 3:19

Eureka!

Your faith [is] of greater worth than gold.
1 Peter 1:7

Kneeling beside a creek in Juneau, Alaska, Kenny held a prospecting pan just under the surface. As the stream flowed over the pan, he stared at the gravelly dirt inside, looking, looking ... "Pull out yer pan and stir things up," said the old man standing behind him. "Use yer fingers to break up clumps and make soupy mud. Sand and dirt will rise, and the heavy stuff—like gold—will sink to the bottom."

"Right," Kenny said and followed his instructions. Dipping his pan into the stream again, he waited for the muddy water to rinse away so he could see what was underneath. Something flashed in the sunlight. "Hey!" he shouted, standing up. "Look at this!" He held up a tiny yellow nugget.

The old man laughed. "Congratulations, son. But when a *real* prospector discovers gold, he hollers, '*Eureka.*' That means, 'I found it!'"

God really likes gold. His temple gleamed with it. There's a golden altar in front of his heavenly throne, and the whole city of heaven is made of gold. Still, there's something much more valuable to him, and that's faith. Jesus was delighted whenever he found that. (See Luke 7:1–10.) As you trust in God, your faith sparkles in his eyes.

Life in Bible Times

In Bible times, goldsmiths used furnaces to refine gold. They melted the gold to remove the dross, making the gold pure. God often uses difficulties to refine people's faith.

The Jitters

> Do not be anxious about anything, but in everything, by prayer and petition, with thanksgiving, present your requests to God. And the peace of God, which transcends all understanding, will guard your hearts and your minds in Christ Jesus.
>
> Philippians 4:6–7

When Jordan arrived for the baseball game, his Little League coach called him over. "Our pitcher can't play today. I want you to fill in for him."

Jordan was thrilled. He was the team's shortstop, but he'd always wanted to be a pitcher. "Thanks, Coach!" he said. Going to the mound, Jordan threw some pitches to loosen up his arm.

"Batter up!" the umpire said. As the first batter stepped up to the plate, Jordan's heart started hammering. He saw the crowd watching him. Throwing four wild pitches, he walked the batter. "Relax, Jordan!" his coach yelled. "Just focus on the catcher's glove!" Jordan took a deep breath and said a silent little prayer. Tuning out the crowd, he wound up and threw his next pitch.

The umpire shouted, "Strike one!"

Sometimes you feel pressure to perform well, whether in school, sports, or spelling bees. When you do, it helps to relax and focus. It helps even more to pray. Ask God to help you handle the pressure. He'll give you a sense of peace that'll calm your emotions and let you think clearly. Then you can do your best!

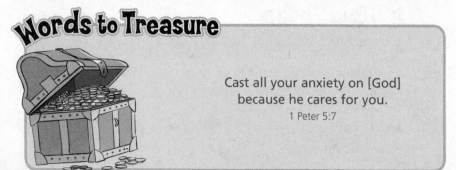

Words to Treasure

Cast all your anxiety on [God] because he cares for you.
1 Peter 5:7

Raising the Big Tent

Everyone who was willing and whose heart moved him came and brought an offering to the Lord for the work on the Tent of Meeting.

Exodus 35:21

The circus was in town! Andy's family went to the fairgrounds to watch workers raise the big top.

The large, colorful tent was spread out flat. The workers used ropes to pull up a part of it that had a doorway.

"Here come the elephants!" shouted Andy. The workers led one elephant into the doorway. They attached ropes to its harness and to the bottom of a pole. As the elephant pulled, the pole stood upright, pushing up one end of the tent. With all the elephants and workers helping out, the big top seemed to rise magically from the ground!

God told Moses and the Israelites to build a special tent for him. It was called the tabernacle, or Tent of Meeting. There God could meet with his people as they traveled through the desert. Many Israelites gave their possessions to supply materials for the tabernacle. And many pitched in to help build it. How about you? Are you willing to offer your time, effort, money, and possessions to do God's work?

Did You Know?

Before the Israelites left Egypt, the Egyptians gave them clothing and things made of silver and gold. Later many Israelites gave these items to God. They were used to build the tabernacle.

Changing Course

> Repent and be baptized, every one of you, in the name of Jesus Christ for the forgiveness of your sins.
>
> Acts 2:38

Mikayla and her parents were out sailing with her dad's boss on his large sailboat. "That pole under the big sail is called the boom," he told Mikayla. "When I turn the boat, it'll swing. Duck your head so it doesn't hit you!"

"Is that why they call it the boom?" Mikayla asked.

The man laughed. "Probably. Now, see those ropes tied to the sail? When we turn, I'll release the one on this side. Your dad will pull in the other one. Your job is to use the winch to help him. Ready?" Mikayla nodded.

He turned the steering wheel. The boom swung over Mikayla's head while she cranked the winch handle. When the sail was in place, her dad tied down the rope.

"Good job, crew!" his boss said as they headed off in a new direction.

In the Bible, *repent* means more than just confessing your sins and asking for forgiveness. It means to "turn from evil and do good" (Psalm 34:14). When you repent, you change course. You start heading in the direction God wants you to go.

People in Bible Times

John the Baptist urged people to repent. Many of them confessed their sins, and he baptized them. He told people to live in a way that proved they had turned away from their sins.

The Great Divide

The Lord God banished [Adam] from the Garden of Eden.... [Then] he placed on the east side of the Garden of Eden cherubim and a flaming sword.

Genesis 3:23–24

"This sure is a beautiful spot," said James, stopping to gaze at the scenery.

Behind him, his father agreed. "It sure is." They were backpacking through Glacier National Park in Montana. The path they were hiking on was part of the Continental Divide Trail.

"Why do they call this the Great Divide?" James asked.

His dad replied, "Because these mountains separate one side of the continent from the other." James stood there awhile, enjoying the view. Then he heard his father's voice from farther up the trail. "Keep up with me, James. *We* don't want to get separated!"

The great divide between people and God is sin. It separated Adam and Eve from God, and it'll separate you from God too. So keep walking with your heavenly Father. Keep obeying his laws. If you do sin and get separated from God, remember that there's a way to get back to him. Just confess your sin and stop doing it. Then Jesus' death on the cross takes away your guilt, and you're reunited with God!

Did You Know?

On the cross, Jesus was separated from his Father. That's because Jesus was carrying the sins of the world. This separation was hard for Jesus. But through it he brought people and God back together.

Choosing What to Keep

Out of the overflow of the heart the mouth speaks.

Matthew 12:34

Standing beside the van outside the amusement park, Audrey dialed her home number. In front of her, the Ferris wheel lights flashed colorful patterns against the night sky. "Hi, Mom. We're leaving. Cami's dad said I'd better call you on his cell phone, since it's late." Climbing in the van, she buckled up next to Cami. "What? Yeah, we had fun! The new water ride is excellent. And there's a roller coaster now with three loops. We went on bumper cars and go-karts and everything!" Audrey listened for a moment, then said, "Okay. See you soon." Closing the phone, she ended the call.

Cami said, "You didn't tell her that your favorite ride was broken. Or that you lost your arcade money. Or that you got sunburned."

Audrey laughed. "Well, my mom always says to only remember the good stuff!"

What are you storing up in your heart as you go through each day? Is it thankfulness for God's blessings, or bitterness over things that go wrong? Choose carefully what to keep in your heart. The things you pack in there determine the kind of words you say and the kind of person you are.

Did You Know?

Believers' hearts should be filled with truth, not lies. Peace, not fear. Love, not hatred. Forgiveness, not anger. Contentment, not envy. Joy, not sorrow. Hope, not despair. Faith, not doubt.

A Perfect Memory

[God] remembers his covenant forever.

1 Chronicles 16:15

Stepping off the high platform, Annette slid onto the elephant's back. Her brother, Andy, got on behind her. The circus was in town, and Annette's family had come to the fairgrounds to watch the elephants help set up the big top. Now that the tent was up, the circus people were letting kids ride the elephants. Annette patted the animal's huge head. "His skin is so rough and hairy!" she said, giggling.

Andy held on to her as the elephant started to move. "I hope you know how to steer this thing," he joked.

Down on ground level, their mom held up her camera. "Wait! I've got to capture this moment. We'll want to remember it." The circus worker leading the elephant stopped so she could take a picture. Both kids smiled and waved, and their mother snapped several shots.

As the elephant began walking again, Andy said, "Hey, Mom. Do you know why elephants don't use cameras?"

Their mother replied, "No. Why?"

Andy grinned. "Because they never forget!"

You don't have to worry about God forgetting things. He's all-wise, so he has a perfect memory. God remembers all of his promises, and he remembers to keep them all too. God won't forget you, and he won't forget to do all the wonderful things for you that he said he'd do.

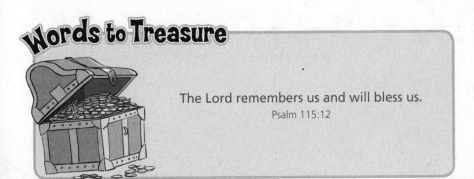

Words to Treasure

The Lord remembers us and will bless us.

Psalm 115:12

Perfect Shot

Be perfect, therefore, as your heavenly Father is perfect.

Matthew 5:48

At summer camp, Sam was getting ready to shoot a .22 caliber rifle for the first time. He leaned on the railing at the rifle range, aiming his gun at a paper target. The other boys from his cabin were doing likewise.

"Line up the sights on the top of your gun with the center of the target," said Mack, their counselor. "Hold the rifle steady, then gently squeeze the trigger." He looked up and down the line. "Okay, begin firing. And remember — best shot wins a prize!"

Sam pulled the trigger. There was a small bang, and a hole appeared near the bull's-eye. He fired again and again. A couple shots hit the bull's-eye, but none perfectly in the center.

Jimmy finished shooting at the same time Sam did. He didn't do so well. As the two boys examined their targets, Jimmy said, "I'll trade you!"

Everybody gets just one shot at life. Jesus was the only person who hit the bull's-eye perfectly. His entire life was holy and sinless. The amazing thing is, he was willing to trade his perfect score for your imperfect one. So you won the prize of being accepted into God's kingdom! Be sure to thank Jesus for what he did for you. And tell others that he's willing to do the same for them.

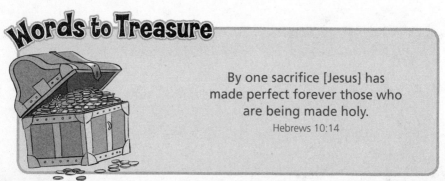

Words to Treasure

By one sacrifice [Jesus] has made perfect forever those who are being made holy.
Hebrews 10:14

At the Olympics

> Do not judge, or you too will be judged. For in the same way you judge others, you will be judged.
>
> Matthew 7:1–2

Morgan and Natalie were practicing their dives at the swimming pool in their neighborhood. Running on the diving board, Natalie bounced once and dove into the water. "That one gets a score of five point two," Morgan said as her friend climbed up the ladder. "You looked like a frog!"

Natalie grimaced. "I know. I always forget to keep my legs together."

Morgan dove in next. Thinking her dive was pretty good, she swam to the ladder and climbed out. With a splash, Natalie dove in again. Morgan said, "That's a six point one." She stepped onto the board, started running, and tried to perform her very best dive. But her foot slipped, and she performed a terrific belly flop instead. As she surfaced, she heard Natalie say, "One point zero!"

At the Olympics, only certain scores count. Those are the ones the official judges give. It doesn't matter what the audience thinks. It doesn't matter what other athletes think. The official judges make the call. It's the same way in life, except there's only one official judge—God! He knows everything, and he's a righteous judge. (See Psalm 7:11.) He's the only one who can judge people fairly. (See 1 Peter 2:23.) So don't judge others, even in your heart. Let God make the call!

Words to Treasure

It is God who judges.
Psalm 75:7

Highlight Video

> I will remember the deeds of the Lord; yes, I will remember your miracles of long ago.
>
> Psalm 77:11

Crack! Standing at the shortstop position, Jordan saw the grounder rip past the pitcher's mound. He dove for the ball and snagged it. Rolling in the dirt, he tossed it to the second baseman, who stepped on the bag and fired the ball to first. Double play! The all-star game was over, and Jordan's team had won.

"Great game, Son!" said his mom as he jogged off the field.

His dad held up a digital camcorder. "It sure was. And now that the season's over, we can put together a highlight video."

Jordan grinned. "You sure love that new camcorder, Dad."

Nodding, his father said, "Hey, why don't you help me edit the footage I took this summer? We can add all kinds of special effects, like background music and graphics. When we're finished, we'll have a cool DVD that shows all your great plays."

God has done many astounding things, and the Bible is a record of his highlights. Read it. Think about God's wonderful deeds as you lie in bed at night. Recalling the great things he's done will help you remember how awesome he is.

People in Bible Times

Before people could write, the stories of God's great deeds were passed down through spoken words. Later, scribes used quill pens and ink to record them on scrolls made of papyrus or parchment.

Inner Beauty

Your beauty should not come from outward adornment.... Instead, it should be that of your inner self, the unfading beauty of a gentle and quiet spirit, which is of great worth in God's sight.

1 Peter 3:3–4

Mikayla stood at the helm of the large boat, hands on the big silver wheel. The owner of the boat, her dad's boss, stood beside Mikayla, letting her steer for a while. Watching for other boats, Mikayla noticed one passing them. It had a huge, colorful sail out front. "That's so cool!" she said. "Can we put up a sail like that?"

Her dad's boss said, "Sure! It's called a spinnaker. Let your dad take the helm, and come give me a hand with it." He carried a bag to the bow of the boat. There he attached lines to the three corners of the spinnaker, which were sticking out of the bag. Mikayla pulled one line to raise the sail. Then he adjusted the other ones.

The wind filled the brightly colored spinnaker, and it billowed out. Smiling, Mikayla said, "Now we're looking good!"

Being gentle and humble makes you beautiful. It doesn't change your outer looks, really. But it gives you an inner beauty that's very pleasing to God. Other people "see" this beauty in your behavior and attitude. When they do, it can inspire them to be gentle and humble too.

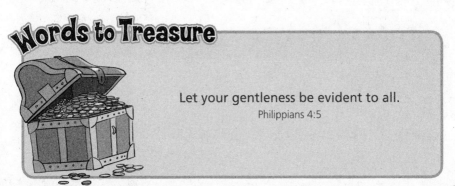

Words to Treasure

Let your gentleness be evident to all.
Philippians 4:5

225

Complicated Choices

> Whether you turn to the right or to the left,
> your ears will hear a voice behind you, saying,
> "This is the way; walk in it."
>
> Isaiah 30:21

As James held the map, his father pointed at the line that ran through Glacier National Park in Montana. They'd stopped to get their bearings while backpacking along the Continental Divide Trail. "We're right here—near Triple Divide Peak," James's father said. Looking up, he indicated a rugged mountain ahead of them. "There it is. An interesting place!"

James gazed at the mountain. "Why is it interesting?" he asked as they resumed their hike.

"It's the spot where two divides meet," his father said. "We're on the Great Divide. That runs north and south across the continent, through this mountain. The Northern Divide starts at this mountain and runs east. These divides determine which way rainwater flows. Water that falls on the summit of Triple Divide Peak can go in three directions. It can go west to the Pacific Ocean, north to the Arctic Ocean, or east to the Atlantic Ocean!"

Making choices can be hard. Especially when you have many options! How will you know which way to go? If you listen carefully, God will tell you. His Spirit will whisper to yours. The Holy Spirit can speak to you directly, or through a Bible passage you read, or through a godly person you turn to for advice.

Words to Treasure

[God] will be our guide
even to the end.
Psalm 48:14

A Shower in the Sky

The heavens declare the glory of God; the skies proclaim the work of his hands.

Psalm 19:1

Lying on a blanket with her friends, Carlie checked her watch. "It's eleven p.m., so our meteor shower party can officially begin. Remember, whoever sees a shooting star first wins a prize!" It was mid-August, and the sky was clear.

"I could spend all night out here," Peyton said.

Carlie reached for some chips. "My dad wouldn't let us. But he said we could stay out till one o'clock. Most of the meteors will come around midnight, so we'll see lots of them." She pointed up. "See Perseus? That's the constellation I drew on your invitations. All the meteors will come from that direction. That's why they're called the Perseids."

Brooke asked, "How do you know all this stuff?"

Carlie smiled. "My dad loves astronomy, and he teaches me a lot. Did you know—"

Suddenly Peyton shouted, "Look!" just as Brooke hollered, "There's one!" A white light streaked across the sky, and they all said, "Oooooh!"

Need a reminder of how wise, powerful, and wonderful God is? Go outside anytime, day or night, and look up. Beautiful clouds. Awesome thunderstorms. Spectacular sunsets. Majestic stars. Through all these, the sky reminds everyone of God's glory.

Words to Treasure

Lift your eyes and look to the heavens: Who created all these? He who brings out the starry host one by one, and calls them each by name.

Isaiah 40:26

Rediscovering a Treasure

> Hilkiah the high priest said to Shaphan the secretary, "I have found the Book of the Law in the temple of the Lord."
>
> 2 Kings 22:8

Well, looky here!" said Shawn's grandfather. "It's my old model train set." He and Shawn had been rummaging through his basement, looking for board games. Holding up the engine, he said, "Wanna see if it still works?"

Shawn grinned. "All right!" They carried the box upstairs. Shawn helped his grandpa lay out the tracks. Besides the engine, there were six railroad cars and a caboose, plus accessories to make a small town. There was even a crossing signal with a gate.

When the train set was put together, Shawn's grandfather plugged it in. "Here, Shawn. You take the controls."

Shawn pushed a lever. The engine's headlight came on, and the train began moving. As it went around the track, Shawn's grandpa said, "I'd forgotten how much fun this is!"

Sometimes valuable things get put away and forgotten. Is your Bible gathering dust somewhere? Have you lost the habit of reading it every day? Are there Scripture verses you used to have memorized but can't remember now? If so, dig out your Bible and rediscover what a treasure it is.

People in Bible Times

When the book of God's laws was discovered, King Josiah realized what a treasure it was. He read it to the people of Judah. Then everyone promised to live according to that book.

Watching the Sky

[Jesus] was taken up before their very eyes, and a cloud hid him from their sight.

Acts 1:9

Andre and Elena lay on the grass, watching the clouds. "That one looks like a castle," Elena said, pointing.

Andre cocked his head. "Nah, I don't get it."

Elena rolled her eyes. "Well, what do *you* see?"

"A ship! It has three sails," Andre said, pointing at another cloud.

Elena stared at the cloud. "Doesn't look like anything to me."

Andre put his hands under his head. "That's because you have no imagination."

Glaring at him, Elena said, "What do you mean? I just imagined a fortress. That beats a boat!"

Laughing, Andre said, "Uh-oh, my ship just ran into your castle. Now the whole thing looks like a snowman."

Elena looked up. "You're right! Ooh, it reminds me of Christmas."

Think about how you long for Christmas during Advent season. It seems that day will never arrive. But you know it will! That's the way it was for God's people before the first Christmas, as they waited for the Messiah to come. And that's the way it's been ever since Jesus left. The present time is a kind of Advent season. Even though it sometimes seems Jesus will never return, one day soon he will.

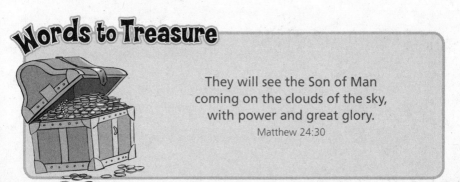

Words to Treasure

They will see the Son of Man
coming on the clouds of the sky,
with power and great glory.
Matthew 24:30

Waiting ... and Waiting ...

Wait for the Lord; be strong and take heart and wait for the Lord.

Psalm 27:14

I s the water boiling yet?" Roger asked.

Standing at the stove, his mother said, "Yes. You can add the ingredients now." They were making rock candy to sell at the arts and crafts fair. Roger poured sugar into the pans. He added a different food color and flavor to each one. Then his mom stirred the pans as the sugar dissolved. "Okay, that's it," she said. "Are the jars ready?"

Going to the kitchen table, Roger said, "All set!" Carefully his mother filled the jars. Across the top of each jar, Roger set a pencil with a string tied to it. He positioned the pencil so that the string hung down into the liquid. Then he sat and watched.

"It'll take days for the crystals to form on the strings," his mom said.

Roger sighed. "I know. I just wish there was more we could do besides wait!"

Waiting for God to answer your prayers can be hard. But it's not like sitting around waiting for rock candy to form. When you're waiting for God to act, there's something you can do. You can go on praying! Be patient, but don't give up. Keep trusting that God will answer your prayers. Even when nothing seems to be happening, he's working. In time that will become crystal clear.

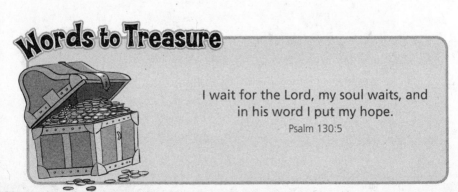

Words to Treasure

I wait for the Lord, my soul waits, and in his word I put my hope.

Psalm 130:5

God's Dark Side?

God is light; in him there is no darkness at all.

1 John 1:5

"I'm glad the moon's full, so we can see all of it," said Carlie.

Aiming his telescope, her dad replied, "Actually, we can only see half of it. That's the near side, which always faces earth. Right now that side is also called the bright side, because the sun's shining on it. In two weeks it'll become the dark side. With no sunlight, it'll be completely black and five hundred degrees colder."

He straightened up. "Take a look at the Sea of Serenity. That's the big spot up there."

Carlie peered through the telescope. "I see it!" she said. It was smooth but surrounded by craters and mountains.

"The Apollo 17 astronauts landed near there," her dad said.

Carlie grinned. "I hope they packed warm pajamas!"

God doesn't have a dark side, like the moon. He is holy, which means he's all good. When you sin, God's holiness can *seem* dark, because it makes you feel guilty and afraid. But when you let Jesus remove your sins, you find that God's holiness is warm and bright. That's the way God wants you to experience it.

People in Bible Times

When Pharaoh and his army attacked, God protected the Israelites. He was there in a pillar of cloud. The part of the cloud facing the Egyptians looked like a terrible storm. To them, God seemed to have a dark side.

"Ghost" Story

> [Jesus told his frightened disciples,] "Look at my hands and my feet. It is I myself! Touch me and see; a ghost does not have flesh and bones, as you see I have."
>
> Luke 24:39

Sam crept through the dark woods with Jimmy, one of his cabin mates at summer camp. "There they are!" Sam whispered, pointing. In a clearing was a cluster of tents. Some boys from another cabin were camping out for the night. Quietly Sam and Jimmy unfolded the sheets they were carrying and slipped them over their heads. Then they started walking around, making spooky noises.

"What's that?" Sam heard someone say. He snickered, then made his noises even louder.

Suddenly a bright light shone on him. "Nice try, guys!" the counselor shouted. "But ghosts don't wear tennis shoes!" Laughing, Sam and Jimmy ran back to their cabin.

Jesus was raised from the dead completely, body and all. He wasn't just a ghost walking around. He proved this by letting his disciples touch him and by eating meals with them. When you go to heaven, you won't be just a spirit walking around either. The Bible says you'll have a body—one that's much better than the body you have now!

People in Bible Times

Jesus let Thomas touch his body to prove he was really alive. Then Jesus said, "Because you have seen me, you have believed; blessed are those who have not seen and yet have believed" (John 20:29).

232

Sailboat Serenade

The wind blows wherever it pleases. You hear
its sound, but you cannot tell where it comes
from or where it is going. So it is with everyone born of the Spirit.

John 3:8

Walking along the pier, Mikayla looked at the sailboats. They were all tied up for the night. She and her parents had been out sailing with her dad's boss. Now the adults were sitting in the boat, chatting. It was a warm summer evening, and Mikayla's mom had let her take a stroll.

There were no other people around, so everything was quiet. Mikayla heard the water lapping against the pier. Then she noticed another noise. *Where is that coming from?* she wondered. Finally she realized what it was. A gentle breeze was causing the ropes to bang lightly against the masts of the sailboats. It made soft, wonderful, dinging sounds. She stopped and listened, feeling as if she were surrounded by a giant set of wind chimes.

You can't see the wind, but you can tell when it's blowing. It's the same with the Holy Spirit. Invite God's Spirit to move in your heart. There the Spirit will produce godly qualities such as love, joy, and peace. And your heart will start ringing with thankfulness, worship, and praise. These are the notes of a beautiful song God loves to hear.

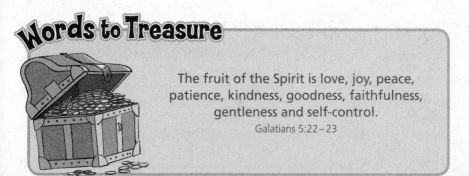

Words to Treasure

The fruit of the Spirit is love, joy, peace,
patience, kindness, goodness, faithfulness,
gentleness and self-control.
Galatians 5:22–23

Greatness on Display

> Faith is being sure of what we hope for and certain of what we do not see. This is what the ancients were commended for.
>
> Hebrews 11:1–2

Jordan saw the pitch coming fast. He swung his bat and connected solidly. "Nice hit!" his dad said. Grinning, Jordan stepped out of the batting cage. They were at the Little League Museum in South Williamsport, Pennsylvania. Leaving that area, they entered the Hall of Excellence. On its walls were plaques honoring former Little League players who'd done great things in life. There were businessmen, sports stars, entertainers, an astronaut, a soldier, a fireman, and a president.

Amazed, Jordan said, "They all played Little League baseball?"

His dad nodded. "Just like you. The values they learned in Little League helped them become outstanding men and women."

Browse through the Bible's hall of fame. (See Hebrews 11.) Each of these heroes of Scripture started out as a kid, like you! Now it's as if they're all looking down from heaven, watching to see if *you'll* become a hero. Ask God to help you follow their example. Ask him to help you learn biblical values such as courage, loyalty, and faith. Then you'll grow up to be one of God's heroes too.

Words to Treasure

Since we are surrounded by such a great cloud of witnesses, let us throw off everything that hinders and the sin that so easily entangles, and let us run with perseverance the race marked out for us.

Hebrews 12:1

Strength to Soar

Those who hope in the Lord will renew their strength. They will soar on wings like eagles; they will run and not grow weary, they will walk and not be faint.

Isaiah 40:31

Shifting his backpack, James let out a long breath. He and his dad were high in the Rocky Mountains on a long hike on the Continental Divide Trail. The path was rugged, and James was tired. Suddenly his father stopped. "Look, Son!" James looked where he was pointing. Over the valley, a large bird was soaring. It was dark-brown with a white head, and it gave a shrill cry.

"Dad, it's a bald eagle!" James said.

His father grinned. "Is that awesome, or what?" Grabbing his binoculars, James watched the eagle. It made powerful strokes with its wings and then glided, the feathers of its wingtips extended.

"It must have a six-foot wingspan!" James said, handing his dad the binoculars. Both of them stood there, admiring the majestic creature. As he watched it fly, James breathed in deeply, his weariness gone.

Even kids get worn out sometimes, especially when the going gets rough. Are you feeling weary? Are you discouraged because of difficulties you're going through? Don't give up hope. Put your hope in God. Remember his promises and keep trusting them. God will refresh your strength, enabling you to soar like an eagle.

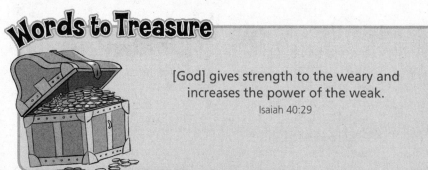

Words to Treasure

[God] gives strength to the weary and increases the power of the weak.
Isaiah 40:29

The Mix Master

> Each man has his own gift from God; one has
> this gift, another has that.
>
> 1 Corinthians 7:7

C assie's grandfather introduced her to the man in the white coat. "This is Mr. Gardner. He's in charge of making all the ice cream I sell at my shop."

Mr. Gardner smiled. "Welcome to the ice cream factory, Cassie. I'm the mix master."

"What do you do?" she asked.

Patting a machine, he replied, "Here, I combine the right amounts of milk, cream, sugar, and egg yolks to make the ice cream mixture." He led them through the factory, pointing out equipment. "The homogenizer pounds the mixture, making it smooth. The pasteurizer heats it to kill bacteria."

Stopping at a silver contraption, Mr. Gardner said, "Here we add colors and flavors. Then the mixture is frozen softly." He walked to another machine. "This shoots in the goodies, like nuts and caramel and chocolate chips. Over there the mixture is poured into containers and frozen hard. And—ta-da!—you have delicious ice cream."

God carefully mixed the ingredients of your personality. He also put some "goodies" in you, called spiritual gifts. Ask God to show you what your spiritual gifts are and teach you how to use them.

Did You Know?

Spiritual gifts include prophecy, serving, teaching, encouragement, giving, leading, mercy, wisdom, knowledge, faith, healing, miraculous powers, telling good spirits from evil ones, speaking in tongues, and interpreting tongues.

Don't Get Hooked

Keep your lives free from the love of money
and be content with what you have.

Hebrews 13:5

C ole and his friend sat on the dock, fishing. Ethan's bobber jiggled, then disappeared under the water. "I got something!" he said, scrambling to his feet.

Cole watched excitedly. "Is it big?"

Reeling in his line, Ethan raised his pole. The hook dangled there, shiny and bare. "Oh, man. The fish ate my worm."

As Ethan reached for more bait, Cole felt a tug on his sleeve. "Hey, you snagged my shirt!"

Turning around, Ethan said, "Oops. Sorry."

Cole tried to remove the barbed hook, but it wouldn't come out. "Now what are we supposed to do?" he groaned.

Just then a fisherman walked up. "Need help, boys? I saw your predicament when I was getting on my boat. So I grabbed these." He held up a pair of wire cutters. Snipping off the barb, he pulled out the hook.

"Thanks!" Cole said.

The man smiled. "No problem. Just be glad it didn't snag your skin."

Don't let greed hook you! People often get hurt by the love of money and the desire to be rich. Greed causes people to sin, and then it pierces them with sadness. You'll be much happier if you avoid greed by living God's way and being content with the blessings he gives you. (See 1 Timothy 6:6–10.)

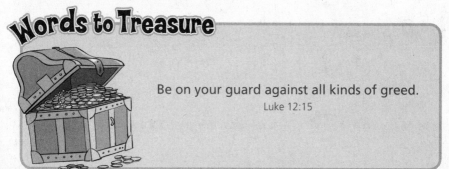

Words to Treasure

Be on your guard against all kinds of greed.
Luke 12:15

A Tree beside the River

Blessed is the man who trusts in the Lord....
He will be like a tree planted by the water that
sends out its roots by the stream.

Jeremiah 17:7–8

Wyatt sat on a branch that hung over the river and tied the rope to it. "What if the branch breaks?" asked T.J. below him, holding the other end of the rope.

"It's a strong tree," Wyatt said. "It'll hold us." He scurried down, and T.J. handed the rope to him. Wyatt gripped it with both hands and jumped. He swung high out over the river, then came flying back. As his feet hit the ground, he said, "What a rush!"

Taking the rope, T.J. leaped. At the height of his swing, however, the rope came off the branch. He cartwheeled into the water. Wyatt laughed as his friend crawled up the riverbank, drenched.

"Well, the tree was strong enough," T.J. said, "but your knot wasn't!"

A person who trusts God is like a tree drawing strength from a river. That tree isn't afraid of heat or drought, and it's always lush and fruitful. Where do you send your roots to find strength? Are you drawing it from your faith in God?

Live It!

Thinking about God's Word helps you trust God and draw strength from him. Draw a big, beautiful tree with many roots. Each week, learn a new Bible verse. Then write its reference on a root.

Someone Special

As [Jesus] was praying, the appearance of his face changed, and his clothes became as bright as a flash of lightning.

Luke 9:29

On a warm summer evening, Juan and Anita were sitting on the patio with their parents. A bolt of lightning lit up the sky.

"Did you see that?" Juan said.

His father nodded. "I sure did. Looks like a storm's rolling in."

Anita got up and walked to the edge of the patio. "I love the way it feels just before a thunderstorm," she said. "The air tingles, like there's all this energy in it!"

As lightning flashed again, their dad stood up too. "Well, there's a lot of power in lightning. It's not just a pretty light show." He gathered up their drinks and snacks, adding, "Which means we'd better head inside!"

Do some of your friends think Jesus is nobody special? Tell them about the time he showed the disciples his glory. They saw his face shine like the sun, and his clothes blaze like lightning! Tell your friends other amazing stories too, like the time Jesus calmed a storm with three words. (See Mark 4:39.) When you think of all the mind-boggling things Jesus did, it's clear he's someone special indeed.

Live It!

Have a friendly debate. Invite a friend to tell you the reasons why he or she thinks Jesus isn't special. Then tell your friend about Jesus' miracles. Can you convince your friend that Jesus *is* someone special?

Love That Spans Light-Years

Your love, O Lord, reaches to the heavens, your
faithfulness to the skies.

Psalm 36:5

Carlie looked up at the observatory as she and her father approached it. The building had a large dome with a slot in its side. Indoors, a man greeted them. "Hi, John. Hi, Carlie. Glad you could make it. The sky is nice and clear tonight."

Shaking his hand, Carlie's father said, "Hello, Ned. Carlie, this is my friend Mr. Thomas. He's a member of the astronomical society."

Carlie shook hands with Mr. Thomas. He grinned. "Let's go have a look, shall we?" He led them upstairs, where a giant telescope was mounted inside the dome.

Making some adjustments, he invited Carlie to look into the eyepiece. She saw a beautiful cluster of stars. "Ooh, it's the Pleiades! They look so close!" she said.

Mr. Thomas laughed. "Actually, they're 440 light-years away."

Carlie kept gazing through the telescope. "Wow. It looks like I could reach up and touch them!"

God's love *can* reach the stars. His love is so big, it would be measured in light-years, if it could be measured. If you ever wonder how much God loves you, imagine him stretching out his arms across the universe, saying, "This much!" When you're worshiping God, stretch out your arms too, showing him how much you love him in return.

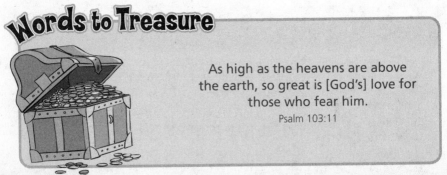

Words to Treasure

As high as the heavens are above
the earth, so great is [God's] love for
those who fear him.
Psalm 103:11

Go-Karts and Real Cars

Jesus called the children to him and said, "Let the little children come to me, and do not hinder them, for the kingdom of God belongs to such as these."

Luke 18:16

Logan's dad was winning as they raced around the track on go-karts. Logan kept trying to pass him. But his father hugged the curves to prevent it. Risking a spinout, Logan took the last curve fast and wide. They were side by side coming out of the turn. Logan floored the pedal, pulling ahead just before the finish line.

"Nice race!" said his dad as they climbed out of their go-karts.

When they got back to the car, Logan slid behind the steering wheel. "I'll drive, since I'm better at it," he joked.

His father laughed and shook his head. "Nice try, kiddo. Move over!"

Is there an adults-only version of God's kingdom? Do kids only get the go-kart version? No way! There's only one kingdom of God, and you're part of it. Your prayers aren't go-kart prayers. They're real prayers. Your Bible isn't a go-kart Bible. It's a real Bible, full of real truth and real wisdom and real power. When children go to Jesus, he makes them real members of God's kingdom.

Live It!

When it comes to faith, don't just ride in the backseat of your parents' car. Pick up your Bible when you're alone. Pray when no one's around. Build your own relationship with Jesus!

Making Blueberries

> God said, "Let the land produce vegetation: seed-bearing plants and trees on the land that bear fruit."
>
> Genesis 1:11

The old car bumped over a two-track road at the U-pick blueberry farm. As Shawn's grandfather drove between the fields, Shawn kept hearing loud screeches. "What's that noise, Grandpa?"

Parking beside the road, his grandfather said, "Those are devices that make hawk calls, scaring away birds so they don't eat the berries." They grabbed their buckets, got out, and walked into the field. Shawn spotted a bush full of big, ripe blueberries. His grandfather picked one and admired it. "Aren't blueberries amazing, Shawn? I always praise God for them. They look great, taste wonderful, and give your body energy. No wonder birds want them!" He chuckled. "Plus, each blueberry has seeds that grow into plants that produce more blueberries. All the berries on this bush came from one little blueberry. And God made them all." He popped it into his mouth and grinned. "C'mon, let's fill our buckets and get back, so your grandmother can bake that pie she promised us!"

Only God can make a blueberry. Or any kind of fruit. Or other marvelous things such as flowers and trees. Think of all the wonderful things only he can create. Butterflies, bumblebees ... even birds. Not to mention people! Whenever you enjoy something only God could have made, give him praise.

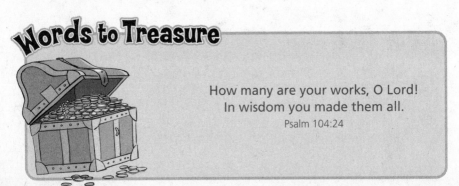

Words to Treasure

How many are your works, O Lord!
In wisdom you made them all.
Psalm 104:24

He's Here!

"I am with you," declares the Lord.

Jeremiah 46:28

Standing inside the ice cream truck, Nolan handed out frozen treats to customers. The truck's owner had asked Nolan's dad to make his rounds while he went on vacation. "How about a Nutty Buddy?" Nolan suggested to a little girl. He pointed at the pictures on the truck. "We also have Popsicles, Choco Tacos, Push-Ups ..."

The girl finally ordered a Klondike. Nolan handed her one. "Thanks," she said, giving him her money.

Nolan smiled. "You're welcome!" His dad drove around the corner. More kids were standing there. "Everywhere we go, they're waiting for us!" Nolan said.

His dad chuckled. "Sure. The minute they hear the music, they know the ice cream truck's here."

Unlike the ice cream truck, God is always near. But are you always aware he's with you? In the 1600s there lived a monk named Brother Lawrence. He taught others how to be mindful that God was with them all the time. His teachings were put into a book called *The Practice of the Presence of God*. You too can practice being aware of God's presence. It's more than just knowing God's with you. It's *sensing* he's there, and sharing every moment of your life with him.

Live It!

Find ways to stay aware of God's presence. For example, start using music kind of like an ice cream truck does. Everywhere you go, hum a song that reminds you God is near!

Crossing the Mighty Mac

[Jesus said,] "No one comes to the Father except through me."

John 14:6

J ared, come over on the grated lane," Emily said, staring between her feet. "You can see the water way below us!"

Her brother stayed in the asphalt lane. "I'm good here."

They and their parents were with a crowd of sixty thousand people walking across the Mackinac Bridge, one of the largest suspension bridges in the world. Today was Labor Day, the one day each year when pedestrians were allowed on the "Mighty Mac." Half of the lanes on the bridge had been closed so people could walk the five miles between Michigan's two peninsulas. Jared gazed at a huge tower holding up the thick cables that supported the bridge. "I can't wait to reach the other side," he said.

"What's wrong, your feet tired?" his mom teased.

Jared smiled. "Uh-uh. I just want to get the certificate that proves I made it across!"

Just as a bridge connects two pieces of land, Jesus connects people to God. Because Adam and Eve disobeyed God, all people were separated from him. Jesus is the bridge that makes it possible for everyone to return to God. If God seems far away from you, ask Jesus to take you back to him.

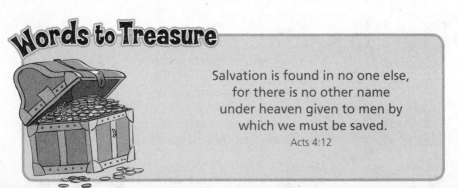

Words to Treasure

Salvation is found in no one else, for there is no other name under heaven given to men by which we must be saved.

Acts 4:12

God's Theme Music

It is good to praise the Lord and make music to your name, O Most High.

Psalm 92:1

D avin's dad backed the minivan into a spot at the drive-in theater. Opening the hatch, Davin unloaded folding chairs for his parents. Then he and his sister, Carrie, spread out sleeping bags in the back of the van. Meanwhile their mom went to the concession stand. She returned just as *Star Wars: The Empire Strikes Back* was starting. They all settled in to watch.

A huge spaceship glided across the screen. Dark, threatening music began playing. "You hear that music every time Darth Vader shows up," Davin said.

His father nodded. "Yeah. It has to be the greatest theme music ever made for a movie villain. That music really conveys how evil he is!"

Have you ever wondered what theme music for God would sound like? He's so good that it's impossible for one piece of music to describe him. Maybe that's why so many different kinds of praise and worship songs have been written for God. Memorize some songs that remind you of all the good things about God. Sing them to praise and worship him. That'll remind you how great and awesome he is!

Live It!

Pick one of God's good qualities. Then make up a melody to express it. Use any musical instrument you have at home. Be creative! Add some words, and use your song to praise God.

Big Boat

The Lord knows how to rescue godly men.

2 Peter 2:9

Douglas stood on the pier at Ludington, Michigan. He watched as all kinds of vehicles paraded along the pier and onto the SS *Badger*. That was a large ferry ship getting ready to cross Lake Michigan. Cars, motorcycles, motor homes, buses, and trucks went up a ramp and through huge doors in the back of the ship. "There goes our car!" shouted Douglas's sister, Cindy.

Douglas said, "Doesn't this remind you of Noah's ark? It's like watching the animals get on before the flood."

His father looked up from a pamphlet he was reading. "Funny you should mention that. This ship is 410 feet long, almost the same size as Noah's ark."

Just then the ship's whistle blew, and Douglas's mom said, "We'd better get on board."

Looking up, Douglas joked, "Yeah. It's starting to look like rain!"

The tale of Noah's ark proves that God is able to rescue his people. Other Bible stories prove this too. God saved Moses and the Israelites from the Egyptian army. He saved Daniel from the lions' den. He saved the apostle Paul from a shipwreck. Through Jesus' death on the cross, God saved all of his people from sin. No matter what troubles you may have, God is able to save you. Whenever you face a crisis, trust him to rescue you.

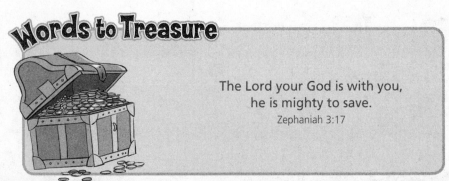

Words to Treasure

The Lord your God is with you,
he is mighty to save.
Zephaniah 3:17

Wind Power

"Not by might nor by power, but by my Spirit,"
says the Lord Almighty.

Zechariah 4:6

Byron let out fifty feet of line as Jeanette held his new delta wing stunt kite. It had two lines Byron could use to make it do loops and dives. "When I say go, toss it up," he said. Jeanette nodded. There wasn't much wind, but Byron wanted to try the kite out. "All right ... Go!"

Jeanette flung the kite into the air, and Byron ran. The kite went up a bit, swerving back and forth. But when Byron stopped running, it fell to the ground. As Jeanette came running up, Byron felt the breeze grow stronger. "Let's try again!" he said.

This time, all Jeanette had to do was lift up the kite and let it go. Byron just stood there holding the lines, watching the wind carry his kite high into the sky.

You can't do anything worthwhile just by trying really hard if God's Spirit isn't helping you. But if God's Spirit is behind you, blowing like the wind, the smallest thing you do will achieve a lot. Always ask God to help you do whatever he wants you to do!

People in Bible Times

God wanted the Israelites to build a special tent for him to dwell in. So God filled Bezalel with his Spirit. That gave Bezalel the skills to work with metal, wood, and cloth. It also enabled him to teach others these skills.

Now and Then

No eye has seen, no ear has heard, no mind has conceived what God has prepared for those who love him.

1 Corinthians 2:9

In the city, Mandy spotted kids romping in a splash fountain. "Mom, can Gary and I play in the fountain too?" she asked.

Her mother hesitated. "I don't know … You guys aren't wearing your swimsuits, like those children are." But since it was so hot out, she finally said yes.

Joyfully they kicked off their shoes and joined the other kids. Mandy put her foot over the water shooting up from the sidewalk. Gary ran through the mist as water arched overhead. By the time they had to leave, they were soaked. Their mother laughed. "If you guys liked that, you're going to love the new water park the city's building. I hear it'll be fantastic!"

Being part of God's kingdom on earth is wonderful. But God has something even more awesome in store for you. In this world you can talk with God through prayer and enjoy his blessings every day. But in heaven you'll talk with him face-to-face and enjoy much greater blessings. There will be things there that you can't even imagine. Life with God here on earth is really good, but heaven will be amazingly better!

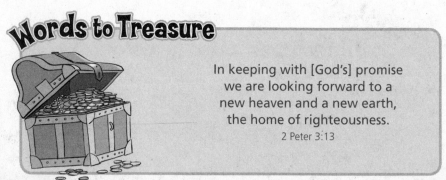

Words to Treasure

In keeping with [God's] promise we are looking forward to a new heaven and a new earth, the home of righteousness.
2 Peter 3:13

Recharging Your Batteries

Because so many people were coming and going that [the apostles] did not even have a chance to eat, [Jesus] said to them, "Come with me by yourselves to a quiet place and get some rest."

Mark 6:31

The car-hopping contest is starting!" Buddy said. He was at the annual car cruise. Once a year, thousands of classic autos paraded up and down the city's main street. In nearby parking lots, there were car shows, concerts, and burnout contests. Buddy and his father found a spot to watch the car-hopping competition. "Look at that!" Buddy shouted. A souped-up car was bouncing on its front wheels. The car kept going higher and higher, until it was bouncing six feet off the ground!

After the contest, they looked at the car up close. "See all those batteries in the trunk?" Buddy's dad said. "They power the hydraulic system that makes the car hop."

Counting twelve large batteries, Buddy replied, "I'll bet it takes some time to charge them all up!"

Like a battery, your spirit needs to be recharged now and then. Jesus will reenergize your spirit if you spend time alone with him, resting. Make time each day for some quiet moments with the Lord. You can read devotions, study your Bible, and pray. Your spirit is powered up when it's rested up!

Words to Treasure

[Jesus said,] "Come to me, all you who are weary and burdened, and I will give you rest."
Matthew 11:28

Using God's Things

The earth is the Lord's, and everything in it.

Psalm 24:1

Honk! Honk! "What's that?" Brock asked. He and Melissa were watching TV after school.

She went to the window. "It's Dad! And he's driving a convertible!" They ran out to the driveway.

Their dad was sitting in a bright-red sports car with its top down. "Hi, guys," he said. "It's so nice out, I left work early. My friend let me borrow his car, so we're going cruising to the shore! Get your mom, and let's go."

Melissa ran back into the house while Brock walked around the car, admiring it. When his sister and mom came out, his dad said, "Get in, everybody!" Brock started to climb over the door, but his dad stopped him. "Whoa there. This car belongs to someone else. So we have to take good care of it and use it responsibly."

The Bible says that everything you have belongs to God. That includes your body, your home, and your possessions. You're not the owner; you're a "steward." God is letting you use his things. He's trusting you to take care of them and use them for his glory.

A steward was a servant who managed his master's things. Joseph became a steward in Egypt. His master put Joseph in charge of everything he owned. He expected Joseph to care for it and make good use of it.

The Family Tree

[Jesus] was the son, so it was thought, of Joseph, the son of Heli, the son of Matthat, ... the son of Seth, the son of Adam, the son of God.

Luke 3:23–24, 38

Adam and his parents were at the park for the big family reunion. In the pavilion, Adam spotted a poster. "Look, it's the family tree! Let's find our names."

His mom traced her finger along the lines. "Here we are! There's your name, Adam. And here are your grandparents and your cousins." Adam liked learning how everyone in his family was connected. When he asked about names he didn't know, his parents pointed out people. Then they explained how those people were related to him.

Soon his head started spinning. "I'll never remember all this!"

Chuckling, his dad said, "I can't keep it all straight either. But your great-grandfather over there—he knows everybody!"

Some parts of the Bible are basically family trees. They're called *genealogies*. These may seem boring to read at first. But every name in them represents a person God knew and loved. God knows and loves you too, and he's glad you're part of *his* family tree. That one includes everyone who has become his child through faith in Jesus.

Live It!

With your parents' help, draw your family tree. Using a colored marker, circle the names of your relatives who believe in Jesus. Pray that the others will join God's family soon.

The Center of the Universe

[Jesus said,] "I am the way and the truth and the life."

John 14:6

Under a starry sky, Carlie watched her father put his camera on a tripod. "What're you doing?" she asked.

Aiming the camera, he replied, "Taking a time-exposed photograph. Have a look." Carlie peered at the camera's screen. In the center was Polaris, the brightest star in the Little Dipper. Her father said, "I'm leaving the shutter open all night. Tomorrow you'll see something interesting." The next morning, he showed her the picture. Polaris looked normal. But all the other stars appeared as white lines circling it.

Carlie said, "Wow, this makes Polaris look like the center of the universe!"

Her father grinned. "That's because it's the North Star. As the earth spins, the other stars seem to rotate in the sky. But Polaris is directly over the North Pole, so it doesn't move. That's why sailors and others use it to find their way. It always points to true north."

On a time-exposed photo, Polaris may look like the center of the universe. But Jesus is the real center of everything. He always has been, and he always will be. That's what he meant when he said, "I am the truth." Keep following Jesus, and you'll always be headed in the right direction. He's the way to eternal life.

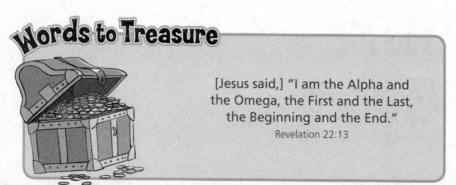

Words to Treasure

[Jesus said,] "I am the Alpha and the Omega, the First and the Last, the Beginning and the End."
Revelation 22:13

Glow in the Dark

God, who said, "Let light shine out of darkness," made his light shine in our hearts.

2 Corinthians 4:6

Coby and his family were at the hot-air balloon festival. Night was falling, and everyone was waiting for the "balloon illume." Up ahead, twenty-five fully-inflated balloons were tied to the ground. They were dark shapes against the purple sky.

"Good evening, folks," said an announcer. "It's time to illuminate the night!" He began a countdown, and Coby and the rest of the crowd joined in. "… three … two … one … Light 'em up!" With a loud whoosh, the balloonists fired their burners. Flames shot up, and the balloons glowed colorfully.

"They look like huge night-lights!" said Coby's sister, Jasmine.

The balloonists began firing the burners in random bursts. As the balloons flickered on and off in the darkness, Coby laughed. "Now they look like giant fireflies!"

God first shone light into the darkness right before he created the earth. He did it again when he sent Jesus here to be the light of the world. Now he's doing it through Christians just like you. Every believer has God's Spirit glowing inside his or her heart. Are you letting people see that light in you?

People in Bible Times

The apostle Paul and Barnabas traveled far. Filled with the Holy Spirit, they shone God's light around the world. Many people were touched by that light, and their hearts also began to shine.

Close Enough?

> Whoever keeps the whole law and yet stumbles at just one point is guilty of breaking all of it.
>
> James 2:10

At the big family reunion in the park, Adam's uncle was teaching him how to play horseshoes.

"A horseshoe that surrounds the stake is called a ringer. It's worth three points," he told Adam. "A horseshoe leaning against the stake is worth two points. The horseshoe closest to the stake is worth one point. Got it?"

Adam nodded. "Got it. Let's play!"

His uncle went first. One of his horseshoes hit the stake but spun off. The other landed near the stake. Adam threw his first horseshoe. It came up short, so he threw the second one harder. That one hit the sand just in front of the stake.

"Good shot," his uncle said. "I think that's close enough to score a point!"

Being close to the target counts in horseshoes, but not when it comes to obeying God. You may think it's good enough to follow all of God's rules except one. It's not! Anytime you disobey God, it's a big deal to him. But God is gracious, and if you confess your sin, he'll forgive you. Then Jesus will "justify" you. That's like moving your horseshoes right over the stake so you get a perfect score.

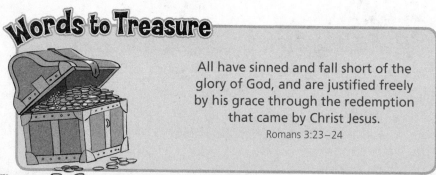

Words to Treasure

All have sinned and fall short of the glory of God, and are justified freely by his grace through the redemption that came by Christ Jesus.

Romans 3:23–24

Working with Good Materials

Each one should be careful how he builds.... If what he has built survives, he will receive his reward.

1 Corinthians 3:10, 14

B obby walked along the shore, admiring the entries in the sand sculpture contest. "Look at that sea turtle!" said his sister, Claire.

Their father gazed at the giant sculpture. "How do they do that? I can't even make a decent sand castle!"

Laughing, their mom said, "It takes talent, I guess." Claire enjoyed the sculptures of ocean creatures best, like the starfish, seahorse, and octopus. But Bobby preferred more exciting ones, like the race car, spaceship, and train.

"What'll happen to the sculptures after today?" Claire asked.

Their father raised his eyebrows. "Well, they're made of sand. Pretty soon they'll turn back into beach."

Grinning, Bobby said, "If I made a sculpture, I'd use metal, so it would last!"

Serving God is like creating a beautiful sculpture. So use the best "materials" you can! In other words, give God your best effort. Not doing your best for him is like building a sculpture out of sand, with sticks and seashells for decorations. A sand sculpture isn't worth much and doesn't last. Doing your best to serve God is like making a sculpture out of gold, decorated with precious gemstones. A gold sculpture is worth a lot and lasts a long, long time. God rewards people who serve him with that kind of effort.

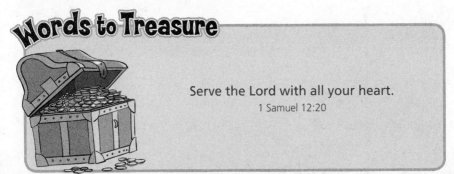

Words to Treasure

Serve the Lord with all your heart.
1 Samuel 12:20

Getting Out the Good Stuff

How sweet are your words to my taste, [O Lord,] sweeter than honey to my mouth!

Psalm 119:103

Wearing a beekeeper's hat, Patricia watched her uncle. He was taking honeycombs out of one of his beehives. First he used a special can to blow smoke on the hive.

"What's that for?" Patricia asked.

As he pulled out the honeycombs, her uncle replied, "It calms the bees down." Patricia followed him into a small building. With a big knife, he cut off the wax caps that sealed the honeycombs. Then he loaded the honeycombs into a machine. It spun them fast, removing the honey. The golden liquid was filtered as it flowed out.

"Try some," he said, filling a little paper cup. Patricia tasted the honey, and it was delicious.

Beekeepers go to a lot of trouble to get honey out of a honeycomb. Are you trying hard to get the good stuff out of your Bible? It's full of great things, like God's precious promises, inspiring stories, and wise rules for living. Don't let your Bible just sit on your bookshelf. Crack it open, and do your best to get everything you can out of it.

Live It!

Buy some honeycomb, and try eating the honey right out of it. Then do the following things to get the good stuff out of your Bible: Read it. Study it. Think about it. Memorize it. Believe it. Pray it. And live it!

The Mansion

[Jesus told his disciples,] "In my Father's house are many rooms.... I am going there to prepare a place for you."

John 14:2

Dillan and Leanne followed their parents through the beautiful mansion. They were at the Biltmore House in Asheville, North Carolina. Although it was finished in 1895, it was still the largest home in America. "Can you believe the size of this house?" said Dillan's dad as they admired the huge library. "Two hundred and fifty rooms. Sixty-five fireplaces. A banquet hall, a billiard room, and a music room. It even has elevators and an indoor swimming pool!"

"Don't forget the bowling alley," Dillan said, grinning.

Shaking her head, his mom said, "I can't get over how big the bedrooms are."

Leanne gazed at all the polished woodwork in the library, and at the thousands of books it contained. "I like the garden best, with all the stone walls and statues." Leaving the library, the family continued their tour. They reached the observatory, atop the main tower. From there they could see woods, meadows, a river, and mountains.

Dillan said, "I'd love to live in a place like this!"

Have you ever really thought about what heaven will be like? The Bible doesn't reveal everything about it. But you won't be living on a cloud, that's for sure. God's home will be an exciting, wonderful place. And he has a room in it just for you!

Words to Treasure

I will dwell in the house of the Lord forever.
Psalm 23:6

Released!

The Lord sets prisoners free.

Psalm 146:7

Donny shouted as he and his dad sped down the first hill of the roller coaster. Then they hit a loop, and the world turned upside down. Strong g-forces pushed Donny's body into his seat. Racing into a downward spiral, they went around and around, faster and faster. Then they flew over some camelback humps. "Air time!" Donny's father hollered. Donny laughed, feeling weightless at the top of each hill. Finally the train of cars started slowing down. Then all at once it halted, close to the ground but far from the station.

"Hey, why did we stop?" Donny asked.

His dad looked around. "I don't know." There they sat, held firmly in their seats by the shoulder harnesses. Donny began to feel trapped.

Finally a ride operator came to talk to the passengers. He explained that a safety system had automatically stopped the train. "Everything's okay," he said. "A maintenance man will restart the ride soon." Minutes later the cars began moving again. They slid into the station, the harnesses lifted, and Donny and his dad climbed out.

Before you became a Christian, you were trapped. You couldn't get out of sin. But when you put your faith in Jesus, he set you free! Don't let the Devil convince you that you're helpless to stop sinning. You're not his prisoner anymore, and with the Holy Spirit's help you can obey God's commands.

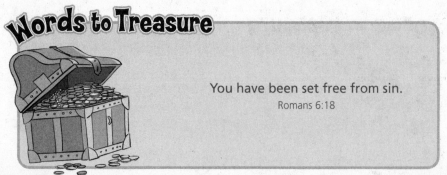

Words to Treasure

You have been set free from sin.
Romans 6:18

Food Chains

Everyone who sins is a slave to sin.

John 8:34

Jody put down her copy of *The Lion, the Witch and the Wardrobe.* "Mom, can we go on the Internet and look up the recipe for Turkish delight?"

Her mother glanced up from a magazine. "Why?"

Bouncing off the couch, Jody said, "Well, the White Witch gave Edmund some in Narnia. He liked it so much, he became her slave to get more. I wanna know what it tastes like!"

Her mom laid down the magazine. "Okay. It might be fun to make some." They found the recipe easily. Soon the kitchen counter was covered with ingredients. They boiled a few, added others, and poured the mixture into a pan to cool. Then they cut the soft, sticky candy into squares. Finally, they rolled the squares in powdered sugar. Jody tried a piece. "What do you think?" her mom asked.

Jody raised her eyebrows. "It's pretty good. But I wouldn't be anyone's slave for it!"

If you keep doing the same sin over and over, you've become a slave to that sin. It has a hold on you the way Turkish delight had a hold on Edmund. The good news is, Jesus can set you free. (See John 8:36.) Ask him to help you escape from the sin that has you all tied up. (See Hebrews 12:1.) That way, you can live the way God wants you to live.

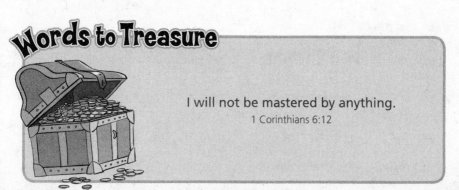

Words to Treasure

I will not be mastered by anything.
1 Corinthians 6:12

Chasing the Wind

Whoever loves money never has money enough.

Ecclesiastes 5:10

Danny and his mother walked into the sporting goods store to buy him some soccer cleats and shin guards. "What's that?" Danny asked. Near the front window was a glass booth with paper money swirling inside!

An employee said, "It's our 'Instant Rebate' program. If you spend over fifty dollars, you can go in the money booth for one minute. You get to grab as many dollar bills as you can."

Danny looked at his mom. "Can I do it?"

His mom laughed. "Sure, if we spend enough."

When they checked out, the employee let Danny inside the booth. Grabbing here and there, he tried to snatch the bills out of the air. When the buzzer sounded, he stepped out. "I got eleven!"

It would be fun to get into a money booth and try to grab as much cash as you could. But don't love money so much that you spend your life chasing it! King Solomon called this meaningless, like chasing the wind. He said that people who live this way are never satisfied. Solomon knew the real purpose of life. It's to "fear God and keep his commandments" (Ecclesiastes 12:13).

People in Bible Times

God told King Solomon to ask him for whatever he wanted. Solomon could've asked for money, but instead he asked for wisdom. God was pleased, so he gave Solomon great wisdom and great riches.

Filled with Hope

May the God of hope fill you with all joy and peace as you trust in him, so that you may overflow with hope by the power of the Holy Spirit.

Romans 15:13

Wow!" Justin said, looking around. He and his sister, Lydia, were at the World of Coca-Cola museum in Atlanta, Georgia. They'd just entered the "Bottle Works" section. In front of them was a huge red and white machine. Overhead, hundreds of glass bottles were moving in single-file lines. Some bottles were empty, some full.

Lydia laughed. "They look like little people marching around!" The kids approached the machine for a closer look. Bottles were winding all around it, going up and down, this way and that. At the top, empty bottles stopped under long silver spouts, which filled them.

"This is great," Justin said. "But let's head to the 'Taste It' section soon. Watching this is making me thirsty!"

Many people in the world are walking around empty. They don't have any joy, peace, or hope inside. That's because they don't have a relationship with God. Aren't you glad you do? Keep trusting your heavenly Father. Let him fill you up each day with joy, peace, and hope. And tell others about how they can know God through faith in Jesus. That way, they can be filled up too.

Words to Treasure

Hope does not disappoint us, because God has poured out his love into our hearts by the Holy Spirit, whom he has given us.

Romans 5:5

Horsepower

> Do you give the horse his strength or clothe his neck with a flowing mane?
>
> Job 39:19

The horse Debbie was riding splashed across the stream that ran through her uncle's ranch in Montana. Cold water soaked Debbie's jeans, but she didn't care. She turned to her cousins Laura and Ben, riding behind her. "Come on, you two. Keep up!"

Debbie's horse was a dappled black steed named Starry Knight. She urged it into a gallop, riding fast just for the joy of it.

Debbie loved horses. She was always reading about horses, drawing horses, and collecting model horses for her bookshelf. Once, when she and her parents traveled to Italy, she'd begged them to take her to the city of Milan. She wanted to see the twenty-four-foot-tall sculpture called *Il Cavallo*, which means "The Horse." Marveling at the huge statue, she'd been impressed by the artist who designed it. But now, leaning into Starry Knight's mane, feeling the power in the animal's legs, Debbie thought about the One who created *real* horses.

"God, you're awesome!" she whispered.

Give glory to God daily for the beautiful world he created. Praise him for all the wonderful creatures he made, and for everything on this earth that you love.

Live It!

Make a poster illustrating Psalm 148, which lists many things God created. Hang the poster in your bedroom to remind you to praise God for all the wonders he's made.

Riling Things Up

A gentle answer turns away wrath, but a harsh word stirs up anger.

Proverbs 15:1

Chris handed his father a large plastic bottle. "Here's the soda you wanted. What are you gonna do with it?" Chris knew his dad was up to something. He was always up to something! Chris's father was a science teacher, and Chris often helped him try out experiments. At the moment, they were standing in their backyard.

In answer to Chris's question, his dad held out a roll of Mentos mints. "Want one?" Chris took one of the candies. "You're gonna love this experiment," said Chris's dad. He popped a mint into his mouth. "It shows a process called nucleation. You know how the carbon dioxide in soda forms into bubbles? This happens faster when you add something with the right kind of surface. It gives the bubbles something to form on." Opening the bottle, he dropped in the rest of his Mentos. The soda fizzed and erupted, creating a geyser three feet high.

Putting harsh words into a person's ear makes anger erupt. But putting in gentle words has the opposite effect. It calms the anger down. Listen to yourself as you talk to your siblings, parents, teachers, and friends. Are you speaking harsh words that cause anger, or gentle words that produce peace?

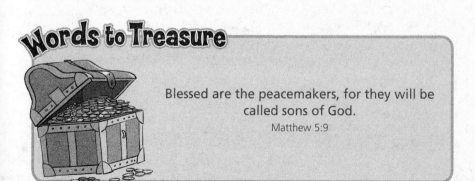

Words to Treasure

Blessed are the peacemakers, for they will be called sons of God.
Matthew 5:9

Getting in Synch

How good and pleasant it is when brothers
live together in unity!

Psalm 133:1

At the church picnic, the pastor dropped his hand. "Go!"

Calvin sprang from the starting line—and fell flat on his face. His brother went down on top of him.

"Get up!" Calvin said, pushing him off.

"Sorry," Brent said. They struggled to their feet. It wasn't easy, because Calvin's right ankle was tied to Brent's left one. This was a three-legged race.

"Listen!" Calvin told Brent. "We have to get in synch." He threw his arm around Brent's shoulder, saying, "Put your arm around me. Now, on one, we'll step with our free leg. On two, we'll step with the leg that's tied. Ready? One … two … one … two …"

They hobbled awkwardly at first, but then they got into the rhythm. And they started passing the kids who were still tripping each other up.

When you're part of a family, you can't live as if you're alone. You and your siblings are closely connected. Unless you work together, nobody will get anywhere. Find ways to cooperate with your brothers and sisters instead of competing against them. Life will be much better!

Did You Know?

The word *unity* means "oneness." Your eye and your foot belong to the same body. Brothers and sisters are part of the same family. Christians around the world all belong to the same church—God's.

Chores before S'mores

If a man will not work, he shall not eat.

2 Thessalonians 3:10

Debbie watched her uncle light the large grill. She and her parents were staying at his ranch in Montana. After riding horses all day with her cousins Laura and Ben, Debbie was starving. "What are we having?" she asked.

Her uncle smiled. "Steak, potatoes, green beans, and biscuits. And s'mores for dessert."

"Mmm!" Debbie said. "When do we eat?"

Her uncle's eyes twinkled under his cowboy hat. "As soon as you three take care of the chores that need doing."

Ben sighed. "Come on, Debbie. The rule around here is, No work, no grub." Debbie helped her cousins put fresh straw in the horses' stalls. While Ben gave the animals some oats, she and Laura filled their buckets with water. The kids were just finishing when the dinner bell rang.

Your home is just like a ranch. There are chores to do! Your parents work hard to keep a roof over your head. Give them a hand by doing your part around the house without complaining or being reminded to do it. This will bless your parents and help keep things at your "ranch" running smoothly. Also, doing your chores diligently will help you develop good work habits. That'll be important later in life. When you're out on your own, you're going to want a good meal now and then!

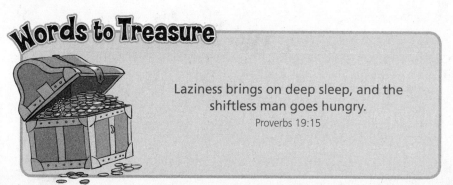

Words to Treasure

Laziness brings on deep sleep, and the
shiftless man goes hungry.
Proverbs 19:15

All Suited Up

> [God's] divine power has given us everything
> we need for life and godliness.
>
> 2 Peter 1:3

It was Wade's first year playing in a youth football league, and this was his first game.

Before leaving home, he'd gotten all suited up. He'd put on his pads, his uniform, and his cleats. Everything except his helmet. Wearing all that equipment made him feel big and strong.

When he and his father arrived at the field, Wade jumped out of the car. Then he stopped. "Oh, man. I forgot my mouth guard! The coach won't put me in the game without that."

Closing the car door, his dad laughed. "Relax. I put it on your helmet while you got dressed. See?"

Wade checked his helmet. The mouth guard was hanging from a strap attached to the face mask. "Thanks, Dad," he said, putting the helmet on.

"You have everything you need," his dad said. "Now go play some football!"

God commands you to be holy, like him. Then he gives you everything you need to live a righteous life. God has suited you up. He's given you all the necessary gear. So get out there and be godly!

Did You Know?

God puts his Spirit in Christians. This gives them the power they need to be godly. But Christians have to *use* that power. They do that by choosing to be holy instead of sinful.

Learning the Hard Way

The Lord disciplines those he loves, as a father the son he delights in.

Proverbs 3:12

At Sleeping Bear Dunes National Lakeshore, Casey stood on a high bluff overlooking Lake Michigan. Staring at the shoreline 450 feet below, Casey heard a whoop. She turned to see two teenagers running down the steep, sandy slope. They went all the way to the bottom, laughing and hopping and sliding. Casey looked at her mom. "Can I go down?"

Her mom said, "No, sweetie. There's a sign telling people not to do that, because it damages the dunes and getting back up is very hard." Looking down, she shook her head. "Those two have a rough climb ahead of them." After they watched the teenagers struggle awhile, they drove to the sand dune that people were allowed to climb. "Come on," Casey's mom said, closing the car door. "I'll race you!" They scrambled to the top of the 150-foot dune. Then they rolled down, giggling and getting sand all over their clothes and hair.

God's rules are like signs showing you where he wants you to go and where he doesn't. If you break his rules, he'll forgive you. But he'll also discipline you by making you face some consequences for your actions. That's because, like a parent, he loves you and wants what's best for you. Follow God's rules—it's easier than learning obedience the hard way!

Words to Treasure

God disciplines us for our good, that we may share in his holiness.

Hebrews 12:10

Dunked by Doubt

> Take up the shield of faith, with which you can extinguish all the flaming arrows of the evil one.
>
> Ephesians 6:16

Calvin sat on a flat seat. He was surrounded by a protective chain-link fence. But there was a round target beside him, and his feet were dangling over water. "You're going down, little brother!" Brent shouted, picking up a baseball.

Calvin laughed. "Give me your best shot!" The dunk tank was the most popular attraction at the church picnic. After the church members dunked their pastor, people started challenging one another to sit in it. So of course Calvin and Brent had dared each other. As the crowd watched, Brent wound up. *Thunk!* His fastball hit the tarp behind the target. "High and outside!" Calvin taunted. "Only two more throws!" Brent hurled another ball, this time barely missing. Calvin started feeling anxious about the target. But he didn't let it show. "Is that all you got?" he said. Seconds later he received his answer. Brent's throw hit the bull's-eye, and the seat collapsed, dumping Calvin into the water. He came up spluttering. "Okay, bro. Now it's *your* turn!"

The Devil tries to knock you down by shooting flaming arrows at you. Hold up the shield of faith! And don't offer the Devil a target by doubting God in any way. As long as you keep believing and trusting God, Satan's shots can't take you down.

Words to Treasure

Stop doubting and believe.
John 20:27

Flying Blind

These commands are a lamp, this teaching is a
light, and the corrections of discipline are the
way to life.

Proverbs 6:23

Sitting in the copilot's seat, Hannah held the control wheel of the Skyhawk.
She loved flying with her dad, who sometimes let her steer the small plane.
"Try keeping us straight and level without looking outside," he challenged.

Closing her eyes, Hannah giggled. "Okay." Her sense of balance told her she
was on course.

But when her dad said, "Open your eyes," she saw she was banking left and
diving toward the ground! As she leveled the plane, he said, "Now watch the attitude indicator. It shows the plane's attitude, or position, in the sky." He tapped an
instrument on the dashboard. It had two short lines representing the airplane's
wings, and a longer line representing the horizon. Hannah stared at it, making
sure the "wings" didn't tip right or left or move up or down. When she looked up,
the plane was flying perfectly.

If you trust your senses to tell you what's right and wrong, you'll make bad
choices and get into trouble. (See Proverbs 14:12.) God's commands are like an
attitude indicator. They keep you flying safe and headed in the right direction.

Life in Bible Times

During the time of the judges, the
Israelites did whatever seemed best
to them. That kept getting them off
track. They were following their own
feelings instead of obeying God's
commands. (See Judges 21:25.)

Chasing Cows

> They worshiped idols, though the Lord had said, "You shall not do this."
>
> 2 Kings 17:12

Rodney eagerly lined up with other kids in the outdoor arena. A rodeo clown spoke into a microphone. "Cowpokes, it's time for the calf scramble! At my signal, five calves will be released. Grab a ribbon off their tail and earn ten bucks. Ready to rustle?" He gave the signal, hollering, "Giddyup!"

A gate opened, and the calves scampered out. Rodney and the other kids ran after them. As the audience cheered, the calves scattered. The kids jostled each other, pursuing the animals. Rodney saw two girls collide and a boy fall in the dirt.

One calf, dodging five children, headed toward Rodney. "I've got him!" he yelled. He grabbed its neck, but the animal dragged him halfway across the arena. When the event was over, Rodney brushed himself off and walked away, empty-handed.

The Israelites had a habit of turning away from God and chasing idols. Idols were carved or molded statues, such as golden calves, that represented fake, powerless gods. Today, idols can be anything you run after harder than you run after God. This includes things like money, toys, or trophies. Pursue God hardest of all! Only he can fill you with true joy. Other things leave you empty.

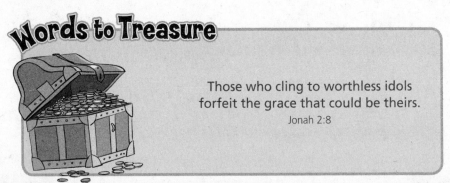

Words to Treasure

Those who cling to worthless idols forfeit the grace that could be theirs.
Jonah 2:8

Setting Up Camp

Lot … pitched his tents near Sodom. Now the men of Sodom were wicked and were sinning greatly against the Lord.

Genesis 13:12–13

Stephanie sat in the backseat with her dog as her dad drove through the campground. Her family was spending a week in the Smoky Mountains. Suddenly she pointed. "There's a good spot! It has lots of shade and a great view."

Her dad slowed down, and they all checked it out. "Looks good to me," said Stephanie's mom. Then they heard a commotion in the next campsite. Four young men were sitting near a fire pit, with empty bottles and trash all around. Two of them had raised their voices, cursing and arguing.

Stephanie's father said, "Let's see what else we can find." Stephanie was glad. Suddenly this spot didn't look so good.

Choosing close friends is like picking out a campsite. It'll have a big impact on your well-being, for better or for worse. Lot pitched his tents near people who weren't living God's way. The foolish, evil things they did really bothered him. (See 2 Peter 2:7–8.) And being in bad company could have ruined his good character. (See 1 Corinthians 15:33.) Pitch your tent near kids who love God and follow his laws! In other words, choose wise, godly people as your closest friends. They're the friends whose character and behavior will affect yours the most.

Words to Treasure

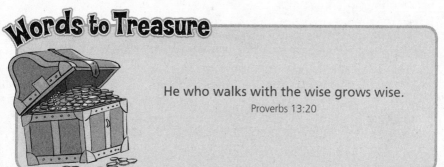

He who walks with the wise grows wise.
Proverbs 13:20

Don't Fall Away

Many of [Jesus'] disciples turned back and no longer followed him.

John 6:66

At the rodeo, Rodney saw a man trying to ride a mechanical bull. The machine bucked and spun, and the man fell off, landing on the padding around it. The crowd laughed as he got up.

"Dad, can I try that?" Rodney asked.

Looking doubtful, his father said, "I'll ask."

He spoke to the cowboy running the machine, who grinned at Rodney. "Sure, son, give it a whirl. I'll slow it down a bit, but hang on tight. This ain't no kiddie ride!"

Climbing on, Rodney grabbed hold. The machine started bucking, and Rodney was tossed every which way. Still, he clung to the bull as hard as he could, and when it finally stopped, the crowd cheered.

Some of Jesus' teachings are hard to understand. And they're hard to live by once you do understand them. Don't let that throw you! Cling to Jesus, just like the apostles did. They refused to let go of him, even when others "fell away" because of what he said. (See John 6:67–69.) If you cling tightly to Jesus, he'll help you understand his words and empower you to live by them.

Did You Know?

When Jesus said he was the Bread of Life, many of his followers were upset and deserted him. Some may have misunderstood his words. Others may have understood them but refused to accept them.

God's Nicknames?

You shall not misuse the name of the Lord your God.

Exodus 20:7

Roly! Roly-poly!" Stephanie called. "Jeez, where is that dog?" Her dad gave her a look as they searched around their campsite in the Smoky Mountains. Suddenly they heard a muffled bark. Stephanie scrambled up the mountainside. "Roly!" Following his barks, she reached a crevice and squeezed through. She found herself in a cave, with Roly jumping on her legs. "There you are." She picked him up, then gasped. "Gah, this cave is huge!"

When she wriggled out, her dad said, "I'm glad you found Roly, sweetheart. But I'm concerned about your language. 'Jeez' and 'Gah' sound like nicknames for Jesus and God—like me calling you Steph. You know how God feels about people using his name the wrong way. Maybe you should use other words to express yourself." Ruffling her hair, he looked into the crevice. "So, what do you say we do some spelunking?"

She gave him a puzzled expression that made him laugh. "That means cave exploring," he said.

Stephanie looked sideways at him. "Well, Dad, maybe we *both* need to start using other words to express ourselves!"

People once thought God's divine, personal name (Yahweh) was so special, they wouldn't say it at all. Do *you* always treat God's name as holy?

Life in Bible Times

Scribes considered God's divine name so holy that they always wrote it in a special way. In the Old Testament of many Bibles today, this special name is printed in small capital letters: LORD.

Shooting Down Sin

> Each one is tempted when, by his own evil desire, he is dragged away and enticed. Then, after desire has conceived, it gives birth to sin.
>
> James 1:14–15

At the skeet range, Ty's dad handed him an orange disk. "These are called clay pigeons. When you yell, 'Pull!' a machine will throw one of them. Then you try to shoot it."

Ty examined the disk. "Sounds simple!"

Laughing, his dad said, "It's not so easy. The trick is to aim ahead of the target. If you aim right at it, you'll miss."

Ty lifted the 20-gauge shotgun and hollered, "Pull!" A clay pigeon took off, and he squeezed the trigger. *Boom!* The "bird" escaped.

"Aim farther ahead of the next one," Ty's dad said.

Ty took his stance again. "Pull!" Another clay pigeon shot into the air. This time when Ty pulled the trigger, the target exploded into dust.

The trick to shooting down sin is to aim a little ahead of it at the evil desire that always comes first. That's the feeling that makes you want to do something God says is wrong. Set your sights on that sinful desire. By aiming at that, you can blast your sinful behavior to bits.

People in Bible Times

Before Adam and Eve ate the fruit God said not to, they *desired* it. They could have stopped themselves from sinning if they'd dealt with their evil desire. (See Genesis 30.)

Billboard Barns

You are a letter from Christ … written not with ink but with the Spirit of the living God, not on tablets of stone but on tablets of human hearts.

2 Corinthians 3:3

"Look," Jody said, "there's a big sign painted on that barn!" She and her parents and her friend Gina were driving through Tennessee.

Gina leaned over to look. "It says, 'See Rock City.' What's that?"

Jody's father said, "It's a place on Lookout Mountain with huge rock formations. From there you can see seven states." As he drove, he glanced at the barn. "There used to be hundreds of barns like that in this part of the country. Many are gone now. My brother and I used to count those signs during road trips."

"So, Dad, did you actually *see* Rock City?" Jody said.

He laughed. "Of course. And you guys will too."

In 1936 a painter named Clark Byers started changing barns into Rock City billboards. Jesus wants to change you into something people can read. He wants to make you like a sign on the highway or a letter in the mail. Then people who know you will want to go to him. Jesus has a message of love for the world. Is it written all over you?

Live It!

Be a billboard for Jesus by wearing a T-shirt with his name on it. Even better, let people see Jesus' love in you, so they'll be drawn to him!

Some Things Never Change

Jesus Christ is the same yesterday and today and forever.

Hebrews 13:8

Adrian stood in his yard, watching the earthmovers. Moose, his family's St. Bernard, stood panting by his side. Backhoes, graders, and dump trucks were crawling all over the vacant land next to Adrian's home. They were preparing the ground so houses could be built.

"There goes our field," Adrian said. He patted the large dog's head. "We had lots of fun playing there, didn't we?" A bulldozer made a beeping sound as it backed up. Adrian shook his head. "I wish things didn't have to change."

Then another thought struck him, and he smiled. "But it'll be nice having more kids around to play with." Moose barked. Kneeling beside him, Adrian rubbed his neck. "Don't worry, big guy. You'll always be my best friend!"

Things around you may change, but Jesus never does. And he'll always be with you, no matter what happens in your life. Try to look on the bright side of the changes that come your way. Ask Jesus to help you cope with the losses they bring. Dealing with changes is easier when you remember that Jesus always stays the same.

Life in Bible Times

When Daniel and his friends were taken to Babylon, their lives changed a lot. Everything was different—their home, their food, their language, and even their names! But one thing stayed the same—their God.

Light of Liberty

The truth will set you free.

John 8:32

Keeshia stood on the deck of the ferryboat approaching Liberty Island. She was getting her first close-up view of the Statue of Liberty. Her father pointed up. "See those windows under her crown? When I was your age, your grandfather and I climbed the spiral staircase inside the statue and looked out from them."

Keeshia brushed a strand of hair from her face. "What was it like?"

"It was crowded—and hot!" He chuckled. "The sunshine heats up the metal. But I thought it was great. I wanted to climb the ladder inside the arm to the little balcony around the torch. But they haven't let people do that since 1916." He looked at her. "Do you know what that flame symbolizes?"

Keeshia nodded. "Freedom."

"That's right," he said. "The actual name of the statue is *Liberty Enlightening the World*. That flame represents the hope that one day the whole world will be free."

Like a shining light saving you from darkness, the Bible's truth sets you free from the Devil's lies. Satan wants to make you a prisoner. So he tries to convince you that you're stupid, ugly, or worthless. But God wants you to live in freedom, knowing that you're his beloved child. (See 1 John 3:1.) Learn the truth, believe it, and be free!

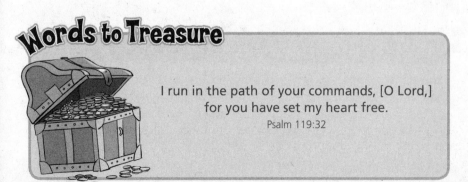

Words to Treasure

I run in the path of your commands, [O Lord,] for you have set my heart free.
Psalm 119:32

Straight-Faced

The One enthroned in heaven laughs.

Psalm 2:4

Lee and Amy were sightseeing with their parents in England. In London, they made faces at the royal guard standing in front of St. James's Palace. They were trying to make him laugh. Or smile. Or do something! But the soldier, wearing a red coat and a tall, furry black cap, just stared straight ahead. Amy did a cartwheel in front of him. No response.

"Come on, kids. Leave the poor fellow alone!" their mom said. "He's on duty."

Shrugging, Lee said to the guard, "Oh well. You can't blame us for trying!" He turned to follow his sister—and collided with a man walking past. Lee fell backward, landing at the feet of the guard. The soldier never flinched.

Lee's family was laughing, though. His dad said, "If *that* doesn't make him laugh, nothing will!"

Some people think God sits on his throne with a straight face, never cracking a smile. If anything (they think), he just gets angry. But the Bible says there are times when God laughs. There are even times when he sings. (See Zephaniah 3:17.) God has many emotions, the deepest of which is love.

Did You Know?

Some Bible stories show God's sense of humor. For example, God made proud, evil Haman throw a parade for his enemy, a good man named Mordecai. Haman had to lead the parade, shouting about how great Mordecai was! (See Esther 6.)

Knocked Around

[Jesus said,] "Blessed are you when men hate you, when they exclude you and insult you ... because of [me]."

Luke 6:22

During recess, Davis saw some older boys getting ready to play marbles. "Can I play?" he asked.

Hugh, the biggest boy, sneered. "Yeah, whatever. But we're playing for keeps!" He drew a large circle in the dirt, and everyone put marbles in the center. Taking aim with his large "shooter" marble, Davis fired. His shooter collided with the other marbles, scattering them. But none left the ring, so he didn't win any. His shooter also stayed in the circle.

"Now it's our turn," Hugh said. Laughing, the older boys ganged up on Davis, each blasting his shooter. Finally one of the boys knocked it outside the circle, and Davis was out of the game.

Kids pick on other kids for lots of reasons. Have you ever been knocked around like a marble because of your faith? Maybe some kids blasted you with mean words because you talk about Jesus. Or maybe others pushed you out of their circle of friends because you wouldn't join in their wrongdoing. If so, you can be glad. Jesus said you're blessed! You'll receive a rich reward in heaven for being loyal to him.

People in Bible Times

The religious leaders had the apostles beaten for preaching about Jesus. The apostles suffered because of their loyalty to the Lord. But they were happy. They knew they were blessed!

God's Eyes

> The eyes of the Lord range throughout the earth to strengthen those whose hearts are fully committed to him.
>
> 2 Chronicles 16:9

In a plaza near the River Thames, Lee stared up. "That's one *gigantic* Ferris wheel," he said. Lee and his family were in England, about to ride the London Eye.

"Actually, it's an observation wheel," said his father. "Ferris wheels have seats. This has pods."

Lee's sister, Amy, ran ahead. "Whatever it is, let's get on it!" After waiting in line, they entered one of the glass pods, each of which could hold twenty-five people. As it rose, Lee stood looking out over London. In fifteen minutes they reached the top, over four hundred feet high. Amy pointed down at a tall clock tower. "There's Big Ben!"

"Why is this called the Eye?" Lee asked.

His father shrugged. "Maybe because it looks like a big eye in the sky."

God is always watching. That doesn't mean his eyes are harsh. God's eyes are loving, and he's looking for people who are true to him. Some people, like King Ahab, do evil in God's sight. But others, like King David, do what's right. They're committed to God, and they've chosen to live his way. When God sees someone like that, he strengthens and cares for and helps that person. What will *you* do as God watches?

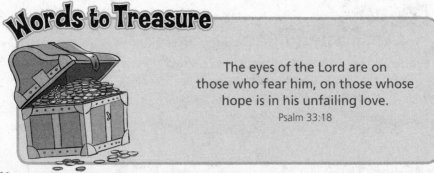

Words to Treasure

> The eyes of the Lord are on those who fear him, on those whose hope is in his unfailing love.
>
> Psalm 33:18

Focusing on What Matters to You

Set your hearts on things above, where Christ is seated at the right hand of God.

Colossians 3:1

What're you gonna do with your birthday money?" Shannon's friend Tracy asked her after school.

Shannon shifted her backpack. "First, I'm buying a CD—"

"Ooh, let's listen to it together!" Tracy interrupted.

Shannon laughed. "No, no. I mean a certificate of deposit, not a compact disc. It's an investment. You put money in it now to get more money out later. I'm also buying more stock. That's another kind of investment. Last year my grandpa bought me some stock in a movie company. We've been watching the company to see how it's doing. The better it does, the more my stock is worth."

Looking amazed, Tracey said, "I didn't know you were interested in that stuff."

Shannon smiled. "I am now!"

Putting your faith in God is an investment. You place your trust in him, and you're rewarded when he keeps his promises. Anytime you invest in something, you pay more attention to it. (See Matthew 6:21.) The more faith you put in God, the more you'll read the Bible and pray and listen for his voice. You'll stay tuned in to heaven because that's where your hope is.

Words to Treasure

Show me your ways, O Lord, teach me your paths; guide me in your truth and teach me, for you are God my Savior, and my hope is in you all day long.

Psalm 25:4–5

Time for Gratitude

> [Paul] took some bread and gave thanks to God in front of them all. Then he broke it and began to eat.
>
> Acts 27:35

I've never seen a shipwreck," said Casey. She and her mom were hiking on South Manitou Island.

"Me either," her mom said, "but we'll see one soon."

The trail was heading toward Lake Michigan. Suddenly Casey shouted, "There's the ship! It's sticking out of the water!" The *Francisco Morazan* was three hundred feet from the island, in fifteen feet of water.

Casey's mom read the sign on the shore. "It ran aground during a winter storm in 1960," she said. "The captain and crew were rescued, but the ship and its cargo were lost."

After gazing at the shipwreck awhile, they sat down to eat lunch. Casey's mom started to take a bite of her sandwich, but Casey said, "Shouldn't we say grace?"

Her mom smiled. "Well, I guess we should. Even if we *are* eating out of brown paper bags!"

The apostle Paul was in the middle of a storm at sea, about to be shipwrecked. Still, he remembered to say grace! (See Acts 27:27–44.) Always take time to thank God for the blessings he provides. Even if you're on a picnic or eating fast food in a minivan on the way to soccer practice.

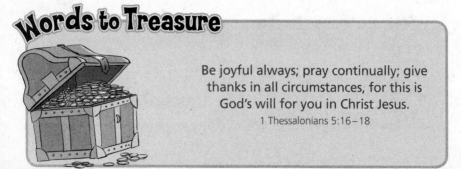

Words to Treasure

Be joyful always; pray continually; give thanks in all circumstances, for this is God's will for you in Christ Jesus.
1 Thessalonians 5:16–18

Super-Catapult Power

With authority and power [Jesus] gives orders
to evil spirits and they come out!

Luke 4:36

At Warwick Castle in England, Lee stood near a huge medieval weapon called a trebuchet. A crowd had gathered to watch the firing demonstration. And Lee was going to pull the trigger!

"It looks like a catapult," said his sister Amy.

"Yes," her father agreed. "But this is much more powerful."

Made of wood, the trebuchet was basically a big lever. There was a six-ton weight on the short end and a sling on the long end. The men in charge cocked the weapon by pulling down the long end, locking it into place. Then they put a thirty-pound stone in the sling. One of the men signaled Lee.

"Here goes!" Lee said, yanking a rope. The massive weight dropped, causing the long end of the lever to swing upward. As the lever reached the top, the sling whipped around over it. This hurled the heavy stone hundreds of feet through the air.

Trebuchets can throw very large stones. But Jesus can do something better. He can throw out demons. If you ever feel you're being troubled by a demon, talk to some Christian adults. They can help you ask Jesus to cast it far away from you.

Did You Know?

Demons are angels who followed the Devil when he rebelled against God. With the Devil, they were thrown down from heaven. They're sometimes called "fallen angels."

Excuses, Excuses

> [God asked the man], "Have you eaten from the
> tree that I commanded you not to eat from?"
> The man said, "The woman you put here with
> me—she gave me some fruit from the tree."
>
> Genesis 3:11–12

Racing down the field, Danny drove the soccer ball toward the goal. Two members of the other team were covering him. "I'm open!" shouted Jerome. Danny knew he should pass the ball. But he'd worked hard to get it, and he wanted to score this point. He was about to take a shot when one of his opponents kicked the ball away.

"Danny, what were you thinking?" said his coach at halftime. "You should've passed to Jerome!"

Danny threw his hands up. "It wasn't my fault. Jerome should've waved his arms."

Jerome gave him a funny look. "I yelled that I was open."

"You should've yelled louder," Danny said, walking away.

Moments later Danny went back and admitted it was his fault. "That's okay," Jerome said.

The coach smiled. "Don't worry about it. Now, get back out there!"

When you sin, don't do what Adam did. He tried to justify himself by making excuses, blaming someone else for what he did. Confess your sins to God, and let *him* justify you! God can do that, because he sacrificed his Son, Jesus, to pay for your sins. If you own up to your sins and confess them, God will wipe your slate clean.

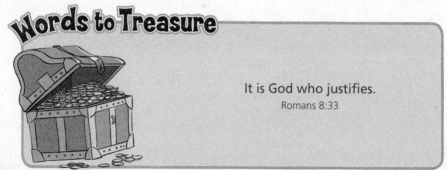

Words to Treasure

It is God who justifies.
Romans 8:33

Calling Heaven Your Home

You are no longer foreigners and aliens, but
fellow citizens with God's people.

Ephesians 2:19

As Keeshia stepped off the ferryboat, her father said, "Welcome to Ellis
Island. This is where millions of immigrants coming to America got off their
ships."

Keeshia joked, "Now I know how they felt!" She and her father entered the
main building. Keeshia was impressed by the Baggage Room. There she saw old
trunks and suitcases and duffle bags the immigrants used. On the second floor,
she stopped at a bronze statue of a girl.

"That's Annie Moore, from Ireland," her dad said. "She arrived on January 1,
1892, the day this place opened. It was her fifteenth birthday. Her two younger
brothers with her were about your age. She got a gold coin for being the first im-
migrant to set foot on Ellis Island." Staring at the girl's face, Keeshia wondered
what it must have been like to get used to belonging to a new country.

You're learning what it means to be a citizen of your country on earth. As a
believer in Jesus, you're also a citizen of God's country. That's the kingdom of
heaven. It's important to learn about the laws and customs of the country you
belong to. Study the Bible to learn about God's kingdom! Heaven is your true
home now, and it will be forever.

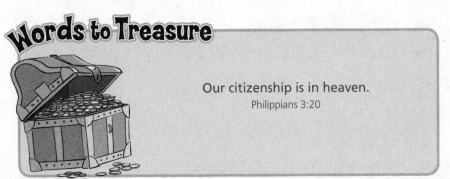

Words to Treasure

Our citizenship is in heaven.
Philippians 3:20

Loyal and True

> Let love and faithfulness never leave you; bind them around your neck, write them on the tablet of your heart. Then you will win favor and a good name in the sight of God and man.
>
> Proverbs 3:3–4

Adrian wandered onto the vacant land next to his house. His family's St. Bernard, Moose, followed him. They used to play in the field that was once there. But now the land was being prepared for new houses, and the ground was all torn up. Adrian was sad about that. But he also wanted to look at the earthmovers parked there for the night.

"Check out this backhoe, Moose!" Adrian said. It was getting dark, and he wished he had a flashlight. "I'd sure like to drive—" Suddenly Adrian fell into a large hole. His ankle was twisted and his side hurt, so he couldn't climb out or yell. Moose stayed with him, barking for help. Finally Adrian's parents came to his rescue. "Good boy, Moose," Adrian said when they pulled him out. "You're a loyal dog!"

St. Bernards are known for their loyalty. God wants you to be known for yours. The Bible says you should strap faithfulness around your neck—kind of like the little wooden barrels St. Bernards wear in cartoons. That means you should practice faithfulness until it's part of who you are. Then you'll have a quality that God values and rewards.

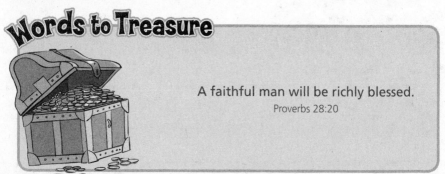

Words to Treasure

> A faithful man will be richly blessed.
> Proverbs 28:20

Because God Says So

Simon answered [Jesus], "Master, we've worked hard all night and haven't caught anything. But because you say so, I will let down the nets."

Luke 5:5

Mira and her family were in a museum next to the Sea of Galilee. There they were looking at an ancient fishing boat. It was twenty-seven feet long, with curved sides and ragged edges. The dark-brown wood looked very old. "Could Jesus have ridden in this boat?" Mira asked her father. He was an archaeologist working in the Holy Land.

"It's possible," he said. "The boat was found nearby, and it's from Jesus' time. In any case, this shows what boats were like back then."

Mira's mother gazed at it thoughtfully. "This reminds me of when the disciples put out their nets one more time, just because Jesus said so. And they caught lots of fish! That story always inspires me to trust God and obey him."

Sometimes you may struggle over whether to do what God tells you to do. Always remember that God loves you. He knows what's best, and things will turn out well if you obey him. The best reason in the world to do anything is because God says so!

Life in Bible Times

A first-century fishing boat could hold five fishermen and a large catch of fish. The fishermen dragged a big net, threw a smaller one, or possibly used a hook and line.

Changing Places

> The last will be first, and the first will be last.
> Matthew 20:16

Libby rang the doorbell of the house in front of the apple orchard. Her best friend, Alayna, had invited some kids over for a hayride-and-bonfire birthday party. "Hello, Libby," said Alayna's mom, opening the door. "I'm glad you're here. Alayna was worried that you weren't coming."

Libby smiled. "Hi, Mrs. Johnson. Sorry I'm late."

Alayna's mom said. "You'd better get out back. They're loading up the wagon." Libby hurried to join everybody else. The horses hitched to the wagon shook their manes and pawed the ground as Alayna's dad sat holding the reins. Alayna sat on the hay, near the front of the wagon, and the other kids were climbing aboard. Libby wanted to scramble for a seat next to Alayna. But she knew that everyone wanted to be close to the birthday girl. So she sat near the back instead.

"Libby, you made it!" Alayna said. "Come up here. I want you to sit beside me. Make room, everybody!"

When it's time to line up or choose a seat or find a place to stand, do you say, "Me first" or "After you"? Jesus taught his disciples that people who say, "After you" will someday hear God say, "You first." And to the "Me first" people, God will say, "After them."

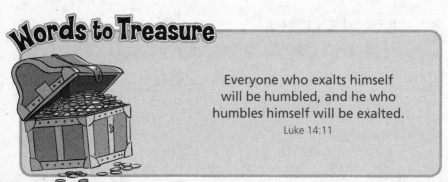

Words to Treasure

Everyone who exalts himself will be humbled, and he who humbles himself will be exalted.
Luke 14:11

Riding the Wind

Cast your cares on the Lord and he will sustain you; he will never let the righteous fall.

Psalm 55:22

Chris stepped into his dad's home lab, carrying a hair dryer. His mom was following him. "I got it!" Chris said.

His father, a science teacher, turned from the workbench. "Good. Bring it here."

Grabbing Chris's shoulder, his mother said, "Wait! What are you planning to do with my hair dryer?"

Chris's dad chuckled. "Don't worry. We're just trying a little experiment I want to show my students. We won't hurt it." He nodded at Chris. "Okay, plug in the hair dryer, turn it on, and point it at the ceiling." Chris obeyed, and his dad held a Ping-Pong ball over the hair dryer. "Now I'll demonstrate Bernoulli's principle." He let go of the ball. It shot upward, then hovered in midair. "See?" he said. "The fast-moving air creates a low-pressure 'tunnel.' And the higher pressure around the ball keeps it in there. The ball is perfectly suspended!"

Pilots rely on Bernoulli's principle to keep their airplanes flying. Air moves faster over the top of a plane's wings, and the higher pressure underneath lifts the aircraft. As you fly along in life, you can rely on God to hold you up. No matter what you fly through, you never have to worry about falling. God will support you!

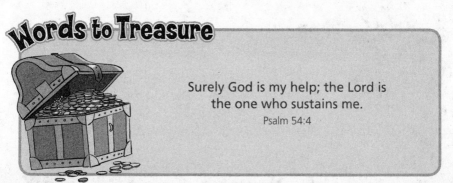

Words to Treasure

Surely God is my help; the Lord is the one who sustains me.
Psalm 54:4

Playing with a Big Fire

> Worship God acceptably with reverence and awe, for our "God is a consuming fire."
>
> Hebrews 12:28–29

Libby was enjoying Alayna's birthday party. After Alayna's father gave the kids a hayride through his apple orchard, he lit a huge pile of brush in a clearing behind the barn. The kids hung out around the bonfire, playing games. Some bobbed for apples. Libby was getting ready for the sack race when she noticed two boys by the brush pile, pulling out burning branches. "Hey, you guys —," she said. Just then part of the pile collapsed, shooting up sparks. One of the boys started yelling. The bottom of his pants had caught fire! Libby used her burlap bag to beat out the flame.

"What's going on?" said Alayna's dad, running up. The boys explained, and as Libby went to join the race, she heard Alayna's dad lecturing them about fire safety.

Kids who goof off during worship time at church would change their ways fast if they could see God's fiery glory. God may not quickly strike down someone who worships him improperly, as he once did. (See Leviticus 10:1–2.) Yet disrespecting God is a risky habit to get into. God may not punish a person for a long time, hoping he or she will change. But what if that person never changes?

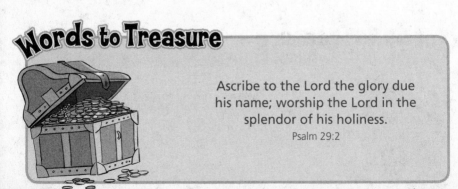

Words to Treasure

Ascribe to the Lord the glory due his name; worship the Lord in the splendor of his holiness.
Psalm 29:2

Strong Support

"I will strengthen you and help you; I will up-hold you with my righteous right hand," [says the Lord].

Isaiah 41:10

L et's sit in the back," said Jody, who had come with her family and her friend Gina to Chattanooga, Tennessee.

"You'll get a good view wherever you sit," said the railcar operator. He pointed at large windows in the roof.

"Is this thing safe?" Gina asked, sitting beside Jody. The seats faced backward. They were tilted back so much, Jody felt like an astronaut about to lift off. They'd boarded the Incline, the steepest passenger railway in the world. It was going to take them straight up Lookout Mountain.

"Relax," the operator said. "The cable pulling us can hold seventy tons." The car started moving. Jody felt herself sitting up straighter as the tracks got steeper. Soon she was looking out the roof, which was right in front of her! Looking down through the rear window, she reminded herself of the strong cable supporting them.

When you're feeling afraid, remember that God has you in his hands. His arms are very powerful. Don't focus on how big your problem is. Focus on how mighty God is. There's no need to fear when you have God's strong support.

People in Bible Times

Running for his life, Elijah was afraid. He wanted to give up. God met Elijah in the desert, fed him, and encouraged him. So Elijah was able to keep on serving God. (See 1 Kings 19:1–18.)

For You or Against You?

God demonstrates his own love for us in this:
While we were still sinners, Christ died for us.

Romans 5:8

Coach Jackson blew his whistle at football practice. "Wade, you're supposed to cut toward the middle of the field!"

Walking back to the scrimmage line, Wade said, "Sorry, Coach."

The coach looked him in the eye. "Mental errors like these are making us lose games, Wade. I want you to hit the bench and review the plays in your head. Send Cameron out."

Wade jogged to the sidelines, taking off his helmet. "Your dad wants you out there," he told Cameron. Plopping down on the bench, he added, "Man, he just likes catching our mistakes. Then he can jump all over us!"

Cameron stood up, strapping on his helmet. "It's not like that, Wade. My dad cares about this team. You should see all the work he does getting ready for practice. He sacrifices a lot, because he wants us to succeed. Believe it or not, he's on our side."

Do you ever think God is just waiting for you to mess up so he can punish you? That's far from the truth. God is *for* you, not against you. He proved that by sacrificing Jesus to make up for your failure to live by his laws. Now God wants you to succeed in following his commands. He wants to give you the rewards that come from obeying him.

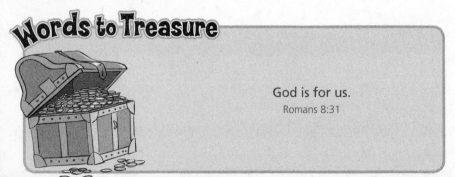

Words to Treasure

God is for us.
Romans 8:31

God's Spotlights

Let your light shine before men, that they may
see your good deeds and praise your Father in
heaven.

Matthew 5:16

Anthony pointed through the windshield of his father's SUV as they left the hardware store. "Dad, check that out!" In the distance, spotlights swept the night sky. "Can we follow them?" Anthony asked. "I wanna see what's going on."

His father said, "Well, we're in no rush. I'm feeling adventurous. Why not?" He turned at the next intersection. "Okay, Son, I'm the pilot and you're the navigator. Tell me where to go." Watching the spotlights, Anthony guided his dad. For fifteen minutes they followed the lights, getting closer and closer.

"It's gotta be just around this corner," Anthony said. "Take a left here." His father turned, and they finally saw what all the hoopla was about. "It's a new skate park!" Anthony exclaimed. They parked and joined the crowd around the large half-pipe. Under the spotlights, professional skateboarders were putting on a demonstration, wowing everyone with their moves.

A spotlight doesn't draw attention to itself. It draws attention to something else. That's why Christian athletes often point to heaven when people applaud for them. When you do a good deed or achieve success, you can be a spotlight for God. Give him glory, and turn everyone's attention to him.

Words to Treasure

Live such good lives among
[unbelievers] that ... they may see
your good deeds and glorify God.
1 Peter 2:12

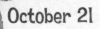

Wondering What's Ahead

> "I know the plans I have for you," declares the
> Lord, "plans to prosper you and not to harm
> you, plans to give you hope and a future."
>
> Jeremiah 29:11

Keeshia peered through the metal gate in the old train shed, staring at row after row of tracks in the Central Railroad station at the New Jersey waterfront. There many immigrants coming to America had started the last part of their journey.

"Just think, Keeshia," her dad said. "These people traveled in ships across the ocean. They passed the Statue of Liberty and landed on Ellis Island. Then they went through a long process of becoming U.S. citizens. After that, they rode a ferryboat to get here. Then they waited at this station for a train to take them to their final destination, where their new lives would begin."

Keeshia whistled softly. "That was some trip." She wondered what the kids her age were thinking and feeling as they waited here. Were they excited about their future? Were they scared?

Facing your future can sometimes be frightening. Maybe you're dealing with some major changes, like switching to a new school or moving to another part of the country. Put your future in God's hands. No matter how things change, you can trust his plans for your life. He has good things in store for you.

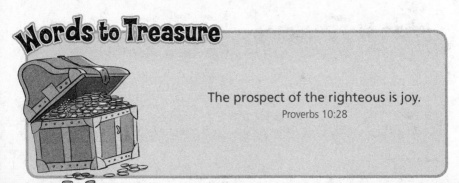

Words to Treasure

The prospect of the righteous is joy.
Proverbs 10:28

Finding Your Way

Trust in the Lord with all your heart and lean not on your own understanding; in all your ways acknowledge him, and he will make your paths straight.

Proverbs 3:5–6

"Does this trail really go all the way to Maine?" Kevin asked, following the footpath through the woods.

"Yes," replied his uncle Bill. "And if we turned around, we could walk clear to Georgia. This trail is two thousand miles long!" They were at the border of New Jersey and Pennsylvania, hiking on the Appalachian Trail. Kevin picked up a stone for a souvenir. Then he hesitated. The path was getting harder to see.

"That way," his uncle said, pointing. "See the white mark on that tree? It's called a blaze. There are 165,000 of them on trees and rocks along the trail. Don't worry, we won't get lost. When we reach that blaze, we'll see another."

God has a plan for your life. All your days were marked in his book before you were born. (See Psalm 139:16.) It's as if God put a white blaze on each day of your life. You don't have to see the whole path at once. All you have to do is look and listen for God's direction every day, telling you which steps to take next.

People in Bible Times

Moses, a great leader, was also a faithful follower. As he led the Israelites through the desert, Moses followed God—who showed him each step of the way.

Searching for Treasure

> The kingdom of heaven is like treasure hidden in a field.
>
> Matthew 13:44

Paige lay on the floor in Ava's bedroom, reading a newspaper article about the county-wide treasure hunt. The friends puzzled over the final clue. "'Amazement in the ears, way ruined for years,'" Paige read. "What does that *mean*?"

Ava stopped spinning in her chair. "I've got it! It's a maize maze!" She headed for the door.

"A what?" Paige asked, following her.

"A maze in a cornfield," Ava explained. "*Maize* is another word for corn … ears of corn … get it? There's a cornfield near school with an old broken gate. That's the 'way ruined for years'!"

The girls jumped on their bikes and raced to the field. Clambering over the busted gate, they saw an opening between the corn plants.

"You're right!" Paige said. They started winding through the maze. At the end they found a box, and inside was the gold coin everyone was looking for.

The Bible has all the information you need to find God's kingdom. God will help you understand his Word if you're willing to study it, then think and pray about what it says. The kingdom of heaven is worth searching for!

Did You Know?

There are tools to help kids understand the Bible. A Bible dictionary explains words and names in the Bible. A Bible atlas has maps and pictures showing places in the Bible. A Bible concordance tells where to find key words in the Bible.

Angels along Your Path

Are not all angels ministering spirits sent to serve those who will inherit salvation?

Hebrews 1:14

Kevin and his uncle were hiking on the Appalachian Trail. They were near the Delaware Water Gap, at the border of New Jersey and Pennsylvania. After a long climb, they reached the top of a rocky ridge. Below was the wide Delaware River. "Look, Uncle Bill!" Kevin said. "Someone left a cooler up here."

His uncle's face brightened. "It's probably a gift from a Trail Angel." He opened the cooler and took out a note. "It says, 'Have some refreshments! God bless you on your journey.'"

Kevin was puzzled. "What are Trail Angels?"

"They're people who care about hikers on this trail and help them," his uncle said. He pulled out two juice packs and two granola bars. Then they sat on the rocks to rest and enjoy the view.

As they munched their snacks, Kevin said, "It's nice to know someone's looking out for us."

There are many stories in the Bible about real angels helping people. Angels helped Jesus in the desert. (See Matthew 4:11.) An angel fed Elijah. (See 1 Kings 19:5–6.) Another angel got Peter out of prison. (See Acts 12:1–19.) When you pray, thank God for taking care of you. And thank him for having his angels watch over you too.

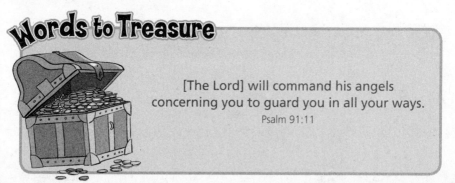

Words to Treasure

[The Lord] will command his angels concerning you to guard you in all your ways.

Psalm 91:11

Walking in Daylight

> The path of the righteous is like the first gleam of dawn, shining ever brighter till the full light of day.
>
> Proverbs 4:18

Ty and his dad walked stealthily through the woods, carrying shotguns. Dawn had broken as Ty's dad parked his truck beside the gravel road. Now the sky was getting lighter. "How far to the cornfield?" Ty whispered.

"Not far," his dad replied quietly. "Now, no more talking. This time of day, pheasants will be at the edge of the field, eating corn off the ground. We don't want them to hear us before we're in position."

Ty nodded, trying harder to walk softly. The sky grew even brighter, and he could see more clearly now. They planned to come out near one end of the cornfield by full daylight. Then they'd walk along the edge of the field. Any pheasants there would be startled and fly into the air.

Finally, Ty spotted the cornfield ahead. Soon they stepped out of the woods. The sun was up, and Ty found himself staring into a dazzling blue sky.

When you're walking with the Devil, life gets darker and darker. You wind up walking in total blackness. But when you're walking with Jesus, your life grows brighter and brighter. In the end, you're walking in shining glory.

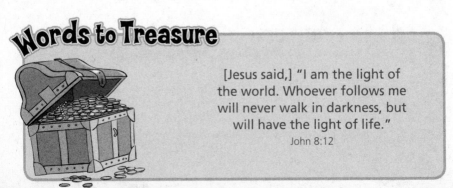

Words to Treasure

[Jesus said,] "I am the light of the world. Whoever follows me will never walk in darkness, but will have the light of life."
John 8:12

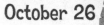

Your First Dime

"Bring the whole tithe into the storehouse.... Test me in this," says the Lord Almighty, "and see if I will not throw open the floodgates of heaven and pour out so much blessing that you will not have room enough for it."

Malachi 3:10

Terri helped her brother Dustin stuff leaves into a bag. From his front porch, their neighbor Mr. Jefferson said, "Have some lemonade, kids."

Wiping her forehead, Terri said, "Sounds good!"

Mr. Jefferson handed them each a glass. "What'll you do with the money you're earning?"

Dustin shrugged. "Buy Rollerblades."

"When I started my business," said Mr. Jefferson, "I planned to frame the first dollar I made. But I knew that God wants us to test him by giving him a tithe, or ten percent, of everything we earn. So I gave my first dime to him and framed the other nine. Then I kept giving God the first dime of every dollar I made. And God has really blessed me."

Giving God ten percent of your income is an act of obedience. It also shows that you trust God to keep his promise to bless you richly in return. And he will! God invites you to test his faithfulness in this matter. You'll be amazed at how many ways he can find to bless someone who trusts and obeys him.

Words to Treasure

Give, and it will be given to you. A good measure, pressed down, shaken together and running over, will be poured into your lap.

Luke 6:38

Eye Protection

> Your eye is the lamp of your body. When your eyes are good, your whole body also is full of light. But when they are bad, your body also is full of darkness.
>
> Luke 11:34

The doorbell rang on the morning of Randall's birthday. When he opened the door, he found a package addressed to him. "It's from Grandpa!" he exclaimed, carrying the long box inside. As his parents watched, he opened it. Then he whooped. "It's a BB gun!"

He eagerly examined the rifle while his dad read the card. "This says, 'Happy birthday, Grandson. Hope you enjoy this BB gun. I gave your father one just like it when he was your age. Use it carefully, and be sure to wear the safety glasses I sent. I wouldn't want you to shoot one of your eyes out!'"

"Amen to that," said Randall's mom.

Grabbing the glasses and the box of BBs, Randall headed for the door. "C'mon, Dad. Let's try it!"

Eye protection is important when you're shooting a BB gun. It's also vital when you're watching TV, playing video games, reading magazines, and looking at websites. Be sure to guard your eyes from anything harmful in those things. What goes into your eyes affects your whole body, especially your heart.

Live It!

Protect yourself. Read Proverbs 4:23–27 and Isaiah 33:15–16. Then draw a picture of yourself. Using arrows, write what the Bible says about guarding these parts of your body: eyes, ears, mouth, hands, feet, and heart.

Saving for the Future

In the house of the wise are stores of choice food and oil, but a foolish man devours all he has.

Proverbs 21:20

When Terri and Dustin entered the house, their dad glanced up from his laptop computer. "How's the lawn-raking business?"

Terri replied, "It's booming!"

Opening the fridge, Dustin added, "We have enough customers to keep us busy all fall."

Their dad smiled. "You guys want to use my computer to manage your money? You can track how much you make and where it goes."

"Sure," said Terri.

As they looked over their dad's shoulder, he explained how the money program worked. "Here's where you enter the amount you're giving to God," he said, pointing at the screen. "Now, the Bible says you should save some of your income. So you could take one or two dimes of every dollar and put it in the bank. If you develop that habit now, you'll be in good shape when it's time to pay for things like a car, college, and a house."

- - - - - -

It's not smart to eat up all the food in your house. You should save some for later. The same principle applies to money. It's wise not to spend all the money you make. Instead get into the habit of saving for the future.

People in Bible Times

Joseph advised Pharaoh to save one-fifth of the food grown during seven years of good harvests. Then Egypt would be ready for seven years of famine. (See Genesis 41.)

Above the Clouds

> The Father of the heavenly lights ... does not change like shifting shadows.
>
> James 1:17

Outside the Skyhawk's windshield, the world looked dreary. But Hannah was in a good mood. She sat happily in the copilot's seat as her dad taxied the small plane onto the runway. He checked the instruments, then revved the engine to test it. "Okay, Hannah. Tell them we're good to go."

Hannah picked up the microphone. "Control tower, this is November three zero niner Victor, ready for takeoff." Her dad had taught her the proper way to say the letters and numbers on the tail of his plane—N309V. She liked saying "November" for *N*, "niner" for *9*, and "Victor" for *V*, just like a real pilot.

The radio crackled. "Three zero niner Victor, clear for takeoff." Her dad pushed the throttle forward.

Speeding down the runway, the Skyhawk climbed into the overcast sky. They flew into the clouds, and Hannah could see nothing but gray. She peered through the windshield, waiting ... until they burst through the mist into a clear blue sky, where the bright, yellow sun was blazing.

Sometimes problems and worries are like clouds that hide the sun. But the sun is always shining. God is the same way. No matter what's happening in your life, he never changes. Prayer takes you above the clouds, where you experience God's goodness, beauty, and love.

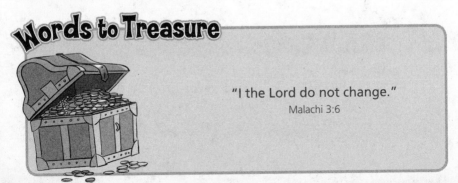

Words to Treasure

"I the Lord do not change."
Malachi 3:6

Teaching Others What You Know

I pray that you may be active in sharing your faith.
Philemon 1:6

At the new skate park, Anthony tried out the mini ramp and worked on his kickflip. He noticed a younger boy watching the other skateboarders zip past, practicing their moves. The boy wore a helmet and pads and held a skateboard, but somehow he looked out of place. Anthony walked over to him, saying, "Isn't this new park great?"

"Yeah," the boy said, "but I'm just a beginner. I wish I could skate like those guys!" They watched a kid slide down one of the grinding rails, balancing on his skateboard.

Anthony said, "Well, I can't do stuff like that, but I can show you what I've learned."

"Okay," the boy said, looking grateful.

Anthony led him over to the mini ramp. "First, I'll teach you how to do a drop-in ..."

You may not know everything about the Bible, but you can help others by teaching them what you do know. Philip wasn't all-wise, but he taught another man what he knew about the Scriptures. He helped the man understand that Jesus died for his sins so he could live forever. The man became a believer. (See Acts 8:26–40.) Through your words and actions, share with others what you've learned about the Bible.

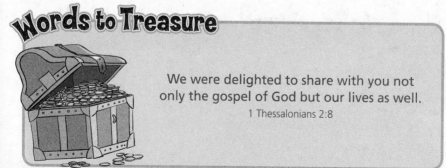

Words to Treasure

We were delighted to share with you not only the gospel of God but our lives as well.
1 Thessalonians 2:8

Riding Aslan

Rejoice in the Lord always. I will say it again:
Rejoice!

Philippians 4:4

Jody and Gina ran around the carousel at Coolidge Park in Chattanooga, Tennessee, trying to decide which animals to ride. Besides horses, there was a giraffe, a zebra, a bear, and many other animals. "I'm riding this one!" Gina yelled, climbing on a colorful elephant.

Then Jody saw the lion. The king of beasts stood strong and magnificent, its mouth open, roaring. When she looked at its name, she couldn't believe her eyes. "It's Aslan!" She loved reading the Chronicles of Narnia. Especially *The Lion, the Witch and the Wardrobe.* Her favorite part was right after Aslan died to save Edmund. It was when Aslan came back to life, and Lucy and Susan took a joyful ride on him.

Jody slid onto the smooth, hard saddle atop the wooden lion. The music started, and the carousel began to move. Jody imagined herself riding the *real* Aslan. As the carousel picked up speed, she tossed her hair back and laughed.

Celebrate your relationship with Jesus! He's your Lord, your Savior, your brother, and your friend. Jesus loves you so much that he died for you. And now his Spirit is here with you to carry you through this life. His presence brings great joy. And that joy gives you the power you need to obey him wherever he takes you.

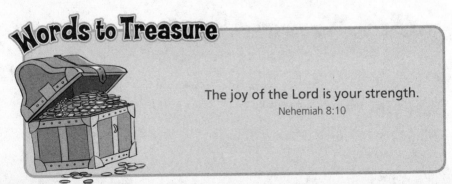

Words to Treasure

The joy of the Lord is your strength.
Nehemiah 8:10

The Real Goal

Whatever you do, do it all for the glory of God.

1 Corinthians 10:31

Kneeling on the fifteen-yard line, Audie set up the football. With a running kick, Brett sent the ball between the goalposts. "It's good!" he shouted, raising his hands.

Audie ran to retrieve the ball. Then he asked, "Have you seen that movie *Facing the Giants*?" Brett shook his head, and Audie said, "It was great. This high school football team kept losing, and their coach was gonna get fired. So he started reading his Bible and praying. Then he switched his goal from winning football games to honoring God. The team did too, and everything began to change."

He set up the ball on the twenty-yard line. This time Brett's kick missed to the right. "Well," Audie said, "I guess we should praise God that you can kick a fifteen-yarder!"

Make it your goal to honor God with your life. Do your best at whatever you do. Keep trying to improve. And leave the results up to God, praising him no matter what happens. Then your life will truly be successful. That's because when your goal is to glorify God, he'll make sure you achieve it.

Live It!

Try kicking field goals at a football field. Start on the ten-yard line and move back five yards at a time. See how long a field goal you can kick! Then pray, promising God that your goal in life will be to honor him.

Watch and Learn

> [The ant] has no commander, no overseer or ruler, yet it stores its provisions in summer and gathers its food at harvest.
>
> Proverbs 6:7–8

"They're here!" Dale said, bursting into the bedroom. He showed Brayden the little plastic tube that had arrived in the mail. Inside were live ants.

"Cool!" Brayden said. "Let's put them in their new home." The boys had pooled their money to buy an Ant Farm. It was filled with clear green gel that gave the insects food, moisture, and a place to build their nest. Brayden opened it and used a little tool to poke three "starter tunnels" in the gel. Then Dale gently shook in the ants that the Uncle Milton company had sent.

Over the next few days the boys watched them, fascinated. The insects worked hard, digging 3-D tunnels that twisted all over. "They never stop!" Brayden said one day after school.

Dale nodded, then looked at the clock. "Well, we've got our own work to do. We'd better quit watching the ants and start acting like them."

Ants work hard, and they don't need anyone to make sure they do their jobs. Try to be like them when you tackle your homework and chores. God wants to bless you with wisdom and success in life. One way he does that is by teaching you to be diligent and responsible, like an ant.

Words to Treasure

Go to the ant, you sluggard; consider its ways and be wise!
Proverbs 6:6

Praying for Healing

Praise the Lord, O my soul, and forget not all his benefits—who forgives all your sins and heals all your diseases.

Psalm 103:2–3

The day before her gymnastics meet, Lillian lay in bed, sick. Her head hurt, her stomach was upset, and she felt feverish. Her mom came in. "How are you doing?"

"Not great," said Lillian. "I won't be able to compete tomorrow if I feel like this."

Adjusting the blanket, her mother said, "Would you like me to pray with you for healing?"

Lillian frowned. "I don't know. I mean, I've heard some people say God heals everyone who asks him to, if they have enough faith. But other people say he chooses not to sometimes. It's so confusing."

"I know," said her mom. "But I also know this: In the Bible, God promises to heal his people. And Jesus healed everyone who came to him in faith. So what do *you* think?"

Lillian was quiet for a moment, then said, "Let's pray."

Christians have different beliefs about God's promises to heal. You'll have to decide what *you* believe about them. Read God's promises for yourself. Pray about them, knowing that "the Spirit ... will guide you into all truth" (John 16:13). You can trust God's Word, and you can trust the Holy Spirit to help you understand it. God will point your faith in the right direction when it comes to healing.

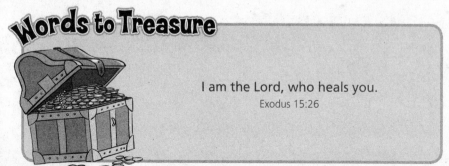

Words to Treasure

I am the Lord, who heals you.
Exodus 15:26

Gutting It Out

> Consider it pure joy, my brothers, whenever you face trials of many kinds, because you know that the testing of your faith develops perseverance.
>
> James 1:2–3

Danny stood on the soccer field in the pouring rain. *I'm freezing out here!* he thought. But he didn't let the weather distract him. "Keep your head in the game," he muttered to himself, focusing on the action downfield. Danny had been in this situation before. The first time was when he started playing soccer, in first grade. He'd just stood there shivering, wishing he could go home. But Danny had grown up a lot since then.

Now a player from the other team was driving the ball toward him, chased by two of Danny's teammates. Out of the corner of his eye, Danny spotted another member of the other team running down the sideline. Danny saw the pass coming and dashed to intercept it. Immediately he blasted the ball downfield, knowing that one of his teammates was open near the goal. His teammate took the pass, made a quick shot, and scored.

When things get tough, in sports or in school or in life, hang in there and stay focused. Quitting will get you nowhere. But gutting it out, with God's help, will build up your character. And having inner strength will give you hope as you face the future.

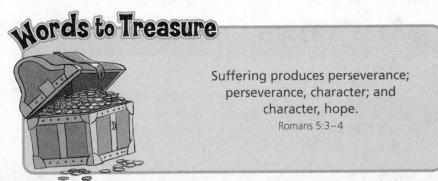

Words to Treasure

Suffering produces perseverance; perseverance, character; and character, hope.
Romans 5:3–4

A Jewel Underground

If I go up to the heavens, you are there, [O Lord]; if I make my bed in the depths, you are there.

Psalm 139:8

The elevator door opened, and Cody saw a different world than the one far above. He swallowed hard. "Hey, Cody, get out so we can see!" said Evan.

"Sorry," Cody replied, stepping forward. His homeschool group followed him.

"Wow, it's cooler down here," Julia said. They were in Ruby Falls Cave in Chattanooga, Tennessee—260 feet down inside Lookout Mountain. Cody's heart was racing. The farther they walked into the cave, toward the middle of the mountain, the deeper underground they'd be. He felt trapped. Then he remembered Psalm 139. He seemed to hear God saying, *Don't worry, I'm here.*

Cody took a deep breath. *Okay, Lord.* Soon he was enjoying himself, walking along and admiring the rock formations. Finally the group reached the cave's end, 1,120 feet underground. Cody stood with the others, amazed at the beautiful waterfall God had created there. And he prayed, *Lord, thanks for not letting me miss this!*

There is no place you can go where God is not present. Whether you're in a jet thirty thousand feet high or a cave a thousand feet deep, God is always right there with you.

People in Bible Times

The prophet Jonah spent three days inside a giant fish deep in the Mediterranean Sea. But God was with him even there. When Jonah cried out, God heard him. (See Jonah 2.)

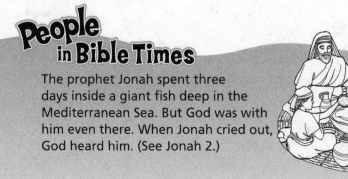

Leaning into the Curves

I have put my trust in you, [O Lord]. Show me the way I should go.

Psalm 143:8

Tiffany's uncle kick-started his motorcycle, and the engine roared to life. "Okay, hop on," he said.

Tiffany tightened her helmet, climbed on the back, and clung to him. "Ready, Uncle Vic!"

"Listen," he said, looking back. "Whenever I turn, I'll lean in the direction I'm turning. When you feel me leaning, lean with me. It might seem scary at first, but it'll keep us balanced. Okay?"

She nodded, and he pulled out of the driveway. For a while Tiffany was afraid to lean. But then she learned to trust her uncle. Soon they were winding through the mountains, enjoying the beautiful scenery. Every time her uncle turned, Tiffany leaned into the curves with him.

Learn to "lean into the curves" with God. Cling to him, trust him, and go in the direction his Spirit is moving you. King Hezekiah did this. The Bible says, "Hezekiah trusted in the Lord.... He held fast to the Lord and did not cease to follow him" (2 Kings 18:5–6). When you sense the Holy Spirit moving you to go this way or that, have faith and follow his lead!

People in Bible Times

One day the Holy Spirit moved Simeon to go to the temple. Trusting God, he followed the Spirit's lead. Because he did, Simeon got to see Jesus when his parents brought him there.

Treasures of the Past

Do not store up for yourselves treasures on earth, where moth and rust destroy, and where thieves break in and steal. But store up for yourselves treasures in heaven.

Matthew 6:19–20

E ver been to a junkyard before?" asked Shane's granddad, parking his pickup truck.

"Nope," Shane replied as they climbed out. "But I always wondered what they look like inside." He gazed at the tall wooden fence. His granddad grabbed a toolbox and led Shane into a small building. The owner of the junkyard gave them permission to search for the part they needed. Walking through the gate, Shane was amazed at all the rusted, broken-down vehicles he saw. It was cool—but a little sad.

His granddad said, "Remember that new truck we were admiring yesterday? Well, all these were just as shiny once." He put an arm around Shane's shoulders. "Here's something important I've learned, Shane. Don't live your life for material things. Sooner or later it all ends up here."

You don't need to visit a junkyard to see that the treasures of this world don't last. Look in your bedroom closet or basement. You'll see toys you begged your parents for. You'll find others you saved up your allowance to buy. Many are gathering dust because they're outdated, worn out, or broken. Heavenly treasures, such as godly character and all the riches of paradise, last forever. It's the only stuff worth living for.

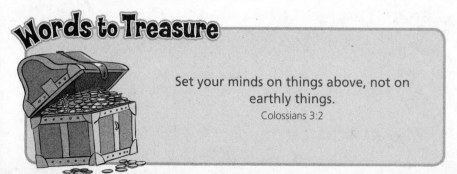

Words to Treasure

Set your minds on things above, not on earthly things.
Colossians 3:2

Open Arms

Everyone who calls on the name of the Lord
will be saved.

Romans 10:13

As the bright-red, two-car train climbed the steep mountain, Carlos asked, "Grandpa, what keeps us from sliding down the tracks?"

His grandfather answered, "There's a middle rail with notches in it. A gear under the train grabs it and pulls the train along. Don't worry, Carlos. This train has been going up and down the Corcovado mountain for over a hundred years. We'll make it." Sure enough, the train reached the top, and Carlos and his grandparents got out. He was visiting them in Rio de Janeiro, Brazil, and they were taking him to see the famous statue called *Christ the Redeemer*, which overlooks the city. They rode an elevator up, then took an escalator farther up.

Carlos stared in awe at the 125-foot statue towering over them. The figure of Jesus, standing with his arms opened wide, seemed to be welcoming everyone. "Look at the statue's shape, Carlos," his grandmother said. "Doesn't it remind you of a cross?"

The word *gospel* means "good news." And the good news is that God sent his Son, Jesus, to die for the world. Anyone who believes in Jesus can live forever. (See John 3:16.) That good news is for everyone! Jesus really does welcome anybody who comes to him, no matter who they are or where they're coming from.

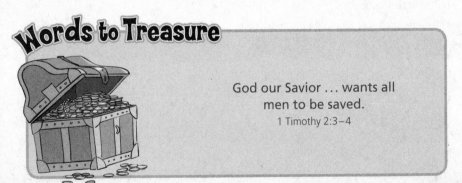

Words to Treasure

God our Savior ... wants all
men to be saved.
1 Timothy 2:3–4

Marked!

Though your sins are like scarlet, they shall be as white as snow.

Isaiah 1:18

Colton leaned around a tree, his eyes darting. *Splat! Splat!* Bright-orange blotches of paint exploded on the trunk. He hit the ground, rolling behind a log. "Almost got you!" yelled his friend Riley.

Colton hollered, "You missed by a mile!" Adjusting his facemask, he checked his paintball gun. Almost empty. He listened. A twig snapped, and Colton jumped up, firing in that direction. Riley dodged behind a tree. Then he shot back, hitting Colton twice. Immediately Colton realized two things: he'd lost the game, and he'd gotten paint on his new coat.

"I win!" said Riley.

Colton sighed. "Yeah, and I'm cooked. My mom's gonna be mad." He considered trying to clean the coat himself, but he didn't know how to run the washer. So he went home and told his mom what he did.

She was angry, but he apologized, and she forgave him. "Don't worry," she said, taking his coat. "I can get this stain out."

There's no use trying to hide your sins from God. He knows what you did, and only he can take away your guilt. Even though sin offends God, he loves you. He wants you to come to him and confess when you've done something wrong. God will forgive you, and he has the power to wash sins away.

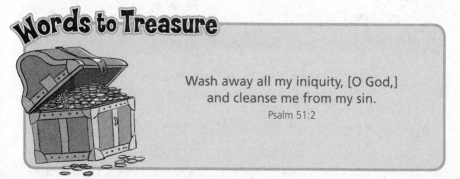

Words to Treasure

Wash away all my iniquity, [O God,] and cleanse me from my sin.
Psalm 51:2

Wandering through a Maze

[O Lord,] I am always with you; you hold me by
my right hand. You guide me with your counsel,
and afterward you will take me into glory.

Psalm 73:23–24

Libby laughed as she and Alayna ran through the cornfield. Then the path they were on suddenly ended. "Another dead end!" Alayna said. The friends were trying to get through the maze Alayna's father had built in the cornfield next to his apple orchard. Backtracking, the girls returned to the last crossroads. "Which way, Dad?" Alayna cried.

From overhead Libby heard a chuckle. "Go right, sweetie." She looked up. Alayna's father was standing in a watchtower that gave him a view of the entire maze.

"He was here the whole time?" Libby asked.

Alayna nodded. "Yep. He put up that tower so he can guide people who need help."

Life is like a maze. You can't see very far ahead, and you constantly have to decide which way to go. But you're not in this maze alone! God is with you. He can see the way and guide you. Each time you reach a corner, he'll tell you which way to turn, until you finally make it through.

Life in Bible Times

The Israelites didn't really wander in the desert on their way to the Promised Land. God led them the whole time. But he took them along a winding, twisting path, like a maze.

Mysterious Things

[God] made known to us the mystery of his will ... [which is] to bring all things in heaven and on earth together under one head, even Christ.

Ephesians 1:9–10

Inside the strange wooden cabin, Johnny rolled a ball down a slanted board. It rolled back up. His mother shook her head. "That's weird."

Across the room, Johnny's dad said, "Watch this, you guys!" Grabbing the top of a doorway, he lifted himself off the floor. Instead of hanging straight down, he was tilted at a bizarre angle.

"Let me try!" Johnny said, and his father lifted him up. Johnny hung at the same angle. Laughing, he said, "This is crazy!"

The tour guide set a chair against the wall, its back legs resting on a beam two feet off the floor. Johnny climbed up on it. "Hey, Mom and Dad!" he shouted, waving. His feet were dangling in midair. Scratching his head, his father said, "Now I know why they call this the Mystery Spot."

Some things are a mystery, but God's will—his chosen plan—isn't. God intends for Jesus, the Savior of the world, to also be the Lord of the world. He wants him to rule the earth, the way a head rules a body. Jesus becomes your Lord when you decide to always obey him. Is Jesus only your Savior, or is he also your Lord?

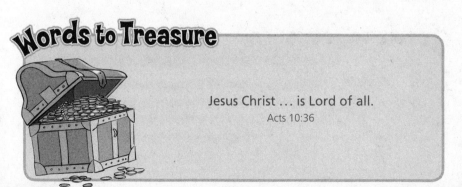

Words to Treasure

Jesus Christ ... is Lord of all.
Acts 10:36

Written in Stone

> When the Lord finished speaking to Moses on Mount Sinai, he gave him the two tablets of the Testimony, the tablets of stone inscribed by the finger of God.
>
> Exodus 31:18

The cement truck's here!" Nate said. He and his parents watched the big truck back up to where their new driveway was going to be.

Nate's dad held up his hand. "That's good!" The driver got out and set up the chute. He pulled a lever, and the gray, slushy mixture started pouring out. Using long-handled tools, he and Nate's dad moved the cement around. When the first section of the driveway was filled, they used other tools to smooth out the cement. Then the driver moved the truck, and they began working on the next section.

Soon the job was done. Nate stuck his palms in the wet cement, then wrote his name and the date with his finger. Everyone applauded. The driver said, "That's going to be there a long, long time!"

God used his own finger to write the Ten Commandments on stone tablets. But what he really wanted to do was inscribe his laws on people's hearts! Are God's laws written on *your* heart, so they're part of you forever? Memorizing Bible verses is a great way to help God put his laws right where he wants them to be.

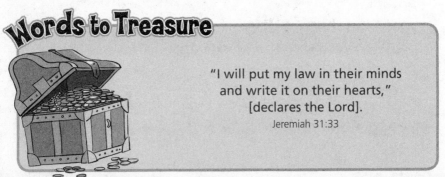

Words to Treasure

"I will put my law in their minds and write it on their hearts," [declares the Lord].

Jeremiah 31:33

Knowing Your Opponent

We are not unaware of [Satan's] schemes.
2 Corinthians 2:11

A s the other football team huddled up, Wade wondered what they were going to do. The game was almost over, and his team was ahead. But their opponents only needed four yards to score a touchdown and win. *Will they try to pass the ball or run with it?* Wade wondered.

He watched them line up on the field. Taking his position, he tried to read their eyes. Wade's team had played this team twice this season. He thought about what they'd done before in situations like this. *I bet they're going to pass*, he thought.

The center snapped the ball, and Wade rushed forward. He collided with the player in front of him. Wade saw the quarterback fake a handoff to another player. But he wasn't fooled. As the quarterback wound up to pass, Wade plowed into him. The quarterback went down, fumbling the ball.

It's easier to deal with an opponent when you know what he's going to do. And you don't have to guess what the Devil will do. That's because the Bible reveals his goals and how he tries to achieve them. Learn Satan's schemes, so you can defend yourself against him.

Did You Know?

What are the Devil's schemes? Satan comes to "steal and kill and destroy" (John 10:10). To accomplish this goal, he lies to people. He tries to scare them. He tricks them into doubting God. And he tempts them to sin.

A Special Kind of Blessing

Blessed is he who is kind to the needy.

Proverbs 14:21

A cold wind was blowing as Natasha and her parents entered the soup kitchen. It was a place that offered free meals to poor people in the city.

Natasha's dad found the woman in charge of volunteers. "Welcome!" she said. "Hang up your coats and step behind the counter, and I'll show you how you can help."

Soon Natasha was spooning out mashed potatoes to people who came in for food. When they thanked her, she smiled. "You're welcome. Happy Thanksgiving, and God bless you!" Serving them made her feel warm inside.

Later she took a break to eat. She sat with a girl named Clara, who'd come through the line with her mom. Clara gratefully said grace, and they all dug into the food, talking and laughing. To Natasha, turkey never tasted so good.

There are many types of blessings you can be thankful for on Thanksgiving Day—and all year round. But there's one special blessing you only get by being kind to the poor. It's the joy and satisfaction God puts in your heart as you help people he loves. That's what Jesus meant when he said, "It is more blessed to give than to receive" (Acts 20:35). Think of ways to reach out to needy people throughout the year. God will be pleased, and he'll bless you for your kindness.

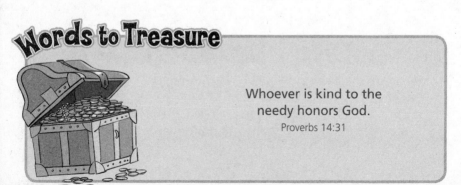

Words to Treasure

Whoever is kind to the needy honors God.
Proverbs 14:31

Getting Pumped Up

Be filled with the Spirit.

Ephesians 5:18

Skyler shivered as his granddad poured him more hot chocolate. The sound of the marching band was fading, and Skyler could hear new music. He pointed up the street. "Here comes the Polar Express float!"

They were standing beside Columbus Circle in New York City, watching the Macy's Thanksgiving Day Parade. His granddad handed him his cup, saying, "It was worth it, getting here early. Isn't this a great spot?" Nodding, Skyler took a sip. His granddad continued. "Next time, we'll come the night before the parade and watch 'em inflate the huge balloons. You should see that! They start out flat, lying in the street. Then the crews pump helium into them from tank trucks. The characters start coming to life, and soon they're looking big and strong and ready to go."

Skyler glanced up the street again. "Look, Granddad. There's Snoopy!" The immense balloon was just coming into view, soaring high above the crowd.

Balloons are designed to be filled with helium or air. God designed people to be filled with his Spirit. When God pumps you up with his Spirit, you're ready for anything. Every night before you go to bed, or each morning when you wake up, ask God to fill you with his Spirit. That'll prepare you for the day ahead!

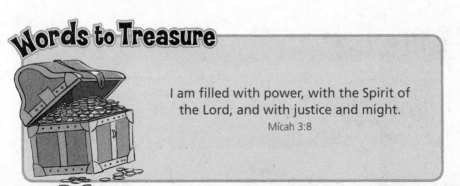

Words to Treasure

I am filled with power, with the Spirit of the Lord, and with justice and might.

Micah 3:8

Showing Your Spirit

[O Lord,] from the lips of children and infants
you have ordained praise.

Psalm 8:2

Look what I got on my way home," said Ronnie's dad, walking in the front door. He showed Ronnie a box.

"A face painting kit? What's that for?" Ronnie asked.

His dad started opening it. "Well, your brother's big football game is tonight. So I thought we'd show our team spirit. Are you in?"

Ronnie grinned. "I'm in!"

Going into the bathroom, they painted the school colors on their faces. On their cheeks they painted the number on the jersey that Ronnie's brother always wore. Then they looked at themselves in the mirror. "Go, Eagles!" they shouted, high-fiving each other. At the game, they sat in the stands and hollered their lungs out.

When Jesus rode into Jerusalem on a donkey, children were shouting praises to him. (See Matthew 21:1–17.) Why not show that kind of enthusiasm at church? Shout out your praise when your worship leader invites you to. And sing with all your heart during praise songs. God wants you to show him your spirit! But remember, it's not just about being loud. It's about worshiping God from the innermost part of your being. (See John 4:24.)

Live It!

Buy a face painting kit. Have everyone in your family paint their faces for a special worship night at home. Use symbols and colors that remind you of Jesus. Then sing loud, upbeat songs praising him!

Fruit on the Vine

[Jesus said,] "I am the vine; you are the branches. If a man remains in me and I in him, he will bear much fruit."

John 15:5

Whoosh! A blue flame shot up into the gigantic balloon above Stacy and her father. The basket they were in started rising. "Away we go!" said her dad. Soon they were high over California's Napa Valley. Jim, their pilot, let the balloon drift quietly.

"It's so peaceful up here," Stacy said. "I can't even feel any wind."

Grinning, Jim replied, "That's because we're moving with it."

Stacy gazed at the valley. "Look at all the vineyards, Dad! You can see rows and rows of grapevines."

"It's almost harvesttime," her father said. "Those vines must be filled with big, juicy grapes."

Handing Stacy a rope, Jim said, "Let's go closer and see. This rope lets hot air out of the top of the balloon. That'll make us go down. Give it a pull!"

God wants to see fruit growing in *you*—spiritual fruit, that is. These are qualities such as patience, kindness, and goodness. (See Galatians 5:22–23.) Stay connected to Jesus, the way a branch is connected to a grapevine. Then the Holy Spirit will produce this fruit in you.

Life in Bible Times

Ancient gardeners pruned the branches of their grapevines. They cut off bad parts so good parts could grow. That way, the branches produced more fruit. God prunes believers for the same reason.

Keeping Score

> "I will forgive their wickedness and will remember their sins no more," [declares the Lord].
>
> Hebrews 8:12

Get him!" Blake yelled at the football players on the field below. He sighed. "Oh, man. Another touchdown against us." Blake pushed a button, and the numbers on the arena's scoreboard changed. He had won, in a drawing, the chance to sit in the control room and run the scoreboard for tonight's game.

The man who usually kept score said, "You're doing great, Blake. But this should be fun."

"It is," Blake replied, grinning. "I just hate giving points to the other team."

The control room was an exciting place to watch the action, but the game wasn't going well. When the final buzzer sounded, the home team had only three points. "We'll get 'em next time," the man said as the crowd began leaving. "Why don't you wipe out that ugly score?"

Blake smiled. "Glad to!" He pushed the reset button, and all the numbers on the scoreboard changed to zeros.

When you sin against God, there's nothing you can do to reset the score. But if you ask God to forgive you, he promises to forget what you did, as if it never happened. Can God really do that? He can, because Jesus died to wipe out the sins of everyone who has faith in him.

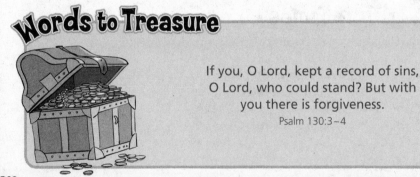

Words to Treasure

If you, O Lord, kept a record of sins, O Lord, who could stand? But with you there is forgiveness.

Psalm 130:3–4

Keeping It Together

> [Jesus said,] "Everyone who hears these words
> of mine and puts them into practice is like a
> wise man who built his house on the rock."
>
> Matthew 7:24

Holly opened the van's hatch, saying, "I hope it's okay." Inside the van was a large gingerbread house.

"Looks good!" said Holly's mom. Holly was happy that the gingerbread house survived. It was a long trip from their home in Kentucky to the Grove Park Inn in North Carolina. That was where the National Gingerbread House Competition was held. She and her mother had spent hours making their masterpiece. First they'd baked gingerbread and cut it into pieces. Then they'd glued the pieces together with frosting and decorated the house with candy.

As they lifted it out of the van, Holly was glad they'd chosen a sturdy piece of plywood for the base. That kept their beautiful creation from wobbling and falling apart.

If you want to keep your life from falling apart, build it on a good base. You do that by listening to Jesus and doing what he says. Jesus' words are the most secure foundation there is. Basing your life on them is the only way to keep it all together.

Live It!

Use blocks to make two houses—one in a sandbox and one on the sidewalk. Jump up and down next to each house. Which one stands? Now test *your* foundation. Are you building your life on Jesus' words?

One-on-One

> Very early in the morning, while it was still dark, Jesus got up, left the house and went off to a solitary place, where he prayed.
>
> Mark 1:35

K.C. was dribbling a basketball in the driveway when his dad got home from work. "How about a little one-on-one?" he asked, tossing his father the ball.

His dad took off his jacket. "You're on!" K.C. liked playing basketball with his father. It was fun, and it gave them a chance to talk. His dad made a fast break, but K.C. blocked him, forcing him to try a jump shot. It missed, and K.C. grabbed the rebound. He dribbled the ball out to their "center court line" (which was just a crack in the cement). Then, with his dad covering him, he looked for an opening. K.C. spun and went to his left. His dad tried to steal the ball. But K.C. ran around him and made a quick layup.

"That's two!" he said.

His dad retrieved the ball. "Nice move. So, how are things at school?"

Jesus spent lots of one-on-one time with his Father. (See Luke 5:16.) God wants to have that same kind of time with you. Enjoy some special moments with your heavenly Father every day, through prayer. That way, the two of you can stay connected. Spending lots of quality time with God is the best way to keep your relationship with him strong.

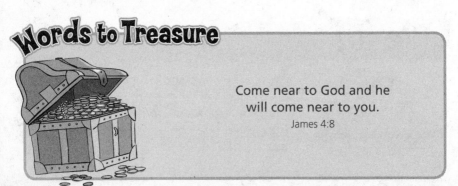

Words to Treasure

Come near to God and he will come near to you.
James 4:8

Being Trained

Train a child in the way he should go, and when he is old he will not turn from it.

Proverbs 22:6

Joel stood with his parents in the last car of *The Canadian*, a train carrying them westward through the Rocky Mountains of Canada. The car was round in back with windows on three sides. Joel watched the track disappearing behind them. "This is the best car on the train!" he said.

His dad nodded. "Wait'll you see the panoramic dome on top." He led them upstairs, where people were relaxing in comfortable seats. There were windows all around, even on the ceiling.

Joel gazed up at the mountain peaks and forward at the tracks ahead. "I'm riding here the rest of the way," he announced.

His mom chuckled. "You'll get hungry and head for the dining car before we reach Vancouver."

"What's that?" Joel asked.

His dad replied, "A beautiful city in Canada, near the mountains and the ocean. You'll love it. That's where this track is taking us."

Because God loves you, he tells your parents to "train" you. He wants them to set you on the path of righteousness so you'll stay on it, like a train on its track. Listen to your parents, cooperate with them, and obey them. The path of righteousness is a wonderful journey. And it leads to a great destination!

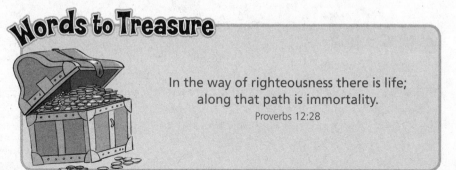

Words to Treasure

In the way of righteousness there is life; along that path is immortality.

Proverbs 12:28

Evidence of the Past

The word of the Lord is right and true.

Psalm 33:4

C hloe and her dad walked around the old drive-in movie theater. It had closed down a long time ago, and they were taking pictures of it. Chloe had a small digital camera. Her father, a news photographer, carried a much larger one. "Come here, Chloe," he said. "You'll want to get a picture of this!"

She took a shot of the broken marquee sign, then went over to him. He was looking into a ticket booth. "See?" he said. "This one still has an old cash register in it!" Lifting his camera, he started shooting. Chloe took some pictures, then followed him toward the snack bar. He stopped to take a close-up of one of the gray metal speakers people hung inside their cars.

"This place is really interesting," she said, looking at the gigantic movie screen.

"I know," her dad replied. "You can almost see everyone sitting in their cars, watching a movie."

In ancient cities, archaeologists have found the ruins of old theaters. They've also found scrolls and pottery. These finds help prove that stories in the Bible really happened. Learning about archaeology helps you understand the Bible better. And it strengthens your faith.

Live It!

The Bible tells about a riot in Ephesus. Using the Internet or an encyclopedia, find a picture of the theater where the crowd gathered. Those ruins are evidence that what the Bible says is true. (See Acts 19:23–31.)

Facing a Lion

Your enemy the devil prowls around like a roaring lion looking for someone to devour. Resist him, standing firm in the faith.

1 Peter 5:8–9

At the zoo, Eddie's little brother Mark spotted some lion masks for sale. "Ooh, can I have one?" he asked. Their dad bought one, and Mark put it on.

As the family strolled around the zoo, Eddie took pictures with his mom's digital camera. "Can you see the animals through that thing?" he asked Mark near the bear exhibit. The little lion nodded. "Show me your claws," Eddie said. Mark raised his hands with fingers curled, giving a muffled roar. Laughing, Eddie snapped his picture. The lion exhibit was next. Eddie zoomed in for a close-up of the king of beasts.

Later, during the drive home, Eddie scrolled through the pictures on the camera's screen. He toggled back and forth between the shot of Mark roaring and the next one. Grinning, he said, "You look ferocious in your lion mask, Mark. But you're no match for the real lion!"

Satan prowls around *like* a lion, but you don't have to be afraid of him. Jesus is with you, and he really *is* a lion. In fact, one of Jesus' names is the Lion of Judah. (See Revelation 5:5.) Ask him to empower you to stand up to Satan, and Satan will leave you alone.

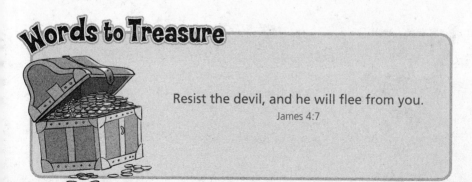

Words to Treasure

Resist the devil, and he will flee from you.
James 4:7

November 24

Carving Character

[God] who began a good work in you will carry it on to completion until the day of Christ Jesus.

Philippians 1:6

Chelsea gazed at the life-sized model of Crazy Horse, the famous Native American leader. The figure was riding a stallion and pointing. Then she looked past it to Thunderhead Mountain. There, carved into the rock, was a sculpture based on the model—only *much* bigger. It was the Crazy Horse Memorial in South Dakota.

"Look, Dad!" she said. "His face is done, and you can see where his arm will be."

"I know," her father replied. "Do you realize how *big* this carving is? It's longer than two football fields. This will be the world's largest sculpture."

"When will it be finished?" she asked.

Her dad shrugged. "Nobody knows. It's taken the sculptors over sixty years to get this far. But they'll keep working until it's done." He took her hand. "Come on, let's leave the Welcome Center and go see the carving up close!"

God has been shaping your character for a long time. In his mind, he has a beautiful image of what he wants it to look like. He won't give up on you until his good work is done and your character is perfect.

Live It!

With clay and modeling tools, make a sculpture of your favorite Bible character. As you work, think about how God is working on you all the time. What tools is he using to mold your character?

You're Not Alone

Elisha prayed, "O Lord, open his eyes so he may see." Then the Lord opened the servant's eyes, and he looked and saw the hills full of horses and chariots of fire all around Elisha.

2 Kings 6:17

Alan and his dad carried groceries up to their house. "I hope you're enjoying your birthday," said Alan's dad. "I know we're not doing much to celebrate it. But you said you wanted a minibike instead of a party."

Alan reached for the door handle. "That's okay, Dad. I love the minibike you and Mom got me. I wanna go ride it!"

"Well, first let's have some of that cake your mother baked," said his father, smiling. "You can't have a birthday without cake."

Alan opened the door and stepped inside. The house looked empty. "Mom, we're back."

Suddenly a bunch of people jumped out from their hiding places. "Surprise! Happy Birthday!"

Sometimes when you're a Christian, it feels like you're all alone. But the truth is, you're surrounded by fellow believers. They're in your family, your church, your neighborhood, and your school. And the armies of heaven are standing by your side, just as they were for Elisha and his servant. (See 2 Kings 6:15–17.) Most importantly, God is with you. So never give up battling evil and trying to live God's way. With all that support, you can't lose!

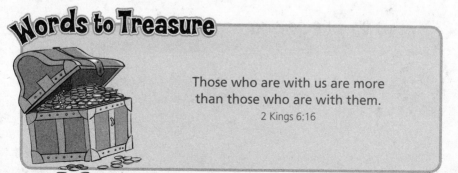

Words to Treasure

Those who are with us are more than those who are with them.
2 Kings 6:16

Making It Hard for the Enemy

Do not let the sun go down while you are still angry, and do not give the devil a foothold.

Ephesians 4:26–27

Alex's friend Jake rappelled down the climbing wall. He came down fast, kicking himself off the wall each time he swung toward it. "I made it to the top," he said after landing on the mat. "Your turn!"

Alex said, "I'll try."

The attendant gave Alex some pointers while helping him put on the harness. "One more thing," the man said as he finished adjusting it. "Always make sure you have a good hold on the wall before you try to climb higher."

Alex nodded. Then he grabbed the highest "rock" he could reach. Putting his toe on the lower one, he started climbing. Things went smoothly at first. But about halfway up he fell. Swinging on the safety rope, he told Jake, "I guess I didn't have a good foothold!"

When you stay angry, you give the Devil a foothold in your heart. A foothold can be the jutting rock a climber uses to conquer a mountain. Or it can be the captured land an army uses when it conquers a country. Don't give Satan a foothold so he can conquer you! Get rid of your anger. Praying about it will help. So will talking with people you're angry at, and choosing to forgive them. That'll make things much harder for the Enemy.

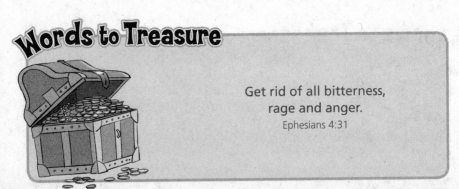

Words to Treasure

Get rid of all bitterness, rage and anger.

Ephesians 4:31

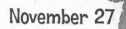

Lost and Found

> [Jesus said,] "Suppose a woman has ten silver coins and loses one. Does she not light a lamp, sweep the house and search carefully until she finds it?"
>
> Luke 15:8

Lindsay led her grandfather through the backyard. He was carrying his metal detector. She stopped in the middle of the lawn. "My pendant fell off here somewhere. Matt was chasing me. He grabbed my necklace, and it broke."

Her grandfather handed her the machine. "Here you go."

"I get to use it?" Lindsay asked, her eyes wide.

He nodded. "Sure! It's your pendant."

Lindsay moved slowly across the yard, waving the metal detector over the ground. The machine beeped. "I found something!" She felt around in the grass, then held up a rusty nail.

Her grandfather laughed. "Keep looking. You'll find it." For fifteen minutes Lindsay searched with no results. Then the metal detector beeped again. She knelt, then shouted joyfully and showed her grandfather the tiny gold pendant. Smiling, he said, "This calls for a celebration. Let's get some ice cream!"

Anyone separated from God by sin is like a valuable lost item he wants very much to find. Tell people about God's love. If someone stops sinning and goes back to him, you'll have helped God get back something precious. Then all heaven rejoices! (See Luke 15:8–10.)

People in Bible Times

When the prodigal son gave up his sinful ways and went home, his father ran to hug him. Then his father called for a celebration. (See Luke 15:11–32.)

Whittling Away

> On the walls all around the temple, in both
> the inner and outer rooms, [Solomon] carved
> cherubim, palm trees and open flowers.
>
> 1 Kings 6:29

Randall's grandfather had flown in from out of state for a visit. "Here, I bought you something," he said, handing Randall a small box as they sat on the porch.

"Thanks, Grandpa," Randall said. He opened it. "Wow, a jackknife!"

His grandfather grinned. "I thought I'd teach you how to whittle. So I brought my knife and the carving I'm working on, and some wood for you to practice with." He showed Randall his carving of a dog. Then, using Randall's knife and a block of wood, he demonstrated some whittling techniques. "Now, I've been doing this awhile," he said, giving Randall the knife and the block. "You should begin with a simple shape."

Randall frowned. "Aw, I want to carve something cool. Wait, I know—I'll make a baseball!"

People in the Bible used their tools and talents to carve lots of things out of wood. Some people made beautiful decorations for God's temple. Others carved images of false gods. What will you do with the tools and talents God gave you? Make a commitment to use them for his glory.

Life in Bible Times

When Solomon built God's temple, the king of Tyre sent him cedar logs. From these logs, boards were made to cover the inner walls. Then the boards were carved with decorations. (See 1 Kings 5–6.)

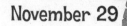

Better Than Radar

The Lord will watch over your coming and going both now and forevermore.

Psalm 121:8

Hannah and her mom hung up their coats and went to the family room. Sitting at the desk, Hannah turned on the computer. She typed in "FlightAware.com," then entered the tail number of her dad's single-engine airplane.

A map of the United States appeared on the screen. A yellow dot indicated the nearby airport in Louisville, Kentucky, where they'd just dropped off Hannah's father. Another dot showed the airport in Albany, New York, where he was headed on a business trip.

"Dad's over Ohio right now," Hannah said, pointing at a green airplane icon. A green line showed his progress so far.

Hannah's mom smiled. "Looks like he has about three hours to go. Why don't you go do your homework? We'll check this later. And don't worry—God will be watching over your dad, even when we're not."

God has you on his radar screen all the time. Actually, he does more than just watch you. He goes with you wherever you go, protecting you and keeping you safe. When you pray for his help, you never have to wait for him to come. He's already there.

Live It!

The next time you travel, write the words of Psalm 121:8 on a map. Use a red marker to trace your progress. After the trip, keep the map as a reminder that God is always with you, watching over you.

A Hand Up

With my God I can scale a wall.

2 Samuel 22:30

Alex clung to the climbing wall, breathing hard. He was near the top, over two stories high. He had a harness on, and a man was holding his safety rope. But as Alex glanced down, he thought, *What if I slip again way up here, and this time the rope comes out of his hands?*

"You can do it, Alex!" shouted his friend Jake, who was standing below.

Alex looked up. Part of him wanted to quit. He was tired, and he couldn't decide which fingerhold to try next. Some were easy to hold on to, but if he grabbed the wrong one ...

God, help me not to be afraid, Alex prayed. *Show me the way to go. Give me the strength to make it.* He studied the fingerholds above him. The one on the left seemed to stand out from the others. Bracing himself, he lunged for it.

His fingers found a good grip! Muscles shaking, he worked his way up the last few feet, then punched the buzzer.

God promises to be with you and help you. He is never afraid, he is never tired, and he always knows what to do. Whatever you're trying to achieve, you can trust God to be there and lend a helping hand.

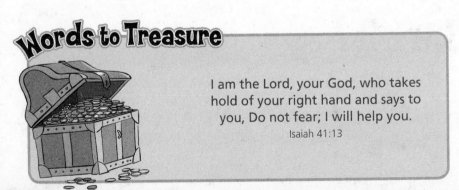

Words to Treasure

I am the Lord, your God, who takes hold of your right hand and says to you, Do not fear; I will help you.

Isaiah 41:13

Mixing with the Right Crowd

Do not be yoked together with unbelievers.

2 Corinthians 6:14

Chris stood at the workbench in his dad's home lab. In front of him was a drinking glass, a pitcher of water, a bottle of cooking oil, and a container of blue food coloring. Chris's father, a science teacher, was trying out another experiment. "Okay, Chris. Fill the glass halfway with water and the rest of the way with oil."

Chris grabbed the pitcher. "Right, Dad."

As Chris followed directions, his dad said, "Everyone knows oil and water don't mix. But let's see what a drop of food coloring will do." Chris finished pouring the oil. The liquids formed two layers, with the oil on top. He squeezed a drop of food coloring into the glass. Without losing its shape, it sank through the oil. Then the drop hit the water and dispersed, mixing with it thoroughly.

Imagine that the kids you know are either oil or water. It's okay to be friends with the ones who are oil (nonbelievers). Just don't get mixed up with them too much. If you do, they'll pull you away from Jesus. Develop your closest friendships with the kids who are water (believers). They'll help you follow Jesus faithfully.

Life in Bible Times

An ancient farmer would join two oxen together with a wooden yoke. The two animals became one team. The apostle Paul wrote that believers shouldn't link up with nonbelievers that closely.

335

Losing Status

> [Jesus], being in very nature God, did not consider equality with God something to be grasped, but made himself nothing, taking the very nature of a servant.
>
> Philippians 2:6–7

Erin and her friend Cathy sat in tilted-back chairs. On the dome above were images of the solar system. As music filled the planetarium, Pluto zoomed into view. "Pluto was discovered in 1930," the narrator said. "At the time, it was thought to be as large as Neptune. But in 1990 the Hubble Space Telescope showed that it was smaller than Earth's moon. Other objects in the solar system were found that were as big or bigger than Pluto. So in 2006 it was decided that Pluto wasn't a planet after all. Now it's considered to be a dwarf planet."

Erin nudged Cathy. "Poor Pluto," she whispered.

Cathy nodded. "Can you imagine? One day you're a planet, and the next you're hardly more than an asteroid!"

When Pluto was reclassified as a dwarf planet, it lost a lot of status. So did Jesus, when he became a human being. As God's Son, Jesus was the prince of heaven. All the angels worshiped him. He had the most status of anyone, except for his Father! But Jesus was willing to give all that up. He left heaven and came to earth so he could save people. Are you willing to give up some of your status to help others?

Words to Treasure

Your attitude should be the same as that of Christ Jesus.

Philippians 2:5

The Authorities

Do you want to be free from fear of the one in authority? Then do what is right and he will commend you.

Romans 13:3

When Cayden's mom dropped him off at his new friend's house, he was surprised to see a police car in the driveway. Russell came out of the garage, followed by a policeman. "Hi, Cayden. This is my dad. He's getting ready to go out on patrol."

Shaking hands with Russell's father, Cayden said, "I like your car."

The policeman grinned. "Want to see inside?"

"Sure!" Cayden replied. Opening the door, Russell's father let Cayden slide behind the wheel. Then he pointed out the radio, the radar gun, and the switches for the siren and the flashing lights. "Do you catch lots of speeders in this car?" Cayden asked.

"Oh yes," said Russell's father. "And I slow down many more. People stop speeding when they see me out there!"

Do you obey the rules all the time, even when nobody's watching? That's what it means to have integrity. It's about always doing the right thing, because it's the right thing to do. If you live like that, you never have to worry about getting into trouble. When people *are* watching, they'll praise you for your good behavior! This is true with everyone in authority over you. That includes your parents, your teachers, and the police.

Words to Treasure

Submit to the authorities, not only because of possible punishment but also because of conscience.

Romans 13:5

337

Secret Identity

> [Jesus] was transfigured before them. His face shone like the sun, and his clothes became as white as the light.
>
> Matthew 17:2

Dean sat at the drawing table, working on a comic book. Physically he was in his bedroom. Mentally he was on the planet Xorkton. With him was Magma-man, the superhero he'd created.

Magma-man was in a hurry. Xorkton had left its orbit around a distant star and was heading for Earth. He had to act quickly, before his coworkers realized he was missing. Otherwise they might guess his secret identity. Thinking fast, he shouted, "Magmatize!" Instantly he changed into a mass of red-hot lava. He flowed into a dormant volcano. Then he erupted out, pushing the planet away.

Returning to normal shape, Magma-man headed back to Earth. At the deli, his coworkers were looking for him. He came out of the back room, adjusting his apron. "There you are, Joe," Janet said. "I was beginning to wonder ..."

Do you know who Jesus really is? When he was on the mountain with Peter, James, and John, he revealed his divine glory. That showed them his true identity. Jesus was actually God, who had become a man so he could save the world.

Did You Know?

What happened to Jesus on the mountain? Jesus began to shine brightly because he was God. His glory was usually hidden. But for a while on the mountaintop, it could clearly be seen.

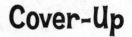

Cover-Up

> Christ Jesus, who died—more than that, who was raised to life—is at the right hand of God and is also interceding for us.
>
> Romans 8:34

Roxanne stood in line with her dad, holding her favorite book. Lots of kids were there, and the bookstore was serving goodies. "I'm so excited!" Roxanne said. "I can't wait to meet the author."

As she sipped her drink, her dad said, "First you'd better wipe those cookie crumbs off your face."

Without thinking, Roxanne wiped her mouth with her sleeve—spilling red punch on her shirt. "Oh no, I can't go up there like this!"

Taking her cup, her father said, "It's all right, Roxanne. I'll take care of it."

She blinked back tears. "How?"

"Just trust me," he said. Soon they were next in line. Roxanne's father put his arm around her shoulder. "Ready, sweetheart?"

Glancing down, she saw he was covering the stain with his hand. She looked up and smiled. "Yes, Daddy." When it was Roxanne's turn, they approached the author's table together.

Right now Jesus is covering your sins, because you've put your faith in him. As God looks at you and talks with you, Jesus intercedes for you with him. That means Jesus stands beside you, covering your guilt with his goodness. So you look perfect to God. Because of Jesus, you don't have to be ashamed in God's presence!

Words to Treasure

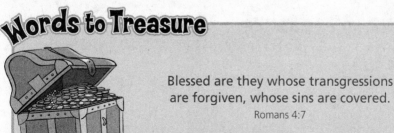

> Blessed are they whose transgressions are forgiven, whose sins are covered.
> Romans 4:7

A Powerful Echo

"My word that goes out from my mouth ... will not return to me empty, but will accomplish what I desire and achieve the purpose for which I sent it," [declares the Lord].

Isaiah 55:11

At the Liberty Science Center in Jersey City, New Jersey, Payton put his mouth near one end of a long metal tube. The tube ran up the wall, went around the ceiling of the room, and came back down. The other end was next to his ear. "Hello!" he said. "*Hello!*" his voice responded. "Give me a cheeseburger!" he said. "*... a cheeseburger!*" his voice answered back. Laughing, Payton turned to his parents. "This is cool. It's amazing how long it takes for the sound to travel around the tube."

"You must have a tube like that between your ear and your brain," his mom joked. "Whenever I ask you to do something, it sure takes a long time for you to do it."

Payton grinned. "Don't feel bad. I just ordered lunch, and I doubt it'll ever come."

God's words never echo back to him uselessly. They always make things happen. That's good news, because it means that all of God's promises will be fulfilled. All of his predictions about the future will come true. And someday everything will be just as he says it should be.

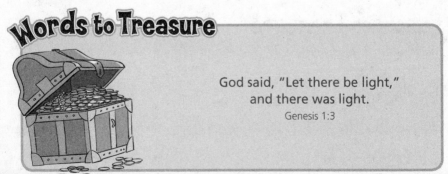

Words to Treasure

God said, "Let there be light," and there was light.

Genesis 1:3

Shipwreck

> Bear with each other and forgive whatever grievances you may have against one another. Forgive as the Lord forgave you.
>
> Colossians 3:13

Leonard heard a crash and ran to his bedroom. His younger brother Peter was holding a damaged model ship. Peter looked miserable. "I'm sorry, Leonard! I didn't mean to drop it."

Leonard grabbed the broken vessel. "You *ruined* it!" he yelled. "Get out of my room!"

Peter left, crying, just as Leonard's mom came in to see what happened. When he told her, she said, "Oh, Leonard. I'm sorry." Then she had him sit next to her on his bed. "I know you're angry," she said. "But I want you to think about forgiving Peter. Remember how you felt when you broke my favorite Precious Moments figurine? I was very upset, but I forgave you. Shouldn't you show the same mercy to your brother?"

God has forgiven all your sins, and that wasn't easy for him to do. For one thing, your sins caused God a lot of pain. Plus, in order to forgive you, he had to sacrifice his Son, Jesus. Now God wants you to forgive others when they do things that hurt you. He understands how hard that is, but he's also willing to help you do it.

People in Bible Times

One servant didn't forgive another one who hadn't paid him back a little money. But the first servant had forgotten something. Their master had forgiven the huge debt *he* owed!

Heads or Tails

If you fully obey the Lord your God ... [t]he
Lord will make you the head, not the tail.

Deuteronomy 28:1, 13

Tonya was excited to be one of two students chosen to wear the school mascot costume during assembly on Friday. She wasn't so thrilled about being the back part of the horse. But she was a good sport. At the rehearsal on Wednesday, Mrs. Deacon helped her and Brandi zip the two halves of their costume together. "Okay in there?" Mrs. Deacon asked.

Her voice sounded muffled to Tonya. "I guess," she answered. She couldn't see. All she could do was follow Brandi around. When Mrs. Deacon finally unzipped them, Tonya said, "Whew! Thanks, Mrs. D. It was getting hot in there." Climbing out of the costume, she saw her dad waiting. "Bye, ya'll. Gotta go."

Driving home, her dad asked, "Who was the other girl in the costume?"

Tonya replied, "That's Brandi. She's pretty and popular, but she's not very nice to people. I wouldn't want to follow her around in real life, like other kids do."

Sometimes it's tempting to follow people who don't set a good example. But you don't have to do that to have friends! If you live according to God's rules, some people will follow *you*. They'll copy your example. You can lead others toward righteousness if you obey God instead of giving in to peer pressure.

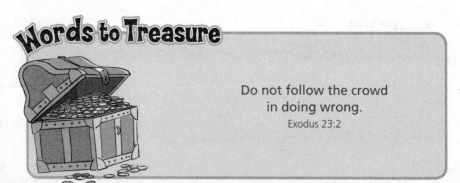

Words to Treasure

Do not follow the crowd
in doing wrong.
Exodus 23:2

False Promises

I am the Lord; those who hope in me will not be disappointed.

Isaiah 49:23

A TV advertisement Roy had seen before came on. He ran to grab a pencil and paper. Racing back to the living room, he scribbled down the phone number. "Dad!" he said, going out to the garage. "Can you help me order something I saw on TV?"

His father looked up from under the hood of the car. "What is it?" Roy described the item he wanted. Wiping his hands on a rag, his dad said, "Are you sure it's everything it's cracked up to be? Ads can be tricky."

Roy frowned, asking, "What do you mean?"

"When I was a kid," his dad replied, "I saw an ad in a comic book. It was for a remote-controlled ghost you could use to scare people. It seemed to be controlled with a radio transmitter. So I sent my money. I got a balloon, a plastic sheet, and some string. The instructions said to put the string over a tree branch, hide somewhere, and pull the string to make the ghost wiggle!"

When someone fools you or makes a false promise, it's disappointing. God is everything he says he is, and he always keeps his promises! He'll never let you down if you put your hope in him.

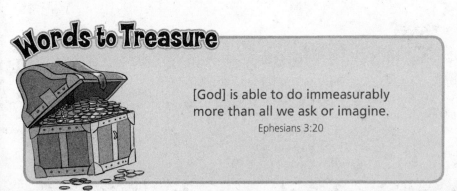

Words to Treasure

[God] is able to do immeasurably more than all we ask or imagine.
Ephesians 3:20

Overcoming Gravity

> Who may ascend the hill of the Lord? Who may stand in his holy place? He who has clean hands and a pure heart.
>
> Psalm 24:3–4

Jumping on their sleds, Heidi and Joey sped down the hill behind their school. It was big and steep, and the snow was hard-packed. Heidi started moving ahead. Grabbing her ankle, Joey pulled her back. "No fair!" she yelled.

But by doing this, Joey put himself into a spin. He wiped out and slid partway down on his snowsuit. Heidi sailed past him, laughing. "Now, that's fair!" Joey threw himself back on his sled. At the bottom of the hill, the friends began trudging up again.

Near the top, Joey pulled off his hat. "Whew! Sliding down is a piece of cake, but climbing up is hard work."

Breathing heavily, Heidi said, "I wish this hill had a rope tow!"

Doing the right things seems like an uphill climb. But doing the wrong things seems as easy—and fun—as sliding downhill. Why is that? It's because everyone was born with a sinful nature that acts like gravity. The good news is, God enables you to overcome it. He pulls you all the way up to the top of his holy hill.

People in Bible Times

The apostle Paul wanted to do the right things, but he found that he kept doing the wrong things. Paul knew that his sinful nature was dragging him down. But he trusted God to pull him up. (See Romans 7:15–25.)

Freebies

You who have no money, come, buy and eat! Come, buy wine and milk without money and without cost.

Isaiah 55:1

Tate gazed into the kitchen at the Krispy Kreme store. His class was there to see how the company used machines to make doughnuts. He watched one machine drop rings of batter into a long vat of hot vegetable oil. As they floated along, Tate nudged a classmate. "They look like little inner tubes going down a river!" A device flipped the doughnuts over. Then a conveyor belt carried them out of the oil.

"Here's where we put on the glaze," said the tour guide. The doughnuts went through a waterfall of sugary icing. The guide said, "See the neon sign in the front window? When it's lit, that means we're making doughnuts. If you come inside then, we'll give you a warm, fresh doughnut—right off the conveyor belt!"

Companies often give away free samples. They hope customers will like them and buy their products. God gives away freebies too. Salvation and eternal life are free gifts from God to you. So are God's forgiveness and his blessings. You don't have to earn them or pay for them somehow. God gives them to you because he loves you! He just wants you to love him back and have faith in him.

Words to Treasure

Whoever is thirsty, let him come; and whoever wishes, let him take the free gift of the water of life.
Revelation 22:17

The Hidden Side

> He who conceals his sins does not prosper, but whoever confesses and renounces them finds mercy.
>
> Proverbs 28:13

Callie was helping her grandfather in his workshop. That's where he fixed up old carousel horses. Using fine sandpaper, she lightly sanded one of the brightly colored animals. "He sure turned out beautiful," she said.

Her grandfather smiled and patted the horse. "He did, didn't he? Wait'll we get this last coat of varnish on him. Then he'll really shine!"

As Callie admired the horse, she noticed something. "Why are there all kinds of jewels and decorations on one side but not on the other?"

"Lots of carousel horses are like that," her grandfather replied. "The side that's all fancy is called the 'romance' side. That's the one everyone sees, because it faces outward on the carousel. The side that's not so nice faces inward, so it's hidden."

Everyone has flaws and failures they don't want others to see. Hiding them makes you look good on the outside, but it hurts you on the inside. That's no way to succeed in life. It's best to reveal your mistakes to people who love you. Then they can encourage you, pray for you, and help you ask God for forgiveness. Don't hide your sins and suffer—confess them and prosper!

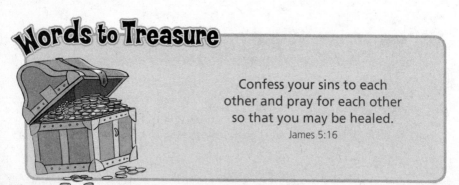

Words to Treasure

Confess your sins to each other and pray for each other so that you may be healed.

James 5:16

Tuckered Out?

Let us not become weary in doing good, for at the proper time we will reap a harvest if we do not give up.

Galatians 6:9

Elliot huffed and puffed as he followed his dad along the trail through the snowy woods. They were cross-country skiing on a bright winter morning. His father had shown him the right technique, and Elliot was getting the hang of it. Pushing himself forward with his left foot and right pole, he glided on his right foot. Then he pushed with his right foot and left pole, gliding on his left foot. He'd gotten into a steady rhythm, but it was still a lot of exercise. "Dad, I'm getting tired. Can we take a break?"

Turning his head, Elliot's dad coasted to a stop. "Sure, bud." The two of them stood there for a moment and rested.

"Whew!" Elliot said, breathing hard. "This is fun, but I like downhill skiing better. It's way easier!"

You can get tired of doing outdoor activities. You can get tired of playing board games. You can even get tired of watching TV. But there's one thing you should never get tired of. That's doing good! There's an eternal reward for people who never give up on that. Keep on living God's way, helping others, and doing the right thing. (Are you starting to grow weary of do-gooding? Read Isaiah 40:30–31 for a little pick-me-up!)

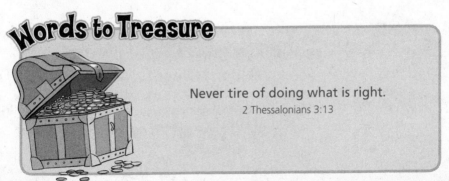

Words to Treasure

Never tire of doing what is right.
2 Thessalonians 3:13

Walking Like Jesus

"Be holy because I, the Lord your God, am holy."

Leviticus 19:2

Ruby watched her feet as she walked. "I love these snowshoes," she said. "It's cool walking on snow!" On a winter retreat at a Christian camp, Ruby and her family hiked across the countryside. Wearing big snowshoes was fun, but Ruby had to walk with her feet farther apart than she was used to.

"How are you doing, Ruby?" asked the man leading their expedition. He'd stopped to check on everybody.

"Great," Ruby said. "But I was wondering. How do these keep me on top of the snow?"

Walking beside her, he replied, "They spread out your weight so your feet don't sink. Amazing, huh?"

Ruby smiled at him. "Yeah. If you think about it, we're actually walking on water!"

Being holy, like God calls you to be, may seem impossible to you. It may seem as impossible as walking across a lake, the way Jesus did. Don't worry. God isn't asking you to do it on your own. He knows you can't be holy without his help. But he also knows you *can* do it with him holding you up.

People in Bible Times

When Peter saw Jesus walking on the water, he wanted to do it too. Peter knew he couldn't do it by himself. But he believed that with Jesus' help, he could. (See Matthew 14:22–32.)

Impossible?

[Jesus said,] "I tell you the truth, if you have faith as small as a mustard seed, you can say to this mountain, 'Move from here to there' and it will move. Nothing will be impossible for you."

Matthew 17:20

The bowling pins exploded. It looked like a strike. But when the dust settled, the seven pin and ten pin were still standing. *A seven-ten split*, Michael thought. *The worst kind!*

There was a big "Ooh!" from members of his junior bowling league. Michael heard whispers. "That's impossible." "No way."

His teammate Albert said, "Don't listen to them. You can do this!" Michael had never seen anyone knock down a seven-ten split. But he knew Albert was right. It *wasn't* impossible. Picking up his ball again, Michael faced the pins. He took four steps and fired it, hitting the seven pin hard. The pin flew into the pit behind it—then bounced out, knocking over the ten pin.

Life is full of challenges. Some are fun. Some are more important and serious. As you go through life, you'll hear two messages about whether you can meet these challenges. One will be from the Devil, who'll say, "You can't." The other will be from God, who'll say, "You can!" You have to decide which one you're going to believe. But before you do, remember one thing. "With God all things are possible" (Matthew 19:26).

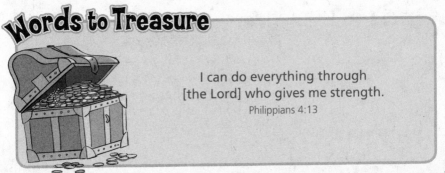

Words to Treasure

I can do everything through [the Lord] who gives me strength.

Philippians 4:13

Backspin

Flee the evil desires of youth.

2 Timothy 2:22

Chase leaned over his uncle's pool table, holding a cue stick. "Eight ball in the side pocket," he announced, happy that he was about to win the game.

"Be careful not to scratch," said his uncle.

Looking up, Chase said, "What do you mean?"

His uncle pointed at the balls Chase was aiming at. "If the cue ball goes into the pocket too, that's called a scratch. And if you scratch when you're shooting at the eight ball, you lose. Let me show you how to put some backspin on the cue ball so that doesn't happen."

Leaning over Chase, he grabbed the cue stick, guiding Chase's hands. "It's simple, really," he said. "Just hit the bottom of the cue ball with your stick, like this."

He struck the white ball. It knocked the black one into the pocket, then rolled back safely.

Learn how to backspin when you're tempted by evil desires. These desires can make evil things seem very attractive. But you don't have to be controlled by them. God can help you control them and escape temptation. If you start heading toward something appealing but wrong, backspin like a cue ball. Get away from it before you fall into sin.

Words to Treasure

God is faithful; he will not let you be tempted beyond what you can bear. But when you are tempted, he will also provide a way out.

1 Corinthians 10:13

In the Know

The very hairs of your head are all numbered.
Matthew 10:30

A little bell jingled as Cheyenne walked into her favorite candy store. "Hello, Cheyenne," said Mr. Whitney, who worked there. He was putting the top on a huge glass jar.

"Hi, Mr. Whitney. Wow, look at all those gummy bears! Are you having a sale on them?"

Mr. Whitney wiped the counter. "Nope. Actually, the store is running a little contest." He pointed at a sign next to the jar.

Cheyenne read it out loud. "'Guess the number of gummy bears in the jar and win them all.' Cool! Can I try?"

"Sure!" Mr. Whitney said. "The contest begins today. Your entry can be the first."

Cheyenne studied the jar. Writing down her guess, she dropped the entry form into a box on the counter. "Do *you* know how many there are?" she asked.

With a twinkle in his eye, Mr. Whitney said, "Of course. I put 'em all in there!"

God knows everything about you, even how many hairs you have on your head. After all, he created you. He knows and cares about everything you think and feel and do. How well do you know him? Get to know God better! Read your Bible regularly. Pray daily. And walk with him every moment of your life.

Words to Treasure

O Lord, you have searched me and you know me. You know when I sit and when I rise; you perceive my thoughts from afar.
Psalm 139:1–2

Standing Together

> Be sympathetic, love as brothers, be compassionate.
>
> 1 Peter 3:8

Terry sat in the barbershop chair, watching clumps of his hair fall to the floor. "That's it," the barber said, shutting off his clippers. "Ready to look?" Gulping, Terry nodded. The man swung the chair around to face the mirror. Terry was shocked. His hair was gone. He hardly recognized himself. Then he grinned. In the mirror, he saw his classmates standing behind him. They were just as bald! They applauded as the barber turned him around and whisked off the sheet.

"You did it, Terry!" said Kathleen.

Standing, Terry nodded. "Yep. Now we all look alike."

Phillip, Terry's best friend, looked around at everybody. "Thanks, guys," he said shyly. "I really appreciate you doing this for me, so I wouldn't feel so weird."

Phillip's medical treatments had made all of his hair fall out. Putting an arm around his shoulder, Terry said, "We just didn't want you to be the only one at school with a cool new look!"

Do whatever you can to support and encourage friends and family members when they're facing hard times. Show them sympathy and compassion when they need it. Stand beside them no matter what they're going through. That's what godly people do!

People in Bible Times

When Ruth's husband died, his mother, Naomi, had no one left to take care of her. Instead of going back to her own mother's home, Ruth chose to stay with Naomi. (See Ruth 1.)

Cleaning Up the Airwaves

Do not let any unwholesome talk come out of your mouths, but only what is helpful for building others up.

Ephesians 4:29

The manager of the radio station led Luis's class into a studio. "Here's where we record interviews. Who wants to help me demonstrate?"

"I do!" Luis said.

The man told him, "Have a seat beside that microphone. What's your name?" As Luis sat, he said his name. Pushing a button, the man nodded. "Okay, Luis. Tell us about yourself."

Luis hesitated. "Well … I like baseball … um … and dogs … uh … oh yeah, and pizza."

The man pointed at a computer screen. "See there, everyone? That's a digital graph of what Luis said. With editing software, I can clean up his answer. I'll just delete all the bad stuff." He made some changes, then played the recording. Luis's voice came over the speakers: "I like baseball and dogs and pizza."

One of Luis's classmates said, "Wow, I wish my mom had a machine like that. She cleans up my language with a bar of soap!"

Need to improve your language? Ask God to help you edit what you say before you say it. Delete unwanted words and sounds. That includes swearing, grumbling, gossiping, lying, and an angry or sarcastic tone in your voice. Then your language will bless and help others instead of offending or hurting them.

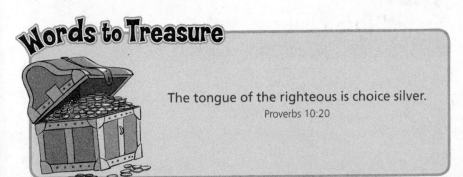

Words to Treasure

The tongue of the righteous is choice silver.
Proverbs 10:20

Sparkling Pure

> Do everything without complaining or arguing, so that you may become blameless and pure, children of God without fault in a crooked and depraved generation, in which you shine like stars in the universe.
>
> Philippians 2:14–15

At the winter festival, Colleen and her brother watched a man cut a block of ice with a chainsaw. "What's he making?" Colleen shouted.

Gabe yelled back, "Watch and see!" Shaved ice flew as the man worked. He sliced big chunks off the block, carving it into a rough shape. Then, using a grinder, he began to fine-tune his creation. The shape started looking familiar.

"Maybe it's an angel," Colleen said.

Gabe laughed. "It's kind of a funny-shaped angel." The man reached for a chisel. For a while he was blocking Colleen's view. But finally he moved.

"Oh, I know," she exclaimed. "It's an eagle!" As the artist added the final details, his sculpture glittered in the sunlight.

A great-looking ice sculpture sparkles like crystal. That's because the ice is made from pure, clear water. God is carving you into a beautiful shape. But is arguing with your parents making you murky? Is complaining to them making you look like ice made from muddy water? Be blameless and pure! Then you'll shine bright.

Life in Bible Times

In the desert, the Israelites argued with Moses and complained. They were upset because there was no water. Their character wasn't shining very brightly. Neither was their faith in God.

Learning to Control Yourself

[God's grace] teaches us to say "No" to ungodliness and worldly passions, and to live self-controlled, upright and godly lives.

Titus 2:12

Dylan loved building electronic gadgets. Today he was putting together a robot while his dad read the directions from the kit. "The right arm's done," Dylan said, testing it.

"Great!" said his dad "We're almost finished. Next, attach the computer chip to the robot."

Following his dad's instructions, Dylan snapped on the chip. Then he connected it to his PC with a cable. Using the software that came with the kit, he programmed the robot. "All done!" he said, disconnecting the cable. "Let's try it out." They went to the kitchen. "Mom, watch this. I built a robot and taught it to do things." Setting the robot on the floor, Dylan said, "Walk." The robot started walking.

Dylan's mom applauded. "That's wonderful, honey!"

"Wait, that's not all," said Dylan. "Turn right." The robot pivoted to the right. "Stop." The robot kept walking, right toward the refrigerator.

Laughing, Dylan's mom said, "Looks like his stomach has taken over!"

Being self-controlled doesn't mean you can do whatever you want to do. It means you can ignore your sinful desires and obey God. Ask God to teach you self-control. Then keep listening to his voice. That way, you can say no to your sinful desires and yes to his commands.

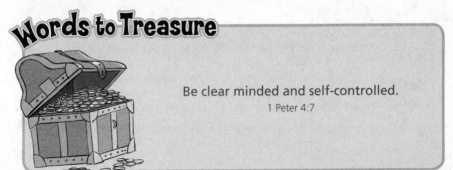

Words to Treasure

Be clear minded and self-controlled.
1 Peter 4:7

Choosing Sides

> This righteousness from God comes through
> faith in Jesus Christ to all who believe.
>
> Romans 3:22

As J.R.'s teacher wrote on the whiteboard, some kids paid attention. Others misbehaved. One boy read comics. Two girls passed notes. A spitball hit the whiteboard.

"Cut!" said J.R., lowering the camcorder. "Okay, good. Next I want the bad guys to *really* go crazy. Tip over a desk. Chase each other around!"

His teacher raised her eyebrows. "Just don't break anything!"

Everyone laughed. It was Saturday. J.R.'s classmates were helping him shoot a movie for a class project. After explaining the plot, he'd let each of them choose whether to be good guys or bad guys.

"Let's finish this shot," J.R. said. "And remember—all you good guys, keep acting good! Ready? Action!"

You don't become one of the good guys by behaving well. First you *decide* to be one, by putting your faith in Jesus. Then God makes you a good person, and you act accordingly. You behave well because that's what righteous people do.

Live It!

Skim through the book of Proverbs. As you do, remind yourself that God has made you a righteous person. The good-guy qualities apply to you! Let them become part of who you are. For example, for Proverbs 10:1 you could say, "God has made me wise. So I'll behave in a way that brings joy to my parents, because that's what wise children do."

The Center of It All

Today in the town of David a Savior has been born to you; he is Christ the Lord.

Luke 2:11

Lydia gazed at big, lit-up characters that seemed to move as her family drove through Lake Lanier Islands, near Atlanta, Georgia. She enjoyed the huge light display put on there every year at Christmastime.

"Look at that jack-in-the-box popping up," said her brother, Justin.

Lydia pointed ahead. "There's one you'll like, Dad. It's a golfer hitting a ball!"

There was a snowman waving, a train chugging along, Santa's sleigh taking off. Lydia kept looking around. Finally she spotted what she was searching for. It was a glowing scene, with angels, shepherds, and wise men gathered around a manger. "There's Jesus!" she said. "Right in the middle of it all."

Jesus is the center of all the celebration at Christmastime. He's the reason for all the lights and decorations and music and gifts. After all, if he hadn't been born, there would be no Christmas. And since he's God, Jesus is also the center of the universe. He's the reason for *everything*. If it weren't for him, nothing would exist. Celebrate Christmas with joy, keeping your focus on the center of it all. Celebrate life the same way!

Words to Treasure

For to us a child is born, to us a son is given, and the government will be on his shoulders. And he will be called Wonderful Counselor, Mighty God, Everlasting Father, Prince of Peace.

Isaiah 9:6

Oh Come, Let Us Adore Him

They saw the child with his mother Mary, and they bowed down and worshiped him.

Matthew 2:11

"Steven, you're here!" said Mrs. Anderson. "Hurry and get dressed." On Christmas Eve Mrs. Anderson was directing the live nativity scene at the Christian school Steven attended.

"Sorry I'm late," Steven said, rushing to put on his shepherd's robe. "I had to run errands with my mom before she dropped me off." He grabbed his staff, ran outside, and took his place next to the stable. Joseph, Mary, and the angels were already in position. So were the animals. People started arriving to see the display. Steven tried to look worshipful, but he was flustered. Besides, he was cold, and the sheep kept biting his robe. Steven sighed. He'd thought this would be fun. And meaningful, like being at the first Christmas. After all, he really did love Jesus.

The angels began to sing. Staring at the manger, Steven started thinking about everything Jesus meant to him. Soon he truly was worshiping his Lord and Savior.

Everyone's busy nowadays—even kids! Take a moment every day to worship Jesus, no matter how busy you are. He is God's Son, who came to save the world. He deserves to be praised. You can celebrate Jesus' birth all year long by coming to him daily and giving him your love.

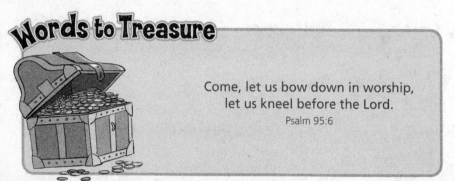

Words to Treasure

Come, let us bow down in worship, let us kneel before the Lord.
Psalm 95:6

Room for Jesus

[Mary] gave birth to her firstborn, a son. She wrapped him in cloths and placed him in a manger, because there was no room for them in the inn.

Luke 2:7

Kip gazed at the huge columns inside the ancient building. He and his family were in Bethlehem, visiting the Church of the Nativity. "According to tradition, this church sits right over Jesus' birthplace," said Kip's father. He was an archaeologist working in the Holy Land.

Kip's sister Mira looked down. "There's a stable under us?"

Their father nodded. "Yes, but not the kind you're thinking of. The stable Jesus was born in may have been a cave. People often kept animals in caves back then." The family went down some winding steps. There Kip saw an altar. In the marble floor underneath, a silver star marked the spot where Jesus was born.

The people of Bethlehem had little room for Jesus at the time of the first Christmas. The only place they would offer him was a stable! How much room do you have for Jesus? Have you given him the most important place in your life? Or are your days too filled with other things? Ask Jesus today if you need to make more room for him.

Life in Bible Times

In the days when Jesus was born, newborn babies were washed with water. Salt was rubbed on their skin. Then they were wrapped snugly in strips of cloth called swaddling clothes.

Shining Stars

> The star they had seen in the east went ahead of them until it stopped over the place where the child was.
>
> Matthew 2:9

Lacey filled a plastic bag with peppermint candies. Laying it on the kitchen floor, she began smashing the candies with a hammer. "I wanna do some," said her brother Tate, dropping his tube of frosting. He'd been decorating star-shaped Christmas cookies.

"You can finish them," Lacey said, handing him the hammer. At the counter, their mom was pouring something into a bowl.

"What's that?" Lacey asked.

"Vanilla-flavored chips," her mom replied. "Here, melt them in the microwave." Lacey did, and her mom said, "Tate, we're ready for the peppermints." He poured in the crushed candies. Lacey mixed it all up, then dropped spoonfuls onto a cookie pan. "Put the pan in the fridge," her mom said. "Later we'll melt chocolate to dip the patties in. Your Sunday school teachers will love these."

Tate said, "Yeah—and the star cookies!"

Which people around you lead you to Jesus, the way the star of Bethlehem guided the wise men to him? They may be your teachers, coaches, or neighbors. Or they could be your parents, relatives, or friends. Thank God for putting these shining stars in your life, and be sure to show them your appreciation.

Words to Treasure

> Those who are wise will shine like the brightness of the heavens, and those who lead many to righteousness, like the stars for ever and ever.
>
> Daniel 12:3

The Loving Thing to Do

The commandments ... "Do not steal," "Do not covet," and whatever other commandment there may be, are summed up in this one rule: "Love your neighbor as yourself."

Romans 13:9

Sheldon stood next to the soda machine, trying to decide what he wanted. After an hour at the skating rink, he was thirsty.

"I know how to get a free can of pop," said a boy, rolling up to the machine. Putting quarters in the slot, he pushed a button. Then he held down the coin-return lever. Sheldon heard a clunk and a jingle. The boy pulled out a can of soda—and took back his money from the coin-return slot. "See? The machine's broken! Go on, try it."

Sheldon thought for a moment, then shook his head. "No, thanks. I don't want to rob anybody." He put in his quarters, pushed a button, and pulled out a soda.

The boy shrugged. "Suit yourself!" he said, skating away.

When you refuse to steal from someone, you're not just obeying God. You're showing love to that person. Love is the main principle behind all of God's commands. Knowing this truth makes it easier to decide if doing something is right or wrong. Just ask the Holy Spirit to help you answer two questions: What do God's laws say about it? Would it be a loving thing to do?

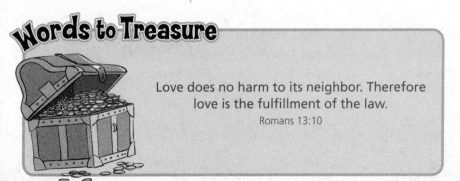

Words to Treasure

Love does no harm to its neighbor. Therefore love is the fulfillment of the law.
Romans 13:10

The Golden Rules

> The ordinances of the Lord are sure and altogether righteous. They are more precious than gold.
>
> Psalm 19:9–10

Leaning over a display case, Mason looked at the old Bible. The book had been made during the Middle Ages. Its words were skillfully handwritten in black ink. Intricate patterns and drawings filled its margins. The colors were bright, especially the gold, which gleamed under the lights. "That looks like *real* gold!" Mason said.

His dad nodded. "It is. Some Bibles were decorated with very thin pieces of gold, called gold leaf." They were at the Holy Land Experience, a theme park in Orlando, Florida. The park had many exhibits. This one was filled with ancient scrolls, manuscripts, and other artifacts.

Mason gave a low whistle. "All that gold must be worth a lot."

"Actually," his dad replied, "the laws in that Bible are much more valuable than the gold!"

Matthew 7:12 says, "Do to others what you would have them do to you." That's called the Golden Rule. But the truth is, this rule and *all* of God's laws are far more precious than gold. Knowing and obeying them makes you wise, protects you, and brings you many blessings. Are you valuing God's laws enough?

Did You Know?

Before he died, Moses reminded the Israelites about all of God's laws. He wanted to make sure they knew how valuable these laws were. He said, "They are your life." (See Deuteronomy 32:46–47.)

Laus Deo

My mouth is filled with your praise, [O Lord,] declaring your splendor all day long.

Psalm 71:8

Addison stood next to the Washington Monument, staring up. "See the little windows at the top?" said Lance, pointing. "Pretty soon we'll be looking out through those."

When their dad waved at them from the entrance, they went inside. There was a statue of George Washington in the small lobby. During the elevator ride up, a guide shared some facts about the monument. "When it was finished in 1884," he said, "this was the tallest building in the world. It's still the world's tallest stone structure."

At the top, Addison peered out the windows. She saw the White House, the Lincoln Memorial, and the Jefferson Memorial. As she looked out the east window at the U.S. Capitol, her father said, "Did you know that there's an inscription on top of this monument? It's on this side—which faces the sunrise. The inscription says, 'Laus Deo.' It's a Latin phrase that means 'Praise be to God.'"

Each day when the sun comes up, take a moment to praise God. He's worthy of it! You could even make a poster or plaque that says, "Laus Deo." Hang it on the east side of your bedroom. Let it remind you to praise God first thing every morning—and keep praising him all day long.

Words to Treasure

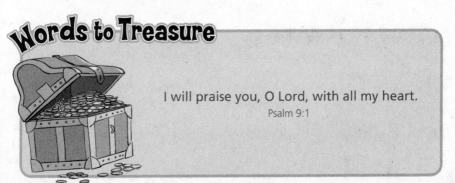

I will praise you, O Lord, with all my heart.
Psalm 9:1

Get Real

Take hold of the life that is truly life.

1 Timothy 6:19

Deep in the ocean, Walt steered toward an undersea volcano. His mini submarine could hold three people, but he was alone. However, he could talk to the crew of the research ship floating far above him.

"Look at those strange formations!" he said. He knew they were watching the images from the cameras on his craft. As the volcano loomed nearer, its mouth glowed red. Walt glanced at the instruments in front of him. The water was getting hot. His vessel began to shake. The volcano was erupting, and he was too close! As he turned the steering wheel frantically, he heard a voice.

"How's your homework coming?"

Walt blinked, and his eyes focused on the math book in front of him. "Uh ... okay, Mom," he said to the closed door of his bedroom.

You know the difference between a real adventure and a daydream. That can help you understand the difference between a life that's real and one that isn't. Living a real life means taking part in the most exciting adventure of all. And that is getting to know God, learning his purpose for you, and fulfilling it. Daydream a little. Get out and enjoy some adventures. But don't just settle for that kind of life. Grab hold of the life that's really real!

Words to Treasure

[Jesus said,] "I have come that they may have life, and have it to the full."

John 10:10

A Special Moment

If anyone is in Christ, he is a new creation; the old has gone, the new has come!

2 Corinthians 5:17

Last New Year's Eve at midnight, Skyler had been asleep on the couch. This year he was wide awake in New York City, watching the ball drop in Times Square. "It's starting to move!" he yelled. The sparkling globe was slowly sliding down a pole atop a building.

His granddad shouted, "In one minute the old year ends and a new one begins."

Times Square was crowded. People were wearing goofy hats and glasses. Everyone started chanting, "Ten … nine … eight …" Skyler and his granddad chanted along. "… three … two … one …" The ball touched bottom, and everyone shouted, "HAPPY NEW YEAR!" Music and confetti filled the air.

Beaming, Skyler said, "This beats watching it on TV!"

Midnight on December 31 is a special moment. That's when the old year leaves and a new one arrives. This happens whether you're aware of it or not. Another special time was the moment when you accepted Jesus as your Lord and Savior. Even if you didn't feel anything, God changed you in an amazing way. He made you a brand-new person—and gave you a while new life.

People in Bible Times

Saul of Tarsus was persecuting believers and putting them in prison. Then Jesus appeared to him, and God changed Saul into a new person. He became the apostle Paul, who spread the gospel around the world. (See Acts 8:1–3; 9:1–19.)

Topic Index

E

F

G

I

J

K

L

m

T

U

V

W

Scripture Index

John 3:16, January 3, February 9

John 4:24, November 16

John 6:65, April 9

John 6:66, September 29

John 6:67–69, September 29

John 7:38, January 26

John 8:12, October 25

John 8:31–32, June 27

John 8:32, October 4

John 8:34, September 16

John 8:36, May 14, September 16

John 8:44, January 24

John 10:3–4, July 11

John 10:4, July 11

John 10:10, November 13,
  December 30

John 10:11, July 16

John 11:25–26, May 3

John 11:41–42, June 1

John 12:32, January 3

John 13:1–17, June 10

John 13:35, April 28

John 14:1, July 23

John 14:2, September 14

John 14:6, September 1, September 9

John 15:5, November 17

John 15:13, January 3, May 8

John 16:33, March 3

John 18:1–13, March 1

John 19:30, April 25

John 20:27, September 25

John 20:29, August 20

John 21:15–17, June 23

John 21:17, June 23

Acts 1:9, August 17

Acts 2:38, June 16, August 6

Acts 4:12, September 1

Acts 8:1–3, December 31

Acts 8:26–40, October 30

Acts 9:1–19, December 31

Acts 10:36, November 11

Acts 12:1–19, October 24

Acts 16:25–34, January 29

Acts 17:11, April 22

Acts 19:23–31, November 22

Acts 20:35, November 14

Acts 27:27–44, October 9

Acts 27:35, October 9

Romans 3:22, December 22

Romans 3:23, April 21

Romans 3:23–24, February 21,
  September 11

Romans 4:7, December 5

Romans 4:20, May 5

Romans 5:3–4, November 4

Romans 5:5, September 18

Romans 5:8, October 19

Romans 6:4, May 3

Romans 6:13, May 23

Romans 6:18, September 15

Romans 7:15–25, December 10

Romans 8:1, April 24

Romans 8:6, February 15

Romans 8:26, March 13

Romans 8:31, October 19

Romans 8:33, October 11

Romans 8:34, December 5

Romans 10:13, November 8

Romans 11:17, May 17

Romans 12:2, February 17

Boys Bible

Hardcover • ISBN 9780310703204

Finally, a Bible just for boys! Discover gross and gory Bible stuff. Find out interesting and humorous Bible facts. Apply the Bible to your own life through fun doodles, sketches, and quick responses. Learn how to become more like Jesus mentally, physically, spiritually, and socially. Part of the 2:52 series for boys.

The Case for Christ for Kids

Softcover • ISBN 9780310711476

Who was Jesus? Using kid-friendly language, Lee Strobel helps tweens understand who Jesus Christ was. "Excellent for Homeschool Use"

The Case for Faith for Kids

Softcover • ISBN 9780310711469

If God loves us, why does he allow so much suffering? Using kid-friendly language, Lee Strobel tells about true stories of how people throughout the world exhibit faith in God. "Excellent for Homeschool Use"

The Case for a Creator for Kids

Softcover • ISBN 9780310711483

Did God create the universe? Or was there a big bang? Author Lee Strobel explains cutting-edge scientific research proving that the universe was designed. "Excellent for Homeschool Use"

Off My Case for Kids: 12 Stories to Help You Defend Your Faith

Softcover • ISBN 9780310711995

Through twelve fictional scenarios written by Robert Elmer, this companion book to the tweens editions of the Case for... series helps kids live out their faith. "Excellent for Homeschool Use"

Available now at your local bookstore!

We want to hear from you. Please send your comments about this book to us in care of zreview@zondervan.com. Thank you.

ZONDERVAN.com/
AUTHORTRACKER
follow your favorite authors